Lake I Love You

Farrah Jane

ASHWING PRESS

LAKE I LOVE YOU

Contents

To my very own J, the keeper of my heart – every emotional, anxious, & messy bit of it.
Thank you for loving, understanding & supporting me through all the highs and lows, & everything in between.
For believing in me, even when I didn't.

I am the luckiest.

(Now let's go tip a kayak.)

Want to dive into the mood music that helped inspire this book?
Check out my FREE, personally-curated playlist for LAKE I LOVE YOU – available exclusively on Spotify!

DIRECT LINK: https://bit.ly/LakeILoveYouPlaylist

or scan the QR CODE:

Prologue

Lizzie

Three months earlier

"Is all of this a dream?"

I repeated the question in almost a whisper as I stood there, staring at my grandmother.

But still, she refused to give me an answer—beyond the usual secretive smile playing across her lips.

It probably wasn't fair for me to feel frustrated. But really, if anyone knew the answer, it would be her. Because without Grandma Cora in my life, I doubt I would've grown up dreaming at all. She'd always been my person, the one who understood me best—even when no one else seemed willing or able.

It was partly the reason she had pushed for those summers at the family lake cabin in Dearing Creek. She knew how important that time—and that place—would become to me, to all of us. And clearly, she knew the day would come when I'd need something to believe in.

For over thirty years, the sprawling blue cabin on the southern shores of Lake Elska had belonged to my grandparents—but when Grandpa Walter retired, they decided to turn it over to my family. Their dream was for the place they'd loved for decades to grow to be just as special for the next generation.

By then, Mariah was fourteen and Ethan and I were twelve, busy with our lives and activities in the suburbs of Minneapolis—a far cry from the sleepy northern Minnesota lake town. Both of our parents were deep into their careers by that point, working long hours and rarely making time in their schedules for anything resembling fun. And we three kids had gotten used to being independent, with things like family traditions or slowing down a foreign concept.

So the odds of the Blake Family feeling gung-ho about driving two hours north to hang out together on purpose—especially in an outdated cabin, with limited technology—was unlikely at best.

Looking back, though, it was clear the five of us had already begun drifting apart. Grandma Cora knew it and urged our mother to make family time a priority. And what better place?

"The cabin's free to use, and so beautiful... remember how you used to love it there?" I'd overheard her saying to my mother. *"Go on, get away from all those distractions and reconnect with your family, Cynthia. You'll never get these days back again."*

But my mom wasn't like *her* mother in most ways. So if it hadn't been for the final push from my father's doctor, I still don't know that we would've done it. Dr. Banks had made it clear, though—if our father didn't find a way to slow down with work, the stress from everything would eventually kill him.

And so our family began committing to a summer schedule that allowed us to spend most of our summer weekends up north. Some weeks, we kids would stay there for longer stretches with our grandparents while our parents headed back to Minneapolis for work.

At first, the three of us grumbled over losing access to our friends and everything we loved about summer in the city. Slowly, though, the magic of Lake Elska won us over. The lazy summer days, floating in the water; the freedom of riding our bikes all around town, ice cream in hand, without a care in the world; exploring in the woods surrounding the town and the lake, pine trees stretching high enough to block out the distractions of real life.

And then there were the evenings spent around a bonfire or laying in the cool grass, gazing up at the millions of stars rarely visible in the city—whispering countless wishes as they were carried off into the great beyond. We'd never known anything like it.

After that first summer, no one could deny that Grandma Cora had been right: this place—this pause—had been what each of us needed, for one reason or another.

But it wasn't really until the summer I turned thirteen that the true magic of this place revealed itself to me, gifting me with most of my best memories.

Because that's when I met my Dearie Girls.

That's what we called ourselves, anyway. Seven girls—some local, others from cabin families like me—named after the small town we'd met in. It was my grandmother who'd coined the name first, calling us her 'little dearies' one pivotal weekend—and, well, the name stuck.

It was a miracle, really, that the group of us came together the way we did. Or maybe it was the magic of that place that did it.

By then, I was a gangly, introverted, and awkward girl with blazing auburn hair, spending most days hiding out with my nose in a book—while simultaneously praying that my boobs would finally show up. Back home, I had a couple of good friends—but for the most part, I'd never quite seemed to find where I fit.

My mother, however, had grown tired of me always hanging around the cabin during her "alone time", while Dad was off fishing—and with my siblings already running around with the local friends they'd made, she was determined to get me out of her hair as well. "Bring a friend along next weekend," she told me at the start of the season—really more of a command than a loving suggestion.

So that was how my good friend Indigo (or Indi, as she preferred to be called) came to be a regular member of Blake family cabin weekends. Indi was a compassionate free-spirit whose parents—hippie-types turned real estate agents—had divorced when she was little but still ran their business together. To her, the idea of going off with her friend to a lake cabin up north—instead of fending for herself all summer—sounded like a dream. And by the end of that first weekend, Indi had fallen under the spell of Dearing Creek as well.

But it still took a visit from Grandma Cora, luring us away from our books and porch loungers, to change everything. She ran us around to all her favorite places in Dearing Creek, making introductions with some of the locals before inviting a huge group to join our family for a bonfire.

That night, while the adults socialized inside with cocktails and gin rummy, the kids all sat together awkwardly around the fire, armed with marshmallows on roasting sticks, five flavors of Shasta soda, and a few bags of Cool Ranch Doritos.

Bit by bit, the group dispersed, until it was down to just seven of us—me, Indi, Brooke, Kait, Tess, Jules, and Lena. Normally, I'd also be looking for an escape back to my cozy, introverted cocoon. But something about those girls made me stay, laughing and chatting as if we'd known each other our entire lives.

It's amazing how a pile of junk food alongside a camp-fire under the stars can be a great equalizer, bringing together the most unlikely of people—almost like they'd always belonged there.

And that summer, our bond was cemented.

Over the years that followed, we all grew into women—and despite our differing personalities, paths and backgrounds, a strong sisterhood formed between the seven of us, traveling far beyond where we'd started.

All of it was thanks to my grandmother, who knew from the start what we'd need most to carry us through life—*love*. True, unconditional, intentional, and steadfast love. The kind that not only lifts you up and carries you away but holds you together when everything else is falling apart.

It was the strongest thing I could think of to believe in.

And my grandmother knew how much I'd need it for when the end of our chapter together finally arrived. I just never believed we'd arrive there so soon.

I stood next to her casket now, continuing to stare at the peaceful, smiling face of the woman who'd loved me best.

Please, Grandma... is all of this a dream?

Because it hadn't seemed real six days earlier, when we'd received the call from her assisted living facility. I'd been with Ethan and Mariah, sitting in vigil next to our dying mother more than a hundred miles away, when my phone rang.

"I'm so sorry, Miss Blake... Cora passed away in her sleep sometime during the night. But it was so peaceful, my dear. No suffering."

I have no idea if I even responded. I remember nothing beyond gut-wrenching pain.

Mom followed her just a few days later, and I'd felt like I was floating along in a fog of grief and disbelief ever since.

And now, here we stood—alone in a blurry sea of well-wishers, none of whom could do a single thing to bring either of them back.

I reached down now to touch my grandmother's hand, lifeless and cold, nothing like the woman she'd been. Wishing more than anything that I could feel her warmth again, squeezing my hand in return. That I could hear her reassuring words, reminding me to never give up on my dreams, to hold tight to what I believed in.

"Don't fret. Nothing is ever truly lost, Lizzie girl..."

But I *had* lost her, hadn't I? There was no going back. Not ever.

Feeling the tears start again, I forced myself to step away. Because wishing for things to be different was pointless—and I already knew the answer to my question. None of this was a dream.

I couldn't have known it then, but Grandma Cora had already been working in the background, writing the outline for my next chapter.

And even I, the writer of the family, couldn't have written—*much less predicted*—the plot twists she had waiting ahead for me.

Chapter 1

Lizzie

"Large decaf, no-foam, brown sugar oat milk latte for Lizzie?"

I took two uncertain steps forward, eyes darting between the coffee cup bearing my name on the counter and the new tattooed barista at Steep & Shot Coffee—apparently named *Heinrik*—who'd shoved the cup in my direction.

"Um, yeah... that's not right."

Heinrik raised a pierced eyebrow, though the rest of him appeared unaffected. "That's what you ordered."

I tried not to wince. The bored affect/vocal fry was *high* with this one.

I shook my head. "No, you just said 'decaf'. What I ordered was extra-caff. As in, an *extra* shot of espresso."

"Sorry... that's not what I heard."

What kind of psychopath orders decaf coffee at seven-fifty in the morning?

Taking a deep, steadying breath, I willed myself to remain calm. "Heinrik... please, help a girl out. I mean, do I look like someone who needs a decaf right now?" I gestured dramatically, shaking the plastic bag containing the box of tampons I'd just picked up from the drugstore. Combined with my rumpled appearance, today's hot-mess version of Lizzie Blake left little room for doubt that caffeine was an absolute necessity.

Though if Fate had proven anything to me over the last year, it was that it had a really twisted sense of humor.

Because not only had I been handed an overnight power outage, leading to a way-too-late wake-up time—but I woke up slammed with pre-period cramps, several days early.

And, yet again, the incomparable baristas at Steep & Shot had given me the wrong freaking coffee order.

Oh, and I was already twenty minutes late to work. *Again.*

But Heinrik just shrugged as he moseyed on back towards the cash register, clearly not here for hysterical women or self-righteous coffee demands. "Beth can make you another one, but..." he said, craning his neck to look past me, "it's gonna be awhile."

I followed his gaze towards the lineup of people also waiting on their orders, which had grown exponentially during the past fifteen minutes I'd spent sucked into another romance novel on my e-reader.

And like me, not a single one of them looked thrilled to be there.

It was like a tragic scene out of what would likely be the worst—or most accurate—book ever: *Death by Nine-to-Five Grind.*

Though I was pretty sure none of the other patrons had been up until two a.m. for the fifth night in a row, trying to make progress on a manuscript that seemed determined to unwrite itself.

Probably because I'm more qualified to write the Death book than my own.

"Ugh, just... never mind." I was already late enough for work as it was. Snatching my cup from the counter, I shifted the strap of my bookbag further up my shoulder before elbowing my way through the crowd towards the door.

For the fourth time in as many weeks, I grumbled to myself about finding a new coffee shop—but who was I kidding? This place was only a block away from my second-floor walk-up apartment. I knew I'd be back again for the same torture on Monday morning, if not sooner.

I rolled my eyes, annoyed at my own sad-sack internal monologue. I was better than this. Mostly, I was tired of feeling so... stuck. And the last few months since losing my mom and grandmother had only managed to amplify all of it.

With a sigh, I pushed open the door to step out onto the sidewalk. Suddenly there was a shout—and the door immediately swung back, smacking me square in the face. My coffee—along with everything else I'd been carrying—flew out of my hand. Cursing loudly, I felt the hot contents of the paper cup spill down the sleeve of my light gray blouse, tumbling down to land amongst the tampons that had, *of course*, fallen out of their box and across the cement.

Eyes tearing up from the pain (both from my third-degree latte burns and the giant goose egg forming on my forehead), I tried to shake off the shock as I bent down to gather my coffee-soaked feminine products, praying nobody saw me.

But of course—*of course*—my request was denied, as I discovered most of them were scattered around a pair of scuffed-up sneakers.

"Jesus... you ok?"

The smooth tenor of the man belonging to those shoes rang out above my head. Looking up, I was met with gold-flecked hazel eyes and a smile that was equal parts sexy and disarming—perfectly framed by a smattering of brownish whiskers and a single dimple that I itched to run my fingers over.

Grabbing the last few remaining tampons and throwing them into my bag, I quickly stood to face him, my traitorous cheeks already ablaze. Fully upright, he still had a good eight inches on me, tall and lean with decidedly better muscle tone—at least, based on what I saw outlined through the thin fabric of the t-shirt and shorts he was wearing.

To sum it up, the guy was hot. Like, really hot—in a ruggedly handsome, *Fourth Horseman of the Apocalypse, sent to deliver my doom with a side order of humiliation,* sort of way.

"Yeah, I'm fine," I said, dabbing at my soaked sleeve with a tissue I'd pulled from my bookbag, but it was pointless—the stain was already set. Sighing, I tossed it into the plastic bag, along with the rest of the coffee carnage. "I just... somehow ran into the door."

Smirking, he ran a hand briefly through his sexy-scruffy golden-brown hair. "Yeah, I figured as much... so did I." He gestured a few feet behind him, where a few boxes lay spilled open across the sidewalk. "See, I was carrying a load of my friend's stuff—that is, until your door swung open and shoved everything into my face."

My eyes drifted towards the welt over his right eyebrow, feeling the teensiest pang of guilt—nevertheless, I bristled at the insinuation that somehow all of this was *my* fault.

But getting upset wouldn't help a dang thing right now, much less get me to work more quickly. *Just keep it breezy and be on your way, Blake.*

"Well, technically, it's not *my* door... unless my name has been changed to Steep & Shot Coffee, which would be great if it came with a discount." With a *breezy* little laugh,

I tossed my empty cup and bag of useless, caffeinated tampons into the trash can nearby, turning back to face him. "Anyway, I guess we both just need to be more careful next time."

But instead of being gracious and moving on, ~~Hot~~ Rude Guy raised an eyebrow—staring at me in a way that felt equal parts uncomfortable and heart-fluttery—and simply said, "Huh."

'*Huh*'? Not even a question—more of a statement, like, '*Well, you're ridiculous*'.

Speaking of which, I caught a glimpse of my reflection in the coffee shop window behind him—stained shirt, black skirt, the messy bun I'd frantically piled atop of my head looking even more disheveled than before. I couldn't have looked more hot-mess certified *ridiculous* if I'd tried.

All things considered, the smart move would've been to walk away right then—especially since this conversation was getting me nowhere. But instead, I tucked a stray section of auburn hair behind my ear, narrowing my eyes at him. "Exactly what do you mean by '*huh*'?"

He shrugged. "Well, it's just that—*you* were actually the one who opened the door. Might not be a bad idea to take a quick glance outside first and make sure no one's within striking distance, ma'am." Now his tone was borderline condescending as he appeared to bite back a smile, cranking up the heat on the irritation already simmering in my chest that was becoming impossible to ignore.

'Ma'am'?! I one-hundred percent did not need this right now.

Crossing my arms, I looked him square in the eye. "I'm sorry, but who walks around Minneapolis without watching where *they* are going? You could've just as easily taken out a small child, restricting your sightline with a stack of boxes like that. Maybe you should be more careful next time, *sir.*"

Now there was *definitely* no mistaking the amusement in his annoyingly-twinkly gold eyes. "Yes, well... it would also be a shame if a small child somehow managed to trip over this," he said, reaching down, "unless you aren't concerned with the aftermath of your lady litter, *Red?*" With a smug smile, he presented me with one last rogue *tampon.* Which *of course* happened to be one from the pack screaming 'HEAVY FLOW' down the wrapper in gigantic, judgy text—probably chosen by some masochistic moron being paid mid six-figures a year.

My face burned as I snatched it from his hand, refusing to break eye contact. "I'll have you know, I care *very much* about children *and* the environment. And I also care too much about my time to waste another second of it on *this* conversation." Pointedly, I dropped the tampon into the trash can and turned to storm past him, his laughter echoing behind me as I made my way towards work—now, later than ever.

I didn't even care that he was attractive... or that both his voice and his smile were kind of sexy, when he wasn't making blatant accusations... *or* that he might have a point, because at the very least, I *had* been distracted.

But it didn't matter. The only words echoing through my head on the remainder of my rush towards work—besides the cute little nickname he'd tossed at me—were *what. an. asshole.*

Ten minutes later and out of breath, the elevator doors opened on the twenty-fifth floor of Woodruff & Shay to reveal the one person I'd most hoped to avoid on my way in.

Constance Quist stood there—all glowering, five-foot-eleven inches of her—dark eyes blazing and mouth turned down in that perpetually disappointed expression she seemed to reserve especially for me. As Chief Marketing Officer for Minneapolis's top-ranked accounting firm, the woman had a reputation for being a shark in male-dominated waters—and she expected no less than perfection from the marketing staff who reported to her.

Worse still? For whatever reason, Constance hadn't liked me from the moment I was hired as lead copywriter three years ago. And now, glancing down at the folder she held in her hands, I knew I was likely circling the drain.

"Ah, Elizabeth... so kind of you to grace us with your presence this morning. Please, follow me to my office, won't you?"

I felt my face and hands begin their usual anxious tingle as I followed her down the long corridor, willing myself to hold it together while simultaneously cursing myself internally. Walking into her spacious-yet-imposing corner office, I let the door close behind me before lowering myself into one of the angular metal chairs.

Constance settled into her high-backed leather chair, resting her arms against the desk with fingers clasped as she stared, waiting to begin the interrogation.

"Listen, I'm really sorry. The power was out in my building this morning, and I—"

"---still had time for coffee, I see," she said coolly, nodding towards the partially dried stain on my blouse. But before I could respond, she continued. "Do you recall the very important meeting that was scheduled with the senior partners this morning, Elizabeth?"

"Yes, I—"

"... and yet, you waltz in here almost–" she glanced at the gold watch on her bony wrist, "—forty minutes late, after leaving myself and the rest of the team to look like complete morons, as we attempted to present the Q4 marketing plan without our completed ad copy?"

"I know, and I'm so—"

"Yes, I know... *you're sorry*," Constance said impatiently, her words dripping with thinly-veiled sarcasm. "I shouldn't have to remind you that the firm has already been discussing the possibility of layoffs. Every single one of us needs to be performing at one-hundred-percent. Which begs the question—-do you even *want* to be here, Elizabeth?" She unfolded her hands now, moving to tap a fingernail against the surface of her desk, each tap pounding like a nail into my coffin.

I paused, heart racing, as I considered my words. Being honest right now would only cause more damage—and like it or not, I *needed* this job.

"Of course I want to be here. I'm grateful for the opportunity I've had to learn from you, Constance."

Lies, lies, lies!

She studied me for a moment in silence, her pale face and narrowed eyes framed by her trademark angular, mahogany bob—looking very much like a black hole, siphoning away what remained of my confidence.

Slowly, she leaned forward in her seat towards me. "Then I trust this won't happen again, yes?" Her tone was softer, which only made it more menacing.

"It won't, I assure you. You can count on me."

"Good. You may go. And have the Q4 materials on my desk before ten." She turned towards her computer and began rapidly typing away.

I rose from my seat and was halfway to the door when she spoke again. "Oh, and Elizabeth?" I braced myself for the inevitable insult that usually followed. "Please tidy yourself up. This is a professional environment, not some millennial rager. You look like you're... *high* or something."

Yep, there it was.

"Of course."

As I shut the door of my own office a few minutes later—with thoughts of scary-ass boss ladies and hot/rude men swirling around in my head—I tossed my bag to the floor and sank into my chair. Slowly, I released my breath, leaning back with eyes shut tight.

What the hell was wrong with me?

I mean, for God's sake, I was thirty years old—and even though I wasn't exactly thrilled with my career, I wasn't *irresponsible*. I'd always worked hard and done the job asked of me, even when I'd rather be doing literally *anything* else.

Clearly, missing that meeting this morning had been a major screw-up on my part. I couldn't fully blame the power outage or my disastrous run-in with Rude Guy. I swear, it was almost like I'd been in self-sabotage mode the last few months. Everything just felt *too much*. And I had no idea how to fix any of it.

All I wanted to do right then was walk out that door—away from this job, away from all of the stress and worries and *grief* that seemed determined to bury me, too. I'd hide out in my apartment, focused on nothing but healing my heart—until I got my spark back. Maybe then all the hard crap from the past year would finally sort itself out.

Maybe then I'd no longer miss my grandmother in a way that made it hard to breathe.

It wasn't that easy, though, was it? Hiding from my problems wouldn't pay the bills—and neither, apparently, would my fiction writing. Because even there, I felt stuck. The words that used to come so easily just didn't flow anymore. Maybe they never would.

I swear, if I listened closely enough, I could almost hear my mom chanting 'I *told you so'* with her megaphone up in heaven—all of her warnings about the '*frivolity of creative careers'* going in one ear and getting lost deep inside my brain, never managing to find their way towards the exit on the other side.

I released a long, slow breath, refusing to allow my thoughts to pull me down further. It had taken everything in me to get to the point of being functional again these past few months. I couldn't afford to go backwards. Not again.

But I knew—neither my grandmother nor my mother would be proud of the road I was on right now. I felt like I was barely holding my life together with a few loose stitches, not even able to finish the first draft of a manuscript I'd been working on since before I'd started this job *three years ago*.

How long, exactly, would those stitches continue to hold?

I squinched my eyes shut, hands clasped in my lap. *Please, God... help me to—*

But my prayers were soon interrupted by a loud pinging coming from my phone. Opening my eyes, I reached down to scoop it out of my bag—groaning out loud as I read the message.

BROOKE: Hey, babe.... where are we going for happy hour tonight?

Shit, I'd forgotten. And I really, *really* didn't want to go out tonight. But before I could reply back, my phone pinged again.

BROOKE: And no, you can't just stay home. You promised, Lizzie. I'm not letting you post-pone a third time. You need this.

Damn it.

Sullenly, I typed in my response.

> LIZZIE: Alright, fine. The Independent at five-thirty?

> BROOKE: Fabulous! See you there. And… wear something cute, ok? NO SWEATS this time.

Setting down my phone, I leaned back in my chair again and tilted my head towards the ceiling, amending my prayer—

Please, God… just let me get through the rest of this day.

Oh, and maybe pass along some divine inspiration while you're at it?

K, thanks.

Chapter 2

James

"Hey, can you hurry it up a bit, old man? I'd actually like to eat before next Tuesday."

I hoisted the ratty old recliner I'd been carrying into the back of the moving truck, wiping my brow with the back of my hand as I shot daggers at my friend. "Piss off, Jack. You know, this city has turned you into an even bigger asshole than you already were."

"Guess it's a good thing I'm leaving then, before I turn into you," Jack said, capping the rebuttal with his usual exaggerated wink.

"You wish." But I couldn't help laughing. Jack and I—along with our friend Jesse—had been giving each other shit for almost our entire lives. And we weren't likely to stop anytime soon.

It was one of the many reasons why they were really more like brothers than friends by this point. Given how small my inner circle was, I wouldn't risk my bond with them for anything.

And now, having Jack back with us where it all began—up north, in our hometown of Dearing Creek—maybe I'd stop feeling so unsettled, like I couldn't find my footing. Maybe I'd even start listening to those nagging thoughts at the back of my mind, nudging me to go after what I wanted instead of treading water where I was.

Maybe, I'd start feeling happy again.

Because if I were being honest, I hadn't really felt that way in quite some time.

Jack shut and latched the rear door to the moving truck, turning back to look at me. "Seriously, James, I'm starving. Where do you wanna go? La Cucaracha? Leaning Tower of Pasta?"

"Nah... let's grab happy hour somewhere. I could use a beer."

Twenty minutes later, we were just about to walk through the entrance of Mac's Bar when a voice called out behind us.

"Well, I'll be damned... is that two of the *Three Js* I see?"

We turned in unison at the sound of our old nickname, spotting a familiar face. Brooke Christenson quickly closed the distance between us, wrapping us up in a quick hug before pulling back with a smile.

"What are you boys doing here in the cities? God, I feel like I've gone back in time about a decade."

Jack laughed. "You're actually catching me on my last day here. I've been living and working in Minneapolis for the past nine years."

"*Seriously?* I've been here for almost seven. How have we never bumped into each other before?"

"Guess you and I were running in different circles for once, Christenson. Gone are the days of Lake View High," he said, grinning. "Anyway, I've been working in finance, but... I recently decided to make a switch. How about you?"

She tucked a strand of her pale blonde hair behind her ear, quite a bit shorter—and lighter—than the long hair she'd sported in high school. "PR. I actually just got promoted to director at Ayvers Agency."

"Hey, congrats, sounds right up your alley. I bet you're great at it."

"Not too shabby." She shrugged—nonchalant, though she looked secretly pleased by the compliment. "So, where are you headed now? And you," she said, directing her attention towards me, "Never thought James Tate would be caught dead hanging out in Minneapolis."

"A one time offense, trust me," I said, chuckling. "I'm just here helping my boy pack up and finally move back home."

"So the *Three Js* will truly be back together again. Better warn my family," she said, shaking her head with a grin. Then she glanced down at her watch. "Shit, I'm going to be late meeting Lizzie. Do you remember her? She and her family used to come up to their cabin a lot during the summers."

I cocked my head. "Not really. But if she's part of that crew you ran around with back then, something tells me she's trouble."

She snorted. "Lizzie? *Hardly*. But she might just kill me if I make her sit at the bar by herself for much longer." She pulled us in for another quick hug. "So good to see you guys. Let's get together for drinks the next time I'm up north, ok?"

"You bet."

I caught Jack watching Brooke as she strode off down the sidewalk, heels clicking along the pavement and hips swaying in the snug bootcut jeans she wore. "Didn't you two date back in high school?"

Jack snorted out a laugh as he started again towards the bar door. "A senior dating a freshman? Not likely. And you know Trent and Dustin would never have let me live if I'd tried." He wasn't wrong—everyone in Dearing Creek knew enough not to mess with the Christensen brothers—especially when it involved their baby sister.

Following him inside, we grabbed the last couple of spots remaining at the bar. This place was just as I'd remembered it—dimly lit but cozy, with a handful of booths and tables spread throughout the room, old Minneapolis photos and local sports mementos lining the dark paneled walls. I hadn't been to Mac's Bar in a couple of years, but I knew without a doubt what I'd be eating tonight.

The bartender walked over to us, wiping his hands on a bar towel. "You two ready to order?"

"Yeah. Juicy Lucy with fries, please, and a tall Stormy Weather IPA."

Jack gestured towards me. "I'll have the same."

A short while later, we were working our way through steaming baskets of greasy fries and molten cheese-filled burgers—along with our half-drained beers—as we sat reminiscing about the old days. Seeing Brooke had definitely triggered a lot of memories for both of us.

More than anything, it was good to see my old friend looking like his happy, relaxed self again. I knew his time in the cities had run him through the wringer in more ways than one—and I was damned glad that soon he'd be back where he belonged. I chuckled under my breath, remembering one particular memory stirred up by our earlier conversation.

"What're you laughing about over there?"

I took a sip of my beer. "Just the whole '*Three Js*' nickname. I haven't heard that one in a long time."

Jack looked amused. "I still say it was Jesse who made up that damn thing in the first place. Mostly to irritate the hell out of you."

"Yeah, well, I think he did a better job of irritating *you.* I actually find it kind of... endearing."

"'*Endearing*'? Who the fuck are you, and what did you do with my best friend?"

I chuckled. "Maybe I've softened my edges the last few years. I've been sending all of my asshole energy to you, remember?"

"Nice try. You'll always be a grumpy bastard, James. Don't fight it." He took a bite of his burger before wiping his mouth on a napkin. "So, are you ever going to tell me what happened with those boxes of my files earlier? They look like shit." He narrowed his eyes as he looked more closely at me. "Come to think of it, so does your forehead."

I smirked, recalling my run-in with the redhead at the coffee shop earlier in the day. Honestly, I'd found her running through my thoughts more than once as we'd continued our work moving Jack out of his condo. With the way she'd looked—both beautiful and chaotic—it had been nearly impossible not to. Especially watching her get all worked up, her green eyes shooting out daggers that I'd have taken gladly, just to keep her focus on me.

But it also made me realize I would've deserved every bit of the resulting pain, acting the way I had. My exhaustion from another long workday—coupled with a two-hour drive to get to Jack's place the night before—had me running on some seriously grumpy energy by the time the two of us crashed into each other. Simply put, I'd behaved like a jackass. And it was far from her fault.

Well... maybe a little bit her fault.

"Yeah, I had a collision with a woman outside the coffee shop near your place this morning. She... kinda hit me with the door."

Jack cocked an eyebrow. "What do you mean, she *hit* you?"

"Well, she whipped the door open on her way out. I just happened to be walking along at that exact moment." I paused, recalling the scene as Red scrambled to retrieve her tampons, finding myself struck more by the delicate flush of her cheeks than the door itself as she stood up to face me. "And I, uh, might've implied that she was the one at fault."

"*Dude.*"

I gave him a sheepish look, rubbing at the scruff along my jawline. "Yeah, I know. It was hard to see while I was carrying your huge ass boxes. Guess I wasn't really watching where I was going."

Jake shook his head, chuckling as he reached for his beer. "I hope you apologized to her, at least."

"Well, no... but I *did* help her to pick up her tampons. That's got to count for something, right? Although, I might've tossed in a lecture on littering there at the end..."

He groaned, covering his face. "I say this with love—you're sounding more like my father every day. If you don't watch it, Jesse and I will soon be the only ones who'll tolerate your sorry ass."

I shrugged, a small smile playing across my lips. "Yeah, we'll see about that." But my mind wasn't focused on anything my friend was saying—instead, I was replaying those few minutes I'd shared with that woman, knowing I wasn't likely to forget it for some time. There'd even been a brief second where I'd had to hold myself back from brushing the hair from her face after it had fallen from that crazy little updo of hers. I hadn't wanted to miss the electricity I saw in those eyes, doling out her final retort before storming off.

In hindsight, she likely would've hauled off and slapped me for it—and I must be some sort of masochist, because I couldn't help grinning at the idea. Even though it would've been worth it, I supposed one smack to the face per day was probably enough.

I shook my head, wondering what the hell had gotten into me. I wasn't the sort of guy who had his head turned easily by *any* woman, much less some city girl.

Not that I had cause to think about anything along those lines, anyway. My workload back home with Aaronson Construction had me putting in long hours most days and didn't leave room for much else. I didn't even *need* much else, other than my friends. Besides, I already had a woman in my life that I loved. And despite questioning where my life was headed lately, I knew I was damn lucky.

Come tomorrow morning, I'd be putting Minneapolis in my rearview mirror for the foreseeable future. And I couldn't get home soon enough.

"Hey, man... Can I ask you something?"

I glanced over to Jack, who was eyeing me as he played with his french fries. "Are you wondering if Dearing Creek is ready for Jake the Hot Shot? Because the answer is probably not..."

"Cut it out. I'm actually being serious." He tipped back his beer, draining the glass before continuing. "Am I making a mistake, abandoning a successful career to go off and start something new? I mean... I'm leaving a lot behind here."

I knew his question was about more than just quitting his cushy, six-figure job in finance to pursue his dream of running high-end guided fishing tours up north. My mind drifted to how messed up he'd been over the last few months, ever since his girlfriend of three years, Dana, had broken up with him. Moving back home would be like cutting the final cord to the secure life he'd been building for almost a decade.

It was hard for me to imagine feeling so affected by a woman in that way—mostly, I guess, because I'd never really allowed myself to go there. But I was happy keeping things casual, way less messy. And it definitely made it easier to walk away when I needed to.

"No, you're not making a mistake. You've thought it through and planned ahead, plus you'll be building something you're passionate about—that's never a bad thing. Honestly, I really envy you, man. Both Jesse and I are proud of you."

"Thanks." He flashed me a quick smile, nudging me with his elbow as he went back to his food. "You could finally take the leap too, you know."

I snorted. "What, start my business? I've got enough on my hands right now. Like getting your ass out of this god-forsaken city."

Jake grinned. "Dearing Creek will rejoice at having the three of us back together again. Just like old times, eh?"

I nodded, reaching for my beer. "Like old times."

It's not like I was lying when I said it—but beneath the words lay the thoughts I'd been stewing over for what seemed like forever.

Why do I feel like all that I have isn't enough anymore?

Chapter 3

Lizzie

It was almost six o'clock, and I was sitting alone in a red vinyl corner booth at the dimly-lit Independent Bar, fiddling with my cocktail straw while trying *really* hard not to feel annoyed. Because my dear friend Brooke—who'd practically begged me to come out tonight—was still nowhere to be seen.

When I'd stopped back at my apartment to change clothes after work, I'd almost talked myself into not even coming out at all. I'd been in a funk all day, and still hadn't quite managed to shake myself out of it. The urge to just curl up in my grandmother's quilt and escape into another fictional world, far away from the problems in my real life, had been way too tempting.

Not that hiding in a book would fix anything, of course. Those were the wishes of a young girl, not a thirty-year-old woman with bills and responsibilities and a career on the brink. But eventually, I knew, something had to give.

Easier said than done, though, when you are a creative, irregularly shaped peg trying to wedge herself into a square-ish corporate hole. How does one even *begin* to feel passionate about writing stale, lifeless ad copy or sitting in strategy meetings all day when your soul is literally screaming out, "*But you're an author, dammit!*"?

I mean, I used to at least be better at pretending—until my mom ended up sick. Once she was diagnosed with Stage 4 colon cancer, though, everything changed.

Me and my brother Ethan found our lives quickly consumed by treatments, appointments, finding hospice care—all while bearing the brunt of her bitterness for the hand she'd been dealt. Especially considering the daughter by her side through most of it wasn't the one she'd have chosen, were it up to her—a fact she reminded me of daily. *That* daughter was off living her best life with her upper-class family in Massachusetts, only adding to our stress the couple of times she came back home to help.

At the end of the day, I'd had no bandwidth left for things like faking excitement for the career I'd found myself in—or time to devote to my own writing. There was no space for *anything*, really, beyond getting through each day. After losing both Mom and Grandma Cora three months ago, things had only gotten worse.

And now, the idea of becoming a writer felt like the immature daydreams of a child—wished for long before life taught you to grow the hell up and be realistic. "*Dreams are like wishes, Lizzie—both are impractical. And both have a way of fading away the moment you wake up to reality."*

How many times had I heard my own mother say this to me, desperate to knock some sense into her youngest daughter? Even now, I could still hear those words echo in my mind—not just in our mom's voice, but my sister's as well.

Both sensible women, yes—but were they actually *happy*? Our mother had never seemed to be, especially after Dad died. Mariah too, for that matter. But listening to their advice meant giving up my dream of being published altogether—and I'd sworn to Grandma Cora I never would, no matter what.

No matter how many hours and months I'd already wasted—or all the words backspaced into oblivion—I couldn't walk away. I couldn't give up, not yet.

But speaking of *giving up*, I glanced down at my phone to check the time—hoping for an encouraging response from my boyfriend to my earlier venting text. Instead, all that stared back at me was a blank screen and a blinking clock, reminding me that I'd been sitting here alone like a sad sack for fifteen minutes now. Just as I was ready to walk out of that damn bar and head home, Brooke finally appeared in the doorway. Her smile lit up her entire face as soon as she spotted me, making a beeline in my direction.

As always, my friend looked effortlessly beautiful—chic, pale blonde bob brushing against the shoulders of her flirty red blouse, her tailored bootcut jeans and heeled sandals making me wish I had at least gone with the green floral blouse instead of the black.

What can I say—I was driven by mood.

"Well, look who *finally* decided to grace me with her presence," I said as Brooke reached our booth, leaning down to give me a quick peck on the cheek before sliding in across from me, breathless. "You're lucky. I was about two minutes away from leaving. It's not like I don't have better things to do than sit around and wait for you."

Brooke rolled her eyes as she set down her purse on the seat next to her. "Oh, relax. I *am* sorry for being late. But we both know you would just be sitting at home, moping with your quilt and nose-deep in a book if I hadn't dragged you out here."

Sometimes, I really hated that my friends knew me so well.

"And besides," she continued, flagging down a server as she scanned one of the menus on the table between us, "it's Friday! And you're barely thirty.... way too young to be acting like some crotchety old lady." Our server arrived at the table, pad in hand. "Hi! I'll take a.... Lizzie, what're you having?"

I raised my glass, jostling around the ice. "An Old Fashioned."

"I was wrong. You're not a little old lady. Your boyfriend has turned you into a *little old man*."

"Hey, now... Old Fashioneds are trending again." I glanced up at the server for confirmation. "Right?"

The server shrugged, looking bored. "Yeah, I guess. But I'd personally go for the blackberry mojito."

Brooke brightened, setting down the menu. "Perfect! I'll take one of those please, and..."

"... cheese curds and a salmon salad to split?" I sighed. It really was impossible to stay mad at Brooke.

"Of course. And you can just bring all the food together at once. Oh, and waters for both of us, please." As the server walked away, Brooke leaned in, waggling a finger in front of my face. "You will be drinking every drop of your water this time, lady."

"No, no, no, *no*... I am *not* getting drunk tonight." I mean, yes, I probably needed to unwind a little. Or a lot. But nights out with Brooke had a habit of going way too far in that direction, despite our best intentions.

Also the reason I'd gone with flats tonight, just in case my *'best intentions'* weren't up to par.

"Who said anything about getting drunk? But I could already feel your energy when I walked in... you definitely need some loosening up."

"Why do I feel like I've heard this pitch before..."

"*Yeah, yeah, yeah,*" she interrupted, waving away my words, "anyway, the reason I'm late is because I ran into a couple of old friends from high school on my way over. Do you remember Jack LeClaire and James Tate?"

"Hmmm.... I don't think so."

"Yeah, I think they were seniors when I was a freshman at Lake View High... so they would've already graduated, maybe weren't around as much during your last few summers at the cabin," she said, shrugging. "Anyway, apparently Jack has lived in Minneapolis all this time, but now he's moving back home to Dearing Creek. Small world, huh?"

"Sure, guess so."

Brooke cocked her head slightly, eyebrow raised. "Ok, seriously... What's with you today? I'm beginning to think a wet blanket would've made a better date."

I sighed, glancing up as the server returned with Brooke's cocktail and two glasses of water. She reached for hers immediately. "Sorry, you're right... My day started off kind of crappy, and I'm having trouble shaking it."

"It's ok, I just had to give you crap," she said, smirking. "So what happened?"

"Well first, I woke up late for work, Constance was on my case again... and along the way, I had a run-in with some guy who made me spill my stupid decaf coffee all over my tampons..."

Brooke snorted out a laugh, nearly choking on her cocktail. "Excuse me, what?"

Feeling my face burn at the memory of it, I continued. "So I was walking out of Steep & Shot, and this guy plowed right into the door. Everything flew everywhere... my coffee, an entire box full of tampons..." *Yep, confirmed*—it was still every bit as humiliating now, replaying the scene in my head for the eightieth time. No doubt my anxiety in the moment had fired off a clear warning shot: *Save yourself, sir... this woman is a freakin' hot mess.*

No wonder Rude Guy had looked at me like I was crazy. Not that I even *cared*, but—if he was now going to be frequenting my coffee shop, I'd definitely have to find a new spot. Which was a shame because he was, well, very nice to look at.

As long as he didn't open his mouth.

"I don't doubt it was embarrassing, you poor thing," Brooke said as she bit her lip, clearly trying not to laugh. "But at least you lived to tell the tale. No doubt this one will be a winner with your kids someday."

"Gee, thanks."

"You're welcome. Now, what happened with Cruella?"

"Constance? Well, I ended up missing that Q4 pitch meeting I told you about..."

She winced. "*Ooof...*"

"I know, I *know*. Her being pissed was justified. But it wasn't intentional. The power went out in my building, so my alarm never went off. And technically, I had the work ready." But the excuse sounded lame, even to me. Because even if I had been on time, I knew my contributions to the project were far from my best work.

"Well, we both know the bigger issue here isn't that you messed up. It's that you'd much rather be doing something else."

It was far from the first time we'd had this conversation—but what else could I do? This was the job. And I had to get my head on straight if I wanted to keep it.

Draining the rest of my cocktail, I pushed the empty glass towards the edge of our table, where it was promptly scooped up by a passing server. "Of course, in a perfect world." *God, now I sound like my mother...*

"And why does the world have to be *perfect*? Lizzie, you've been wanting to be a writer ever since I've known you."

"Yeah, well... I *also* need a paycheck, remember? Which this job provides me with, every two weeks. Besides, at the rate I'm going with my book, the only way I'll get paid for fiction writing is if I print it out and sell it for literary kindling."

She snorted. "Come on. How far along are you now?"

"Considering I've basically started over *again*..."

"Hmmmm." I noticed she was studying me now, head cocked.

"What?" But I already knew what was coming.

"I'm just wondering how long you're planning to avoid the obvious."

"Which is what?"

She leaned in closer. "Come on, Lizzie. You're not getting anywhere trying to force yourself into loving that book. Despite what Randall may be filling your head with, we all know what you'd *rather* be writing. Pretending doesn't change that."

I felt my body tense, thinking again of all the work and painstaking research I'd already put into my Depression-era tale about two sisters—as well as the conversations I'd had on this very topic with my boyfriend. A literature professor at my alma mater who was also twenty years my senior, Randall Price always had plenty to say when it came to both my writing and my career.

And I couldn't bear to see the look on his face if I told him *yet again* about my dream to write romance novels.

"Well, like I said before... *this* is the sort of book I should be writing, if I want publishers to take me seriously."

Brooke sighed. "Look, I get it... and if you keep at it, I have no doubt you'll make that book come together. You're an amazing writer... I wish I had even an ounce of your talent." She took a sip of her mojito, dabbing her lips with a napkin after setting the glass down. "But I can't help thinking you're taking the hard road here, holding yourself back from what you love." She paused. "Maybe it would also help you to feel closer to your grandmother."

I twirled the straw around in my water glass, watching the ice cubes clink and dance before my blurry eyes as I thought about Grandma Cora. She'd been the one who first introduced me to romance novels when I was around fifteen years old—and it wasn't long before the two of us were devouring piles of books together, sharing little handwritten notes written in the margins, and giggling together over the particularly swoony parts.

Thinking about it now, the constant ache I'd felt over the past few months pulsed even deeper—and I flinched from the pain of it.

Looking up from my glass, I forced a smile. "Well, there'll be plenty of chances to write in other genres down the road if I manage to secure a publisher with this book."

Brooke sighed. "Honey, I promise... I'm not trying to discourage you. I just want you to be happy, ok?" She reached a hand across the table, giving mine a comforting squeeze. "Besides, any publisher worth their salt will see how talented you are... no matter what sort of book you choose to write."

"Thanks." What I didn't say was: *I don't know if I believe that anymore.*

But anyway, what the hell was I doing? I'd made the effort to yank myself out of my apartment—I *should* be focused on having a fun night out with my best friend—not stewing in my problems, like a character in some melodramatic tragedy that would inevitably result in a big ol' DNF.

Straightening in my seat, I smiled at the server as she arrived with our food. "Hey, any chance I can get another Old Fashioned? Another for you, too?" I glanced at Brooke, who nodded.

As the server walked off, I took a deep breath, eager to shift the topic away from all the ways I seemed to be falling apart lately. "Look, let's just have some fun tonight.

We both need it. And besides, don't we have a *promotion* to celebrate?"

I noticed Brooke eyeing me closely, clearly recognizing my diversion tactic—but I was relieved she let it slide this time. "Ok, fine… Let's just relax. *But,*" she pointed a finger at me sternly, "I'm buying."

"I am *not* letting you pay when we are supposed to be celebrating you…"

She interrupted me with a dismissive wave. "And why not? I earned a sweet raise with this promotion and I wanna spend it. Who better than my dear Lizzo to help me do it?"

I giggled. "Fine… you win. But I've got the next one, Ms. *Director of Public Relations.*"

"That *does* have a nice ring to it, doesn't it?" Brooke giggled, raising her glass. "Now let's show Minneapolis how the Dearie Girls kick back…"

Chapter 4

Lizzie

Four hours and *way* too many cocktails later, I watched as Brooke headed off down the road in her Uber, cackling and calling out "*Lizzo! Everyone, look... it's Lizzo!*" while waving dramatically from her rolled-down window.

Not quite drunk enough to dodge embarrassment, I did my best to avoid the stares as I stood waiting for my own ride outside Bar Kumquat, the final spot we'd landed at. But attempting to focus my blurry vision on my phone screen felt like a lesson in futility.

I mean *seriously*, I never should've let myself order that last drink. After all these years, you'd think I would learn. I was still such a lightweight compared not only to Brooke, but all of my friends—well, except for Lena. One drink, and that girl turned into an emotional mess, every freakin' time.

Thankfully, the Dearie Girls had mostly slowed down from the shenanigans of our younger years. But tonight, I definitely wished I had behaved more like thirty-year-old Lizzie, rather than a long-buried version of myself.

Because now that Brooke had gone, I was starting to feel not only the brandy hitting me, but also my somber mood from earlier. I leaned against the side of the brick building, longing for my bed—and possibly a lobotomy.

Ten minutes later, a notification popped up on my phone screen—the Uber driver had canceled my ride request.

Fuckity-fuck-fuck.

As I tucked my phone away, the fog in my head cleared just enough for me to realize where I was—and that my boyfriend Randall's townhome was only a handful of blocks away in his posh Loring Park neighborhood.

I'd been feeling so disconnected from him lately, what with the end of the trimester approaching. He'd been so caught up in preparing for finals that he'd barely even taken time to call, much less initiate spending any time together. So even though I was a little hurt that he had yet to respond to my text from earlier—-I also wasn't all that surprised. And now, it hit me just how much I'd actually been missing him.

Actually, it was right in this very spot that we'd first come together. I'd had the hots for the silver fox professor ever since my second-year twentieth century lit class—though in a huge auditorium, there was no reason for Randall Price to ever notice the quiet redhead sitting near the back of the room.

So when I nearly plowed him down while exiting girls' night at Bar Kumquat years later—-*apparently a common theme in my life*—-I couldn't have been more mortified.

But instead of being annoyed, Randall's face had lit up in a sexy smile, his gray eyes crinkling at the corners as he held me steady, taking me in.

"Whoa... where are you rushing off to?"

Face blazing, I'd been about to attempt a coherent response when I saw the recognition flash in his eyes. "Wait, I know you. St. Kate's, right?"

"You... know who I am?"

He chuckled. "Of course I do. I recall having you in at least one of my classes. You were always so... engaged. But it's been a while..."

"... Elizabeth."

"Yes, that's right. Elizabeth Blake."

He remembered my name?? "Well, I graduated over five years ago now."

"Then it's been far too long." He then glanced down, and I remember feeling very self-conscious in the little black dress Brooke had convinced me to wear out that night. But there was something in the way he'd looked at me that made me glad I'd given in. "Don't suppose I could convince you to join me for a night cap? I'd love to hear what you've been up to all these years." He leaned in. "I recall a spark of talent in you, Ms. Blake."

I mean my God, who *wouldn't* have said yes to that man? Confident in all the areas I was lacking, it was like an instant boost to my self-esteem, being noticed like that. I remember accepting his offered hand, feeling the other rest on the thin material at the small of my back—and I was a goner.

At least—-I'm pretty sure that's how it went. Right now, standing outside in the dark in another time completely, the details felt a little... fuzzy.

All I knew was that drink turned into three years of being wrapped up in the arms and the life of that man—and while every moment wasn't necessarily perfect, being with Randall made me believe I could become exactly what I dreamed of. I just needed to stay focused.

And get some damn face time with my boyfriend.

I was about to pull out my phone again and send him a text when I heard another notification sound from my purse.

BROOKE: I'm home!

KAIT: Congrats. Any particular reason for this special announcement?

BROOKE: Huh?

INDI: You texted our Dearie chat, love.

BROOKE: Oops! That message was meant for Lizzo.

INDI: Okay...

KAIT: Okay...

LIZZIE: Alright...

BROOKE: LIZZO! It's about damn time...

Giggling in spite of myself at the ridiculousness of my friends' never-gonna-die joke, I closed out of the chat, at least feeling in a better mood.

And the more I thought about it, the idea of cozying up with my sexy boyfriend at his place sounded *infinitely* better than hiding from my life under a quilt. Plus, maybe I could pick his brain on that sticking point I'd hit in Chapter Three.

But that could wait until morning... I had far better ideas in mind for what I wanted to do with my boyfriend tonight. And none of them had a single thing to do with writing.

Maybe this time he'll be willing to do a little extra so I get my happy ending, too...

Slowly, I made my way through the neighborhood, my head a little swimmy as I stumbled through the first few blocks. After a while, I could see the row of townhomes slowly growing closer off in the distance, lamps glowing alongside each door.

In my head, my friends' joke had transitioned into the melody. *"Turn up the music, I'm gonna celebrate..."*

Humming to myself, I shimmied with a saucy little step into the final intersection, feeling my left sandal slip off the edge of my heel. A moment later, I'd tumbled to my knees in the middle of the street.

"It's *ok! I'm gonna be ok!"* I said loudly to no one in particular as I lay sprawled face-first on the pavement.

Jesus—Pull it together, Lizzo.

Standing up gingerly, I brushed the dirt from the knees of my jeans before taking a quick scan to see if anyone had watched me biff it. By some miracle, this part of the neighborhood seemed mostly deserted.

All the old folks have gone to beddy-bye, a voice trilled in my head, and I snorted—totally something Brooke would've said about Randall.

Usually, I was a little defensive about our age gap. But for some reason, tonight that shit was *funny.*

Yanking off both shoes and looping the straps around one finger, I chose to ignore the fifty million disgusting city germs I was probably exposing myself to and continued on, barefoot. A few minutes later, I finally found myself standing in front of his place.

No matter how many times I'd been there, I still marveled at the beauty of it. Randall had moved into the historic brownstone long before we'd started dating, and it was where we continued to spend most of our time together.

Sometimes, I wished we'd go out for dinner, a show, or *something...* but he'd usually talk me out of it.

"Then I can keep you all to myself," he'd always say.

As if I could argue with that. Randall knew all the best takeout places, besides being a decent cook himself with an impeccable wine collection. And really, I didn't mind staying in all that much. I'd always been a homebody.

Plus, his place *was* gorgeous—though maybe a *bit* stuffy compared to the eclectic boho style of my apartment, which he jokingly referred to as '*a glorified dorm room*'.

And tonight, *Chez Randall* also happened to be *very* convenient.

Gripping the handrail as I made my way up the concrete steps, I paused in front of the imposing black door to test the handle. Finding it locked, I began digging around in the ceramic planter on the stoop where I knew he kept his hide-a-key. Randall had never actually given me my own copy—even after two years together, he was still weirdly private about that stuff.

Snorting out laughter as I rummaged around in the plant, my fingers finally closed on the hollow frog.

'*Hide-a-key*'. *Such a silly word...*

I flipped open the lever beneath the toadstool, letting the key drop into my hand before chucking Mr. Froggy back into the planter. After a couple of jiggles and pauses to steady my hand, I heard the lock click open, and I slowly made my way inside.

The place was quiet and mostly dark, outside of the warm light emanating from the living room at the end of the hallway, bathing the wood-paneled walls on either side of me in a soft glow. As I gently closed the front door behind me to block out the noise of the city, I could hear low jazz music playing. *Good, he was still up.*

I began tiptoeing my way along the carpeted hallway, anxious to surprise him. Pausing at the hallway mirror to take a quick peek at my blurry reflection, I took a moment to tidy the mess on my head left by my earlier tumble.

No, *wait—I need sexy hair!*

I ran my fingers into my long, auburn waves, flipping my head downward to shake it all up.

But of course, I once again overestimated my ability to keep myself upright after four—*or was it five?*—cocktails.

I toppled forward, taking a sloppy nosedive onto the padded antique bench against the wall before rolling over onto the floor. As the shock wore off over what I'd just done, a giggle burst out—and I quickly clapped a hand over my mouth to muffle the sound.

It was then that I heard it. A loud grunt, one that I'd become *very* familiar with over the past couple of years.

Was he seriously having fun... without me?

Scrambling up off the floor, I crossed the remaining length of the hallway and rounded the corner, ready to interrupt his playtime with some of my own.

Problem was, somebody had already beaten me to it.

A topless brunette had her back to me on the dark leather sofa as she straddled my boyfriend's lap, pants pooled at his feet and hands grasping her waist as they moved together. Scattered across the wooden coffee table behind her were piles of papers and two, half-filled stemless glasses—along with the two hundred dollar bottle of wine (*which I really couldn't afford in the first place*) I'd given him for his birthday a few weeks earlier.

I could even see the tiny card still hanging by a red ribbon from the neck of the bottle, with the note I'd handwritten—

'*Happy Birthday, my love.*'

My... love.
"*My favorite wine... you remembered,*" he'd told me that night with a smile. "*You're always noticing things like that, Elizabeth...*"

Always noticing—except, apparently, for *this.*

I felt like I was having an out-of-body experience—seeing and hearing opposing messages—face and hands all numb and tingly as my brain tried to make sense of what was happening.

Then, somehow, I found my voice.

"*What is this...?*"

I'd intended to sound more shocked, more angry. Instead, my voice came out in a breathy whisper—as if the rest of me were still caught in the tipsy stealth mode of two minutes ago, still hoping to surprise my boyfriend with my sexy entrance.

But my feeble confrontation was enough to get their attention. Instantly, the brunette's head whipped around, and I caught a glimpse of her familiar face, eyes widening.

Oh my God.

"You're sleeping with Jessica!?"

Randall's head craned to the side to gaze past his teaching assistant's naked body, and he had the absolute fucking *audacity* to look annoyed.

"Calm down, Elizabeth."

Head spinning, I found myself hovering somewhere between my worst nightmare and disbelief.

Calm down? Was this actually happening right now? Or was it all an incredibly vivid hallucination, thanks to the alcohol pickling my brain?

And was it completely irrational and off-topic that I couldn't help but compare the shortcomings of my own short, curvy body to the slender, leggy one perched on his lap?

I stared at him. "You did not seriously just ask me to calm down while your *number two pencil dick* is still inside another woman."

Randall released a sigh, as though I were just another moody freshman he'd been forced to tolerate in his classroom. "Come, now... we're all adults here. This was nothing... just letting off a little steam in between grading papers."

He reached across the sofa to grab a throw blanket, handing it to Jessica—who quickly wrapped it around her body as she scrambled off his lap. Judging by the horrified look on her face as she rounded the end of the sofa towards the bathroom, the fact that they'd been doing *'nothing'* was news to her.

"*Nothing...?*" I echoed numbly under my breath as Jessica slammed the bathroom door behind her. With a jolt, my heart finally caught up with my brain.

This is real, Lizzie. Your so-called gentlemanly boyfriend is actually a cheating asshole.

At some point during my last thirty seconds of rapid awareness, Randall had arisen from the sofa and pulled up his pants. Now he just stood there, arms crossed, silently observing me with his steely-gray eyes. He hadn't bothered to button his shirt, so I was forced to witness not only his indifference but also his perfectly sculpted chest on full display—still tan from his week-long conference in Maui.

Which Jessica had also attended, as his assistant.

God, I was such an idiot.

I felt the initial shock dissolve into shame as one of the last remnants of my life I'd believed I could count on began to crumble—followed by the inevitable tears.

It was moments like these that I hated how easily the tears seemed to come. Sadness, anger—it didn't matter.

But I couldn't stop any of it, could I? Not the crying, not the humiliation—nor the betrayal, the loss.

Finally, Randall closed the distance between us, pulling me into his chest as I closed my eyes, furious at myself for being unable to keep myself from falling apart. Then I felt his breath, hot against my ear.

"Elizabeth, there's no need to get emotional... you and I, *we're ok.*"

Ok?

It was enough, at least, to mostly sober me up. Wiping the tears from my cheeks with the back of my hand, I maneuvered myself out of his grasp, backing away from the man who I thought had been my everything.

"How can you *possibly* think we are ok? None of *this*," my voice cracked as I gestured wildly towards the after- math on the sofa, the wine, the bathroom, "is ok. *Lying to me is not ok. Having sex with other people* when you are supposed to be in a committed relationship is *not ok*, Randall."

He ran a hand through his perfectly styled, salt-and-pepper hair, groaning in frustration. "There you go again, with your romanticized ideals. Elizabeth, sex can truly be *just sex*. This doesn't change how I feel about you. And besides, you're making an assumption here. We've never actually discussed being exclusive."

"Yes, *we have*. Don't you recall that weekend up in Duluth last year?" My eyes widened, realization dawn- ing. "Wait... are you telling me you've been seeing other women the *entire* time we've been together?"

He was silent.

Jesus Christ.

"Do you even love me at all, or has all of this just been... *convenient* to you?" I heard my voice waver, and I dug my nails into my tingling palms to keep myself from unraveling.

Randall's eyes avoided mine—and for once, the man accustomed to commanding a room with his words looked as though he had no idea what to say. "*Elizabeth...*"

But before he could finish his sentence, we heard a door open as Jessica walked out of the bathroom, partially dressed. As she continued to hunt around in the background for the rest of her things, I could see tears streaming down her face as well—and for a moment, I felt bad for her.

And slowly, all the pieces clicked into place—it all made sense.

Why we rarely spent time together outside of his place.

Why he'd never shared a key.

Why he'd acted so fiercely private about the rest of his life.

I had never been enough for him.

I turned my gaze back towards Randall, now feeling nothing but disgust.

Actually... oh God, I'm going to be sick...

And before I could consider my next move, I heaved the contents of my stomach all over his feet—along with his antique beige Persian rug.

"*Fuck, look what you've done...!*"

It was the first time I'd seen the esteemed Randall Price truly freak out. For some reason, it made me feel just the *teensiest* bit better.

I mean, I hadn't intended to vomit. But it was a suitable exclamation point to cap off the worst day I'd had in a long time. I was done here.

As he hurried off towards the kitchen to find something to save not his relationship but his precious rug, I stepped around the mess to reach for a tissue from the box on the coffee table. Wiping my mouth, I noticed Jessica watching me. Her expression seemed to volley between pain, fear and humiliation—and I felt myself soften.

"Lizzie, I'm... so sorry. He told me the two of you weren't seeing each other anymore..."

I held up a hand. "Please... don't say any more. It's ok." Then my eye caught on something else. As Randall rushed back into the room with rags and a bucket, I grabbed the bottle of wine from the table, tossing the gift tag at him. He caught it, briefly scanning the message inscribed on it before glancing back at me, realization dawning.

"Elizabeth, don't do anything stupid..."

"Too late... you've already beaten me to it." Then I held up the bottle, waving it between us. "There's seventy-five dollars of wine left in here that I paid for. That makes it mine, so I'm taking it home to celebrate the fact that I am no longer *yours*. Goodbye, Randall."

With way more confidence than I actually felt, I turned on my heel, picking up my sandals from where I'd deposited them. I offered a silent prayer of gratitude as I left the room that—*this time*—I didn't suffer a single misstep.

And as I crossed the last stretch of hallway towards my freedom, I may have *accidentally* tilted the bottle just a smidge, leaving behind the sort of deep-set stain that only a ninety-five point Pinot Noir could do.

Anyway, it was fitting, wasn't it? And reminiscent of the mark left upon the heart of a thirty-year-old, would-be *hopeless romantic* by an inadequate jackass who—as it turned out—had never really loved her at all.

Chapter 5

James

I took a deep breath, releasing it into the air around me in one long, slow exhale. It was exactly the kind of late spring morning I loved most—a slight chill in the air, fog hanging heavy over the glassy surface of the water, the sun easing up along the horizon.

I dipped my paddle into the water, reaching with my other hand to push off from the dock. Within moments, I was floating out into the mist, the fog quickly enveloping my kayak in its folds until I could no longer see the shore.

But after all these years, I knew Lake Elska like the back of my hand—even in the dark, I always managed to find my way home again.

I fell into a steady rhythm of slicing the water with my paddle in alternating movements, gliding along silently. In the distance, I could hear the haunting call of the loon—Minnesota's state bird and common resident on our lake—echo across the water. A few others called out in response, and soon, a chorus began.

Sometimes the weekenders who drove up here to their cabins found them annoying, but I'd always liked them. The loons belonged here, on the water, like nowhere else. And probably far more than most.

I could relate to that myself.

I'd been eager to shake off the city as soon as Jack and I had pulled into Dearing Creek late yesterday—but I'd been forced to deal with another issue on the Kinney project and wasn't able to get out here on the water like I'd hoped.

It was just as well—I'd been tired anyway, and in a mood.

Sure, I was happy to have Jack home again. And not just for myself—I knew it was something he'd been needing, too. A fresh start, closer to me and Jesse as well as his dad, who hadn't been in the best of health these past few years. And God knew his baby sister, Lacey, could use the support—especially now, with her two-year-old, Eli. He'd have plenty to keep him occupied in his new life, beyond starting his fishing charter business.

No, it was the text from my boss, Mel Aaronson, that had set me on edge—it's like I couldn't take two goddamn days off from work without getting harassed about something.

I shook my head, irritated at my own crankiness. None of this was Mel's fault, really. I knew he had his hands full, as I did, dealing with the clients on this particular remodel. I'd been assigned as Lead Designer on the project four months ago—but with how high-maintenance Joe Kinney had been with all of his demands, I'd also been having to spend way too much extra time on the job site lately. Even Jesse, who was in charge of the plumbing work, had been fed up with the guy.

Just another rich asshole who thinks his time's worth more than the rest of us.

Feeling my jaw clench, I took another steadying breath to relax myself. Out here on the lake was meant to be *my* time. I wasn't going to let the frustration from one job take that from me.

I had to admit, though—the voice inside, nagging at me to branch out on my own, had been growing louder these days. Already thirty-four, I'd been working for Mel almost since I'd graduated from Lake View High. I was grateful because the man had taught me a lot, even beyond my training at the tech college. Mel gave me opportunities that others maybe wouldn't have, allowing me the opportunity to learn and master various skills within the company before I landed on design. I owed him more than I could ever repay.

Even still, I'd spent much of the past few years imagining what it would be like, owning my time, my success... my future. Too much of what had happened up to now had felt beyond my control. Maybe it was time to prove to myself that I could be more.

But the pull towards starting my own business was only the half of it. The reality was, I was trapped in an impossible situation—-with no idea of how to move forward without making things even more complicated.

I mean, don't get me wrong—I was happy living in Dearing Creek. It was my home, and I had no intentions of leaving this place that had welcomed me with open arms back when I was a young boy, grieving the loss of his mama. And I'd always been somewhat of a loner, outside of the guys—another reason why the idea of being my own boss—-and having a greater stake in my success and career path—-was definitely tempting.

But all the same, I still wasn't sure I was ready to face the main hurdle that was necessary to get me there.

I began to turn the kayak around slowly to head back. The fog had mostly lifted by this point, the surface of the water sparkling with the soft yellow glow from the early morning sun, peeking up over the horizon. I could see Mervin Flenderson sitting on his dock with his usual cup of coffee aways down the shoreline, and I waved as he tipped his hat in my direction.

Then I felt my phone buzz in my pocket, piercing my solitude. Resting the paddle on top of my kayak, I pulled it out to see a message from GiGi:

GIGI: Morning, love. Do you have time to sit and have a cup of coffee before you head off to work?

I glanced at the time—six forty-five. Time to wrap things up here so I could get myself cleaned up.

Chuckling to myself, I pocketed my phone and resumed paddling. I don't know what I'd ever done in my life to deserve her, but thank God for that woman.

I really needed to get my head out of my ass and stop feeling restless or worrying about what came next. I knew I was lucky to even have options to consider.

Things could've turned out so much differently for me, considering how they'd started.

That's what everyone said, anyway. I didn't see any reason to believe otherwise.

"James, can you give me a hand?"

Jesse's voice filtered out from the Kinney's new master bathroom, where the plumbing was finally being completed today. Walking in, I saw his denim-clad legs sticking out from beneath the cabinets of the newly installed double sink.

"Yeah? What do you need?" From my angle, I could see my friend trying to position one of the sinks properly into the countertop, but he appeared to be losing the battle.

"What does it look like? Just hold this in place for a minute while I line up the pipes. Tim was supposed to be up here helping me, but he left early."

I wandered over, grabbing hold of the sink's porcelain edges to steady it. "Alright, I've got it. Do what you need to do."

"Thanks, man."

As Jesse worked to maneuver things down below, I glanced around the room. The master suite was the part of the remodel I was most proud of—probably the most beautiful bathroom I'd designed to date. It was simple, modern—clean lines and brass fixtures, softened by pale green and white tile work, warm wooden cabinets and a custom walk-in shower that could easily fit two or more people.

I smirked. It'd been quite some time since I'd attempted a two-person shower of *any* kind. And the last certainly wasn't as comfortable as I'd made this one. I made a mental note that if I ever decided to upgrade the shower at my place to add some solid grab bars.

Because you just never know when you might need them.

"What're you laughing about up there?" Jesse's voice echoed up through the drain. I hadn't even realized I'd made a sound.

"Just thinking about the shower install. Nice size, isn't it?"

Jesse made a noise as he tightened the last of the sections. "You can let go now." As I stepped back, he shimmied out, dropping his wrench into the toolbox at his feet before pulling up to standing. As he brushed himself off, I watched the residual sawdust from the new baseboards float around his short, sandy blonde hair like a halo. "Believe me, I've been taking photos and sending them to Tara. She's already informed me that she expects an upgrade to ours after the baby arrives this fall."

I raised an eyebrow. "She knows that'll probably just lead to more babies, right?"

He shrugged, grinning. "I dunno... I kinda feel like it's worth it either way, don't you?"

Chuckling, I clapped him on the back. Of the three of us, Jesse had always been the most easy-going and never let too much ruffle his feathers. But as much as I enjoyed giving my friend crap, I couldn't wait to see him as a dad—-I knew he was going to be amazing at it. Even if he ended up with an entire army of Baby Sundgaards, due to his and Tara's inability to keep their hands off each other.

"Well, I feel like I'm missing out on all the fun in here."

Jesse and I locked eyes for a moment at the familiar voice before I turned towards Denise Kinney, who stood leaning elegantly against the doorframe of the bathroom, eyeing us with an amused expression.

Her husband Joe had been traveling for most of the week for his manufacturing business, so we'd been dealing with his wife in his absence. I didn't know if it was better or worse—in a way, I'd almost prefer Joe's hovering demands over Denise and the way she looked at me as though I were her next meal.

I noticed her dark hair was hanging loose today, and that she seemed to have missed a couple of buttons on her white blouse. For a moment, one could almost forget that she was the mother of two college-age boys. The years—or rather, the enhancements—had worked in her favor.

Anyway, dodging Denise Kinney—including whatever she was gunning for, outside of this remodel—was a headache I didn't need right now. Already, her '*design questions*' over the last several days had kept me anchored on site more than I liked. All I wanted was to wrap up my part of the project and move on.

Because at this point, I was nearly at my limit.

"Jesse and I were just talking about family stuff, Mrs. Kinney. But we're about done with this part of the remodel. Just need to install the vanity lights tomorrow, and you're good to go."

Denise wandered over to the sink, lightly tracing the countertops with one hand as she studied the space. Then she turned back towards me. "Glad to hear it. But I have an issue I need to address. Can I borrow you for a few minutes?"

Jesse picked up his tool bag and started towards the door. "I need to check in with Mark before we shut down for the day anyway. See ya." Nodding briefly at Denise while pointedly avoiding my glare, he walked out the door, leaving me to deal with Cougar Town on my own.

Traitor.

I sighed. "Of course, Mrs. Kinney. What's on your mind today?"

She looked at me pointedly. "I thought I asked you to call me Denise, James." Walking past me, she pushed the bathroom door shut, and the noise outside of our crew packing up became muffled. "So noisy out there," I heard her say.

Shit.

"Sorry, Mrs. Kinney. I told you we like to keep things professional on these jobs," I said, forcing a friendly tone into my voice.

"I see." Her tone was cool, but I still noticed the corners of her mouth curled into a smile as she returned to face me. "So, I'm wondering about this shower. Can you come take a look at this, please?"

This woman seemed to enjoy making me feel uncomfortable and under her control. But wasn't that the Kinney way? Between them and the Taylors, all of Dearing Creek was built and run by their money.

Exactly how they liked it.

"Is there an issue with the shower? I thought you signed off on that yesterday."

Denise had stepped inside the shower now and was gazing upwards at the massive, rain-style shower head. "The shower itself is fine, James. I'm wondering about the shower head. Take a look."

The absolute last thing I wanted to do was obey her command and find myself cozied up to this woman.

"It's a bit of a tight fit in there. Can you just point out your concern, and I can take a look at it tomorrow?"

She raised an eyebrow. "Are you afraid of me, James? I promise, I won't bite."

"No, ma'am." I sighed, then took a step inside. *Just get this over with quickly*, I told myself.

Once inside, I immediately felt the energy shift. Though there was plenty of room for her to move over and make space for me, Denise kept her feet planted in the center. Awkwardly, I maneuvered myself as far away as I could manage, pressing my back against the glass side wall to avoid contact.

"So, what's the issue with the shower head?"

Denise pointed upward. "Take a look at the spray holes... don't they seem... blocked to you?"

Begrudgingly leaning over, I craned my head to inspect the underside of the shower head—when suddenly, I felt a hand on my chest. Before I could react, Denise Kinney had pressed her lips hungrily against mine, her hand now grasping the front of my shirt to pull me in closer while the other trailed down towards the crotch of my jeans.

I tore myself away, practically leaping through the glass walls like a battering ram. *What the fuck was she doing?*

"Mrs. Kinney, what the hell are you trying to do here?"

Denise slowly, deliberately, stepped out of the shower, her eyes blazing as she looked straight at me. "Come now, James... don't tell me you haven't been feeling a little blocked up yourself? You've been sending me signals for weeks—let's not pretend any of this is a surprise."

"It damn well is to *me*. The only signal I've been trying to communicate to you is that ours is solely a professional relationship, ma'am, and I'm only here to do a job. And *none* of what just happened is appropriate."

She crossed her arms, eyes narrowing. "So exactly what are you saying?"

"I need to go. Enjoy the rest of your evening, *ma'am.*"

Before she could say another word, I opened the door, storming my way towards the main staircase, where Jesse was just a few steps ahead of me, making his way down to where the rest of the crew was loading up materials. Jesse took one look at my face and immediately knew that something was up.

"You ok?"

"I'm fine. You got the rest covered? I'm headed out," I said, not bothering to wait for his answer.

"Yeah, ok." I could feel his eyes follow me, as I passed down the stairs and towards the door. But no way in hell was I sticking around for a chat.

As I started up my truck a minute later and put it into drive, all I could think about was putting as much distance as possible between myself and this house.

I was *done.*

Chapter 6

James

Thirty minutes later, I was standing beneath my own shower head, letting the hot water wash away the frustrations of the day, when I heard my phone vibrating on the counter. I reached for the knob and turned off the water, leaning forward to rest my head against my arm on the tiled wall.

As I stood there watching the suds swirl down the drain, I could almost see my career swirling down along with them. Because my time spent in here ruminating had done nothing to prove otherwise.

What the hell was I going to do?

Feeling no less tense than I had when I started my shower, I gave up and opened the door, reaching for the dark green towel I'd left hanging on the nearby hook. After drying off, I stepped over to the sink to check my phone.

Shaking my head, I set down the phone and started drying off. No sense pissing her off by being late again.

Besides, I could use a break from focusing on everything that had me feeling off lately.

Thank God for living in a small town with well-traveled short cuts.

Twenty minutes later, I pulled into the open parking space behind the cabin, straightening the collar of my blue button-down shirt as I stepped out of the truck, paper bag in hand. I didn't always make as much of an effort for our dinners, but I figured I should tonight—she deserved to see a better side of me than the one I'd been showing lately.

The door opened in front of me before I could even make a grab for the handle. Then GiGi stepped out, dressed in her typical loose-fitting floral dress, and pulled me in for a hug.

"Well, it's about time you got your ass over here for dinner, Tater-tot."

"I figured if I didn't, I'd be on your shit list forever," I said as I pulled back, grinning.

"Don't worry, you're still at the top," GiGi laughed, swatting at my arm as she took the bag from my hand, shooing me inside.

"How's the new faucet sprayer working out?" I asked over my shoulder as I took off my shoes. I was greeted by the aroma of roast chicken, garlic mashed potatoes, and string beans coming from the kitchen. After all these years, GiGi—*Grandma Georgia* actually, but I don't think I'd ever actually called her by her given name—-knew well enough when I was in a funk. And it never failed that she'd start pulling out my favorite meals.

"*Food is mood,*" she'd always say, and she wasn't wrong—as a small boy, there wasn't much in my world that couldn't be soothed by my grandmother's hugs and home cooking.

These days, both still had a way of lifting my spirits—but the problems of her thirty-four-year-old grandson were another matter entirely.

Knowing GiGi though—if there was a meal powerful enough to fix everything that needed fixing in my life, she was likely to find it.

After all, nobody would dispute the fact that Georgia LaMott was a force of nature, and not just in my life. A lifelong resident of Dearing Creek, she was a pillar of the community who'd built herself a salty/sweet reputation—she didn't take guff from anyone, but she'd also be the first to step in with loving advice or help.

Being raised by such a woman had its advantages—and likely explained a lot. A lesser woman wouldn't have been able to do it, considering where we'd started together—but GiGi and I, we were kindred spirits.

Deep, excruciating loss was something we both had in common.

"It's working perfectly, love... Thanks for getting me all set up. Those dishes won't know what hit 'em." She tucked a section of white hair—flowing in its usual loose waves above her shoulders—behind one ear.

I smiled, nodding towards the kitchen. "Roast chicken, huh?" I said, casting her a suspicious glance as I followed her.

"Chicken was on sale this week at Filbert's," she said, shrugging. "You have something against chicken?"

I smirked. "You know I don't."

"Then stop your belly achin' and help me set the table."

An hour later, we sat there together, bellies stuffed and finishing the last of our ciders. GiGi was in the middle of regaling me with the sordid details of her friend Doris's latest romantic entanglement over in Heartwood, our rival town just to the west.

But my mind was far from Doris, or anything to do with the latest gossip. I had replayed that scene with Denise Kinney over and over in my mind, trying to determine if I'd somehow misled her—though I already knew I hadn't.

Just another fucking entitled person taking what they wanted—what they believed was theirs, just because of their name or that their bank account had more zeros behind it than any decent person needed. The control somehow always ended up in the hands of the wrong kind of people.

And I was goddamned tired of it.

Being fed up wouldn't solve anything, though. Because right now, what I needed to focus on was the security of my job at Aaronson Construction.

It was then that I heard my grandmother sigh. "Alright, out with it."

I glanced over at her across the table, where she sat with her head propped on one hand, staring at me. "What?"

"I've been sittin' here talking about Doris for fifteen solid minutes, and you haven't once asked me to change the subject."

"Would it've stopped you if I had?"

"Not likely. But blathering on about local gossip has always been my barometer to see if you're actually paying attention."

I rolled my eyes. "I *was* listening. Doris and Hank Ressler have been hooking up on Tuesday nights after bowling league."

"It's cute that you think I'm going to let up on this."

Sighing, I set down the bottle of cider in my hand. "Fine, *you win.* I had an incident today at work on the Kinney project. Denise... well, she hit on me."

GiGi didn't even bat an eye. "Of course she did. That woman always has her eye out for her next bedwarmer."

"Sometimes, I wish you'd at least *try* to have a filter."

"James, dear... don't be so innocent," she said, shaking her head in amusement. "Besides, if you would actually take my advice for once and find some nice girl to marry, maybe the cougars in town would start leaving you alone."

"I already told you, GiGi, it's not up for discussion. One woman in my life is enough," I said, crossing my arms in an attempt to look stern. "And besides, you keep me plenty busy."

"I'll wear you down eventually, my boy." She sighed. "Anyway, how'd you respond? And more importantly, does Joe know?"

"He's been out of town this week... and of course I immediately put a stop to it, told her she was being inappropriate. That it was only professional between us."

She let out a low whistle. "I bet that didn't go over well."

"I wouldn't know... I left right after," I said, fidgeting with my fork. "But I have no idea what I'll be walking into tomorrow. She may try to turn this around on me with Mel."

"She might. So, what're you going to do about it?"

"Not much I *can* do. I don't see how this ends well, unless she's embarrassed enough by her own behavior to keep it to herself. Otherwise, she'll probably report it to Mel or Joe."

"Probably. Either way, you might be out of a job."

"Yep."

"Want me to kick her ass?" Her brown eyes narrowed with determination, and I laughed in spite of myself.

"Not this time. I just... need to figure out what to say to Mel."

GiGi was quiet for a moment, considering. "Have you thought any more about what we talked about?"

I raised an eyebrow. "What, starting my own business? I don't know..."

GiGi knew it was pointless to push me into anything. Even still, this had been a persistent topic of conversation at this table for well over a year now—especially during the past few months, while I'd been grumbling about the Kinney project.

We both knew being my own boss—having the autonomy to choose my clients, and the projects I felt passionate about—was everything I wanted.

But I wasn't naïve enough to ignore the realities of what came with it. Striking out on my own carried a great deal of risk. And in my case, it was also deeply personal. What if I fucked it all up?

My grandfather was a good man, working hard his entire life for other people. There was no shame in that. So why did I keep feeling like I needed more? Was it pride?

Either way, I wasn't sure if I was ready to face what I needed to in order to make it happen. Maybe I never would be.

GiGi took a sip of her cider before continuing. "You'd be great at it, you know. And I'm not the only one who thinks so."

Who else had she been talking to about this?

I felt myself tense. "I don't want to discuss this right now."

She rested her hand on mine, her eyes solemn. "You can't run away from it forever, James."

Moving my hand away, I stood up. "I need to head home. If I want to talk to Mel tomorrow, I better do it first thing." Before she could respond, I grabbed my dishes and carried them to the sink, feeling her eyes on the back of me as I rinsed them off. She knew well enough by now that when I didn't want to discuss something, it was best to leave it.

Drying my hands, I paused to kiss her cheek on my way out. "Listen GiGi, I appreciate the advice. I just... can't right now, ok?"

"It's ok, Tater-tot," she said, reaching her hand up to pat my arm. "Good luck tomorrow, ok? And stand up for yourself. Nobody but you gets to choose your outcome."

"I know. G'night then."

But as I drove along the roads towards my own home a few minutes later, my mind was stuck back in GiGi's cabin, the first home I could recall, thinking about what she'd said.

She'd been there for me my whole life, knew me almost better than I knew myself. After my mother—her only child—had died when I was eight years old, and my father bailed shortly after, she and Pops became my whole world. They went through all the hard shit raising me, a broken boy whose whole world had imploded.

And then we lost Pops too, when I was barely eighteen.

It was then that I knew I'd never leave her, never leave Dearing Creek. She and this town had taken me in after I'd lost it all. And going back to where I'd started was something I never even considered. There was nothing left for me there.

But now, all these years later, I wondered if resenting what had been left behind was doing a damn thing—except holding me back.

Chapter 7

Lizzie

"So, Lizzie girl, what are you working on today?"

I looked up at Grandma Cora, who'd walked into my bedroom and now stood peering over my shoulder as I typed away. "It's that story we were brainstorming last week. The one about the awkward baker and the hunky captain? He just walked into her shop for the first time, and they crashed into one another."

"Oooh, yes, that was a good one. So, tell me... what happens next?"

I laughed, now turning fully in my seat. "Like you don't already know..."

"Wake up, Liz... you've got company."

I opened my eyes barely a crack to see Ethan standing next to my bed—wearing his favorite Foo Fighters concert t-shirt, his tousled auburn hair sticking up in the back, identical in shade to my own—and, best of all, holding out a steaming cup of hot coffee.

I glanced at the time on the mint green, old-timey clock sitting on my nightstand—*nine a.m.* For a moment, I was confused why my twin brother was at my apartment so early.

Scratch that—Why was he here at all?

But then slowly, like maple syrup, the memories of the previous day began oozing over me in all of their sticky glory: my humiliating run-in with the rude stranger at the coffee shop; everything terrible that had happened at work; then my overzealous happy hour with Brooke, which every fiber of my hungover self was currently regretting.

And for the final *pièce de résistance*—catching my philandering asshole of a boyfriend in the act, concluded by vomiting five fingers' worth of brandy all over his precious vintage rug.

Hours later, I could still hear his words on repeat: *"There you go again, Elizabeth..."*

Indeed.

After storming out of Randall's place with my bottle of wine and tiny remnants of pride, only to realize I had no way home, I did the only logical thing my shell-shocked/half-tipsy brain could manage: I called my very patient and understanding brother to come to my rescue.

If the entirety of it all—and the aftermath—hadn't been so completely awful, I might've been more impressed with myself for even waking up this morning.

As it was, I gingerly lifted my head from my pillow, fairly certain it had been shot full of angry birds on a merry-go-round while I'd been sleeping. Groaning, I looked up at my brother.

"*Please* tell me time travel exists, so I can go back and redo the last twenty-seven hours."

Ethan shook his head, not bothering to hold back his smile. "Sorry, Sis… as much as I wish that were true, I'm afraid you're stuck here with me here in the present time. But, hey… at least reality comes with fresh coffee?"

I rubbed my temples as he handed me the mug, flashing a quick, grateful smile before taking my first sip. "Did you really stay here all night?"

He shrugged. "Yeah… I slept on the sofa. I was worried about you."

"You know you're the best brother ever, right?"

"Just consider us even, since you covered my ass last week when I couldn't find my car keys," he said, smiling. Then his face grew serious. "Speaking of asses, you know I'm going to kick Price's, right?"

Hearing his name once again triggered my stupid, traitorous tear ducts—though this time, I had no idea if the culprit was anger, humiliation, or heartbreak. I couldn't *actually* be crying over that man again, could I?

Ethan sat down next to me, wrapping an arm around my back to pull me against him, the way he always had. Even now as adults, our bond was strong, closely resembling each other in so many ways—except for our seven-inch height difference.

I rested my head in the comfortable nook of his shoulder, reaching up to wipe away a stray tear that had escaped down my cheek. "Sorry, Liz. I don't know everything that went down between the two of you, but I never trusted the guy. And you deserve way better than what you got. So next time I see him, I promise—his ass is mine."

Lifting my head, I managed a weak smile at the idea of my brother and my ex in a fight—mostly because I knew without a doubt who the winner would be. "Thanks. Randall will never know what hit him." As he stood up again, I shifted my butt towards the side of the bed to do the same. "Anyway... I should probably shower or something." Taking another quick sip of coffee, it suddenly clicked that my brother had served it up in my favorite mug, a gift from Randall—covered in classic literature quotes, with a curved pencil for a handle.

Now the coffee tasted like things I'd rather forget—like the memory of me screaming, "Number two pencil dick!" at my ex as my love life imploded.

Looking up at my brother, I handed the mug back to him. "Actually... I know this is *completely* irrational... but can you please pour my coffee into a different mug? And then chuck this one in the trash?"

One of the many great things about our relationship was that Ethan didn't even question it—just shrugged as he grabbed the mug, turning back towards the kitchen as he called out over his shoulder. "Anyway, a shower isn't a bad idea... because Brooke just showed up."

"She's here? Why?"

"I guess you were sending texts to the Dearies all night, and she was worried... but why don't you ask her yourself?" his voice filtered in from the kitchen.

My eyes darted over to my phone, still laying on the bed. *Oh, boy.*

"Morning, Sunshine!" Brooke's head popped around the corner, just as I was settling back onto my bed, phone in hand, to review the damage from last night. It was annoying, really, how my friend could out-drink me two to one—yet still manage to look chic and refreshed the next morning, like a sporty, blonde Audrey Hepburn in her black athleisure outfit.

Meanwhile—after a quick glance in the mirror—I more closely resembled *the Lorax.*

If I didn't love her so much, I'd be forced to hate her.

She sat down beside me, brushing the wildness of my hair back from my face as she wrinkled her nose. Grabbing a tissue from my nightstand, she began wiping at the streaks of makeup that remained around my eyes. "So, before I ask what the hell happened last night, go ahead and get yourself caught up there first."

With a sigh, I began scrolling through my messages.

Friday, 11:30 p.m.

LIZZIE: MEN SUCK.

TESS: Agreed.

KAIT: I thought we'd already decided this?

LENA: Wait, did I miss something here?

TESS: Possibly. Far as I know, men have been sucking since the beginning of time.

KAIT: Just not the way we want them to. HAHA

INDI: No, I'm with Lena. Lizzie… What's up, sweetie?

LIZZIE: I barfed all over Randall's rug.

KAIT: Ummm… is this code for something? Some new-fangled sex act you city girls dreamed up?

LIZZIE: No. I literally barfed. Right after he pulled his dick out of the girl he's apparently been banging behind my back.

KAIT: Jesus, way to bury the lede, Blake.

INDI: Wait, are you serious?

LIZZIE: :(

LENA: Oh, sweetie… I'm so sorry. <3 What can we do?

KAIT: Grrr…. I knew that guy was an asshat. We're gonna kill him, Lizzie. Don't you worry.

INDI: Lizzie. Where r u now?

TESS: I'll send an Uber. What's the address?

LIZZIE: E picked me up. I'm home now…never leaving my bed ever again. Way too many old drinkies with Brookie. Worst. day. ever.

INDI: Ok, good. Stay there. We've got you.

LIZZIE: fml

KAIT: No, fuck RANDALL and his dick. I hope he wakes up covered in scabies.

INDI: Ok, I've treated scabies…dick scabies are disgusting.

KAIT: Even better. But seriously get some rest, ok, Lizzie? Love u, hon.

LENA: You can tell us all about it tomorrow. <3 <3

Saturday, 1:30 a.m.

JULES: Omg, just left the premiere. WTH happened? #dickscabiesforever

JULES: Wait, nvm. You're probably all asleep by now. Stupid time difference. I miss everything. Are you ok??

KAIT: Just closing bar, but I'm hoping our girl's asleep. We'll strategize the man whore's demise tomorrow.

JULES: Ok, count me in. Love you, Lizzie. <3

Saturday, 7:30 a.m.

> *BROOKE: WTH, just waking up and reading through messages.*

> *BROOKE: Fucking Randall... I'm gonna break his scabies-covered dick.*

> *BROOKE: Don't worry, girls... won't actually break his dick. But I'm headed over to Lizzie's tout de suite.*

> *INDI: Ok... PLEASE keep us posted. Love you both.*

Before I could say a word, Ethan walked around the corner. "Hey, now that Brooke's here, I'm gonna get going. I... have something I need to get to."

I looked at him curiously. "At nine a.m. on a Saturday morning?"

Ethan averted his eyes, looking uncomfortable. "Yeah, I'm meeting someone in an hour to go biking."

"Who, Andy?" Andy was my brother's roommate—kinda awkward, but sweet. I'd always liked the guy.

"No. It's... a date, actually. Sorry." He looked embarrassed. "Crappy timing, I know."

I gave my brother a weak smile. "No... just because my life is stupid at the moment doesn't mean yours is by extension. This is a *good* thing." Reaching up, I pulled him into a hug. "I expect PG-details, ok? And I mean it... thank you again for last night."

He returned the squeeze before releasing me. "Always, Liz. Oh, and don't forget, Mariah flies in tomorrow afternoon. You can still pick her up from the airport, right? The meeting with the lawyer is at nine a.m. Monday."

Ugh. For a moment, in all the chaos, I *had* forgotten. And I didn't know if I had it in me to deal with both my sister and the settling of our family's estates.

"Yeah, I've got it. I'll do the pickup and make reservations for dinner tomorrow. Any preferences, or can I just book Amore Victoria?"

"Nope, sounds good to me. And Mariah can just deal with it." He grinned, then held up a fist. "Wonder Twins Activate?"

I connected my fist with his, ending with our usual *'pow-pow!'*. Then, with a wave, he left the room.

As I heard the front door shut behind him, I set down my phone with a sigh, flopping backwards onto my bed.

"You two are *forever dorks*." Brooke lay down beside me, snuggling in. "So, you wanna tell me about it?"

And so, I replayed for my friend everything that had happened during the hour or so after the two of us had parted ways last night—every painful, humiliating detail. Brooke patiently listened, gasping aloud at a few parts like the amazing friend that she was.

As we lay there talking, however, I realized I wasn't feeling as heartbroken as I thought I'd be. Pissed off? Yes. Humiliated? Definitely.

But if I were being honest with myself, I knew Randall wasn't the love of my life, even though I'd tried to convince myself that he was. On paper, it seemed like we'd be the perfect match—the aspiring author and her handsome, experienced Lit professor, showing her the way towards... *what, exactly?*

Even now, I had no idea how to finish that sentence. Other than, 'The End'.

It had never been about '*keeping me all to himself*'. He just didn't want to advertise the fact that he was spending his time with an aimless thirty-year-old who had nothing impressive or interesting to add to his life beyond sex. Nor did he, apparently, want our relationship to cramp his style of man-whoring around Minneapolis.

It was hard not to feel gross, used... *unworthy*.

But more than anything—ashamed that I'd somehow turned a blind eye to every bit of it.

"Well, I officially hate him," Brooke declared, sitting up. "And you, my dear, deserve so much better than that man."

I hoisted myself up as well, shifting until we were facing each other. "Maybe. I don't know."

"What?"

"Maybe the problem is me. Maybe my idea of love is... I don't know... *unrealistic*."

Brooke narrowed her eyes. "Stop that right now. I will *not* let that man destroy all the beautiful parts of my best friend."

"I'm serious. Look at me—I'm thirty and *still* floundering. What the hell am I even doing?" I trailed off, twisting my hands in my lap.

"Lizzie, listen to me. I mean, truly listen. *You. Are. Amazing.* Even on your worst day. And don't," she pointed a stern finger towards me, "roll your eyes at me. You deserve to be loved completely, to be someone's priority. And even to have the big, passionate love that you used to write about in your books. Randall's problem was that *he* wasn't worthy of *you*." She pulled me into her arms, hugging me tight. "I love you, ok? And we're all here for you. You'll get through this. And there are *much* better dicks out there, just waiting for you. Even non-diseased ones."

"Thwanks," I mumbled, my face squished against her shoulder.

"Anytime. But... I gotta tell you something else."

"What?"

She backed away, her nose wrinkling again. "Honey, you stink."

I made a face. "Gee, thanks for being so sensitive in my hour of need."

She giggled. "You're welcome. Now, go take a shower; it'll make you feel loads better. I'll update the rest of our Dearies. Then you and I will grab brunch at that new place on the corner, so we can prepare you emotionally for your sister's arrival and the lawyers on Monday. Deal?"

"Fine, bossy."

Blowing me a kiss as she leaned back against my headboard and pulled out her phone, I gathered up my clothes and walked into my tiny bathroom.

As I stood in my shower, letting the hot water rain over me a few minutes later, I had to admit—I was starting to feel a little better.

I tried to wrap my head around everything that had gone down with Randall, and the part I had played in it all. Hard as it was to admit, I'd allowed myself to be treated that way.

Regardless, I was sick to death of playing the victim, not really believing I could have what I wanted—or holding myself back because I was so damn afraid of failing. It was time to make some changes—most of all, within me.

Now all I needed to figure out was *how*.

Chapter 8

Lizzie

"So, Lizzie, how's work going?"

It was Sunday night, and Ethan and I—along with our older sister, Mariah—were sitting in the corner booth at Amore Victoria, one of my favorite spots in Uptown. After picking her up from the airport earlier in the afternoon, Mariah had insisted I drop her off at a proper hotel rather than bunk together at my place—"*I'm thirty-two, Lizzie. Isn't a slumber party a little ridiculous?*" And then she asked if I'd thought about cutting my hair, as it would help me to look '*my age*'.

So, yeah, that's how *that* was going.

Not that any of this was a surprise. My sister was her mother's daughter, no question—but the divide became even greater in our late teens, once she transferred from her college in Minneapolis to one thousands of miles away in Massachusetts.

We'd come off of a difficult year after losing Dad to a heart attack up at the cabin, and like the rest of us, Mariah just wanted an escape, a fresh start.

Four years later, she came back with a brand-new life, engaged to an investment banker/trust fund boy. Her upper-class world in Boston had been all about social events, fundraisers and living the carefully cultivated life of a socialite ever since.

Before all of that, though, she was just my big sister—and growing up, I had idolized her. Even back then, things seemed to come so easily for Mariah—beautiful, popular, well-liked. It was such a harsh contrast to how I saw myself, and hiding out in her shadow became my safe space.

But after things began to shift for our family, something fractured between us as well. I'd never understood why or how to return to the way things used to be.

And now, aside from making a couple of trips home during Mom's cancer treatments, as well as attending the joint funeral a few months back, it had been over two years since the three of us had spent any time together on purpose.

But this homecoming couldn't *really* be classified as a happy reunion, either. Our family attorney at Brooks & Morgan had finally assembled the wills and assets from both our mother's and Grandma Cora's estates—and as Mariah, Ethan and I were the sole inheritors for both, we were set to meet with Bill Hawkins to sort out all the details of their final wishes tomorrow.

"Work is... *fine*, I guess," I said, shoveling another forkful of bolognese pasta into my mouth so I wouldn't have to discuss it further. Mariah watched me chew, her nose wrinkling, before taking a dainty bite of her wedge salad—as if to provide further evidence that the only thing my sister and I shared in common was DNA.

I mean... who doesn't like bolognese?

Dabbing at her mouth with her napkin, she continued. "Have you thought anymore about looking at Marcus & Associates in St. Paul? Brad would be happy to put in a good word for you—as I mentioned, their managing partner was his fraternity brother at Harvard. Last year, our families summered together at the Cape."

I tried very hard not to roll my eyes at hearing about summers at the Cape or her husband being a Harvard alum for like the seven-thousandth time. I mean, I liked Brad well enough, but come on.

No, that's a lie. My brother-in-law was an entitled douche canoe.

I smiled brightly at my sister. "Thanks, but I'm good. I've been debating shifting away from copywriting, anyway."

Ethan, who'd been enjoying his lasagna without any sort of third degree, glanced over. "Really? You never mentioned that."

I shot my brother a pointed look, trying my best not to glare. Apparently, our twin telepathy had malfunctioned. "Well, I'm... trying to diversify. Add more skills to my resume."

I noticed Mariah studying my face, trying to sort out whether this was actually true or not. I kept my face neutral, grabbing my glass of Malbec and taking a huge swig before changing the subject. "Anyway, how's Nora been doing? It's been ages since we've seen any recent photos."

Mariah offered one of her rare smiles—when she wasn't focused on the next social soirée, we knew our sister lived and breathed for her five-year-old daughter, Nora.

Unfortunately, since Mariah rarely came back home to Minnesota these days, Ethan and I had only met Nora a handful of times. With strawberry blonde hair and blue eyes just like her mother—and a spunky attitude to match—Nora was already a force to be reckoned with.

"She's wonderful, actually, and so excited about her first sleep-away camp this summer."

I raised an eyebrow. "Wow, at five? Isn't that a little young?"

"Not at all. We could have started sending her last year, but she wasn't quite ready yet. And it's only two nights."

"Sounds fun," Ethan said, grabbing another breadstick from the basket between us as Mariah rolled her eyes.

"Anyway, I'm hoping to also get her in for some tennis lessons, too. Brad thinks she's already got quite a swing."

I knew she had to be delighted, envisioning another tennis protégé. "I bet that'll be fun for her. Hopefully, she'll have lots of time to just run around and get her hands dirty this summer, too?"

"Yes, we'll see." Taking another bite of salad, she set down her fork, clearly ready to move on. "So, for tomorrow's meeting with Bill, I think we need to prepare ourselves."

Now it was my turn to look curious. "What do you mean?"

"Well, Mom's in-home hospice care and cancer treatments were expensive. Combined with the fact that she'd been unable to work at the clinic for the last year due to her illness, that likely ate up much of what was left behind from Dad's pension from the state." Mariah took a sip of her own chilled glass of Sauvignon Blanc before continuing. "And as for Grandma Cora, well... she and Grandpa lived comfortably off his small medical practice, but I wouldn't expect they had a tremendous amount left in their accounts. Plus, didn't Mom mention the assisted living facility in Dearing Creek was kind of pricey?"

Our grandparents had lived in a nearby suburb to our family in the Twin Cities for most of our lives, only going up north to their Dearing Creek cabin in the summers. But after the three of us had grown—and both Dad and Grandpa had passed away—Grandma Cora decided to move up to Dearing Creek full-time, so she could be closer to her friends from the old days.

Ethan shrugged. "So? We've already put Mom's house on the market and had that estate crew donate or sell most of what we didn't want. As long as we can pay off the rest of the bills from both funerals and the hospital from the proceeds, we can split whatever is left. I never expected some big inheritance, anyway."

Mariah sniffed, setting down her fork. "That's not what I'm trying to imply here, Ethan... but it would be nice to know they left us *something*. All I'm saying is, I don't want either of you to get your hopes up."

Annoyed at my sister's implication that somehow Ethan and I were the ones desperate for more money, I held back my words with another sip of wine. I didn't have the energy to fight. "Agreed," I said, glancing across the table towards my brother.

No matter how tomorrow's meeting played out, the only thing I cared about was not inheriting even more heartache and complications than I already had.

"Sorry, sorry, I'm here." I bustled into the conference room at the offices of Brooks & Morgan the next morning, ten minutes late and frazzled after being delayed by Constance on my way out. Apparently, she'd found it necessary that I print all the ad copy files from the past two years before I left the office.

Mariah, of course, looked annoyed at my tardiness. Ethan gave me a small smile before pulling out the empty chair to his right, and I took a seat to face our attorney.

Bill Hawkins had worked for both our grandparents and our parents as the family attorney for decades and was due to retire himself soon. For now, he sat across from us, shuffling through paperwork and looking about as excited as we felt to be stuck in that room on a Monday morning.

Even still, he offered a smile as he peered at me over the tortoise-rimmed glasses perched on the end of his nose. "Glad you could make it, Elizabeth. Shall we get started?

We nodded, waiting expectantly as Bill picked up one of the documents that lay in front of him.

"Alright, we'll start with your parents' estate. I will read directly from your mother's will, which includes assets from both parents."

"*I, Cynthia Blake, residing at 2112 Wayzata Way, Minnetonka, Minnesota, declare this to be my last Will and Testament, and I revoke any and all wills and codicils previously made.*"

Bill had just flipped the page to continue when my phone started ringing from my purse. *Shit, I forgot to turn off the ringer.* Pulling it out, I saw Constance's name flashing across the screen.

I glanced up, all eyes on me. "I'm really sorry, but it's my boss. I have to take this." I scooted my chair back and walked out of the room, shutting the door behind me as I answered the call.

"Hello?" I spoke in hushed tones, trying to find a quiet spot where I wouldn't be disrupted. Thankfully, I spotted a kitchenette just around the corner.

"Elizabeth? Where are you? I just stopped by your office."

I worked to contain the sigh that was fighting its way towards the surface. "Sorry, I had that meeting with our family attorney for the estate this morning. What did you need? If it's not urgent, I'll be back in a couple of hours."

Clearly, Constance didn't feel the need to mask her own frustration as she heaved her own heavy sigh on the other end of the line. "This is all very inconvenient, but it'll have to do."

"What are you talking about?"

"I'm sorry, Elizabeth, but the firm has made the difficult decision to terminate your position."

I felt the blood drain from my face as I stood there, unmoving.

Holy shit, holy shit, holy shit.

"Elizabeth, are you still there?"

Finally, I found my voice. "Um... *what?* I don't understand..."

"It means you no longer have a job here, my dear." Constance's voice was slow, patronizing. "The managing partners have deemed it necessary to downsize each department, based on the firm's performance in Q1 and Q2. Yours and one other position in marketing were determined the least crucial, so... there you have it."

My brain was racing, trying to make sense of all of it. So that's why she wanted those files before I left.

"Anyway, the decision has been made, effective immediately—with a generous, one month severance package. And, as you are not currently here at the office, I'll have someone from security box up your personal effects. You may grab them when you turn in your badge, which you're required to do by noon tomorrow. Someone from human relations will also be in touch regarding transitional benefits." She paused. "Alright, I think that covers it. Do you have any questions?"

'*Questions*'? I still couldn't form one single coherent thought, other than the 'holy shit' screaming on repeat in my head. "I... no."

"Well, then, Woodruff & Shay would like to thank you for your three years of service. Best of luck to you." I heard a click as the other line disconnected, and I lowered the phone from my ear.

What the hell am I going to do now?

As if in a trance, I returned to the conference room, sinking back into my seat.

Ethan could sense by the expression on my face that something was wrong, but I shook my head. I couldn't deal with this right now. "Sorry for the interruption, please continue."

Bill nodded. "We continued on through the portion detailing funeral expenses and debt repayment already. I was just explaining to Mariah and Ethan that there was already an amount your parents had set aside for this purpose which more than covers everything, as neither parent had yet to retire or required skilled nursing care long term.

"Next, continuing on to the money, personal property and real estate portions..."

We sat listening as Bill detailed what remained of our parents' designated personal items, savings, investments, and other assets. Their home had been paid off for a few years, which would mean full profit after the sale, divided evenly. Combined with their savings and current investments, each of us was to receive approximately $1.3 million, depending on the final sale price of the house at closing.

All three of us sat in stunned silence, not having any idea that we would be hearing figures anywhere close to that.

Then he set the document aside, moving on to our grandmother's will. As he read through the list of investments, assets and real estate proceeds from the sale of our grandparents' home a few years prior, our jaws were quite literally on the floor.

Apparently, our grandparents had amassed a small fortune during their marriage—whether it be from our grandfather's medical practice or from crazy investments, we'd never know.

But all things considered, we were each to receive an additional $8.1 million.

Holy shit, indeed.

"How is this possible?" Mariah exclaimed.

Bill shrugged. "Your grandparents did very well for themselves... and it seems that for many years—through last year, actually—there were also automatic annual transfers of one hundred thousand dollars made to a separate investment account. The source of that transfer is confidential, with specific instructions not to be disclosed, however."

Ethan just sat, shaking his head. "This is just so..."

"... unreal?" I murmured, finishing my brother's sentence.

"Just wait, we aren't quite done yet," Bill said, handing us each an envelope. "These were written by your grandmother when she finalized her will a few years back. She asked that these be given to the three of you after she passed. I believe they are regarding a few personal effects."

Taking our envelopes, we each sat reading in silence.

After a moment, Mariah slammed her letter down onto the table. "What do your letters say?"

Ethan cleared his throat. "She's giving me grandpa's gold bar and his antique gun collection." I knew from the tears welling in his eyes that the gift meant a great deal to my brother. He'd been close with our grandfather and loved history, and had spent years admiring the guns he'd never been allowed to handle as a boy. "How about you?"

Mariah shrugged. "Grandmother's china and her jewelry. I don't know what the hell I'm going to do with all of that." She leaned forward to look past Ethan as I sat in silent shock.

"Is something wrong?"

I swallowed hard, shaking my head. "She's giving me the cabin in Dearing Creek and her book collection." My voice was raspy, barely audible.

Bill nodded. "And I'll have the deed transferred over to you by tomorrow, along with the authentication documents for the other items."

"The cabin? I thought that was sold off years ago?" Ethan said, the shock evident on his face.

"No, it wasn't. After your father died, your mother wanted to sell it... but technically, it still belonged to your grandparents. And Cora had explicitly stated that the cabin would never be sold, only passed down within the family, unless there were no remaining descendants to take on the property. In which case, it would then be donated to the community of Dearing Creek as a rental property for new families to enjoy."

"This is bullshit." Mariah whipped her head over again to look at the two of us. "How did we not know the cabin was still ours? And you," she said, her gaze fixed on me, "Why did Grandma Cora choose *you* to inherit it?"

"I don't know any more than you do, Mariah. This is total news to me." Inside, my head was still buzzing—*the cabin?*

But Mariah was still shaking her head. "No, this is… not right." She looked at Bill. "Can you do anything about this?"

Coming out of my fog, I turned to look at my sister. "What exactly are you upset about here? Grandma Cora and Mom just changed our entire lives with these gifts. Even if you don't want or need the money, you should still be grateful. And you know if you ever come to Minnesota to spend actual time here, you can use the cabin, too. We'll work something out."

"I don't need *anything* from you." She stood up, looking across at Bill. "Is there anything I have to sign?" He nodded, sliding a few documents across the table towards her. She hastily scrawled her signature, then turned to grab her purse from the seat next to her.

"Where are you going?"

"To the airport. I'm done here."

Ethan looked confused. "But your flight isn't until tonight. Aren't we going to have lunch, talk through everything like we'd planned?"

Mariah shook her head. "I can't do this right now. I need to get home. I'll just switch to an earlier flight." She turned and walked towards the door.

"Mariah!" I called out to her as I stood up from my seat. She froze mid-stride but didn't turn around. "This is ridiculous. Don't leave like this. Please, stay."

"I... can't," she said, and I heard a tremor in her voice. Then she walked out the door, closing it behind her.

"What the hell was that all about?" Ethan said as I sat back down, still reeling from, well, everything.

"I have no idea," I murmured.

But if Mariah was feeling even a fraction as shell-shocked as I was in that moment, I couldn't blame her for walking out.

Because my life, as I'd known it, had somehow been completely upended in a matter of months.

First, I lost my grandmother—the person I trusted more than anyone.

Then, my mother.

Followed by... my boyfriend.

And... *my job*, as of five minutes ago.

And now I was supposed to be some millionaire saddled with a risen-from-the-ashes lakefront property, tied to nearly every single one of my most precious memories?

The only thing I knew for certain was this: I needed a very, *very* strong drink.

Chapter 9

James

I pulled into the driveway at the Kinney's house bright and early the next morning, turning off the ignition to sit in silence for a moment. I'd been up late the night before, doing a lot of thinking after leaving GiGi's cabin.

No matter how I looked at it, I had to be done with the Kinney project. I couldn't stay there, now that the line had officially been crossed. And who knows, maybe Denise had already approached her husband or Mel about what had gone down in that bathroom. Either way, my job was on the line.

Best thing to do now was walk away from this project, while I still had a shred of dignity left, and prevent any issues for Mel.

I wished that the choice between staying with Aaronson Construction or venturing out on my own was easier. Truth be told, I still didn't know if I was a hundred percent ready for it.

But the alternative—working for clients I didn't respect or feeling like I had to just take whatever crap they threw at me—didn't feel like something I could do anymore.

Taking a deep breath, I hoisted myself out of the truck. I had hoped to avoid this place after what happened yesterday, but in my haste to bolt out of there, I'd left behind my own tool kit. Normally, I wouldn't care all that much—but Pop's hammer and wrench set were in there. And those were irreplaceable.

"I wasn't expecting to see you here so early today." While I'd been stuck in my thoughts, Denise Kinney had stepped out onto the front stoop with her cup of coffee, the steam curling upwards in the early morning air. It would already be May in a few days, nearly summer—though mornings that time of year still hung onto the remnants of winter's chill.

But the air wasn't the only thing giving me a chill at that moment. As I approached, I could sense that a shift had taken place between myself and my client. "Morning, Mrs. Kinney."

"Exactly what is it you're needing before eight a.m., might I ask?" The look in Denise's eyes was both arrogant and challenging, and I wanted no part in it.

"Apologies, ma'am. I left behind my tool kit. Do you mind if I grab it from the kitchen?"

"I'd rather you didn't."

I cocked my head. "Why's that?"

Denise shrugged. "I'm sorry, James… but after what happened yesterday, I'm not sure that I feel comfortable being alone with you in my house anymore."

"Pardon me?"

"Do I need to remind you about the incident? Surely you can't expect me to just forget what happened, James."

I felt a knot begin to form in the pit of my stomach. I *fucking knew it…*

"I'm sorry, but it almost sounds as though you are blaming *me* for what happened."

Her eyes narrowed. "I *am* the client, James. It's *my* money that is paying your wages, is it not? And regardless of what you may believe, the way you spoke to me was completely inappropriate."

Taking a deep, steadying breath to calm the tension mounting within me, I stared at her straight on. "The only thing *inappropriate* was you crossing the line, Mrs. Kinney."

She laughed then, like a thousand tiny knives laced with malice. "Well, believe what you will, but I've already spoken to my husband about this. And he's *furious*. I'd hate to think of the damage this might inflict on Mel Aaronson's business once the word gets out."

I glowered at her. "Mel's a good man. You leave him and his business out of this."

"I don't believe you're in a place to be giving the orders here," Denise said, her lips curled into a sneer.

Just then, Rick, our master electrician, pulled up in his truck. As he approached, I turned towards him, breaking the tension. "Hey, man. Do you mind grabbing my toolkit from the kitchen? I need to wrap things up with Mrs. Kinney."

"Sure thing." Rick walked past Denise into the house, and I locked eyes with her again, feeling the anger flicker within me.

"I am done letting you and your family treat the rest of us like shit. Just because you're a Kinney doesn't mean you own me... or this town."

She raised an eyebrow as she stared at me. "Don't I?" She leaned in closer now, her voice softer, though infinitely more menacing. "Is this really the road you want to head down, James?"

"I'm already halfway there, ma'am... and I am *done* with you."

Thankfully, Rick appeared in the doorway at that moment, bag in hand. "Thanks, Rick."

He nodded as he handed the kit to me. "You taking off or something?"

"Yeah, I have something I need to take care of. Good luck today." Then I turned on my heel, crossing the driveway towards my truck.

But as I backed out a moment later, I caught a glimpse of Denise in my rearview mirror—like a hunter, poised for attack.

And for the first time in ages, I was finally clear on what I needed to do next.

****

"Listen, James, this isn't what I wanted to happen."

I was sitting in Mel's office across town at Aaronson Construction an hour later, having just handed him my resignation notice.

"I know, Mel. And I'm sorry that Joe Kinney is putting you in a tough spot. I just wanted to make sure you knew the truth about what happened."

Mel sighed, leaning back in his seat as he rubbed his temples. "*Fucking Kinneys.* They've always been a damn thorn in my side. And now they're losing me the best man on my team." He lowered his hands to his lap, looking at me. "So, what'll you do now? Finally start that business of yours?"

I raised an eyebrow. "You know about that?"

Mel chuckled sadly. "Honestly, I've been expecting it to happen for years now, son. Just never felt ready to see you go. But I'm happy for you all the same."

"Thanks. Honestly, I'm not sure that I *am* ready for it."

"I wasn't either. But sometimes, we all just need a little push." He stood up from his chair, walking around to the front of his desk as I rose up to face him. "I never had sons of my own, and... well, after all these years, I've always thought of you as one of mine, James. I'm proud of you, and I've no doubt you're ready for this. Your granddad would think so, too." My breath caught in my throat as he reached out, pulling me into a hug. Then, with a quick pat on the back, he released me. "Now get your ass outta here. And don't take away all of my business, you hear me? Or I'll come after ya." His voice was gruff, but I caught the classic Mel twinkle in his eye.

Smirking, I gave him a nod. "I'll do my best, sir."

As I walked out of Mel's office for the last time, I felt a wave of nostalgia hit me and a stinging behind my eyelids. The old man's guidance had helped shape me into the man I was today, and along with Pop—who'd been his master electrician for years before he passed. He'd taught me most everything I knew about this business.

It was a debt I couldn't possibly repay.

But leaving to venture out on my own, despite the circumstances that led to it, felt more exciting now than terrifying.

I just hoped I'd make both men proud.

Later that day, I sat in the chair opposite Tony Miller, bank manager at Twin Lakes Credit Union. On the desk between us lay all the business paperwork I had filed to secure my LLC nine months before, which I'd let collect dust on the shelf in my home office until I felt ready to show up here.

Because now, I was taking the necessary next step, setting up my small business checking, credit and savings accounts. This was the most difficult part by far, and one that I'd hoped to avoid.

But I needed the money. Couldn't deny it or hold myself back any longer.

"Ok, James... so we are pretty much good to go here on these accounts, and you should have your check blanks, credit card and debit cards mailed out to you within ten business days. How much are you looking to transfer from your personal savings into the checking and savings accounts today?"

I took a deep breath. "Let's do half of what's there now into checking, a thousand into savings, and hold the rest where it is for now."

Tony smiled. "Not a problem. Let me run and grab the last of the paperwork, and I'll print you out a receipt."

Twenty minutes later, I sat in my truck in the parking lot, much like my day had started. But this time, I felt something resembling hope.

I stared down at the receipt in my hand—Six million dollars, transferred into the business checking account for Horizon Remodeling, LLC.

One thing I'd been clear on—I wouldn't be incorporating my last name, Tate, into the name of my business.

Because if I was going to do this, I needed it to be about a fresh start—eyes focused straight ahead, no credit given to the past.

I didn't need reminding of the man who'd given me my name, along with the inheritance I'd deeply resented for the past five years—and now found myself needing for the first time.

But in the end, William Tate had his chance. He'd made his choice. And he'd given me nothing else that mattered.

As I shifted my truck into drive, I held my phone up to my ear, waiting for her to answer.

"GiGi, you home? I've got some news, and you're gonna want to sit down for this."

Chapter 10

Lizzie

"Find anything interesting yet?"

Ethan and I sat on my sofa with laptops open, Jules' latest rom-com, *Anyone But You*, playing on the TV screen in the background. If asked to choose a favorite out of all the films my friend had starred in since her career had taken off, this would be the one.

In my opinion, it had everything—a picture-perfect small-town setting, a grumpy-yet-redeemable gorgeous male lead, and a brilliantly performed heroine who was relatable, intelligent and lovably awkward.

Giles—the male lead—was also the quintessential romantic hero. Not only did his character fall in love first in the film, but he then expressed his love to Mira in countless ways. Helping her through tragedy; choosing the perfect gift, because of course he pays attention; working through his own demons so he can become worthy of her.

And then at the end, he makes a grand, romantic gesture that sweeps her off her feet, promising to love her forever in the way she'd never been but had always deserved.

It was no wonder I kept this film on repeat. And by now, I'd nearly gotten to the point where I could watch Jules—practically my sister and whom I'd known since she was thirteen—perform the spicier scenes without outright cringing.

At least Ethan was a good sport and would usually watch it with me whenever he was over. Even though my brother was a sensitive guy, I knew he'd prefer an action movie or something. Sometimes, I even compromised. Especially if it meant something in the Marvel universe. What can I say? I love me some sexy hero action.

But when your life falls apart at the seams, the only reasonable option is a cozy quilt of rom-com comfort. Especially when you are in desperate need of a little hope and inspiration.

We'd been parked with laptops in this exact spot all afternoon and evening, ever since I'd returned from the offices of Woodruff & Shay one last time with my pathetic, half-full box of personal effects in hand.

The fact that I'd never bothered to bring more photos or favorite items into my office in over three years probably said something about the level of my professional commitment. And it was hard not to feel like I was the one who'd actually screwed it all up.

Grabbing a few of the remaining cashews from the bowl between us, I continued scrolling to the end of the current browser page on my laptop screen before clicking through to page five. It was the third job site I'd scoured so far today—but unless I was looking to train as a grant writer or become the admin for an erotic fan fiction site, there was nothing available remotely close to my field. "Nope... nada. Anything over there?"

He cast me a sideways look. "Nothing yet. But don't worry... *we will.* There's got to be something out there for you, Liz."

My brother, the eternal optimist.

Usually, I loved that about him. Once upon a time, we were twins in that regard, too. But at the moment, his optimism felt wasted on me.

After we'd left the lawyer's office the day before, I'd confessed to Ethan about my being fired during our very long lunch, most of which we'd spent trying to wrap our heads around our unexpected inheritance.

I mean, what normal person expects to become a millionaire at the age of thirty—especially moments after being fired from their career?

Not that the windfall could in any way replace all we'd lost, of course. I would have given anything to have Grandma Cora sitting here instead right now, reassuring me the way she always had.

"Chin up, Lizzie girl... your next eureka moment is just around the corner, I know it. You will take the world by storm."

And *God*, did I miss her words, her encouraging presence. *All of it.*

I shut my laptop with a sigh. "It's getting late. Don't you work tomorrow?"

Ethan set down his laptop on the chest I used as a coffee table, glancing at his watch. "Yeah, but it's only eight. How about we grab a late-night happy hour from Edie's before I head home?"

I frowned. "I don't know..."

"What if I told you I'm buying?" he said, waggling his eyebrows at me.

I shook my head, rolling my eyes. "Ok, *moneybags*. Deal."

*****

Fifteen minutes later, the two of us sat in our usual spot at the bar counter, munching on a couple of shared appetizers as we sipped our drinks—a beer for him, a glass of house red wine for me.

"Have you heard from Mariah yet?"

I looked at my brother. "Not yet. You?"

Our older sister had been silent ever since walking out of Bill Hawkins' office without a backwards glance the day before. I'd been worried she was upset with us for some reason—though for the life of me, I couldn't understand why.

"No, nothing. It's weird, huh?"

"Yeah, very. Normally, I'd expect her to have formed a game plan by now, with a zillion instructions on how we should invest and organize our inheritance. But... do you really think she's mad about the cabin?"

Ethan shrugged. "I don't know. No one's even been up there in over ten years—plus, we had no idea our family even still owned it. How could she possibly be angry with you for that?"

"Because it's *Mariah*. You know she's always finding some reason to be mad at me." *Just like Mom.*

I'd long since given up hope for a closer relationship with my sister than I'd had with our mother. The way it was between us when we were younger.

And now, with just the three of us remaining, I guess I'd thought maybe it would be possible again.

But apparently not.

"Lizzie, you know Mariah loves you. She probably just needs time to process everything, like we all do."

I sighed. "Yeah. Maybe."

"Anyway, I have a proposal for you. And brace yourself, because I'm about to channel our grandmother here."

"Is now a good time to tell you that I'm not really into voodoo, *seance-y* stuff?"

He shook his head in amusement. "How about *instead* I tell you exactly what she would have said, were she here with us?"

"Which is...?"

"I think her giving that cabin to you specifically is a *sign*, Liz. And the fact that you also lost your job on the very same day. Normally I don't put much stock in things like Fate, but this… it's almost *uncanny*." He leaned closer, eyes intense. "I think you should move up to Dearing Creek, fix up the cabin with some of that inheritance money, and finally write your book. Go all in."

I looked at my brother, eyes wide. I mean, I'd be lying if I said I hadn't been dreaming about the *exact same thing* for the past twenty-four hours. Wondering what life could look like, if I had the time and space to give everything to my writing.

But that would be *crazy*, right?

"I don't know. Doesn't that seem… *irresponsible*?"

"Now *you* sound like Mom."

"Yeah, well… maybe the reason my life has been kind of a mess is because I should've listened to her more."

Ethan smirked. "Not likely. You and Mom couldn't have been more different if you'd tried. When has following her advice about your life ever actually made you happy?"

I played with the edge of my napkin, sorting through the hundreds of objections filtering through my head. "And what the heck do I know about renovating a cabin, anyway?

He snorted out a laugh, almost choking on his French fry. "Oh, believe me, I'm not in *any* way suggesting that you do the work yourself. I've seen you with a hammer, Liz. Don't think I've forgotten about this." He gestured towards the small scar above his right eyebrow, looking at me pointedly. For a second, a flash image of

Rude Guy—arching a similarly-injured eyebrow—raced through my mind.

At least I'm consistent.

With a roll of my eyes, I sighed dramatically. "Geez, let it go, man. I'm not *that* bad with tools. Besides, wasn't that your own fault for getting in my way?"

"Nope, you *definitely* are that bad." He grinned as I scowled at him, feeling the corners of my mouth twitch. Even when he was being a total butt, I couldn't help giggling, knowing he was right. "But with that money, you could actually afford to hire a professional. Turn the place into a real home."

"I don't know..."

"No, I think you *do*. I swear, Lizzie, it's like Grandma Cora has lined up everything perfectly for you. There's nothing holding you here in the city anymore. And most of your friends are up there, anyway. Other than the fact that I'll miss having you live fifteen minutes away, what possible reason would there be for you *not* to do it?"

After a moment, he turned back to his food, the surrounding noise in the bar filling in the gaps as together we finished eating in silence. After he had paid the tab a short while later, I glanced over.

"We should probably get going... it's been such a long day. And I bet you're as exhausted as I am."

He studied my face for a moment before nodding. "Yeah, fine. I have an early start tomorrow, anyway." We both stood up, Ethan waving at the bartender on our way out the door. Once outside, he pulled me in for a quick hug. "Look... I know you're scared," he said, leaning back again to face me, "but maybe that's even *more* reason to do this."

As always, my brother got me. *Of course* I was scared. Scared of wanting something so badly, of loving so hard, and losing it all over again.

I am so tired of losing.

"Just promise me you'll at least consider what we talked about. I'll even come up north when I can and help out. I've missed it, too."

I nodded. "I will, I promise." Giving him a quick peck on the cheek, I waved as he headed around the corner towards his car.

Turning to start the walk down the block towards my apartment, I felt my phone buzz in the pocket of my jacket.

Glancing down at the screen, I tensed when I saw the familiar name—Randall.

What the hell could he possibly want?

Deciding it was high time I focused on self-preservation, I silenced my phone, tucking it back inside my jacket.

But that moment was a clear sign that for me, *self-preservation* had become more about hiding than healing. Maybe Ethan was right. Despite everything that had happened over the last several months, I still believed in Fate and that the signs were always there... if you were ready to see them.

And maybe Grandma Cora had somehow understood I would need a fresh start, even before I did.

By the next afternoon, I had spoken to my landlord about the possibility of a shorter vacate notice on my rental agreement—hoping to work something out before a new month began. By some stroke of luck, his niece was in need of a one-bedroom apartment, and he was more than happy to be flexible. We agreed he'd release me from my lease early, with no penalty.

That was the last piece. Now there was nothing holding me back.

I almost couldn't believe it—I was going to do this.

I called Ethan with my decision—he sounded even more excited than I felt, offering to get me hooked up with a truck for moving day, two weeks from now.

Two weeks.

But I had one final task to take care of, in order for it to feel real. After first talking with Brooke, it was time to tell the rest.

Wednesday, 7:00 p.m.

LIZZIE: Soooo…what're you ladies doing on Saturday the 12th?

BROOKE: (Pssst…Tell her you have no plans.)

KAIT: I feel like this is a trap. More details, please.

INDI: That's my weekend off from on-call. Why? You coming up for a visit?

TESS: We're actually in town that weekend as well. Dinner?

LENA: I'm doing flowers for a wedding, but I wanna see you!

LIZZIE: ok… so, what if I told you I'd just inherited over $9 million two days ago, along with our old family cabin?

KAIT: I would ask if you are, in fact, high right now.

INDI: Wait… you're not, right? Have you already forgotten the gummy bear incident from Dearie Weekend last summer?

TESS: SMH… this is Lizzie we're talking about. #neverforget

By the time I lay in bed that night, it was settled.

Farewell, Tragic Lizzie. My next chapter has arrived.

Chapter 11

James

"Ok, so spill it. There's gotta be some big reason why you dragged us out here tonight, James."

I'd texted the guys earlier in the day about meeting for dinner at Dearing Creek's finest—and only—steakhouse, Loon's Landing. I knew Jesse was already suspicious as to what was going on—seeing as I had stopped showing up for work. Based on his texts, all he knew was what Rick had told him—he'd caught me meeting with Denise Kinney early yesterday morning, and that I'd left with my tool bag shortly thereafter.

And nobody had seen or heard from me since.

I smirked at Jack across the table. "Why, you got somewhere better to be?"

"Actually, not this time," he said, grinning. "Marty and I were planning to grill up some brats tonight, but I told him I needed a night out with my boys instead." Jack had been staying with his father at the old house since he'd moved back to Dearing Creek a week ago, but their roommate situation was only temporary—he'd already been working with a realtor to scout out a property somewhere near my place, west of Lake Elska.

He and his dad had a complicated history, thanks to Marty's past alcoholism—which led to his parents' divorce when Jack and his sister Lacey were just kids. And while they'd mended fences several years ago after Marty sobered up for good, both men needed their own space.

"Well, I, for one, will be going home to a pissed-off pregnant wife," Jesse cut in, setting down his beer as he wiped the foam from his upper lip. "But I told her I needed to find out what James is up to, since he refuses to give me a straight answer over the phone."

"Relax, man. I wanted to break the news to you in person." I took a breath to steady my heart rate—*why was I feeling so damn anxious?* "So, I met with Mel on Tuesday morning."

"And? Are you finally talking to him about a promotion? God knows you've been there forever..."

"No. I quit, actually." I picked up the oatmeal stout I'd ordered, taking a sip. "Mmm, this is good... have you two tried this one yet?"

"Hold up, did you seriously just try to divert our attention with your questionable taste in beer?" Jack shook his head, raising a hand to flag down the server.

I shrugged. "What? It's a really good beer." I took another swig to hide my smile, but it was more to calm my nerves than anything, considering I was about to reveal the other piece of my news.

Our server, Tina—an old classmate from high school—arrived at our table with a smile. "You boys ready to order?"

His expression suggesting I'd officially gone insane, Jesse finally looked away, glancing down at his menu. "I'll take the steakhouse special burger with mushrooms, garlic mashed and a side salad, please."

I set my menu on top of his. "I'll take the same."

"What the hell... I will as well."

"Oh, and another round of drinks, please, Tina." Grinning, she nodded, walking off towards the kitchen. Turning my attention back to the guys, I noticed Jesse was still staring at me. "What?"

"Nope, you don't get to say *'what'*, not after dropping a bomb like that." Jesse paused, then lowered his voice. "Was this about the other day in the shower with Denise Kinney?"

"Wait, you saw that?"

Jack's eyes bugged out of his head, holding a hand to his mouth to stifle his shocked laughter. "*Holy shit, man...*"

Jesse shrugged. "I wasn't watching, but I heard it. I thought she might try to pull something with the way she'd been eyeing you the last few weeks. Especially with Joe being out of sight this week." He motioned towards his phone, laying on the table. "I recorded your conversation. Even with the door shut, you can still hear most everything."

"Wait... exactly *what* did you do with Denise in the shower?"

I glared at Jack. "Keep it down, man." Then I leaned back in my seat with a sigh. "Like Jesse said, she'd been giving me a bad vibe for a while. That day, she asked me to take a look at her shower head... Anyway, she had me cornered."

"Was her '*shower head*' up to code, then?"

"Knock it off, Jack. I'm being serious here."

But Jesse was nodding, now looking serious as well. "So let me guess... she threatened to turn it around on you with Mel to get you fired?"

"Yeah, basically. So, I got ahead of it myself and told Mel everything. Quitting on my own was just the better solution all around. He wasn't happy about it, though."

"Course not, you're practically family to the guy," Jesse said, shaking his head. "I'm really sorry, man. Fucking Kinneys."

"Thanks. Over and done with."

Jack eyed me. "I'm sorry, too. You didn't deserve any of this."

"Didn't deserve what?"

I tensed at the interruption, praying the voice didn't belong to who I knew it did. Sure enough, Luke Hardon had paused next to our table, decked out in a suit with his typical air of 'God's gift' surrounding him. Another guy that I didn't recognize stood just behind him, looking on curiously.

"This conversation is none of your business, Hardon." I gritted my teeth as I said it, keeping my eyes locked on his.

Luke, however, seemed unaffected. "Come on, just trying to be friendly, Tate," he said, returning my gaze with a smile. Then he glanced back at the man standing behind him. "I went to high school with these guys. And gentlemen," he said, turning back to us, "this is a good friend of mine, Sam Lennon."

Jesse gave the pair a quick smile. "Nice to meet you, Sam."

"Yeah, welcome." Jack gave a small wave.

I said nothing, staring sullenly at my traitorous friends until I finally sighed. *Fuck, I was letting that guy get in my head, just like I always had.* Of course, it was with good reason. But that didn't give me permission to be rude to his companion.

"Hey."

Sam gave me a quick smile and nod, sensing the tension.

It's not like it was much of a secret, anyway. Everyone from around here knew Luke Hardon and I had butted heads for most of our lives—starting from the moment I became a resident of Dearing Creek over twenty-five years ago.

And even though the Hardon family reigned over the neighboring town of Heartwood, our two small communities shared a school system—so he and his brothers had been a constant presence in my life.

But only Luke had decided it was his job to make my life hell. I could still hear his voice echoing down the hallways of LakeView Middle School, piercing through me worse than a dagger ever could—though I never let it show.

"Poor James, his own parents wouldn't even stick around for him... what a loser..."

"So, anyway, what are you men up to tonight?"

I yanked my mind out of the memories I'd rather forget, giving present-day Luke a stony look. "What does it look like?"

Jesse muttered under his breath, "Dude, don't..."

I held up a hand, forcing a smile onto my face as I looked back to Luke. "Please, don't let us hold you up from your dinner. Why don't you move along and enjoy your night?"

Luke paused, looking for a moment like he wanted to say something, but instead gave a quick tip of the head to the table before the two men walked away.

Jack leaned across the table, his voice low. "You have to stop letting Luke Hardon rile you up. I told you, he's not the same asshole he was back in high school."

"Yeah, well... he hasn't given me any reason to think otherwise," I said, giving my friend a look. "Anyway, doesn't matter. I'm fine, as long as he stays out of my way."

But I knew Jack was right. The past may have made it impossible for me to forgive Luke Hardon or the rest of the rich assholes he was related to—but letting him get under my skin accomplished nothing.

"Ok, let's just forget Luke and get back to the conversation," Jack said, leaning back again. "You quit Aaronson Construction. What now?"

I took a breath, working to hold back a smile. "Well, that brings me to the second part of my news..."

Jesse paused, his pint glass halfway to his lips. "Wait, you don't mean..."

"Horizon Remodeling is officially open for business, boys."

Jack let out a whoop, slapping me on the arm. "Yes! It's about damn time. Congrats!"

Jesse was grinning. "I'm really happy for you, man. Seriously."

I smiled at my friends, feeling the tension in my gut finally begin to dissipate. "Thanks. It took me a while, but... I'm finally ready."

"So, I assume you finally dipped into the inheritance, then, for seed money?" Jack kept his voice light, but both he and Jesse knew how much I'd resented that money—how bitter I still felt towards the man who'd left it for me.

I nodded. "I did. But I'm still not looking to make it known around here that I have it, ok?"

"Of course not. You don't need to worry about any of that." Jesse's eyes were sincere, and I was grateful—but ready to change the subject.

"Thanks. Anyway, tomorrow I'll be picking up a bunch of equipment and supplies I had on order. And then, I'll be needing some crew so I can start drumming up some business..." I glanced at Jesse, not bothering to hide my smile this time.

"Damn it, James... you better not be messing with me..."

"What d'ya say, brother?" And as I waited for his response, I noticed my friend had tears in his eyes.

"You already know I'm in. All the way, until the end." He reached over to place a hand on my forearm—after a beat, Jack did the same.

"You've got my support, too. Any financial advice you need, figuring out profit-and-loss statements, business projections, you know I've got your back."

I smiled at him gratefully. "Thanks. But just so you know, this doesn't mean that you're losing my help on your fishing charter venture. I'm still here for anything you need, got it?"

"Oh, I'm not worried. I know where to find you, brother." He grinned. "Look at us... The Three Js, taking Dearing Creek by storm once again."

Jesse grinned. "They won't know what hit 'em."

The three of us laughed, settling back as Tina returned to the table with our meals. As we fell into excited conversation and making plans, I felt lighter, more hopeful than I had in a long time.

This was my chance to clear out the cobwebs and finally forge ahead.

And I wasn't about to fuck it up this time.

Chapter 12

Lizzie

"Lizzie, Indi, put down the books and grab your bikes! We're gonna go over to the pier and check out the new guy from Heartwood that Lena's dad hired to sell minnows."

"Nah, maybe later... I'm all comfy out here on my floaty..."

Brooke crossed her arms and glared at us from the dock. "As your friend, I refuse to allow you two to miss out on this opportunity to see Scotty McHottie without a shirt on. He has actual <u>abs</u>, Lizzie... think of the inspiration for your next book! Even if he does smell a little fishy..."

I stood along the edge of the shore, gazing out across the water. Off in the distance, the sun was starting to sink lower, casting an orangey glow across Lake Elska.

Breathing in deeply, I felt the warmth settle inside of me, illuminating countless memories that made up the best parts of my growing-up years.

God, it felt so good to be back.

My grandparents' cabin—*technically my cabin now, but would it ever feel right to call it that?*—looked exactly the way I remembered it, for the most part. Dark blue wood siding, now with peeling paint; the white shutters, hanging a bit crooked; the wooden front porch bleached and sagging. Some of the shrubs and trees were overgrown, though clearly some care had been taken with the yard over the years. And the grass had already started working its way up, with daffodils sprouting up amongst the dead leaves that lay beneath the large front window.

And I was so happy to see my favorite trees—the tall river birches—were looking as healthy and majestic as ever along the eastern edge of the property, separating what used to be my friend Jules' family cabin from ours.

I couldn't wait to see them showing off their vibrant gold color in the fall. It had been way too long.

Inside was like stepping back into a memory. The cheery, yellow kitchen with white cabinets, wooden dining set and circa 1979 avocado fridge; the large, wood-paneled living room with its stone fireplace and the old green sofa I'd spent countless hours curled up on with a book, gazing out the front bay window onto the lake; the back hallway splitting up three light-filled bedrooms and a yellow-tiled bathroom, along with the door that led out back.

Closing my eyes, I could almost hear the sounds of my brother running out that door, letting it slam behind him as he had so many times before, our parents hollering at him to '*slow the hell down*'. And I very nearly could smell my grandmother's famous pumpkin pancakes, puffing up on her electric griddle.

All of it was familiar, but not. It almost felt as if this place had been holding its breath, waiting for me to return all these years later.

And now, *finally*, I was home—and ready to start fresh.

Even though I'd been back to Dearing Creek many times to visit my friends over the past decade or so, never once had I allowed myself to stop by our cabin. After Dad died, we never came back here again as a family—and until a few weeks ago, I'd believed this property wasn't even a *part* of our family anymore.

Coming here, just to stare at a place that represented a life I'd never know again, had been too painful. Even Jules couldn't coax me over to their place for summer weekends. It was just too close to home.

So instead, I'd come up to stay with Brooke's family, or sometimes, Lena or Kait—out of sight of the old place. Most of the time I'd bring Indi along with me, as I'd always done. Throughout our college years, and then our twenties—as wings were spread and new homes were created, and biannual Dearie Girls weekends became our new tradition—this town had become my home as much as any. Maybe more than the rest.

Even with so much having changed over the years, the cabin had seemed frozen in time, isolated in its own grief. Maybe that's part of why it felt so right being here now—the cabin and I, we understood one another. We'd both lost plenty, each with our own issues to work through. And there was comfort in not having to go it alone.

But if I was going to do this, I had to pull my head out of the past and focus on looking forward—to give this 'fresh start' of mine the fighting chance it deserved.

I had to admit, though—having my brother and these friends surrounding me here today made me feel stronger than I had in ages. Like maybe, I actually *could* do this.

"Ok seriously, Lizzie. How many freakin' books does one person need? I think it's time to stage an intervention..." Kait grumbled as she stomped past, schlepping yet another box filled to the brim with a mix of hardcovers and paperbacks.

Shaking my head, I bit my lower lip to hold back the laughter. Kait was always so surly when she was hungry. "Hey, back off. I donated a bunch before I even left Minneapolis. And anyway, half of those belonged to Grandma Cora." For a moment, I thought for sure I'd hear another snarky retort fly out of her mouth—instead, a chunk of her wavy brown hair cut her off at the pass, making it literally impossible for me to *not* giggle as she sputtered her way back into the cabin.

While Ethan had started unloading the moving trailer this afternoon, Brooke and I had stopped to pick up her collection from the assisted living facility just north of the lake, where they'd been storing Grandma's remaining possessions for the past few months. Combined with my own, I knew the bookshelves inside would be overflowing.

"I don't know why you're griping, Kait." Indi's voice was muffled as she shuffled past, her arms laden with dresser drawers stacked all the way up to her chin. "Considering I literally have Lizzie's entire underwear collection all up in my grill right now."

I rolled my eyes. "For the love of God, they're obviously *clean...*"

"Yes... and they smell amazing, by the way. I need to know what essential oils you're using on those dryer balls!" she called out over her shoulder, disappearing inside through the front door.

I heard the sound of a vehicle coming from the cabin on the other side of mine. Turning, I saw a gray sedan park and an older woman with shoulder-length white hair and a flowy blue dress step out. A moment later, she was bustling across her lawn towards me, as if returning from the past.

"Elizabeth, dear, so good to see you finally moving in! I don't know if you remember me after all these years, I'm—"

"—Georgia! Of course I remember. It just took me a minute." I smiled at her, squeaking out a note of surprise as she pulled me in for a quick hug.

Pulling back, Georgia rested her hands along my arms, studying my face. "You're looking more like Cora every day, young lady," she said, shaking her head.

I felt myself blush. "Thanks. I'll take that as a compliment."

"Good, because it was," she said, hazel eyes twinkling. Then a shadow flitted across her expression, the light in her eyes seeming to vanish. "Losing her has been so hard, hasn't it? I still can't quite believe she's gone."

A lump formed in my throat as I met her gaze, sad and knowing. Then I nodded. "Yeah, it's been really hard. I miss her so much."

"And then your mother too, sweet girl, on top of everything." She reached out to fold my hands up into hers.

"Such a tough time for you all. How are you kids holding up?"

"It's been a rough year, but... it feels good to be here now. I've missed it."

"I'm sure you have. But good that you're here now." Releasing my hands, she patted my cheek tenderly, glancing over my shoulder to where Ethan continued unloading the trailer. "Good to see your brother here as well. I know it made Cora happy to see the two of you grow up so close."

I smiled, shaking my head as my brother awkwardly dropped my bike onto the ground. "Yeah... he's pretty great."

Georgia looked like she was about to continue when all of a sudden, her smile dropped, something catching her eye over my shoulder. "God dammit, that dog is headed back to the Weaver's place again... I swear, he's determined to knock up poor Lulu, too." She held a hand to her mouth. "*Boner! Get outta here, you big dumb mutt!*"

I had to cover my mouth to keep from laughing outright. "'*Boner?*'"

Georgia turned her gaze back to me, exasperated. "Yeah, he's the town stray... well, most everyone calls him Boner *Jr. Jr.*, after both his daddy and granddad. The name's stupid, but it stuck." She held her hands around her mouth like a megaphone. "*Boner! Go on, git!*"

I watched as the mutt scampered off in the opposite direction, looking very dejected at not being allowed to complete his mission. Rolling her eyes, Georgia released a sigh. "There's something wrong in those dogs' DNA... not one of 'em can hold back from humping every four-legged bitch in a five-mile radius."

I snorted out a laugh, trying to compose myself. "Can't animal control bring him in, so a vet can at least get him neutered?"

"Yeah, easier said than done, though many have tried." She had her hands on her hips now as she watched the dog disappear off into the woods behind our cabins. "I swear, though... one of these days, those balls of his will finally get snipped. This town just isn't big enough for any more Boner babies."

Our conversation was interrupted yet again as we heard a crash coming from inside the cabin. With a shake of her head, she chuckled.

"Anyway, sounds like you've got your hands full here, dear. I'll let you get back to it. Though, just curious... have you found anyone to help fix up the place yet?"

"No, not yet. I was going to first g—"

Georgia waved her hand. "Of course, you've been busy. Well, never you mind. I have the perfect person for the job. I'll send him over sometime tomorrow, ok?" Before I could say another word, she turned to hustle back towards her cabin. "Feel free to stop by if you need anything!"

I couldn't help but smile at the whirlwind of the past few minutes.

Georgia LaMott was just as I remembered her—kind, funny, full of spirit. I didn't know why, but it felt oddly comforting, having her as my neighbor. She and my grandmother had been good friends since before they were my age—so it felt a little like having a part of her back with me again.

"Lizzie, where do you want us to put your jackets?" Lena's face peeked out through the open bay window.

"You stay put. I've got it covered," Brooke said as she sidled past me, carrying the fiddle leaf fig plant from her car to rejoin the chaos inside. A moment later, I could hear her voice filtering out through the many windows we'd left open to air out the place as she continued doling out instructions to the others—though I was pretty sure I heard some definite grumbling in the background.

Giggling to myself, I returned to the trunk of my light gray hatchback to grab the last few bags that remained. Behind me, the door to the trailer slammed shut.

"Well, Liz… I think that about does it," Ethan said, wiping his brow as he hopped off the back. "I'm going to start heading back, if that's ok. I want to get this dropped off before the rental place closes."

"Sure, that's fine. Drive safe, ok? And you'll let me know how that second date goes with… wait, what was her name again?"

"Calliope."

"Are we *sure* that's her name?"

Ethan grinned, shaking his head. "Yes, I'm fairly certain. At least, I better be."

"Ok, fine. Let me know how things go with *Calliope*," I said as I leaned in for a hug, feeling the tears prick behind my eyelids. "And thank you. I mean it. I couldn't have made it through these past few weeks without you."

"Of course. And I've told you before, you're never getting rid of me. So never fear, *I'll be back*," he said in my ear with his best *Terminator* impression as I groaned. Chuckling, he pulled away, keeping one arm looped around my back as the two of us gazed at the cabin together. "She needs some work, but... it still feels a little like old times, doesn't it?"

I leaned into his shoulder, a million memories filtering through my mind. As much as this place felt familiar, there was still so much of the old days missing. I couldn't help but wonder—would it ever feel the same again?

But... one step forward, not back.

"Yeah, a bit." I took a step away, offering a small smile. "You better get going while it's still light out. Love you."

"Love you, too. I'll text when I get home." And after our usual *'pow-pow'* fist bump send-off, he climbed into his car.

I stood there waving until the black SUV and trailer had disappeared from sight, past the tall pines surrounding the cabin and the gravel road. The dust and the noise kicked up from his tires filtered away until the air was still once more.

Taking a deep breath, I turned to head back inside.

And as I entered into the cozy living room, I found my-self engulfed in a giant group hug—Indi, Brooke, Kait and Lena wrapping their arms around me, and each other. They knew how bittersweet this day was for me, without me having to say the words. And for a woman who knew the power of words better than most, I loved them all the more for it.

"Ok, I think we've officially succeeded in suffocating her. *Lizzie, give us a sign... are you alive in there?*" Kait's voice came out muffled, and I started giggling again as I felt multiple arms relax their hold around me.

"For the most part," I said, wiping my cheek with the back of my hand. "Who's hungry?"

"Oh, Tess said she won't be here with dinner for an hour yet, so let's finish cleaning up, and then we can crack open a few bottles of wine when she gets here."

Two hours later, the cabin was fresher-smelling and a lot less dusty-musty. Now the space was filled with the sounds of chatter and laughter, remnants of salad and pizza scattered in containers across the floor as we sat on pillows and cushions pulled from the old sofa.

I had sold most of my own furniture before leaving Minneapolis and planned to order new things at some point—but not until after most of the renovation had been completed. Until then, I'd be roughing it with the existing shabby pieces that had always been here. Not that I minded so much.

Tess—somehow managing to pull off elegance while perched on her ratty cushion, her white fitted sheath dress and long, shiny mahogany hair cascading over one shoulder a dead giveaway of her social status—reached over to grab her red Solo cup of wine. As always, she looked the most out of place sitting on the floor of a rustic Minnesota lake cabin—but then, that was sort of the beauty of our mish-mashed group of women. Only the parts that mattered made sense. And it was all any of us cared about.

She'd just finished regaling us with another story about her horrible sister-in-law, Carmen—who, apparently, was in the midst of her third divorce. "So anyway, she asked Carlos if she could just move into our house in Malibu. When she heard he'd already sold it, she was *livid*. And blamed me for it, of course."

Kait glanced over, her look curious. "I didn't know you guys had sold your place, either."

Tess shrugged. "Carlos thought we should downsize a bit. And obviously, we still have our main home in Rochester. It was an opportunity for a nice cash in-flux back into Dominguez Enterprises, while real estate prices were still up. The company took a bit of a hit during the pandemic, after all."

"Ah, to have rich people problems," Indi said, sighing dramatically.

Lena threw a pillow at her, coughing as she waved away the resulting cloud of dust. "Don't be a brat. We all know how hard this recession has been for *all* business owners." Lena knew this better than most—she'd struggled to keep her floral shop afloat when in-person events had halted for over a year during the pandemic.

"Sorry... you're right."

Tess gave her a small smile. "It's fine. But," she grabbed one of the open bottles of wine from the floor, refilling all of our glasses, "let's not talk about boring business stuff. Instead, we should be celebrating Lizzie's return to Dearing Creek. How are you feeling about everything?"

"Honestly? I'm thrilled to be back, but..." I broke off, feeling the tears start to crop up again.

"You miss her, don't you?" Indi said, her smile sad and knowing. She'd loved her, too.

I nodded, taking a deep, steadying breath. "I feel her around me so much, especially here... you know?"

Brooke leaned over to brush back the hair that had once again fallen into my face—I could only imagine what I looked like by this point. "Of course you do. Cora was a huge part of your life and your time here. But maybe that's a good thing?"

Lena smiled encouragingly. "Yes... and now, since you can finally focus on writing your book, it'll be like she's here, cheering you on."

"Like we *all* are," Kait said, reaching across to squeeze my hand.

"*Me too!*" Jules' voice filtered out through the iPad perched on the floor, as she'd insisted on a Facetime call with us from her set trailer in L.A. Her face took up most of the screen, blue eyes twinkling with her long blonde hair done up in rollers, while someone off-camera worked on her makeup. It was such a bizarre sight, not one of us could help but laugh.

As for me, I'd given up on holding back the tears. "I don't know what I'd do without all of you."

"Well, we're family, aren't we? Dearie Girls forever." Brooke's eyes were also shining—I knew how hard this transition was going to be for her as well.

"Dearie Girls forever," I said, making my best attempt at a smile.

And true sisters, in every sense of the word.

Chapter 13

Lizzie

Early the next morning, I sat alone on the dock, dangling my legs over the edge as I relaxed with a cup of coffee, already two chapters into my grandmother's worn copy of *The Lord & The Lady*.

It had been late by the time things wound down and everyone had dispersed the night before. Brooke had decided to stay over with me at the cabin—but then left early to head back to the cities for some important networking event she couldn't miss. It was a tearful goodbye for both of us, despite her promise to be back again soon.

And now, watching the mist dance across the water, I found myself settling into a feeling of melancholy. It was the first real moment that I'd had in weeks to just be *still* and to begin processing everything that had transpired.

I wanted this fresh start more than *anything* and to find a clear way forward. But so much change also felt overwhelming—I mean, my entire life had essentially been flipped on its head in a matter of weeks. And the more

I rehashed everything, the more I couldn't help but wonder—*what had Grandma Cora been thinking?*

Shaking my head to try to clear the voices of doubt that had been threatening my peace this morning, I returned my focus back to my reading. But I felt her there with me as I continued on to one of our favorite passages in the book.

"Lizzie girl, look at this part... Lord Pemberton has just arrived at the ball—you see how the author describes how he looks at Lucille? She can feel him watching her, in what she assumes is disdain. But from his perspective, he's been struck by the sight of her. It's the first moment, Lizzie, that he starts falling..."

"Hey."

"Jesus Christ!" The booming voice came at me out of nowhere, of course scaring me shitless. It knocked me out of my memories as well as off-balance, as my coffee mug flew from my hand. I lunged forward, making a frantic grab for it—and then, in a slow-mo comedy of errors, I found myself also tumbling face first, off the dock, and into the water.

As I resurfaced in shock seconds later and glanced back towards the dock, I realized—-not only had I lost my mug, but I'd managed to take my grandmother's book down with me as well. *"Damn it!"*

"Jesus, you ok?"

Overcome with panic, I ignored both the question and the person, desperate to find what I'd lost. "*Shhhh, just... be quiet. I need to find it...*"

No, no, no...

I went back under, the water now murky from the muddy lakebed being kicked up around me. A few feet away, I could see the glinting white handle of my mug laying next to a rock, and I swam over to grab it.

But where was the book?

Suddenly, someone else dove into the water just ahead, the water now next to impossible to see through.

What the hell were they doing?

And then, I spotted it—the swaying, frayed turquoise ribbon of my bookmark, miraculously still tucked inside the cover of the black-bound book. Running out of air, I reached out—but another hand beat me to it.

Resurfacing and gasping as the air filled my lungs, I swam back towards the dock, mug in hand, a splash sounding behind me as the other person surfaced as well.

"Is this what you were looking for, Red?"

Wait... 'Red'?? Why do I know that voice?

Setting the mug down on the wooden planks above my head, I spun around, ready to confront the stranger—*rather than the memories*—that seemed intent on destroying my peace this morning.

And that's when I saw him—waist deep in the water, golden brown hair dripping into his face—with a grin that was equal parts sexy and smug, and all-too-familiar.

Rude Guy—from the coffee shop?

Not only that, but in his hand was my grandmother's book, dripping water steadily down his arm. As we locked eyes, I saw the recognition all over his face as well.

"*You!?*"

Rude Guy grinned, waving my book in front of him like it was some prize he'd won. "Hello again. This yours?"

Reaching out with my free hand to snatch the book from his grasp, I set it down next to my mug, climbing up the rungs of the ladder until I was standing above him on the dock. Squeezing the water from my hair and clothes, I watched as he swam towards the shore, walking through the shallower water.

"What the hell were you trying to do—*scare me half to death?*" I stormed down the length of the dock towards him, book and mug in hand, annoyed at his smile and that he was finding *any* sort of delight in this situation.

"In my defense, all I said was '*hey*'. I can't help that you're so... jumpy."

I crossed my arms. "Well, for your information, this is *private* property. I was hardly expecting a stranger to come waltzing across it before the sun was barely up." As I said it, I felt a shiver from the slight chill that still hung in the air—suddenly all too aware of the fact that I was dressed in nothing but a thin, very soaked light blue t-shirt and pajama pants.

And seeing as how I was getting a very clear repeat peek of Rude Guy's muscles beneath the thin fabric of his own t-shirt, I hugged my arms to my chest even tighter—simultaneously willing myself not to continue my gaze past his waistline.

His head was cocked to the side now as he looked at me thoughtfully. "Yep, it all makes sense now. You *did* sort of look familiar that day we ran into each other…."

Just then, I heard a door slam as Georgia made her way from her cabin towards my dock. "Ah, good, you're here already, James. And you two have become reacquainted, I see?"

My eyes darted between Rude Guy and Georgia. "Wait a minute… how do you know each other?"

She smiled. "James is my grandson, dear. He grew up here. And," she said, patting him on the shoulder proudly, "he's the owner of Horizon Remodeling, your new contractor." Then she furrowed her brow, finally seeming to notice the state we were in. "Hang on, were you two out there swimming at this hour?"

But I barely heard her question, my head still spinning. "What do you mean '*my new contractor*'?"

Rude Guy—I mean, James—glanced over at me, at least having the decency to look somewhat embarrassed. "Yeah, sorry… did I forget to mention that?"

Un-fucking-believable.

"Ok, let me sort this out. My neighbor—*Georgia*—is your grandmother?"

"Yes."

I paused, looking at him. "But I just saw you in Minneapolis, like, three weeks ago."

"Yeah, well... like I told you before, I was helping my friend move. Dearing Creek is my home." He shrugged, like all of this was completely logical. I flexed my fingers at my sides as they began tingling again, working to slow my breathing—even as my brain argued loudly over how completely illogical this situation was.

"Oh, this couldn't be more perfect." Georgia grinned, clasping her hands together like this was the best day ever.

I interrupted her. "I don't know about that. '*Perfect*' might be a stretch. As for Minneapolis, we just... ran into each other."

James was smirking now. "Right... something like that."

Did he have to sound so goddamn cocky?

No, no, no... Deep breaths, Lizzie.

Crossing my arms, I eyed him straight on. "Ok... *James*, is it? Are you an actual home remodeler? Like, licensed and everything?"

He nodded. "Yes, and insured—all the necessary legal and business operation pieces are in place. But," he paused, "you would actually be my first client."

"Come again?"

Georgia, sensing that her well-crafted plan might be disintegrating, stepped in. "Oh, James is very qualified. He's been doing this sort of work professionally for years now. Just finally took the leap to go out on his own. But he's the best." She motioned behind her proudly. "Did some work on my place, too."

I hesitated, thinking about this cabin and how much it meant to me. Sure, now I had the money to make this place mine... but not a single part of *any* of this felt real to me yet. And more than anything, I didn't want to screw anything else up, regardless of how much Georgia seemed to be pushing for it.

If I hired James and it went badly, I'd still have to face *years* of awkwardness, living next door to his grandmother...

"I don't know..."

James held up a hand, his entire demeanor shifting. "Listen, I don't want to waste either of our time if you aren't interested. Good luck with your project, Ms. Blake." Then he turned on his heel to head back towards the road, his sneakers making wet squishing noises as he set off across the grass.

"Wait," I called out after him, "... I didn't say *no*, exactly." He paused mid-stride, slowly turning as I continued. "I was just... I don't know... caught off guard."

"See? You two just need to sit down and talk things through," Georgia said, all smiles again. Then leaning towards me, she continued in a loud whisper. "But, Elizabeth... you might want to throw something decent on first. You're... nipping out a bit there, dear."

Eyes wide, I pinned my arms back over my chest, feeling the humiliation wash over me in bright shades of blush.

Oh... my God.

And watching James shift from prickly to struggling to hold back laughter wasn't winning him any points, either—beyond the fluttery feelings in my chest as his stupid hazel eyes crinkled up at the corners.

Georgia, however, was undeterred. "Go on, you two. Clean up, and I'll put on a pot of coffee."

I looked back to James, who was just standing there, waiting for me to answer.

"Alright, fine. It can't hurt to talk, I guess," I sighed, throwing up my hands. "Let me go in and take a quick shower, and I'll be out in a bit."

James shrugged. "Fine, I guess that works."

But as I trudged towards my cabin, my grandmother's book still seeping water between my fingers, I could feel his eyes burning a hole in the back of me.

And I couldn't help but wonder if I was about to fall face first into my biggest flop yet.

Chapter 14

James

"Exactly what is it you're trying to pull here?" I walked into GiGi's cabin, the door slamming behind me as I yanked off my wet sneakers. She was already busy by the stove working on a fresh batch of coffee, humming as though she hadn't a care in the world.

But I knew better—she was up to something. And whatever it was, I wasn't having it.

"Don't know what you're talking about, Tater. But can you pass me a fresh filter?"

I stood there, arms crossed, until my grandmother finally looked over.

"What?"

"Don't play innocent with me. Why didn't you tell me that your 'mystery client' was our former neighbor?"

"Didn't see a need to bring up the past," GiGi said, shrugging. "Besides, I doubted you'd remember who she was, anyway. You're a good four or so years older than she is. Pretty sure you were already off taking classes at that technical school while she was doing most of her running around here with those Dearie Girls."

Suddenly, hearing that name made the pieces start to click into place. "Wait, wasn't Brooke Christenson a part of that whole thing?"

"Was, and still is. Half those girls still live up here, y'know."

I shook my head and couldn't help but marvel at the irony of running into Brooke for the first time in years just weeks ago, all the way down in Minneapolis—and now having her best friend living here, right under my nose.

And also quite possibly your first client—if you don't fuck it up.

"Well, anyway, can you lay off a bit? I appreciate the help in promoting my business, but I don't want you nosing around in this. If I'm to take on this project, it'll be because it's a good fit for me and because I earned it outright. Not because you're trying to manipulate one or both of us with whatever convoluted plan you're concocting in that head of yours."

GiGi's expression now shifted from playful to stern. "James, I love ya, boy... but you can really be a self-righteous grump with a chip on your shoulder sometimes. All I'm trying to do here is *help*. Whether or not Elizabeth Blake chooses to hire you is up to her." She turned back to the stove, making a racket with the coffeemaker. "And now I'm thinking I should maybe advise her *not* to."

"No, no… just stay out of it. I've got this. And while you're at it, can you also try to avoid embarrassing our neighbor?" That moment—watching the flush of color spread across Elizabeth's face as GiGi blatantly pointed out the transparency of her wet t-shirt—wasn't one I'd forget for some time.

But now, hearing my grandmother muttering under her breath, I turned my attention back to our conversation, leaning against the counter with a sigh. "Look, I'm sorry. I was just… caught off guard, is all."

GiGi started the coffee and turned back towards me. This time, her gaze had softened. "I know, honey. I'm just so proud of you for finally doing this. Your mama would be, too. I know how hard it was for you to give in and accept that money."

I felt my insides clench again at the thought of it, but I managed a tight smile. "Thanks. You might be a pain in my ass sometimes, but I do love you."

"Love you too, Tater-tot. Now go and get changed. You smell like dead fish."

Shaking my head with a laugh as I wandered back towards my old room for fresh clothes, I couldn't help but wonder again if I'd made the right choice by dipping into that inheritance.

All I could do now was hope that any chaos it managed to kick up in my life would be worth it.

Twenty minutes later, I wandered over to the Blake cabin, two coffee thermoses in hand, along with a Tupperware filled with fresh rhubarb scones—a GiGi specialty. Knocking on the front door, I stood waiting until she approached a moment later, towel-drying her hair. I couldn't help feeling a momentary pang of disappointment that she'd heeded GiGi's advice about her shirt.

"Come on in, I was just finishing up." She held the door open, and I sidled in past her. Inside were stacks of boxes, piled amongst an assortment of old furniture. "Why don't we sit in here?" she said, motioning to the small table in the kitchen area. "Sorry it's such a mess... we were just getting everything moved in yesterday."

I gave a little shrug as I pulled out the chair across from her. "No problem, Elizabeth. Believe me when I tell you, I've seen much worse."

"Oh, you can just call me Lizzie. Everyone does, for the most part." She smiled, seeming hesitant. "Listen, I'm sorry about earlier. I mean, you *did* scare me half to death, and yeah, I was kind of upset after you ruined my grandmother's book..."

"... wait, wait, *I* ruined her book? I mean, I'm sorry for startling you, but I'm pretty sure it wasn't me tossing her book into the lake after you."

Lizzie held up a hand, and I could tell she was doing her best not to get herself riled again—her pert, freckled nose twitching as her lips pulled together in a barely contained scowl. For some reason, I found it all kind of... *adorable.* "*Nope, not again...*" she muttered under her breath, clear as day. Then she exhaled, wrestling out a smile. "Agree to start over?"

"Sure, why not?"

"Good." She finally took a bite of the scone I'd offered her, and I watched as her body relaxed, bright green eyes rolling back in her head. "*Oh my God,* this scone is amazing. Remind me to stay on your grandmother's good side. Forever."

I smiled wryly. "I have to remind myself of that every day."

Laughter bubbled up from her throat, warm and melodic—and it made me glad to have broken the tension. After another sip of coffee, she continued. "Anyway, do you mind telling me about some of the projects you've worked on?"

As we sat there together with our breakfast, I flipped through the portfolio I'd brought along with me—filled with blueprints and snapshots of all my best work through the years. Mel had been generous in allowing me to keep a record for my own use—it was clear now he'd always expected me to branch out on my own one day and wanted to give me a leg up. I was grateful for it.

Lizzie nodded along as I explained the various projects I'd designed or led, studying the photos and pointing out various aspects she liked. I was impressed by how she seemed to take an interest in everything, asking thoughtful questions about my design process, along with my favorite types of materials. I had no idea what she did for a living, especially now that she'd landed herself all the way up here in Dearing Creek—but it seemed obvious to me that she was creative as well.

And even though I'd had my doubts earlier, it felt fucking validating to see someone—outside those who'd known me forever—actually appreciating the skills I'd worked hard to hone over the years. Like maybe I hadn't been crazy to take the leap and start running with this on my own.

As I watched her flip through the last few pages in my portfolio, I found myself studying her face as my mind wandered, now able to recall a few fuzzy mental snapshots of her from many years ago—a bespectacled girl with a wild mane of coppery hair, hanging out on the porch—or floating around the dock with a handful of other girls. I would've been in high school or college by then, several years older—like GiGi said, we'd never had reason to interact much. She'd always seemed friendly, though—it made me wonder about the rest of her family. Not that I had much to speak of there, either.

This fully-grown version of Lizzie, however, was messing with my head. Not just in our last two disastrous interactions—*though who's keeping count?* No, it was more in what I noticed as we sat here together, finally relaxed and not snarking at one another. Teenage Lizzie may have been cute, but the woman before me now was lovely, the juxtaposition of her vivid hair and eyes against her pale skin making it a challenge for me to concentrate and do my job.

Especially if she kept smiling at me like that.

It had been a long time since a woman had brought about thoughts like this in me—maybe I'd been letting myself fly solo for too long. I was bound to get rusty.

After a while, she leaned back in her chair. "Well, I have to admit... I was kind of hoping I'd hate everything you had to show me." She grinned, giving me a sidelong glance. "But you're really talented, James. I'm super impressed with your work. And I can tell you love what you do."

"Thanks... I think," I said, smirking.

She blushed. "I promise, all of that was meant to be a compliment."

"Of course." I took a sip of my coffee, watching as a flock of Canadian geese passing over the lake outside the window also caught her eye. In this light, her eyes almost seemed to have a trace of gold in them. I liked it. "So, Lizzie... What is it that you do for a living? You seem like the creative type."

She returned her attention to me. "Me? Well, I spent the last few years working as a copywriter for an accounting firm in Minneapolis."

"Sounds... fun."

She made a face. "Let me assure you, it one-hundred percent *wasn't*."

I chuckled, feeling myself begin to relax more, too. "So why'd you leave? Just needed a change?"

"Honestly, I'd been wanting to move on for ages, but they kind of made the decision for me—I was just laid off a few weeks ago, while meeting with our family lawyer about my mom and grandmother's estates."

I let out a low whistle. "Ouch... rough day."

"Definitely not awesome," she said, raising her coffee to her lips. "Anyway... it was a blessing in disguise, I guess. It allowed me to move up here after I inherited my grandparents' cabin... and now, I can finally focus on my book."

"Ah, so you're an author, too." My mind flashed back to earlier, replaying the panicked moment when she dropped her book in the water. Now her reaction was starting to make more sense—and I felt a brief pang of guilt for the callous way I'd behaved. Books were clearly important to her, beyond the sentimental. "What kind of book are you writing?"

"As of now, a novel about two sisters, set in the Depression-era Midwest. But things haven't been clicking with this one for a while, so..." she shrugged, "that remains to be seen."

"Well, I hope you can work it all out. Feeling stuck is a hard place to be." Then I hesitated, trying to choose my words carefully. "Sorry to hear about your family, too. I know what it's like to lose the people you love."

As her eyes welled up, I felt immediate regret for bringing up such a sensitive subject—especially with someone I hardly knew. But then she gave a small nod. "Thanks... I appreciate that." Pausing, she chewed on her lower lip—appearing to wrestle with something in her mind.

Watching her do that, however, seemed to be making me wrestle with something else entirely. *Move things along, Tate.*

Especially since now she seemed to be studying me, too. "Look, I want you to know... most of why I was hesitant to hire you is because your grandmother lives right next door."

I nodded. "Sure, makes sense."

Lizzie looked at me straight on now, her emerald eyes now appearing almost faceted as the morning light filtered in through the kitchen window. "And it's been a rough year. I honestly can't deal with any more complications in my life right now."

"I think I understand that better than most," I said grimly. I began to gather my things—better to leave graciously, not force her to decline my services outright. She was right—living next door to GiGi for the foreseeable future might make things messier than they needed to be. What if the job didn't go well?

But I didn't allow myself to linger too long over the other questions in my mind—like, what was it about this woman that pulled at me?

Closing my portfolio, I stood up from my chair. "Well, thanks for your time, Lizzie. I truly do wish you all the best. Let me know if I can recommend a contractor who'd be a better fit. Happy to help."

"Wait... what? Why are you leaving?"

"Uhhh... because, like you said, this seems *complicated*?"

She groaned, burying her face in her hands for a moment. Then she raised her head again as her cheeks flushed, something that seemed to happen often. "*Ugh*, I'm sorry. I really do mean well... but whenever I'm anxious, I'll usually end up saying the wrong thing at least fifty-percent of the time. Please, let me try this again." She cleared her throat. "What I was *actually* trying to do was... offer you the job."

I raised an eyebrow, amused. "You sure about that? Because that's not what I heard."

"What can I say. I'm better at writing." Shrugging sheepishly, she held out a hand. "So, what do you say? Can we give it a go?"

I hesitated again as I stared at her—a confusing mix of '*I really want to get to know her*' thoughts and '*what if I fuck it all up?*' scenarios racing through my head. *Would I really be able to do this with her?*

But maybe it was time to stop worrying and start *doing*. Fact was, I needed the work if I was going to start a business. And Jesse had just quit his job with Mel to join me. He—*and* his pregnant wife—were relying on me to bring in clients. Walking away from a paying gig would be a pretty stupid move. Especially when it was someone I didn't *want* to walk away from.

What else did I have to lose at this point?

"Alright. I'm in," I said, reaching out to shake her offered hand—immediately jarred by the crackle of electricity I felt run through me as my rough palm met her much softer one. I saw her eyes widen—*she had to have felt it too, right?*

Shaking off the reaction as static electricity from the dry and dusty interior of the cabin, I willed myself to relax as I sat down again with a smile. "Now, how about we start with going over all the work you are hoping to have done..."

We talked for another hour, touring the cabin both inside and out while making a wishlist of the projects she'd hoped to tackle, as well as a few recommendations of my own. I was happy to see the love she had for the old bones and character of the structure, and how she was determined to keep as much of it original as possible. And the updates we'd landed on were manageable for Jesse and me to handle on our own, with the exception of a few larger projects: Review and make any necessary updates to all electrical and plumbing; build on a bathroom addition to the master bedroom; refinish the hardwood floors throughout the cabin; create a custom built-in bookshelf wall in the living room; replace all the light fixtures; replace the tile and fixtures in the bathroom; repair the exterior chimney; repaint both the interior and exterior walls; replace the windows; install an air conditioning unit and inspect all duct work; re-shingle the roof, adding gutters and downspouts; rebuild the small front porch; and lastly, repaint both the exterior of the cabin and all the interior rooms.

It was easily a few months' worth of work between the two of us (along with a couple of subcontractors, as needed), enough to keep busy for most of the summer. And Lizzie's budget seemed flexible enough, which I found interesting since she'd mentioned a job loss. But as long as she paid her invoices on time, how she handled her money was none of my business. Just like I didn't need anyone questioning mine.

It was easy talking with her, though, now that we'd moved past our initial head-butting to share in a common goal. And our shift from would-be adversaries to long-term collaborators was going way better than I'd hoped. She was bright, friendly—open to ideas and eager to share hers.

Considering how we'd started off twice, I had to admit—it was a pleasant surprise. More than pleasant.

In the end, we shook hands, with me promising to drop off the estimate of work and contract before the end of the week and a plan to start work on Friday.

"I'm really looking forward to working together, James," Lizzie said, smiling as she leaned casually against the frame of her front door.

Pausing on the wooden porch, I turned around to face her. "Same here. And I promise, we'll make this cabin feel like a real home by the time we're done." As if on cue, the board I was standing on released a loud creaking sound—grimacing, I gave it another bounce, detecting a definite crack this time. "Though *maybe* we better move your porch towards the top of the list, before it kills someone."

She laughed, brushing back her hair as the light breeze passing through swept it across her face. "You're the expert, sir." With a wave, she walked back inside, closing the door behind her.

Shaking my head, I continued on towards my truck, finding it hard to wipe the smile off my face. I thought about stopping in to talk with GiGi before heading home—but I knew she'd likely launch into another one of her interrogations. Right now, all I wanted was some time on my own to collect my thoughts.

Because I had to admit—I was *really* excited about this project. It could be the start of something great, and I felt driven more than ever to build a business I could be proud of—something I created.

The scarier truth? I hadn't even begun the work here yet, and I was already sensing my client was going to be an unintentional distraction.

I mean, I knew I'd been attracted to her from that first moment we'd butted heads in the cities. It was hard *not* to be. Back then, though, I'd also assumed her to be uptight or a handful. And, of course, someone I'd never cross paths with again once Minneapolis was in my rearview mirror.

But now that I'd be spending every weekday near her for the majority of the summer, the problem was no longer about her being difficult. It was more the fact that she *wasn't*. Instead, she seemed pretty great, like someone I'd enjoy hanging out with. I had no idea if I could do that without getting myself caught up in something I shouldn't.

When was the last time I'd spent this much time pondering a woman? It was honestly hard to remember. Beyond a handful of dates here and there, I hadn't made much time for women my own age the last couple of years. And other than missing the physical side of things, I didn't see much of a need. Especially when opening myself up to more brought the risk of—as Lizzie put it—*complications.*

GiGi took enough of my time and attention anyway, and rightfully so.

Besides, regardless of how I'd felt during our few interactions so far, I was smart enough to know—crossing any kind of line with Lizzie would be a bad idea, probably for both of us. Not only that, wouldn't it also make me a hypocrite, considering what I'd just gone through with Denise Kinney?

All I needed to worry about was keeping myself focused on what mattered most—a job well done and a happy client. Which meant maintaining friendly, yet professional, boundaries. Nothing more.

Even if I couldn't help but wonder what *more* might be like with a woman like Lizzie Blake.

Chapter 15

Lizzie

Saturday, May 12th
8:45 p.m.

BROOKE: I cannot believe you hired James Tate to remodel the cabin! I forgot he used to live next door. What are the odds?

LENA: I've heard he's really talented, Lizzie. Your place will look amazing when it's done!

TESS: I heard another thing about James Tate…

LIZZIE: Wait, what did you hear?

INDI: Here we go again…

TESS: Hold up… who said it was anything negative? My friend Lani over in Heartwood went out with him a handful of times last year. Apparently, he's an incredible kisser.

> *LIZZIE: Not exactly the credentials I was looking for…*

> JULES: C'mon, you deserve some good loving in your life after Ol' Pencil Dick.

> *LIZZIE: *sigh* I really regret sharing that story with all of you.*

> BROOKE: No regrets. But I like the way you're thinking, Jules…

Thursday, June 4th
10:10 p.m.

> BROOKE: Ok, fess up. The last three messages from you have been all about a certain contractor. You wouldn't be… I don't know… *into him*, would you?

> KAIT: She thinks he's gooooorgeous, she wants to kissssss him….

> INDI: I would tell you both to knock it off, but I've kinda been wondering the same thing…

I plopped my phone down next to me on the sofa, slamming my laptop shut with a sigh. I'd been getting nowhere with writing tonight, especially now that my brain was being flooded with thoughts of James Tate.

Or now, to be more specific, *kissing* James Tate.

Thanks a lot, Kait.

Though I'd be lying if I said I hadn't already been thinking about it anyway—or of James as more than just my contractor. I'd done that all on my own these past few weeks, without any prompting from anyone.

I mean, from the first moment we *literally* ran into each other in Minneapolis, I'd found him crazy-attractive. Granted, the chaotic circumstances of our little 'meet cute' *may* have overshadowed my initial impression of the guy.

Ok, yeah... I thought he was *the worst*.

But even after starting off rocky yet *again* that day on the dock, there was no denying it—that spark I'd felt was still there. Tall and athletic, with the hint of whiskers on his face and short-ish, wavy-tousled golden brown hair that made me want to weave my fingers through it—James was the vision of the quintessential Minnesota boy with a scruffy Northwoods edge that somehow made him even sexier.

I had to admit, though—it was the way I'd caught him looking at me that got to me the most. I couldn't decide if he found me completely ridiculous, or if he maybe felt something between us, too—the former of which was probably true, and neither of which would help me to write this damn book.

Of course, this made the fact that all I wanted to do was replay our conversations and figure out what made him tick—or how to make him smile in that way that made his eyes all crinkly—*really* problematic.

Even still, James and I were learning how to work around one another, quickly navigating our way from a cordial, professional rhythm towards something that could be called an actual friendship. And being around him all the time felt good, like a place I wanted to stay in.

So, sure—I guess he wasn't the beast I'd first assumed him to be. In fact, far from it—and I was more than happy to be proven wrong. He'd gone from 'Rude Guy'—seemingly intent on driving me crazy—to a man who had proven himself hard-working, thoughtful, playful, and kind. Heck, I'd even call him *funny*.

Which is exactly why I had to be careful and not let myself get carried away by thoughts of sexy smiles, flirty innuendos, and dreamy hazel eyes.

I didn't even know if he was actually *doing* those things or if it was my imagination making it all up. Either way, I felt like I needed blinders around this guy if I was going to keep myself in check.

Because getting caught up in another man wasn't what I came up here to do. I'd spent way too much of the last few years wishing things could be different, believing I should be different. And now that I'd been given this gift of a fresh start, I couldn't screw it all up. Even if a man like

James had me tempted to rewrite all the plans I'd made for myself.

Things felt *right* here, though. And so much had already changed in a matter of weeks. The more time I spent in Dearing Creek, the more I could feel myself re-learning how to relax and just *be*—like I could finally take a full, deep breath without the fear of drowning.

And now, for the first time ever, I had the time and space to give my writing—*this book*—everything I had. I owed that to myself, right?

Maybe if I did, everything else in my life would start falling into place, too.

"Turkey or BLT?"

I'd walked into the kitchen to see James standing at the table, pulling sandwiches from a paper sack. Grabbing the water pitcher from the fridge, I filled two glasses. "I thought we discussed this. Bacon trumps *everything*. Always."

As I set the glasses down on the table, he tossed a sandwich in my direction—which, thankfully, I managed to catch this time. "I know. That was a test to see if you could resist Delilah's Turkey Dinner Wrap."

I unwrapped my BLT as I lowered into my seat, smiling as I noticed he'd requested extra avocado for me as well. "Ok, I'll admit, you almost had me. The TDW *is* my second-favorite. But..."

"... *'no bacon'*, I got it." he said, chuckling as he pulled out the chair next to me.

"You learn fast, Tate."

"Doin' my best, Blake."

We grinned at each other for a moment before each taking a bite. Lunching together had quickly become a habit over the past month, with Jesse usually heading to home or the clinic to have lunch with his wife, who I'd learned a couple weeks back was expecting their first child this fall.

Even though I hadn't met Tara yet, I envied the two of them—how incredible to have found the one you not only wanted to share every lunch with, but a future family, too? And Jesse was such a great guy, so laid-back and happy—I had no doubt he'd be an awesome dad.

I could tell he was good for James, too. They seemed to balance each other out, in all the ways only an old friend could. Kind of like my Dearie Girls.

"So, I was thinking... do you think GiGi would let me pick some of the rhubarb from her garden?"

He sniffed back a laugh as he finished his bite. "I think she would *pay* you to take it. She practically has an acre's worth on the west side of the cabin by now."

Laughing, I plopped a piece of avocado that had fallen from my sandwich into my mouth. "Good, I was hoping that might be the case. I was thinking of taking a crack at my grandmother's rhubarb pie one of these days."

"The custard one? GiGi said Cora finally gave her a copy of the recipe a few years back... practically had to fight her for it."

I giggled. "Yep, that's the one. And I'm not surprised. Pretty sure I'm the only other person who managed to get that recipe out of her." A sudden movement near the fireplace on the other side of the cabin caught my eye. I vaguely reached towards James, blindly swatting at his arm as I kept my eyes glued to the spot.

"What? You trying to fight me, too?"

"No... I think there's a mouse..."

"A mouse?" James pushed back his chair, standing up quickly. "Where?"

I pointed towards the far wall, and at that exact moment, I saw the little guy dart across to hide behind the curtains of the large picture window. "Over there! Under the window!"

Grabbing the nearby pail I'd planned to use for collecting rhubarb, he crept slowly in that direction, gently poking at the fabric of the curtains with his foot until the mouse came flying out. In one swift motion, James quickly dropped the pail over his path, trapping the critter inside as he gave a triumphant whoop. He glanced back towards me, one hand on hip, victorious. "You're safe, m'lady."

Half-laughing as my heart continued racing, I crept over to where he stood. "Thanks, but... now what?"

"What do you mean?"

"I mean, how are you going to get him out of here?"

He glanced down, crossing his arms. "Well, to be honest, I hadn't thought that far ahead."

"Yeah, me neither. Are you sure he's in there?" Chewing on my lip as I dug my fingernails into my tingly palms, I gently tapped the side of the bucket with my foot—the resulting scratching noise from inside making my skin crawl. "Eww, no... this is not ok. We need to get him out of here."

"Alright, well... do you have rat poison?"

My eyes widened as I looked at him. "What, and *kill* him?"

He chuckled. "Ok then, Snow White, how about a *live* trap? We could slide one underneath the bucket and release it outside later."

"Um... no. I don't have anything like that."

"Something tells me a trip to the hardware store might be in order after this conversation," he said, smirking. "Ok, let's try a piece of cardboard from the box of tiles. We can jimmy it underneath, hopefully trapping the little guy between that and the bucket, then rehome him out in the woods."

"Fine."

Moments later, I was crouched on the floor next to James, tilting up the edge of the pail ever so slightly as he began to slowly slide a cardboard panel underneath. Which was going great, until suddenly—I caught a whiff of dust from the cardboard, and I sneezed.

It was just enough to both startle James and jerk the pail upwards, giving Mr. Mouse the sweet taste of freedom as he raced around the corner towards the bedrooms. James fell backwards onto the floor as I squealed, laughing hysterically at the look of horror on my face.

"Ok, cabin life's been *real*. I'll be leaving for the city now."

Pulling himself together, he stood up, reaching out a hand to pull me up as well. "Naw, we just need to get you some supplies so you're better prepared for critters. I'll drop off a few live traps tonight."

"And *in the meantime?*"

He shrugged, grinning. "Maybe leave out a bedtime snack for your furry little roomie?"

James roared with laughter as I threw the cardboard at his head, his whole body shaking—and then *damn it*, I couldn't stop myself from laughing, too.

And despite the fact that I would never be able to sleep in this cabin *ever* again, I couldn't help thinking how great it felt to be here like this, laughing at the ridiculousness of life, with someone like James.

Chapter 16

James

By mid-June, everything was well underway on the Blake project. As Lizzie sat typing away on her laptop each day—often with a snack of some sort and a huge mug of coffee by her side—we'd been slowly transforming the cabin around her.

Once she'd signed off on the blueprint layout I'd worked up for her in early May, we started off with demoing the section of wall in the master bedroom that would lead into the new bathroom addition and building out the structure. Another week was spent scraping and repainting the exterior wood siding in a deeper navy, touching up the white shutters as well. We quickly followed that with a full rebuild of the front porch, with a new overhang for shade—ready for the long summer ahead.

Jesse also had a friend, Chris, who'd started up a landscaping business—so we worked out a deal with him to tidy up the yard, adding some rock-bordered plant beds and a stone path connecting everything. Before he wrapped up, we also had him trim a few of the trees along the property—though Lizzie insisted the river birch not be touched.

"They're my favorite," she'd said, *"and they deserve to reach as far and wide as they wish to go."*

Seeing how the outside of the property was coming together already, I was glad we'd opted to start there—as temperatures had already started climbing. I knew we'd be better off working indoors as much as possible during the hotter summer months—especially now that I'd had my buddy, Art, take care of installing the A/C unit.

The day after he'd finished up the project, I knew right away that eating the cost to hire another contractor had been the right move. Watching the satisfied grin light up Lizzie's face as the stuffy cabin filled with cooler air made it worth every penny of his fee.

But it was only partly about practicalities and cooler air, though. Making her happy had become just as much of a motivator—so much so, it surprised me.

Six weeks in, she and I had settled into a relaxed sort of rhythm together—and for maybe the first time ever, I was excited to come to work each day. Not only was Lizzie gracious and flexible, her warm, laid-back personality made her easy to be around.

More than 'easy'—I *wanted* to be around her. Probably more than I should. Definitely more than felt profession- al. And plenty that felt borderline inappropriate, though I'd obviously kept myself in check.

But as we spent day after day coexisting with one another, I couldn't help learning what made her tick. Like her weird addiction to cashews (*it was borderline obsessive*), or how I'd sometimes catch her humming to herself when she was alone outside or working on something in the kitchen. And there was no doubt she was a hard worker, rarely without her laptop or a book—both almost an extension of her. It made me think of my mom, who'd been a librarian—a core memory I hadn't called up in a very long time.

And whenever I could tell she felt stressed by something, I'd see her alternating between flexing her fingers and balling them into fists, like the rhythm of it somehow soothed her. But when she was *really* focused on a task, like her writing, she'd wrinkle up her nose just a bit while chewing on her lower lip, oblivious to the world around her as she typed away.

I had to admit—all of it made me like her even more.

Our lunch breaks, though, were what I looked forward to most. The two of us would sit at her little kitchen table together—or sometimes, if the weather cooperated, out on the covered porch. It was there that we opened up around each other even more, talking about our lives, how we spent our free time, along with random stories about friends and locals in Dearing Creek. Sometimes our talks went deeper, and it always left me wanting to know even more about her.

And for probably the first time in my life—or at least, beyond GiGi—I actually enjoyed the process of getting to know a woman, digging into what mattered. Or more specifically, *this* woman. There was nothing pretentious about her—and the questions she volleyed back made it seem like she really cared about who I was, beneath all the small talk. Not just for show, or to get something out of me I didn't want to give.

As the weeks passed, I knew it wasn't just because Lizzie happened to be the one right there in front of me, easily accessible, that drew me in.

It was *her*.

Maybe believing she could feel it too was wishful think-ing. It also treaded dangerously close to the boundaries I'd set.

But each day, it was becoming harder to remember why I'd even drawn the line in the first place.

One afternoon, I decided to let Jesse take the lead on overseeing the roofers, giving me space to plan out a smaller project I'd been most excited to dig into. And I had to admit, it was mostly because I knew how much it would mean to Lizzie. I couldn't wait to see the look on her face once it was done.

I was out on the porch, taking a break on one of her new Adirondack chairs when I heard the front screen door swing open. Glancing up from the sketch pad in my lap, I saw Lizzie step out, two glasses of lemonade in hand.

Today, she had her long hair pulled back in a low pony-tail, over her usual tank top and shorts. I couldn't help but notice how today's pair hugged her curves in a way that made me irrationally jealous of a simple piece of fabric.

All that was to say, she looked beautiful—but in her relaxed, natural sort of way, without trying too hard. I liked it, way better than the overdone look most of the women I'd known seemed to go for. Like everything else with Lizzie, she didn't *need* to try. She already stood out, in the best ways possible.

However, that also made it much more impossible to *not* notice her. Especially now, as she gave me a smile that nobody in their right mind could ignore. "Hey, there, want some lemonade? I thought maybe you guys could use a drink."

"Awesome, thanks." I smiled and accepted the glass gratefully, taking a deep swig. God, it tasted good—espe-cially with how unseasonably hot it had been all week. I pressed the cool glass against the side of my face, feeling the droplets of perspiration roll down my cheek. "Want me to take the other one over to Jesse? I think he's in the back, wrapping things up with the roofers."

"No, that's ok. I already brought the whole crew a glass through the back door. This one's all mine." She grinned, motioning towards the empty seat next to me. "Care if I join you?"

"Not at all, you know I love the company." As she lowered herself onto the chair, I held out the small bag of cashews I had in my hand towards her. "Hungry?" She nodded as I bit back a smile, and I dumped several into her outstretched hand.

"Thanks. They're my favorite."

"Yeah, I've kinda noticed."

Grinning, she tossed the nuts into her mouth and leaned back, chewing as she trailed the bottom of her glass along her thigh, leaving a glistening trail. "God, it feels so good not to be staring at that stupid computer screen right now."

I chuckled as I closed the cover on my sketch pad. "Book still not going well, I take it?"

She groaned, rolling her eyes as she munched on a nut. "You could say that. A documentary on the sexual lives of mealworms would probably be more riveting than the chapter I've been trying to write all week."

"Yeah, I've heard those mealworms can get pretty kinky."

She laughed along with me for a moment, but her eyes still looked sad. "Honestly, I think it might be time to pull the plug and put the entire book out of its misery."

I glanced over at her. "I was thinking last night… Maybe a longer break would do you some good. Could help you to feel re-energized or find some inspiration?" I gestured towards GiGi's dock, where my kayak was drying out from my early morning paddle. "Whenever I need to work out something in my head, time out on the water is usually what I need."

"Right, I've noticed you out there a lot of the mornings. Not that I'm some creeper spying on you or anything," she explained in a rush, but she was blushing again. I did my best to hold back the smile. "I just mean, sometimes when I'm up making coffee, I'll see you out on the lake. It looks like it would be peaceful."

"It is. You ever been kayaking before?"

She shook her head, making a face. "Don't get me wrong, I've always thought it *looked* fun… just not sure I'm coordinated enough to paddle and keep myself afloat at the same time."

I leaned over, side-tapping my foot against hers as the skin of our legs brushed against each other, my rough to her smooth. I couldn't help wondering what it would be like, feeling more of her.

Which, of course, was a thought I needed to push straight out of my head—before it became impossible to hide how much she was affecting me at the moment.

I cleared my throat, shifting slightly in my seat. "Happy to teach you sometime, if you're ever interested in learning. I'll even throw in a one hundred percent no drowning guarantee."

Lizzie smiled, her eyes now playful. "How about this... I'll make you a deal." Her gaze briefly flickered downward, and I prayed to God she hadn't noticed the bulge forming against my will beneath the glass I held in my lap. "If you'll read a book I recommend, I'll go kayaking with you sometime."

"I don't know... I've never been much of a reader."

"Yeah, *I've kinda noticed*," she said, echoing back my earlier words with a wink. I couldn't help but laugh.

"Alright, deal. Just tell me what book I need to read."

"Great! I'll have something for you by tomorrow." She beamed, pausing for a moment before continuing. "And listen, I really appreciate the advice, too... It makes sense. I guess I hoped moving up here would be enough to help me get out of my writing rut. The lake has always been my happy place. But looks like I still have more to work through. Maybe it wouldn't hurt to try something new." She gave me another quick smile. "Lord knows ignoring my problems has never worked out anyway."

I met her eyes, with a look that I hoped appeared sympathetic. But deep down, her words had struck a chord—almost like they were meant for me.

How long had I been trying to do the same?

The two of us sat there together for a while in comfortable silence, allowing both the sweet coolness of the lemonade and the sounds of nature filtering through the air to fill in the gaps.

Of course, I knew exactly how Lizzie felt. This lake—the entirety of Dearing Creek, really—had always been *my* happy place, too. Even with the unrest I'd been dealing with over the past couple of years, I needed to remember how lucky I was to be here.

Of course, I'd never wish to repeat the circumstances that had landed me here with GiGi and Pops twenty-six years ago—without question, I'd do pretty much anything to have my mom back. But I was grateful, at least, to have this place. It was my home, and I never wanted to be anywhere else.

I peeked at her again out of the corner of my eye, noticing that her eyes had closed as she relaxed against the back of her chair. I couldn't help but smile at her earlier confession—because, of course, I'd been watching her, too.

No matter how much I tried to pretend otherwise, there was something about her I felt a connection with. It was impossible not to like her. But maybe I was making all this too complicated. I could *like* her... didn't have to mean anything more than that. Right?

I took another long, slow gulp from my glass, leaning back against my chair as well. From a few houses down, I could hear the Weaver kids giggling and splashing around in the water without a care in the world. How incredible it was to be a kid—just happy in the moment, with nothing heavy pulling at you. Sometimes, I wondered if I'd missed that part of my childhood entirely.

But right now, I could see it was Lizzie who needed the help finding her way through whatever was weighing her down so she could find her own happiness.

"Can I ask you a question?"

She opened her eyes, turning towards me again. "Sure, unless it's about mealworms. I don't *actually* have an opinion on their sex lives... though I'm sure theirs are far more interesting than mine." She froze, cheeks blazing. "Oh, my God... forget I said that."

"Oh, I don't know, I'd say that comment alone qualifies you as plenty interesting," I said, unable to hold myself back from laughing outright—though my insides did a funny little twist at the same time. "But my question was actually about your book... and I've been wondering about this for a while now. Does the Great Depression... interest you?"

"The answer should probably be yes? But if I'm being honest, not really."

"Then why the hell are you writing a book about it?" I hadn't meant for the words to come out with as much force as they did, but at least it made her laugh.

"Another good question... and before you ask, I don't know the answer to that one, either." I watched her turn and smile as we both heard Jeremy Weaver release a loud yodel, making one of his signature cannonball leaps into the water. "I mean, at first, I loved the idea of tackling a strong relationship, which is why I started with the two sisters. Having the book set back then was mostly because of stories my grandma used to share about her mother. I'd hoped to write something that would draw people in." Looking back at me, she made a face. "But I'm having a hard time even getting *myself* to want to read it."

I paused for a moment, considering. "So it's the relationships that get you excited about writing, then?"

"Absolutely... which is why I've always loved romance novels. Grandma Cora and I used to have an ongoing reading list that we shared, too. She was always encouraging me to write one myself one day." Her eyes lit up, as they often did whenever she talked about her grandmother. "And since she and my grandfather were basically the perfect couple, I figured they'd serve as my inspiration... if I ever got around to it."

"Yeah, I remember you saying that. So, then what's stopping you?"

"Well, it's kind of embarrassing." Lizzie stared down at the glass resting in her lap, tracing a pattern in the condensation. "My creative writing professors in college drilled it into my head that romance novels are basically... trash. My ex too, for that matter... called them the 'bottom feeders of literature'. That I'd never get published if I didn't get serious."

"Jesus, what an asshole," I said, my words again bursting forth more forcefully than I'd intended. "Sorry, that was rude. But I hope that's the reason he's your ex."

"It's ok. And I know, that probably should've been enough, right?" This time, her eyes were sad. "But no... there were other things, in the end."

Instantly, I felt a knot form in my gut at the thought of someone causing her pain. I'd known Lizzie for just over a month at this point, but it was enough to realize she deserved far better than how she'd been treated.

Of course, the irrational part of me wanted to find that asshole and remind him of who the bottom feeder *actually* was.

Draining the rest of my lemonade, I rested the bottom of the glass against my leg before looking over at her. "Listen... I think if your dream is to be a writer, write what you're passionate about. Don't listen to the noise from everyone else. Only *you* know what's right for you."

She gave me a small nod, her cheeks still flushed. "Thanks. I guess you're the one I should be listening to, anyway. I mean, you made it happen, right? You're living your dream."

"Yeah, well... like I told you, I never really wanted to do anything else. But that doesn't mean it was easy, getting to this point." I shrugged. "You know what it's like, making something from nothing. It's that process of creation that really gets me going. There's nothing better than having an idea in my head come to life in something I've helped build."

"I totally get it. You're an artist," she said, matter-of-factly. "It's obvious, looking at what's already been done here, how thorough and talented you are." She smiled. "I hope you know how grateful I am, having you here. Best decision ever."

I felt my face grow warm at her compliment. I'd never really had someone describe my work in that way before. It felt... a little unnerving, but also really *good*. Though it was hard not to wonder if the job was the only reason she was glad I was there. "Well, thanks. I mean, I can't take all the credit here. Jesse is one of the best. And between my formal training and Pops teaching me when I was growing up, I've had plenty of help along the way."

Her eyes twinkled. "Maybe... but I think we both know you're being too modest. You really put your whole heart into everything, James... like you were *meant* to do this."

She had an almost dreamy look on her face as she said it, her full lips slightly parted, and it made me wonder how much of her statement was really directed at herself. Her eyes were on mine, though, as if hoping she'd find the answer there.

And I was looking at her too, not quite knowing the right words to say. Finally, I got my wits about me again. "Well, like I said... it's taken me a long time to get here, but I'm glad I did. I think everyone assumed I would've gone out on my own a lot sooner than I did. And I would have, if it weren't for—" I froze, realizing what I'd almost just admitted aloud.

If it weren't for being focused on my resentment towards the man who abandoned me.

Standing up, I felt the tension rise within me quickly as the moment of vulnerability between us evaporated like a cloud of humidity. "Sorry, I just realized how late it's getting. I better check in on Jesse to make sure the roofing crew wraps up everything properly." Forcing a smile, I set my glass down on the small table between the chairs. "Thanks again for the lemonade."

Of course, it was hard to miss Lizzie's confused expression as I turned to step down the porch stairs, feeling her eyes follow me as I walked around towards the backyard, my mind racing.

Because for as much as I'd already shared about myself with Lizzie, I hadn't yet been able to unbox what I'd gone through as a kid. But it was becoming clear—the further I continued down this path, the harder it would be to hold myself back with her at all.

Or maybe... I was just tired of feeling like I *should.*

I found Jesse standing near the driveway as I rounded the corner, talking to the lead from the roofing crew as the rest finished loading up their gear. As I approached, he shook the crew leader's hand, walking over towards me.

I nodded my head towards the truck. "Everything done already?"

"Yep, this was an easy one for Val and the guys, pretty straight-forward. Told him to just email us the invoice to your business account... that ok?"

I nodded, my mind a million miles away from invoices. "Yeah, fine."

"I'm going to wrap up and head out too, if that's cool. Tara's making meatloaf tonight," he said, grinning. "I tell ya, her pregnancy cravings are working out really great for me."

I smirked at my friend. "We'll see if you're still saying that after she sends you out to Filbert's for a tub of ice cream every night."

"Naw, I think I'll benefit just fine from that, too." Jesse winked, and I couldn't help but laugh.

"Of course you will." Shaking my head, I watched my friend strut away with the confidence of a man madly in love with his wife.

It was hard not to feel a little envious. And to wonder for like the billionth time if I'd ever have it in me to end up like my friend.

For some reason, the idea of it didn't seem as far-fetched as it once had.

Twenty minutes later, I was in my truck and on the road as well before I realized—I'd taken off without telling Lizzie. Pulling out my phone, I scrolled through until I found her number.

JAMES: Hey, I just left for the day, realized I forgot to check in. See you bright and early in the morning.

A moment later, I heard a ping as her reply came through.

LIZZIE: Sounds good. Hope you have a great night… thanks again for the advice. Currently on the hunt for a documentary on mealworms… I'll keep you posted.

JAMES: I await your report on the sexual habits of mealworms with bated breath.

LIZZIE: Also, no signs of Renaldo the Mouse yet. But if you hear screams from across the lake, you'll know we finally had our rendezvous.

JAMES: Renaldo is a great name for a male lead. Maybe your mouse buddy was sent to you as a creative muse to inspire your first best-seller?

LIZZIE: Don't hold your breath. I bought more mousetraps. #CanYouHearTheTrapsRenaldo

Chuckling as I dropped my phone into the cupholder, I turned off the gravel road from the cabins and headed east through the pines along County Road Three.

It was strange how it all came so easily with her, how sharing all the parts of me felt inevitable. It was hard to know exactly what all this meant yet, but one thing was certain—when I was with her, I felt happier, lighter. It was a feeling I hadn't known much, and it made me want to chase after it. Even more, I wanted Lizzie to know *me*, as much as I wanted to know more about her. And not just as my client or my friend.

Just a handful of weeks with her was all it had taken for me to want to finally let all that other shit go and focus on moving forward.

There was one more question that still nagged at me, though—did I even know who I was, without the rest of it?

Chapter 17

Lizzie

I sat in bed that night, having nearly given up on writing as the blank Google document glared back at me from my laptop. My brain was refusing to cooperate—per usual, it was focused on James.

This time, however, it wasn't about his dreamy eyes or how I loved the way he smelled whenever we were sitting close to one another. It was because I'd managed to somehow shove my foot in my mouth during our last conversation.

It had been another great talk, like the many we'd shared over the past month. I loved how easily he could make me laugh, how thoughtful he was—even up for trying something outside his wheelhouse, like reading a book I'd recommended. I don't think any guy I'd known before would've been willing, not even my own brother. Definitely not Randall.

And I already had the perfect book laid out, ready to hand over to the next day. It was ridiculous, really, how excited I was to present it to him. Even though this meant I'd now be forced to try kayaking in exchange. Because yeah, there was a reason I didn't participate in most physical activities. I was pretty much the most uncoordinated person on the planet.

The thing that had struck me most today, though, was how encouraging James had been while we talked about my writing. Even if the idea of abandoning my book to switch genres still terrified me, he actually made me believe I could do it.

It made me wish for a brief moment that Randall had believed in me that way, too. That I'd felt more at ease with myself around him, the way I did with James. Would we have made it? I doubted it. I could see now that our problems had been deeply rooted in incompatibility.

It was crazy, though, how three years with my ex couldn't measure up to a handful of weeks with a man like James.

There had been a definite shift, though, when James and I had started discussing his work again—his reaction making me wonder if I'd said something wrong. I mean, it's not like we hadn't talked about this very topic plenty of times before—but this time, it just felt different. It was clear he'd been upset, and the idea of it was making me crazy. I needed to make things right.

Because James was a good man. Anyone could see that he cared about the people in his life, based on everything I'd seen in his interactions with Jesse and his grandmother, Georgia (*who now insisted I call her GiGi—since most everyone else did*). So the absolute last thing I wanted was to mess up what we had going.

Because as the weeks raced by, I was finding myself really, *really* liking him. It wasn't only about being attracted to him, like I was at the start. Those feelings had already tiptoed beyond friendship.

Which made having him contractually obligated to be near me, day in and day out, tricky. Not just because of the professional side of things, but also—hadn't I promised myself I wouldn't get distracted?

Even though writing this book on the shores of Lake Elska had proven every bit as difficult as writing in Minneapolis, I had to keep trying. It was the whole point of me moving up here, to prove that I could do this. I owed that to myself. Otherwise, what was the point of uprooting my life and starting over, if I was just going to create the same mess I'd left behind?

And logically, I knew I was getting *way* ahead of myself anyway, throwing around assumptions that had no basis in reality. James was kind, friendly and attentive towards me because I was *his client*, that's all. The fact that we got along so well—and had become friends in a matter of weeks—was a bonus. It didn't need to be more than that. It *shouldn't* be more than that.

But even now, despite everything, a *teeny-tiny* part of me still held out hope that moving to Dearing Creek would bring about more than one positive change in my life. Like Grandma Cora had always said, this place had its own kind of magic.

And I *really* needed to believe in something right now.

A loud squawking sounded outside my window, making me jump about a foot off the bed. Realizing it was nothing but a stupid bird, I snorted out a laugh, shaking my head at how jumpy I'd been lately.

Damn you, Renaldo.

I was still getting used to being here at the cabin on my own. Lately, I'd been debating getting a dog so I would feel a little less alone—especially at night and now that my cabin included a mouse squatter. It had been almost eight years since our beloved family mutt, Missy, had crossed the rainbow bridge—maybe it was time to spring for a pup of my own.

Glancing over at my mint green alarm clock in its new home on my grandmother's old oak nightstand, I realized it was already after eleven. Maybe I'd relax and do a little reading, and make a fresh attempt at writing in the morning.

Hoisting myself out of bed, I shuffled over to the corner where I'd stacked the boxes containing most of my grandmother's book collection.

This room had been my grandparents' back in the day. The cabin itself had three bedrooms, but this one was larger than the others, so it always served as the master. Growing up, Mariah and I had usually bunked together in one of the smaller rooms, with Ethan in the other—or on the sofa, if my grandparents joined our family, too.

But everyone who had once laid claim to this room was now gone—the first time this room had ever been mine. It felt odd, almost as though I was intruding where I didn't belong. I half expected my mother to walk in at any moment and shoo me out the door, hollering, "Just give me some damn space."

And as much as I'd hated all the yelling, a small part of me would've given anything to bring it all back.

Sometimes, when it was just us kids with our grandparents at the cabin, I'd crawl into bed with Grandma Cora early in the morning, after Grandpa Walter had gone off fishing. We'd lay there together while Mariah and Ethan slept, flipping through our latest books and giggling at the racy bits.

Now this room lay silent—*too silent*.

But even though the woman was gone, Grandma Cora's touches were alive everywhere—the white, gauzy curtains with hand-stitched lace along the edges; the pale blue quilt, pieced together in a pattern that mimicked the ripples of the lake; the original white porcelain and brass lamp on the dresser. Even the dresser itself had been hers, a wedding gift from her mother—all warm wood and subtle curves, with a matching oval mirror hanging on the wall above.

The only thing different now was the section of wall missing on the far left corner, which now led to the new addition. When James and I had first discussed the idea of adding the bathroom, I'd been hesitant—it meant changing something about this room that held so many memories for me.

Would my grandmother approve?

Of course, it didn't matter—not everything could be about the past. I also had to think about my future. And if I wanted this cabin to be both my full-time home and a place to share on the weekends with my brother and friends—a second bathroom was needed.

The harder part, though, was feeling my grandmother's presence diminishing over the past few weeks. But here in this room, she felt closer—maybe, if I really focused, I would hear her voice whispering in my ear.

"Lizzie, girl... what should we read next?"

Lowering myself to the floor, I reached for a box I hadn't yet opened, ripping off the strip of packing tape. One by one, I pulled out her books, a handful of which I didn't recognize. Must have been some she had picked up towards the end. At first, the thought of it made me sad—these were books that weren't a part of our story together.

Then again, maybe reading one would complete the circle, bringing her closer?

I reached inside the box again, pulling out a clothbound book with gold leaf pages, wedged halfway down. Despite the thickness of the book, however, it felt... lighter than I'd expected. The title on the cover read, "Love & Other

Tales". As I began flipping the book over to inspect the back cover, I heard an odd sort of clunking sound coming from inside.

What the hell was that?

I tilted the book upright again, gingerly opening the front cover. And that's when I discovered it.

This particular book wasn't a book at all. It was one of those fakey-books used to hide precious items on book-shelves from would-be thieves. And this one held a dark green velvet pouch, nestled with a tiny, folded piece of paper. Fumbling as I worked to unfold it, I recognized my grandmother's handwriting, her cursive scrawl spelling out a handful of words on the page. Without meaning to, I murmured the words aloud: *The key to my heart.*

Key to my heart?

Suddenly, I felt wide awake.

Loosening the ribbon closure, I reached inside, my fingers closing around what felt like... a brooch, maybe? But what I found instead was a small, ornate golden key, hanging from a gold chain—almost like... a necklace?

I lifted it by the chain so that the key dangled before me, watching as it twirled and sparkled in the dim lamp-light. Odds are, this was some random piece of jewelry that Grandma Cora had picked up from a flea market over the years. Maybe even a gift from Grandpa?

Though, if that were the case... why would it be hidden away in this book, like some secret?

But right then, it didn't matter. Discovering this small, hidden relic that had once belonged to her felt almost like a sign that she was still with me, still cheering me on.

And it was exactly what I needed.

With a burst of determination, I decided to forgo reading and head straight to bed. If I was ever going to make a dent in my word count, I needed sleep and focus.

It was the whole reason I'd moved here, why I'd left my entire life behind in Minneapolis. Not to wallow in self-doubt, or give up when things felt hard, or fall into temptation. This was meant to be my fresh start. And I wasn't going to achieve that by allowing myself to get distracted by someone else who didn't want me all over again.

Besides, I had a feeling the fall would hurt far more with a man like the one who'd recently taken up residence in my mind and heart.

Chapter 18

Lizzie

Well, promising myself that I wasn't going to let that man distract me was one thing.

Actually being able to *stick* to a ridiculous declaration like that? Quite another.

To be fair, it wasn't really my fault. I'd had the best of intentions when I set up camp on the sofa with my laptop later the following week, with the goal of getting through one full chapter of my book.

I'd been trying my best to recommit to my *sisters-meet-Great Depression* novel for several days now, as the windows were being installed around me throughout the cabin. Writing had continued to feel like trudging my way through literary mud—but I wasn't ready to give up just yet. I'd even resorted to going full-out '*woo-woo*'—wearing Grandma Cora's key necklace as a sort of creative talisman, praying for divine inspiration. I was sure it would make my friend Indi—the *woo-est* one of us all—proud.

But for some reason, this morning I was having a hell of a time getting my manuscript file to even *open*. Inwardly, I was doing everything I could not to panic, considering that all the work I'd put into this book for the past *three years* was in that file.

I could hear Mariah's voice in my head: "*Come on, Lizzie, you always have to back up your files. Everyone knows that.*"

Needless to say, I was in the middle of some witty retort in the fictional argument I was having with my sister when a noise from outside charged like a battering ram through my frustrated focus.

Looking up, there he stood—James, in all of his muscled, shirtless glory, throwing the shirt he'd just peeled off at Jesse before leaning down to grab his water bottle.

As he tilted his head back to take a drink, I watched the lean muscles along his neck ripple with every swallow—rhythmically, like a dance, bass thumping.

Wait—was the music just in my head?

Lowering the bottle, he wiped at his forehead with the back of his hand, hazel eyes crinkled at the corners as he laughed at something Jesse said.

And then—I *kid you not*—James lifted the bottle upwards and *fucking poured* the rest of the water over his head. It trickled down his body, almost in slow motion, as if the water didn't want to stop touching his body either—the spray floating around his head like a halo as he shook his hair, wiping his mouth.

All of this, framed perfectly in the large bay picture window across from me—like some sexy velvet painting ripped straight from a nineteen-seventies flea market.

Even worse? When I reached up to touch my own lips, I realized I'd been drooling a little.

Jesus Christ.

How the hell could anyone be invested in anything to do with writing serious literary fiction after watching that *Brawny Man thirst trap?*

And of course, he chose that exact moment to look up and catch me staring out the window at him, like some horny teenager. Grinning as he retrieved his shirt, he gave me a quick wave and a wink before wandering off towards the backyard—leaving me to die of humiliation.

So, yeah... that's how *my* day was going so far.

But I had to admit—if I were writing a romance novel right now, the entire book would've practically written itself.

"Alright, I'm done venting about work. It's your turn." Brooke leaned over to top off the wine in my glass after filling her own, spilling down the side. "Oops! Sorry about that," she said, giggling. "But while we're at it, you may as well spill it, too. How's it been going up here with James and Jesse working on your renovations?"

It was Friday night, and I was out on the porch for a much-needed girls' night, breaking in the new outdoor furniture set that had just been delivered. The red Adirondack chairs had rejoined the other seven around the old fire pit, waiting for new memories to be forged. It had magical properties, after all—without it, the Dearie Girls wouldn't even exist.

Maybe a bonfire would have the power to magically fix my writer's block, too. I was desperate enough to try *anything* at this point.

Brooke had decided to drive up for a couple of days after a rough week at work, and I'd been overjoyed to see her—she and Indi *both*, for that matter. I'd been keeping myself pretty holed up between attempts at writing and the cabin renovation, which meant I hadn't seen much of my friends since they'd helped move me into the cabin over a month and a half ago.

In fact, the only people I'd been interacting with at all lately were mainly GiGi, Jesse, the cashiers over at Filbert's Grocery & Liquor—and yes, James.

But James was the entire reason I was grateful for tonight's distraction. Because ever since yesterday, it wasn't prose or plot points that popped into my head as I stared at my laptop screen. It was a replay of shirtless James standing outside my front window, hot and dripping with muscles on full display as he caught me staring—-over and over and *over* again.

And the only thing *that* visual had in common with the Great Depression was the feeling I'd been left with, knowing I had no business ogling my friend and contractor when I was *supposed* to be, you know, *authoring*.

But not tonight. Tonight was my time to decompress and get my head out of whatever tangle it had been in since I'd arrived in Dearing Creek.

"The guys? They're... great. Very skilled at their jobs."

"*Mm-hmm.*"

I looked over at her, the very picture of denial. "I mean it... you saw what they've already done with the exterior. It's gorgeous, right? And how about my new windows?"

"Yes, yes, it's all *lovely*. Which I already told you when I arrived an hour ago," Brooke said impatiently, waving away my words. "What I meant was..."

"...how are you enjoying the hot male company?" Indi said with a wink, clinking her glass against Brooke's before tipping it back for a celebratory sip.

Yeah, no. Even though that scene of sexy James was on its seven-hundredth loop through my head, I knew my friends would lose their ever-lovin' minds if I told them about it—*or* the fact I was having all these feelings about him in the first place. Which is exactly why I was keeping my mouth shut. For now.

"You two *do* know Jesse is married, right? With a baby on the way?"

Brooke stared at me for a moment, eyes dancing, before leaning in. "You, my dear, are being purposely obtuse. Clearly, I'm talking about James."

Just be cool.

"Oh, yeah... James is great. He's done a great job with everything so far." I tried to keep my expression neutral as I raised my own glass to my lips, but I knew it was pointless with these two. I figured I only had about thirty seconds before they pounced on me, anyway. "And before you say anything else, *yes*... he's friendly. And funny. And attractive. He's a really great guy."

Brooke's eyes hadn't wavered. "I think I clocked three mentions of '*he's great*' in that little speech of yours..."

Indi grinned as she started braiding her waist-long curly blonde hair into a long plait. Resembling spun gold and *never* frizzy, I'd lusted after that hair my entire life. "I knew it."

"Knew *what*, exactly?"

"That you and James would be the *perfect* fit for each other."

I held up a hand. "*Whoa, whoa, whoa,* missy... back that cart up. Just because I agree that he's good-looking—and nice to be around—does not mean I'm agreeing we belong together or anything close. That would be... ridiculous."

But I could already feel the heat spread across my face as I said it, the words '*liar, liar, pants on fire...*' echoing as Horny Lizzie sashayed her way through my mind.

Brooke's expression was smug as she held up her glass, pinky pointed outwards. "*Methinks the lady doth protest too much.*" A little wine sloshed out of her glass as she waved it around—laughing, she quickly grabbed another napkin to sop up the mess.

"Ok, stop, I'm serious. Besides, I doubt he thinks of me in that way. Sure, we get along great... but he's behaved like a total pro this entire time. Why spoil everything by trying to cross a line that I shouldn't? And anyway, I have more than enough on my plate at the moment."

Of course, I knew blatantly drooling over the guy probably qualified as '*line crossing*'. But *no way* was I going to give my friends even more ammunition by admitting that I couldn't stop thinking about him. Or his laugh. Or his thoughtfulness. Or his crinkly, twinkly eyes.

And still, that little voice whispered in my ear: *This could be something amazing, if you let it.*

Indi patted my arm. "Well, for what it's worth... James *is* a great guy. I actually think you two have a lot in common."

"Yes. What she said. It's not like you're *actually* his employer. He's a free agent. And you, my dear, deserve to have a little fun," Brooke said, booping the tip of my nose playfully. "Especially if he's as great of a kisser as Tess's friend claims. Probably means he's good at plenty of other things, too," she said, grinning wickedly.

"*Objection! That is hearsay and speculation.*" By now, I was smiling as well—but also in desperate need of a change in topic. "So, Indi... how's Callum been the past couple of weeks? Did he start that rock climbing camp yet?"

Callum was Indi's twelve-year-old son—we all loved that kid as our own, his aunties by choice. But life hadn't been easy for our friend, becoming a single mom at a time when the rest of us were heading off to college and new beginnings. Even still—as moms go, she was one of the best.

"Nuh-uh. My turn will come later. We're doing *your* updates now. You know the drill," Indi said, waggling a finger at me. "We'll leave you alone about James—for now. But tell us about the book."

I averted my gaze yet again, reaching for my wine glass. "It's going... alright."

Brooke sighed. "And you wonder how we can always tell when you're hiding something..."

"She's not wrong, Lizzie. You've always been a terrible liar."

"Whatever." I leaned back in my chair, enjoying the warm evening breeze flowing through, now that the early summer heat wave had finally ceased. Feeling their eyes on me, I sighed. "Ok, maybe everything isn't completely 'alright'. More like... I think I'm done with this book."

Indi's eyes widened. "You've finished writing it already? That's amazing, Lizzie!"

I shook my head. "No, no... I mean, I'm officially *done* with it. As in, I'm giving up. The entire project is dead." I hadn't planned to say it, or even allowed myself to think it—but as soon as the words tumbled out of my mouth, I knew they were true. Not even a power as great as Grandma Cora's key talisman could save it.

Judging by the looks on my friends' faces, they weren't prepared for my little confession, either.

Maybe dissecting how I felt about James *would* be less painful.

"Ok, Lizzie... what's going on?" Brooke's expression had now shifted from teasing to one of concern as I felt the anxiety bloom in the center of my chest. "You've wanted to do this forever. Just because it hasn't happened yet doesn't mean your dream is dead. Give it time."

"Maybe... I don't know. I guess I thought coming up here would make it a lot easier for the words to flow. But it's been harder than ever. I just feel so... lost."

Willing myself not to cry for the millionth time in the past year, I trained my eyes on my hands. They were tingling again, the way they always did whenever anxiety took root within me. I flexed my fingers, working to bring back the feeling to them. But feeling almost made it worse.

I envisioned thirteen-year-old Lizzie, always with a pencil and a notebook in hand, mind and heart full of stories, with dreams of becoming the next Great American Author. *What happened to that girl?*

Part of me wished that I could go back in time, wrap my arms around her, and warn her that life doesn't turn out that way. *Would she even listen?* I wondered. Probably not. Because giving up on a dream before life gave me a good enough reason would've been nearly impossible for *teenage Lizzie.*

But *grown-up Lizzie* had had enough.

"Oh, honey… I was worried something like that might be going on. You've been so cooped up out here, putting so much pressure on yourself. Especially after the year you've just had." Glancing up, I caught Indi's reassuring smile. "Give yourself some grace. Maybe a little break is all you need to get your spark back."

"Absolutely—a break is a brilliant idea." Brooke squeezed my hand. "Remember—we're all rooting for you, ok? And we're here, don't forget that. You can do this." She leaned in closer. "But no more hiding up here all alone, got it?"

"And the rest of us are going to be checking on you more frequently, so be prepared. If you ghost us, you're done for." Indi tried her best to scowl—but seeing as it was completely out of character for her, I couldn't help but laugh.

"Yes, yes… understood," I said, reaching for my glass. "And actually, speaking of being alone… I've kind of been thinking about adopting a dog. Partly for the company, but also so I feel a little less anxious here on my own. I was never allowed one at my apartment, and I've missed having a dog around since Missy died. Is that a completely insane idea?"

"Not insane at all. I love this for you!" Indi said, clapping her hands.

"Yes, I agree, one hundred percent! Let's all run over to the Lakeview Humane Society tomorrow, before we head to my parents' place for dinner." Brooke poured the remainder of the bottle across our three glasses. "In the meantime, what do you say to a bonfire?"

"Deal."

But as we cleaned up the table to move closer to the lake, all I could wonder was: *What if it really was over?*

I'd always dreamed of being a writer, and here I was, letting every little distraction throw me off, already failing not even two months in on my first true attempt.

Which meant the even bigger question was—if this dream of mine had all been more of a *pipe* dream than anything, what was I supposed to do with the rest of my life?

Chapter 19

James

"Ok, Tater. Are you going to just sit there and stare out the window at those ladies all night?"

My grandmother's voice pierced through the fog in my head as I realized I'd been holding my fork—with the last bite of corn salad—midair. Completing the pass, I finished chewing as I rested the fork on my empty plate.

"For your information, I wasn't *staring*. At least, not at them. I think there's an eagle's nest now in the Grimm's pine tree a couple hundred feet down—do you see it?"

"Uh-huh... a *nest*. That's what held your attention for three solid minutes." GiGi chuckled, shaking her head. "You must think me senile, my boy."

"Not senile... at least, not yet. But you've been known to be wrong."

"Not about you. Don't forget, I've known you your whole damn life. You think I wouldn't notice you showing an interest in our Elizabeth?" As I opened my mouth to speak, she held up a firm hand. "Don't waste either of our time denying it. It's clear as day that you like her. And anyway, I'm old... give your grandmama something to feel excited about."

I groaned, rubbing at my face with both hands, as if trying to wipe away the evidence from my eyeballs that I had, in fact, been watching Lizzie and her friends out on her porch throughout most of our meal.

"Alright, fine. So I was looking. But that doesn't mean that I'm interested in Lizzie the way you're thinking. We're friends."

"Of course you're friends. Doesn't mean you aren't wanting more than that, though."

"Are you already forgetting what made me lose my job with Mel? I told you, I won't start off my business by crossing the line with a client."

GiGi rolled her eyes. "Are you really comparing Elizabeth to that old cougar, *Denise Kinney*? That was practically predatory behavior on her end, and you know it."

"No... it's just, I promised myself I'd keep things professional. I'd be a total hypocrite if I just tossed out the rule book with my very first client, just because I happen to like her."

"You'd be a complete *idiot* is more like it. I've seen how you look at her, James. She even got you reading a book. *You.* Just admit it... you care about her."

"So what if I do?" I crossed my arms, my mind flashing back to a memory of my eight-year-old self, pouting at this same kitchen table. It was enough to make me relax my posture. "It doesn't mean that I have to act on it. Or that she'd even want me to, anyway."

"Oh, I'm pretty sure she would. I've been watching her too, you know. What else does a retired old lady have to keep herself busy with?" GiGi said with a sly wink. "Problem is, you two would dance around this spark between you forever, unless I gave you a little push in the right direction. So, consider yourself *pushed.*"

I narrowed my eyes. "Meaning, *what?*"

"Meaning, stop being chicken shit and ask the girl out. The rest will work itself out, you'll see."

"I don't know..."

"Tater-tot, listen to me—you're thirty-four years old already, almost thirty-five. You haven't been serious about a woman... *ever.* All I'm saying is, maybe it's time to do the work and figure out why that is. Because I'm damned tired of seeing my grandson so unhappy."

I didn't answer, instead looking back towards the window, wishing I could pinpoint the one, insurmountable thing that kept pulling me towards her. Was it just proximity? Or a sum of all her parts?

Maybe all it boiled down to was shared tragedy. Over one of our earlier lunch chats, she'd shared more about not only losing her mother and grandmother, which we'd already discussed—but her father as well.

I remembered hearing about Greg Blake's death fifteen years back—it shook my grandmother too, and not just because he was the son-in-law of her dearest friend.

He'd had a heart attack out on the dock next door, so similar to how we'd lost Pops. Somehow, I hadn't made the connection before that he was Lizzie's father—or that it was the reason we never saw much of her family at the cabin after that.

It made me wonder how much all of that loss had changed the trajectory of that girl. Because it certainly had torn apart mine.

I watched as Lizzie, Brooke and Indi—who I also knew from around town—made their way down to her fire pit. Lizzie had her head tilted back, laughing as she awkwardly carried an oversized log, dropping it with gusto into the pit, shouting what sounded like, "*I carried the watermelon!*". And I wasn't close enough to get a good look at them, but I was certain her eyes had to be sparkling, like they always did whenever she laughed.

It made me wonder what they looked like now, by the firelight.

It was then that I felt my brain come to a complete halt. Because *Jesus Christ*... what the hell was I doing sitting here, ruminating on the shiny eyes of my client?

But she's not just a client to you anymore, and you know it.

Those were the words that kept playing on a loop as I made my way home an hour later, after helping GiGi with the dinner cleanup. She'd had a smug look on her face the entire time, but she hadn't pressed me further.

Anyway, I knew she was right, even if I'd refused to admit it to her then. Getting too close to a woman had always seemed like something I couldn't manage, especially after my own father fell apart from losing his.

And I'd had too much loss in my life already, with little proof that things ever actually worked out.

It's why I'd always kept women—well, most people—at arm's length. The therapist I'd seen off and on throughout my teen years had said as much—'*a protection mechanism*', she'd called it.

I wondered if, at this point, I even knew where to find the switch to power it off. Or if I was brave enough to try.

But what would my life look like in another thirty-four years if I didn't?

Early the following morning, I had parked my truck and was starting to make my way down to GiGi's dock for some time out on the kayak when I saw her.

Lizzie was camped out, legs crossed, on her own dock, wrapped in a quilt with her back to me. But I could see the steam rising from her mug of coffee, knowing she likely had a book in hand as well—much like she had the day we'd crossed paths for the second time. I smiled to myself at the memory of her tumbling into the water and seeing her all fired up afterwards.

It made me glad I'd decided to stick it out here with her. And yes, it was less about the project or my *'client'* now—and more about being granted the chance to continue getting to know the woman.

And, of course, I knew well enough by now not to sneak up on her.

I made it down to my kayak, making a point of being a little louder than normal this time, hoping she'd notice me on her own.

"Hey, there, you're out early for a Saturday." Lizzie had turned at the sound with a somewhat sleepy grin. Taking another sip of her coffee, she set it down next to her book before walking over, her quilt still draped across her shoulders. "You must not be able to sleep in on the weekends, either."

I smiled at her as I bent down, turning my kayak until it was upright again. "Nope, never been able to. Of course, it didn't help that neither of my grandparents believed in it either. Becoming a permanent early riser was sort of a foregone conclusion in my family," I said, making a face.

She laughed. "It was the opposite in my house—everyone else loved sleeping in, except for me. But when we came up to the cabin with my grandparents, I'd usually hang out with my grandmother and read while everyone else snoozed." She paused, and for a moment, she felt far away again. "Those are actually some of my favorite memories with her."

"I'm sure she'd love seeing you here, reading her books again and enjoying the cabin."

"You're right... she really would," she said, beaming. "Speaking of which, how are you liking *your* book?"

It was impossible not to feel the warmth from a smile like hers. "Actually, I'm liking it quite a bit. Never thought of myself as a poetry fan, but... I have to admit, Robert Frost may have done it." I grinned. "So, thanks for coercing me, I guess."

"You flatter me, sir." She made a comical half bow from her seated position as I laughed. "But seriously, I'm really happy you like it. *Birches* has always been one of my absolute favorites. It reminds me of this place."

"Me too." I knew what she meant, of course. But for me, the beauty I saw right then couldn't be captured by a single poem. Though if it were possible, Frost would've come the closest.

"So, listen... I wanted to bring up something." She seemed to hesitate, chewing on her lower lip for a moment before continuing. "I feel like maybe I pressed too hard the other day when we were talking about your business. The last thing I wanted was to make you uncomfortable or share more than you wanted. So if I did that, I'm really sorry."

Shit.

I sighed. "No, Lizzie, *I'm* the one who should apologize. The problem wasn't you asking me... I know I can get kind of weird, because I'm just not used to sharing a lot about myself. But I don't mind it with you. You're... very easy to talk to." It was true. I liked talking to her. And the very fact that she cared about how I felt in a simple conversation like the one we'd had made me want to trust her with the darker parts of me even more.

Even if it feels so fucking hard.

We stood there for a moment, smiling at one other as a breeze came through, twirling and twisting the strands of her hair into a dance around her as an idea popped into my head.

"Say... since I've been holding up my end of the deal with the book, what do you say we try going out on the kayak today? It could be your first mini lesson before going solo."

She gave me a wary look before glancing down at the kayak. "That thing fits two people?"

"No, don't worry, I also have a two-seater up in the garage," I said, chuckling. "And I've done this a million times before. Trust me, you'll be perfectly safe. Unless... you're afraid of getting a little wet?" My grin widened, waiting to see if she'd take the bait.

She arched an eyebrow, head cocked. "Oh, I'm an excellent swimmer. I just don't know how good of a paddler you are."

I smirked as I watched her blush, once again realizing her choice of words. Though I had to admit, I was having a hard time keeping my brain from imagining what sort of paddling was racing around in *her* head.

I was having a difficult time not imagining a *lot* of things having to do with her lately. It had become impossible to keep her out of my mind—not that I really wanted to try.

"Come on... you'll never know unless you try."

Lizzie chewed on her lower lip for a moment, in that way she had that drove me crazy—and I willed my body not to respond. I'd scare her off from tandem kayaking for good if I kicked things off with a hard-on. "Alright, fine." Pulling off the quilt to reveal her usual tank top and shorts, she folded it before setting it on a wooden chair next to the dock. Then she paused. "Wait, Brooke stayed over last night. She's still asleep. Maybe I should let her know where I'm going?"

"Sure, if you want... but we won't be gone long. I'll keep this first run to twenty minutes, I promise."

She looked uncertain for a moment, then shrugged. "Ok, let's do it."

"Great."

I walked back up to GiGi's garage, moving a tarp to pull out the old red tandem kayak Pops and I had used when I was younger. I hadn't pulled it out in years, so it was pretty dusty—-but nothing a little lake water wouldn't take care of.

Walking back down to the water, I handed Lizzie the extra paddle I'd grabbed for her, carrying the kayak along with my paddle into the water as she trailed behind. Setting both down into the water, I turned to her. "Ok, first you're going to want to take one foot and step gently into the front seat there..."

"... wait, what? Why the front seat?"

I smirked. "Because that way, I can help you. It'll be too difficult if you're behind me. Plus you'd be stuck staring at my back the entire time."

I heard her mutter something under her breath, but after a moment, she gingerly extended a leg into the front pocket. Reaching out, I took her hand to steady her—feeling that now all-too-familiar jolt of electricity passing between us.

Or maybe it was all in my head. Who knows? But judging by the look in her eyes, it didn't seem so.

Leaning heavily on my arm, Lizzie settled herself into the front seat, and I handed her the paddle. I took my seat behind her, doing my best not to rock the boat too much—and a minute later, we pushed off.

"Ok, now take your paddle and sort of slowly dig backwards into the water on the left, followed by the right." I watched as she awkwardly dipped her paddle into the water and began alternating her strokes in somewhat jerky motions. "Back and forth, port to starboard... yep, that's it."

Lizzie squealed as she felt the kayak wobble a bit with her strokes. "Are you sure I'm doing this right? I... I feel like we're going to tip over."

I chuckled. "Yes, you're doing fine... just keep the movement in your arms nice and even. Don't lean over too much."

"But we're barely even moving..."

"I'm going to start paddling now, too. Keep going, and I'll match your rhythm."

The mist still hung heavy over the water as we glided further out onto the lake, just the way I liked it. I heard Lizzie gasp as our kayak soon became enveloped in the fog.

"Oh, my God... this feels... almost *magical.*"

"That's because it is." I felt the light breeze carry strands of her hair across my face, teasing me with the soft scent of early summer lilacs. Breathing in deeply, I let my eyes drift over the curve of her shoulders, her arms—the softness of her skin begging me to reach out and touch what lay so close, I could almost feel her warmth radiating from it.

This was better than kayaking alone. I could almost stay here forever in the silence, with her.

Off in the distance, the long, slow call of a lone loon shook me from my reverie. I reminded myself that I just needed to keep moving, one stroke at a time.

We paddled in spurts, sometimes in silence and other times chatting about people we both knew or teasing one another about our stroke styles. Mine were even and deliberate—but Lizzie's continued to lean more on the erratic side, and I couldn't stop chuckling over it. If I left it up to her alone, we'd likely create some sort of whirlpool, pulling every loon and duck in the area down towards the lake bottom. At one point, I actually worried she might tip us over; but I managed to right the vessel before it had dipped too far.

Using my paddle, I made a slow, wide turn to head us back towards shore. The sun was halfway up by now, burning off most of the remaining morning fog.

But still, it felt as though we were the only two people in the world. The surrounding lake was silent but for the sounds of our paddles slicing through the lake's surface, the birds chirping off in the distance. Despite the feelings I had churning inside me, I felt more of the weight I'd been carrying begin to lift. Being here with her, I felt peaceful, content—and I didn't want it to end.

It was then, about fifty feet out from the dock, that Lizzie spotted a small wood duck swimming a few feet away on our left. "Hey, little guy," she cooed as she leaned a hand out towards him, her voice soft, inviting—but somehow, in doing so, she must've shifted her legs just enough towards the far left that I felt us beginning to tilt.

And before I could even react or try and stop it from happening, our entire kayak flipped over.

Crashing below the surface, the sounds around me became muffled as the lake water flowed in and pressed against my ear drums. Shaking off the initial shock, I quickly slid out of the cockpit, noticing Lizzie seemed to be panicking a bit as she hung upside down, disoriented. Reaching an arm around her waist to help her out as well, I pulled her upwards as we broke through the surface together.

Both of us gasping for air, we locked eyes for a moment as we tread water. Then we burst into peals of laughter, slowly making our way towards shore as we towed our gear behind us. The sounds of our laughs echoed across the lake, likely scaring away both the duck and the loon we'd encountered—but I didn't care. I couldn't remember the last time I'd laughed like this, *felt* like this.

Like I was actually, *truly*... happy.

Once we'd reached the point where we could both touch the sandy bottom with our feet, I turned towards her again, grinning. "Seriously, are you ok?"

Lizzie nodded, catching her breath as her giggles subsided. "I'm fine, really. Though I think I failed at my first kayaking mission, Captain."

"No, that one was on me. I let myself get... distracted."

"I mean, that duck *was* pretty cute..."

"It wasn't the duck." Now my face was serious as I reached out a hand, brushing away a section of wet hair that had fallen across her face. The tiny droplets of water clinging to her eyelashes dazzled in the early morning light, bringing out flecks of gold amongst the green.

Later, as I reflected back on this moment, I wondered if it was actually her eyes, or the way she shivered as her top clung to her in wet patches—maybe even the way she chewed that damn lower lip—that had finally done me in.

Because right then, I couldn't help myself. No, scratch that. I was tired of my brain having a million reasons not to do it. I wanted to listen to the much louder voice, screaming on my shoulder, "*Do it, you idiot.*"

So, I did.

Placing a hand on each cheek, I lowered my face towards hers, pausing only a second as I felt her breath hitch... and I kissed her.

And God, why had I waited so long? Because her lips—they were as soft and strong and delectable as I'd imagined them to be. No, better. *Definitely* better.

But then I felt them responding to mine, matching my movements—both hungry and gentle, nibbling and pressing, the slight flick of her tongue and whisper of a moan threatening to make me lose any shred of control or decency I had left. *Had she been as hungry for this as I'd been? Was it even possible?*

It wasn't protests of fear or responsibility in my head now as I reached a hand up to thread through her wet hair, the other pressing against her back to bring her closer. The only thing I could hear, the only thing that *mattered*, was this simple truth: *I never want this to end.*

"*Lizzie! Is that you out there?*"

Hearing Brooke's voice floating out across the water, we instantly broke apart, gasping for air as our eyes met again, the fire stoked and burning in both. It was clear neither of us knew what to say or do next, other than to turn and continue the last stretch towards shore in breathless silence, with me holding a paddle to conceal what that kiss had awakened in me.

As we stepped up onto the sand of the beach, Lizzie set down her paddle before turning back to me, cheeks flushed. "Um, thanks again for the ride." Then with a quick smile, she darted up the grass to retrieve her sandals and quilt, making her way up across the slight slope to where Brooke stood watch. As Lizzie passed by her to continue on towards the front door, Brooke turned her head towards me again, making the '*I'm watching you*' sign with the V of her fingers before following her inside. Never before had Brooke Christenson more resembled her two brothers.

After the screen door swung shut a moment later, I turned to start packing up my gear, my head racing in a million different directions. I didn't even know the right way to feel about what just happened, but one thing was certain—-I damn well didn't regret it. I just hoped Lizzie didn't either.

There was no point in denying the truth anymore—I was falling for her, plain and simple.

Hearing GiGi's words echo through my mind as I drove home a few minutes later, I hoped she was right—that the rest *would* figure itself out. Because that kiss had accelerated Lizzie's and my relationship way past professional—and way the hell south of simple.

And for the first time, I felt like I might actually be ready for it.

Chapter 20

Lizzie

Brooke shut the front door behind us, pulling me by the arm into the living room, where I now stood dripping. "Ok, you little hussy, spill it. After *allll* of your denials last night, did I seriously just catch you making out in the lake with *James freakin' Tate?*" Her tone was accusatory, but by the look on her face, I knew—Brooke was thrilled.

And if I'd been blushing before, it was nothing compared to the inferno now spreading across my pasty-pale landscape. And how was she *not* reacting to the sounds of my brain screaming, '*what the hell just happened?*' Because even *I* could barely hear her question over all that racket.

Breaths. Deep breaths. Just be cool.

"Ummm... *would* we call that making out?" Making a lame attempt to appear nonchalant, I walked past her towards the bathroom, grabbing a towel from the closet to wrap around me. Now that I was out of the water and back in the air conditioning, I was beginning to feel the cooler air overtake the heat, still radiating throughout my entire being following that kiss.

Because, OMG, that kiss.

"Oh, *no, no, no*... you do *not* get to be coy right now." Brooke crossed her arms as she examined me. "This is *me*. Your best friend. I know you better than anyone. So seriously, wha—"

Ever-so-gently, I closed the bathroom door in my friend's face, turning on the shower to further drown out her interrogation—I knew I'd pay for that one later. For now, I leaned my head against the tile wall behind the door, finally releasing the breath I'd been holding as I held my fingertips to my lips.

All I needed was a few moments to process everything on my own—and figure out how I felt about the fact that *James freakin' Tate* had kissed me. *Me.*

Or the even more surprising fact that—despite everything I'd promised to myself—I'd also *very willingly* kissed him back.

Three hours later, Indi and her twelve-year-old son, Callum, met me and Brooke at Lakeview Humane Society, following our early lunch with Kait at her family's bar, The Thirsty Beaver. Although using the term *'lunch'* was a bit of a stretch, considering it had been more of an interrogation—with fries on the side.

It took me finally admitting to what had happened—and insisting to both Kait and Brooke that *no, I wasn't ready to talk about it*—before they let it drop.

Right now, all I wanted to focus on was finding my dog.

Walking over, I gave both Indi and Callum a quick squeeze. She was still wearing her scrubs, having just finished an early morning on-call shift after last night's bonfire. Towards the end of the night, she'd finally confessed that the roof of her house had started leaking during the last storm, so she'd been taking on extra shifts to cover the upcoming repair expenses.

Indi was one of the hardest working people I knew, and she took both her job and her role as a single mom seriously. She also had the most generous soul, which is why she'd insisted on being here today, instead of at home resting.

But even though my friend looked tired, she and her son seemed as excited as I was to find me a companion. I glanced over at Brooke. "Hey, why don't you and Callum head in... I want to talk to Indi for a sec."

Giving me a knowing look, Brooke nodded, throwing an arm around Callum as the pair walked inside.

"Alright, what's up? Is something wrong?" Indi's eyes were concerned, ready to help. My oldest friend had always been there for me, without question or hesitation. Which is why it was now my turn to do the same.

I pulled out a small envelope from my purse and handed it to her. "I wanted to give you this without Callum around."

She looked at me curiously for a moment, then opened the envelope, her eyes growing wide. Inside was a check for twenty thousand dollars, which I'd pulled from my inheritance fund at the bank before brunch that morning. Immediately, she started shaking her head. "Are you insane?? No, no... I can't accept this."

"Why not? You need a new roof. And there's plenty of other things you've had to put off for way too long." I placed a hand on her arm, giving it a slight squeeze. "What good is this inheritance if I can't do good things with it? You're my family, and this is what family does. Please, let me do this for you guys."

She stood there, the shaking of her head slowing as the tears came. "I... don't know..." She paused, taking a breath. "Thank you. I don't know how I can ever repay you, Lizzie."

"You're not allowed to," I said simply. "My only requirement is that you help me find this dog."

Throwing her arms around me, she whispered into my ear. "Deal. Love you so much."

Pulling back, I gave her a watery smile. "Love you, too. Now let's go in and make sure Brooke hasn't convinced Callum he needs eighty-seven kittens."

And that's exactly where we found them, Brooke peering into the kitten pen as Indi's son poked a finger between the metal bars and played with one very cute and fluffy gray kitty. Callum was tall for his age, his dark brown hair in clear contrast to Indi's blonde, but just as curly. He was a great kid—thoughtful, easy-going and kind—in those ways, very much like his mother. And for someone who'd been surrounded by six unofficial aunties for his entire life, he never seemed bothered by the fuss.

Indi had chosen not to reveal the identity of his father—not even to me, her oldest friend. I'd never pressed her on it—though, sometimes, I wondered how much time she had before Callum started asking more questions about who his father was—or wanting a relationship with him.

For now, though, he seemed content to walk alongside me, his mom and Brooke chatting behind us, as we followed the staff person back towards the kennels.

"Auntie Lizzie, what kind of dog are you looking for?"

I thought for a moment, scanning the cages. "I'm not sure, really... I guess I'm hoping that I'll connect with one of these pups, and just know that they're *The One*. That we're meant to be together, you know?"

How ironic that I was standing here—thirty years old, waxing poetic about Fate, like I knew what the hell I was talking about—when my only source material came straight outta the pages of romance novels. What else did

I have, really? Because outside of my dead grandparents' marriage, real life had fallen pathetically short.

But did it *have* to be fiction? Why was it so unreasonable for actual relationships to work out that way? Twenty years of filling my head and heart with these stories had made me want to believe it. By now, though, that belief was starting to feel, I don't know, *ridiculous*.

"Lizzie in the clouds with daydreams..." Dad would often sing as he walked by me, to the tune of the classic sixties' song. I used to like it. Now, I wondered if all it had done was to keep me up in those clouds, floating in a state of false belief.

But obsessing over any of this in the middle of an animal shelter—including how it might apply to a certain contractor—was pointless. I was here to find a *different* love of my life—of the four-legged variety, that is.

We walked along one side of the kennel area, both Indi and Brooke cooing at various dogs, pulling me over to take a look, eager to get me to commit. And sure, many of them were cute, every single one of them worthy of love. I just hadn't felt that spark yet.

After a few more minutes, my friends became distracted by a cage filled with newborn kittens. Callum and I continued on, rounding the corner towards the last corridor.

And that's when I saw him—lying in the rear corner of his cage, with the name *Garbage* tacked up in big letters next to the door.

Oh my God... who names their dog 'Garbage'?

Immediately, I knew this dog needed love more than all the others.

He was a mutt-astic mix of breeds, but I could tell there had to be some Australian Shepherd, maybe even some Golden Retriever in his lineage. Noticing us, Garbage lifted himself up off the floor to mosey on over to where we stood by his cage door, sniffing at my outstretched hand.

Now that he was more visible in the light, I noticed his fur was a shaggy mix of white and chestnut splotches—his sad eyes, a vivid blue.

And—he was missing his front right leg. A *tripawd*.

What can I say? It was love at first sight.

I lowered myself to the cement floor and Callum followed suit, reaching out a tentative hand through the wire grate. Garbage sniffed at his fingers for a moment before giving them a sloppy lick, Callum giggling.

"How are you doing, sweet boy?" I murmured softly as the pup turned his eyes back to me, tongue hanging out. "What's your story?" He cocked his head then, as if he understood my question. It was freaking *adorable*.

I glanced up at Mark, the staff member who'd brought us back here. "Can you open his cage? I just want to interact with him a little more, make sure he's comfortable with me."

"Sure." He unlocked the door, and Garbage came bounding out, almost knocking me over as he kiss-at-tacked my face. Giggling, I held out a hand to hold him back a bit, stroking his head with the other hand at the same time. Callum sat down next to me and began petting him, too—until Garbage surprised us both again by flopping over onto his back, exposing a fluffy white belly. Laughing again, we both gave it a good rub.

"You're such a good boy, Ga—" I glanced up at Mark, "—is his name really supposed to be *Garbage*?"

He sighed. "Yeah. He was dropped off by some frat boys that came over from Duluth a few weeks ago. Probably thought it would be funny to name a dog something stupid."

"Do you know anything more about his story?"

"Not really. The vet tech said he's probably around three years old, based on his dental... and that he likely lost his leg as a puppy. Probably why he can move so well without it. Otherwise, he's a healthy, normal dog. Real good-natured and everything." He shrugged. "The only reason he's still here is because most people assume a tripawd would be harder to care for. But that's definitely not the case. Dogs are very adaptable."

Indi and Brooke were behind us now as Callum and I took turns scratching Garbage's ears, his tail wagging and tongue lolling off to the side. "Those dumb boys didn't know what they were missing. You're perfect." I looked up at Indi and Brooke. "He's the one."

"I'm pretty sure he thinks so, too," Indi said, smiling.

Callum looked up at his mother as he stood up, clearly in heaven himself. "Mom, can we please get a dog, too...?"

She met my eyes briefly before giving her son a sad smile. "Sorry, bud... we've talked about this. It's just too hard with our schedule. But... maybe we could try a cat?" Rustling his hair, Indi glanced over at me again. "And I bet Auntie Lizzie will let you hang with her pup anytime you want..."

"Yep! As much as you want. And you can be my number one dog sitter too, if it's alright with your mom."

"Ok." Callum seemed satisfied. With a quick smile to his mom as Indi took him by the hand, the pair wandered around the corner to take a look at the kittens again.

Mark shut the door of the cage and hooked a leash to Garbage's collar as I hoisted myself up off the floor. "So, should I go ahead and get the paperwork ready?"

"Definitely."

"Great." Handing me the leash, he headed off towards the office.

Now that we were alone, Brooke gave me a sideways glance as she scratched behind my dog's ears. "Did you give her the check?"

"Yep... and as predicted, she tried to refuse. But I still won."

"That's my girl." She paused. "Listen, about earlier..."

"... it's fine, really. I just want to focus on this little guy right now."

She reached out, giving my arm a squeeze. "I get it. But... you know I'm here for you, right?"

"Of course I know that."

Brooke gave me a quick smile, turning back towards the dog. "So... it's *'Garbage'* then, huh?"

I grinned. "Yep. But that's not his name."

She looked at me, eyes curious. "Oh, yeah? Then what will we call him?"

"Bucky."

"Uh... I'm not following."

I knelt down again in front of my dog, giggling as he gave my face another lick. "As in Bucky Barnes. The Winter Soldier. Cap's best friend. He lost an arm, remember?" Bucky almost seemed to smile as I shared his much-improved origin story, and I knew I'd made the right choice. "He was a complex hero, just like my Bucky. And Ethan's gonna lose his mind when I tell him." I was already itching to send the text, thinking about my comic book-obsessed brother's inevitable reaction once I gave him the news.

For now, though, I looked straight into my pup's dreamy blue eyes. "What d'ya say, Bucky?"

Much to my delight, Bucky—*the dog formerly known as 'Garbage'*—tilted his head upwards, releasing a long, soulful howl. Brooke and I both started laughing, and I roughed the fluff on his head.

"Come on, Bucky boy... let's go home."

Chapter 21

Lizzie

"Lizzie, can I get you to take a quick look at something when you get in?"

"Yes, just a sec!" It was Monday, and Bucky and I had just returned home following his initial vet visit. It had been a busy two days of setting up the cabin for my new roomie, picking up supplies, and just getting used to one another. He'd ended up sleeping with me the past two nights since his bed hadn't arrived yet. All it took was one look at his furry grin—as he stretched out to spoon me—to realize that doggy bed was a total waste.

Anyway, I was making my way from my car to the front door—Bucky's leash and probiotics in one hand, my coffee and a sack full of strawberries from the Hanson's roadside stand in the other—when I heard James' voice filter through my open bedroom window.

I'd sent him a text the night before, letting him know that I wouldn't be there when he and Jesse arrived for work. Since he had a key of his own, I knew it wouldn't be an issue. I had yet to share the news about Bucky, but I secretly couldn't wait for the two of them to meet.

As I rounded the front corner of the house towards the porch a moment later, I let out a surprised squeal as my face met the very muscular chest of my contractor.

"Whoa, sorry…" With a short, surprised laugh, James reached out a hand to hold me steady, even managing to grab my iced coffee with the other before it dumped all over me—in a moment that had me feeling all kinds of déjà vu. "You ok?"

"Cripes, yes. Guess I should've been watching where I was going." I peeled myself from his chest, realizing only afterwards that I'd taken a deep whiff before doing so. Normally, I would've felt more embarrassed—but God, he smelled *so damn good*, it was criminal.

Like fresh air… and cedar… and… mountain rain, which is impossible, because we are in Minnesota…

As Bucky continued pulling hard at his leash to sniff away at something much less appealing in the grass ahead of him, I noticed James' lips curving upwards into a hesitant smile. Almost like he was uncertain if he should be caught smiling at me at all.

Yep, I wasn't the only one thinking about the last time we were this close.

But unlike before, I now knew what kissing those lips felt like—and there were no take backs. Willing my pulse to slow down, I returned his smile, wiping a small drip of iced coffee that had trickled down my bare arm. "Anyway, sorry I'm late… the vet took longer than I expec—"

Of course, before I could even finish the sentence, James was already on the ground, receiving a kiss-attack of his own from Bucky. I sighed. My wingman would be the only one getting any kind of action today. What can I say—after many years as the best friend of some very beautiful women, I was used to it.

At least, judging by the laughter pouring out of James, the feeling towards my pup was mutual. "So, this is the secret you were keeping," he said, looking up at me with a grin. "Well done, Ms. Blake. He's perfect." He ruffled my dog's ears, while Bucky continued gazing up at James like he was pretty much the best thing he'd ever seen.

You and me both, boy.

James stood back up, brushing off the back of his shorts. "So, what's his name?"

"Bucky. You know, like…"

"Cap's buddy. Yeah, that's perfect for him." He leaned over to give him a little chin scratch as Bucky rubbed his head against his hand in a state of bliss. "You keep our girl safe now, got it, Bucky?"

Our girl?

Right then, I was even more grateful to have Bucky there as a distraction, and not only because of that statement. This was the first time James and I had talked—or even seen each other, period—since our kayaking 'inci-

dent' two days prior. Not a peep via text either, outside of my heads-up about this morning.

Though honestly, what were we even supposed to say after that?

"Yeah, sorry for totally losing control with that kiss in the lake. My bad."

Except, I wasn't sorry. Not one bit. I'd be more than happy to kiss him again, if he'd let me. Because right now, with the way this man was staring at me, it felt like a foregone conclusion. And I knew I was rapidly losing every remaining bit of my very weak self-control.

Would he let me? Or did he regret that it had happened at all?

The look on his face didn't seem remorseful—he really did seem happy, relaxed. Like maybe calling me *'his girl'* felt natural.

In reality, though, it was probably a momentary lapse of judgment. And I *was* still his client. I shouldn't even be thinking about kissing that man again, much less willing it to happen. It's most of the reason why I'd avoided digging into all of this with Brooke and Kait the other day. I knew they'd try to talk me into it—with the best of intentions, of course. They loved me, wanted me to be happy.

But what would make me happiest right now is for something to go smoothly for once, without ending up knee-deep in complications. And I wasn't only thinking about my career.

Our Dearie Girls' biannual ladies' weekend was coming up quickly at the start of September—and after I'd inherited the cabin back in April, I'd made the pitch about hosting it here for the first time. Of course, everyone had been totally on board about the idea.

Now here we were, with the Fourth of July only four days away, and at least a couple months' worth of work remaining before we could officially tie a bow on this remodel, along with our working relationship. I couldn't afford to lose a contractor at this point.

Not to mention, I was only a couple of months removed from the whole mess with my ex, Randall—who, for whatever reason, was still continuing to reach out in the form of unanswered calls, months after I'd stormed out his door. Like he refused to just let me move on.

I *needed* to move on.

But was kissing another man—a palate cleanser, of sorts—the right way to go about it?

Because despite the fact that I was on a temporary writing hiatus, there were still plenty of other things I should be focusing my attention on at the moment that wouldn't wreak havoc in my life.

Like, um, my dog.

Personal development to help me to work through my issues? *Possibly.*

Maybe taking up gardening?

No, like... his lips.

No. NO.

Suddenly, I became very aware that I must be staring at them again as the image of James waving a hand in front of my face came into clearer focus.

"You still with me, Red?"

I gave him a sheepish look. "Sorry. I'm just… tired. Guess I didn't sleep well last night."

"Guess so." He had that half smile on his face again, studying mine intently. Then, with a shrug, he turned, motioning for me to follow. "Anyway, let's go inside for a moment. We found something you need to see."

"Sure, ok." We walked together up the porch steps and through the front door, Bucky leading the way. "What is it?"

"Well, you know how Jesse and I were planning to move the furniture out of the master bedroom this morning to start painting, now that the walls are finished in the master bath? Well, we started before you got back, and … you need to see this for yourself."

Passing through the short hallway and into my bedroom, we intercepted Jesse walking in the opposite direction, carrying the mirror that had previously been hanging above my grandmother's dresser.

"Did you tell her yet?" Jesse moved past us with the mirror, on his way to hide it somewhere safe until the work was done.

"Not yet," James called out after him. Then, grabbing my hand—with another one of those jolts I still hadn't quite gotten used to—he pulled me over to the empty spot where the mirror used to be. "Check this out," he said, eyes twinkling as he motioned towards the bare wall.

Except... the wall wasn't bare at all. Because hanging there was a small painting of what looked to be Lake Elska, no more than a foot across in either direction and surrounded by an ornate gold frame. Around the painting, the wall appeared brighter, as though the mirror had hung over it for a lifetime—concealing its secrets, until this very moment.

It was... odd though, wasn't it? *Why would a random painting be hanging behind the mirror?* I wondered.

I glanced back at James. "So... you found a painting," I said, as if it were obvious. "Kind of strange, huh? I guess we should probably take it down before you get started."

But he just grinned at me. "Nope, we can't. Come on... look closer, Lizzie."

Giving him what I'm sure had to be a look of total confusion, I stepped closer to inspect the painting further. As my fingers grazed the surface, that's when I realized—this wasn't a normal piece of artwork at all. For starters, I spotted two brass hinges attached to the left side of the frame. And the surface of the painting itself wasn't made of canvas at all—it seemed to be painted directly onto a piece of wood.

But then I noticed the small gold handle, bolted to the right side of the frame. *It was...a door?* Intrigued, I pulled at the handle—but it wouldn't budge.

"It's… I mean… what do you think it is?" I turned to look back at James, who was watching my reaction with interest.

"I have no idea… maybe a safe or something? Definitely strange," he said, shrugging as he looked back at the painting. "Anyway, I figured you'd want to see this before we got going in here. And don't worry, we'll make sure it's protected."

"Yeah, ok…"

I felt him move closer until he was standing right next to me, the scent of him once again making me a bit dizzy. "I have to admit, though, I'm intrigued… makes me curious about what might be inside." His voice was low but close, almost directly above me.

It should be illegal for someone to smell this good while sweaty from manual labor, damn it.

"Yeah, me too." But even though his proximity had my senses swimming, the voice in my head couldn't help wondering—What in the world could possibly be hiding behind a tiny door that nobody had likely seen for decades?

What secrets had my grandparents been keeping?

I turned towards James, so close that I had to crane my neck to look upward at him. I took a small step back. "Thanks for showing this to me. And…"

"… listen," James interrupted me, but his voice was gentle. "I just wanted to say, I'm sorry if I caught you off guard or overstepped after kayaking the other day. I… kind of lost control out there for a moment." He gave me another one of his awkward sort of half smiles.

But what he saw in front of him had to be way more awkward by far, as I felt my cheeks return to their perma-embarrassed shade of rosy pink—trying my damndest now to avoid his gaze.

Because I knew looking into those eyes of his would inevitably lead me to take whatever remained of my self-control and chuck it straight into the *'fuck it bucket'*, as my friend Kait was so fond of saying.

"It's... ok. Don't worry, I'm not upset or anything... I mean—"

"Good."

Now I met his eyes. "Good?"

"Yeah. Because I'm not sorry that I did it." He took another small step closer to me.

"You're... *not?*"

Jesus, Lizzie... Could you sound like more of an idiot right now?

"Nope. In fact, I'm hoping... maybe you'll let me do it again sometime."

Ok, I am definitely having a stroke or something.

"Are you... asking if you can kiss me again?"

"In a roundabout way." James smiled. "But first, I'd like to make you dinner... if you don't mind."

I just stared at him. "You want to cook... for me?"

"Yes, I do. Would that be alright with you?"

"Well, sure, but..."

"... because if it makes you uncomfortable to have dinner with the guy you hired to work on your house, Lizzie, I promise... I'll respect that. I know I'm crossing a line here. Just say the word and you won't have to worry about me bothering you again." He paused, taking a deep breath. "But I'll be honest... I'm really hoping you'll say yes."

James' face looked serious now, and he seemed almost... nervous? It was the first time I'd seen him like that, and it actually helped to diffuse the anxious energy buzzing around inside of me.

This was the moment, though, where I needed to decide if I was willing to take on this risk. Because once we stepped onto this path, there'd be no going back. It could no longer be considered an accident.

And I'd have to own whatever the outcome might be.

Just then, I felt Bucky nose his way in between the two of us—weaving through our legs, one at a time, before sitting like a good boy to stare at me expectantly.

And it was clear that he had an opinion on what my answer should be.

Glancing back up at James, I pushed through the last shred of doubt, tentatively offering a shy smile. "Alright. Yes, I would love to have dinner with you."

His entire body seemed to relax before me, the relief evident on his face. "Good. You busy tonight? Say, seven o'clock?"

"Sure, that works." I hesitated. "Is it ok if I bring Bucky? I don't want to leave him home alone just yet."

"Of course, Bucky's more than welcome." As if on cue, Bucky licked James' hand in approval as he smiled at him. "Alright, then. Seven it is. I'll text you my address." With a quick nod, he turned to walk out of the room, calling out over his shoulder. "Jesse and I are going to get started in there, alright? Just so you have someplace to sleep tonight."

It wasn't until I'd heard the front screen door swing shut that I finally let myself relax, leaning against the wall to try and process everything that had once again transpired in a very, very short period of time.

First, a mysterious door—quite possibly left behind by my grandparents. *But what lay behind it? And why was it locked?*

And then, in an unexpected turn of events, I find out the man I'd been secretly crushing over for weeks... liked *me*? And wanted to make me *a meal*?

Any objections I'd thought seemed responsible and logical prior to this conversation now felt completely lame. Because the only reason I'd made them was to cover up the fact that I really, *really* liked this man.

It wasn't just that I found James a hot and sexy distraction. Turns out, the promises I'd made to myself to ignore whatever I was feeling for him had fallen on deaf ears.

Because, yeah—I was already starting to fall. And the thought of how quickly it seemed to be happening was both overwhelming and terrifying. Especially when I didn't know if I could trust myself—*or anyone else*—with my heart just yet.

But at the very least, I was definitely certain of one thing—as scary as it felt to jump into something that seemed so tenuous, I couldn't *wait* to kiss James again.

I just prayed that it wouldn't end up hurting me in the end. Because after everything I'd gone through over the past year, I didn't think I could bear to lose one more thing.

Chapter 22

James

Well, I've done it—consider the line officially crossed, times two.

I walked out of the cabin, the screen door slamming behind me as I crossed over to where we'd laid the tarp out on the grass, along with the first few cans of paint. Lizzie had opted to stick to a similar creamy white shade for her master bedroom, and I noticed Jesse had already pried that one open. We'd need to tackle both the master and the other two bedrooms before calling it a day.

"Hey, man, do you think we should pour the p—"

"I just asked Lizzie out." The words tumbled out of my mouth ahead of me, before I could even think of stopping them. Not that it was likely I would've—I needed to get them out of my head.

Jesse nodded slowly, pausing for a moment to take in what I'd said. "You asked Lizzie out." Matter-of-fact, like he was confirming that the paint color in front of him was indeed called 'Sour Cream'. Who names these things, anyway?

"Yeah. And... I kissed her a couple days ago."

A slow Cheshire grin stretched across my friend's face, like a fat cat sunning itself. "Yeah. I know."

"What do you mean, 'you know'? Why the hell aren't you acting more surprised? Or telling me I just fucked everything up?"

Jesse shrugged, leaning down again to start gathering supplies. "It's mostly because I'm not surprised. Watching you two, you should've done it weeks ago already." He glanced up at me for a moment, amused. "And before you say anything else... yes, it's obvious that you're into her. GiGi, Jack and I all had a bet going to see when you'd finally break."

"You were fucking betting on me?"

He laughed. "Relax, it was all in good fun. If it makes you feel any better, Jack actually thought you'd cave a month ago already."

I groaned, shaking my head. "Exactly how is that supposed to make me feel better?"

"Because now it means I won the bet instead of him. I figured it would take you until right around the Fourth of July," he said, grinning. "Now that you finally admitted it, I'm fifty bucks richer. Thanks, man."

"Awesome. Glad my half-assed love life could make all your dreams come true," I said, my voice dripping with sarcasm. Then it dawned on me. "Wait, how did you even know that I kissed her in the first place?"

"GiGi saw the whole thing and texted us. She was kind of pissed that she'd lost the bet, actually."

I rolled my eyes. "Of course she was. What was her guess, anyway?"

"Well, she said you're a stubborn ass, so it would take you forever... her pick wasn't until the end of August."

I couldn't help but chuckle. "Well, good... she's always more unbearable to be around after winning."

"Not wrong about that one. But you know she's fucking celebrating that you've finally shown an interest in some-one." He tossed a brush into the pail, sneaking a quick glance at me. "It's been a long time, huh?"

Yeah... maybe too long.

I stood there, quiet for a moment, watching as Jesse finished filling the bag with all of our paintbrushes, then handed it to me.

"You just going to stand there staring, or are you going to help me haul this stuff in? We only have five hours to get those rooms painted... and Tara will kill me if I make us late for dinner at her parents' house again."

"Yeah, sorry." I grabbed the bag from his outstretched hand, then paused. "It's just... Do you think I made a mistake? I know I said I'd never get involved with a client, and here I go back on my word with our very first one..."

Jesse held up a hand to stop me—and this time, his expression was more kind than playful. "James, you're one of the hardest working people I know. And you're also one of the smartest. You think things all the way through, and you care about damn near everything... maybe sometimes more than you need to." He took a step closer, smiling. "It's why Tara always knew I'd follow you anywhere, how we both knew it was a good move joining you with this venture. You wouldn't do anything to risk it, not for any of us."

I nodded, considering his words. "But what if I *do* mess things up with her?"

"With Lizzie? You won't," he said, shrugging as if it were obvious. "Just stop second-guessing yourself and give yourself a chance to be happy, alright? It's what we all want for you. And nobody deserves it more than you do, brother. Except for my wife, who now gets to book herself a pedicure with my winnings." Grinning as he gave my arm a quick pat, Jesse grabbed the paint and trays and began walking towards the house. After a moment, I picked up the rest of the supplies and followed him inside, giving Lizzie a quick smile as I passed her on the sofa.

I was relieved that Jesse was supportive, but not surprised—he and Jack had always had my back, no matter where the road ended up taking us. And he was right—I'd never allow myself to mess things up for him and Tara, especially with their first baby due to be born in less than four months.

There was a small part of me that still felt afraid, though, and would probably always wonder if I had what it took to make a relationship work. If I could actually open up enough with someone without always feeling like it wouldn't last.

To *truly* be happy.

But if I was going to try and do this, I was going to do it right.

Starting with tonight.

Chapter 23

James

I had just slid the veggies into the oven when I heard the doorbell chime, barely audible over the music playing in the living room. Wiping my hands on a towel, I did a quick survey of the kitchen to make sure it didn't look like a total mess and that the green button-down shirt I'd chosen wasn't stained. After sweeping the contents of the cutting board into the trash, I walked through the living room towards the front door.

Pausing for a second to take a breath, I pulled the door open to reveal Lizzie standing on the other side, looking almost as nervous as I felt. Bucky sat politely by her feet on his leash, tail wagging and ready to get the party started.

But her anxiousness wasn't what I noticed first. Gone were her usual tank top and cargo shorts, ponytail and flip-flops. Now, her hair flowed loose and wavy past her shoulders, the color even more of a deep amber thanks to the glow of early evening sunlight behind her. And she was wearing a dress, in a dark blue fabric held up by exceptionally thin straps, the top of it hugging her curves before flowing downward over her bare legs.

Her skin had a glow to it tonight as well—not so much from the bit of makeup she was wearing, more from within her. I'd always found Lizzie beautiful, but tonight—well, tonight she was luminous.

I doubt I'd ever used that word before in my life. But who the hell cared—it was the only one I knew of worthy of describing her.

"Hey."

"Hey."

The expression on her face now appeared to shift from anxious to amused as we stood there, awkwardly staring at one another, until Bucky let out an annoyed bark. "Um, do you think we could come in, maybe?"

"Yeah, sorry." I stepped aside to let them pass, the soft floral perfume intermingling with her own scent, as it had that morning on the lake.

And like before, it was intoxicating.

Closing the door, I turned back towards her with a smile. "Glad you could make it. You look... great."

'Great'? Are you going to keep throwing out the lamest words ever? It's amazing you even got this woman to agree to a date with you, Tate.

"Um... thanks."

I saw her blush a bit as she unhooked Bucky from his leash, praying it wasn't over my own stupidity. Why did

I feel so damn nervous? I decided to change the subject. "Did you find the place ok?"

"Yeah, piece of cake. Brooke's brother, Dustin, lives just up the road. But you probably knew that."

I exhaled a quick laugh. "Yeah, Dusty and I go way back. He's a good guy."

"He is... I actually had a crush on him a long time ago, when I was around sixteen or so."

I raised an eyebrow. "Really? I didn't see you as being into burly, firefighter types."

She giggled. "Definitely not. But he didn't exactly look like that when he was nineteen."

"Fair point." I grinned, while also thinking it boded well for me that Lizzie was no longer into uber-muscley types. Even though I was active and kept myself in good shape, I was nowhere near as built as Dustin Christenson—or his brother Trent. Those boys were of a different breed entirely. Probably why they'd found their calling fighting fires and operating heavy equipment.

I glanced down, noticing the bottle in her hand for the first time. "You brought wine... that wasn't necessary."

"My grandmother taught me never to come to dinner empty-handed. What can I say? I'm a little old-fashioned that way." She shrugged, looking sheepish. "But I hope you like Sauvignon Blanc. I didn't know what we were having tonight."

"It's perfect. Dinner's almost ready. Come have a seat in the kitchen, and I'll pour you a glass while I finish up. I've got a water bowl for Bucky, too."

I led her into the kitchen, motioning for her to take a seat at the barstool at the counter, as I opened the bottle and poured us each a glass. With each glug from the bottle, I felt my pulse escalate even faster—especially when I saw the way she was looking at me. Setting the bottle down, I handed her a glass.

"How about a toast?"

She cocked her head, her expression now playful. "Ok. How about... to keeping ourselves afloat from now on?"

I laughed, feeling some of my nervousness begin to dissipate as I clinked my glass against hers. "Come on... where's the fun in that? Besides," I said with a wink, "it's fun to get a little wet sometimes, isn't it?"

Her eyes twinkled as she took a sip, then lowered her glass. "You make a very compelling argument."

Was she blushing right now over the memory of our kiss, or was it because she could feel the same energy I did?

Bucky, who'd wandered over from his water bowl, nudged at my hip with his nose before I could make up my mind, one way or the other. Looking past him, I saw he'd already spilled half of the contents of his water bowl onto the floor around it. "Looks like Bucky took the concept too literally," I said, chuckling as Lizzie hopped out of her seat, scolding him as I wiped up the mess.

Twenty minutes later, we were sitting together at the dining table next to the living room, with me watching Lizzie's face as she took her first few bites. I'd grilled salmon out on the back deck, served alongside balsamic roasted Brussels sprouts and a Caesar salad.

Since my dinner invitation had been kind of spur of the moment, I went with what I had on hand—and I was grateful that GiGi had taught me how to cook well enough over the years.

"James, this is delicious. Honestly, I don't think I've had salmon this good *ever*." If Lizzie's expression was any indication, I knew she had to be telling the truth. It helped that my grandmother's seasoning recipe really *was* the best.

I smiled, now feeling relaxed enough to start eating myself. "Thanks, glad to hear it. GiGi was determined to raise a man who could cook for himself and others, so I've never suffered too badly on my own."

"I have no doubt." She grinned, reaching for her glass of wine. "So how long have you owned this place, anyway? It's beautiful."

"About five years. I always knew I'd want a simple, single-level home surrounded by a ton of trees... makes me feel grounded. Though if I had my way, I'd own some lakefront property as well. But it's become difficult to snag property on Lake Elska these days."

"Yeah, I can see that, growing up where you did." She gave me a shy look. "You really love being out on the water, don't you?"

"I do. Kayaking has become a passion of mine over the years... especially lately." I couldn't help myself, nor did I regret the way my comment seemed to make her squirm just then. It was hard to hold back the smile, along with everything else I was feeling.

But I'd be taking it slow with Lizzie. This was something I didn't want to mess up for either of us.

We spent the next hour alternating between talking, laughing, and making our way through the remainder of the bottle of wine she'd brought, moving on to some ciders I'd already had chilling.

And just like every other time over the past couple of months, spending time with her was so... easy. This woman had no false pretense about her—so open and warm, you almost couldn't help but feel relaxed and open around her. Even her nervous and awkward moments were endearing.

Did she think the same thing about mine?

And that smile of hers—it was hard to play it cool and casual when I felt this deep need to be the reason for it.

"So, can I ask you something I've been wondering about? It's kind of personal."

I glanced at her, curious. "Sure, go ahead."

She paused, as though figuring out how best to phrase her question—always the writer. "How did you come to live with your grandparents?"

Looking away, I could feel my body tense. But when I saw nothing but compassion reflected in her eyes, I knew her question wasn't born out of gossip—just a way of continuing to get to know me better.

As much as I wanted to dive deep into all that she was, I guess I wasn't used to a woman caring to dig past the surface stuff I usually allowed on a date—the small talk that served only as foreplay or the prelude to an inevitable goodbye.

And it wasn't like my story wasn't already known throughout town—or at least, the part where I'd lost my mother. And GiGi and Pops, their only daughter.

By now, more than twenty-five years had passed. I'd always avoided thinking about it, much less talking about it. Most folks around here had learned not to ask questions. It made it easier to keep those feelings private.

But maybe it was time to stop hiding. From all of it.

"It's not a pretty story... you sure you want to hear about it?"

"I'll always want to hear anything you're willing to share with me. Even the hard stuff."

Hearing her words, I could feel myself relax, just enough. Releasing a long exhale, I began.

"When I was eight, my mom and I came up here for a week to visit my grandparents over Christmas. One afternoon, we decided to go ice skating. My dad was planning on driving up to join us after work the next day. I remember him always being gone a lot for work."

I paused again—but this time, I fixed my gaze on the window, where the sky outside was almost orange now. The warmth of it felt comforting.

"Anyway, I'd been begging her to go skating for days, and she finally gave in. We drove over to that section of Dearing River leading off Lake Elska and over into Heartwood. I'd heard some kid in town talking about it being a good spot, and we'd already skated on the lake dozens of times by then. But we'd been having a warmer winter than usual that year, and neither of us realized how thin the ice had gotten. I was about twenty feet out on the ice when I fell through."

I heard her sharp intake of breath. "Oh, James..."

By now, the words were rushing through me. I couldn't pause to look at her—I had to keep going. "So my mom right away started screaming out for help... I was barely hanging on to the edge of the ice, and I remember the current being really strong, and so cold. She crawled across to try pulling me out of the water... it took a while, as she was a small woman, but she finally did it." I took a breath. "But as soon as I'd made it most of the way out, the ice cracked beneath her too. She fell in, and... I couldn't stop it. I couldn't..." I heard my voice crack, splintering all the way through in a long, jagged line.

I couldn't save her.

There it was, the memory I never allowed myself to revisit. It had always been too painful. Even in the many sessions with my therapist, I'd mostly dodged the topic, instead choosing to focus on the anger I felt towards my father.

But I could see that image of my mother's face clearly now, as I made a desperate grab for her hand, realizing she was too far away without me letting go myself. The moment right before she disappeared beneath the surface—her soft hazel eyes no longer afraid but looking at me with calm acceptance—was one that would be imprinted in my mind forever.

And I didn't save her.

That day, the river had pulled my heart under, too. I think it had stayed there, frozen, for a very long time. Probably *too* long.

Vaguely, I felt Lizzie squeeze my hand. Even though I could sense the same tingling in our connection as before, the rest of me felt very far away, caught in the memory of it all. But I felt grateful that she was here, listening, but saying nothing—allowing me to be as I needed to be at that moment.

She wasn't trying to fix me or convince me that what happened to my mom wasn't my fault. She was just there, sitting in all of it, *with* me.

I'd never had someone do that for me before, not ever.

I remembered how my dad drove up that night, right after the recovery team found my mother's body. It had gotten caught up against a rocky area in the river, about fifty yards down. I was at the cabin by then—no one would allow me to help or to be there when it ended. I just sat there on the sofa, numb and alone, waiting for the one person who would never be coming home to me again.

I felt something fall against our clasped hands—a tear. Looking up, I caught Lizzie staring at me and realized she was crying, too.

But there was no pity in her eyes—only compassion.

"James, I'm... so sorry. I can't even imagine how painful that had to have been for you to go through, especially so young. For your whole family, too."

I nodded, reaching across towards her face to wipe away her tears with the pad of my thumb, then resting my hand on top of hers. "We were all pretty broken after that, especially GiGi and Pops... Mom was their only child. The three of us became a new family that night."

"Your grandmother is an incredible woman... it's clear she did an amazing job raising you." She gave me a brief smile. "What about your dad?"

I held her gaze for a moment, the scene of that night playing out in the background. "He walked away. He went back to his life, his house, his company... and forgot I ever existed." But what I didn't say was that he couldn't deal with losing my mother and blamed me that she was dead.

Maybe I was a hypocrite for holding onto this anger towards my father. Because he wasn't wrong.

I blamed myself, too.

The sound of her breath told me Lizzie felt the pain of my words along with me. And oddly enough, in doing so, I felt even more of the heaviness float away. She leaned over, pulling me into her, her arms wrapped around me. "Thank you for trusting me with this... I'm so sorry for everything you've lost. I know nothing can fix that. But I'm still glad you're here." Her breath was soft and warm against my ear, and I reached around to pull her towards me even closer, breathing in all of it.

And I knew—I could trust this woman. With my thoughts, my secrets, my scars.

Maybe even with what remained of my heart.

Somewhere in the background, I could hear the opening melody of a song I hadn't heard for a while begin to play. I finally released her, reaching down to take her hand in mine.

"Will you dance with me?"

She looked surprised. "I'm not that great of a dancer..."

I smiled. "Don't worry, I'll carry you with me. Just follow my rhythm."

Pulling Lizzie along towards the empty space behind my leather sofa, I turned to bring her back into my arms. The curves of her body molded to mine as we moved together, the lyrics saying the words I never believed I'd feel safe enough to feel—until now.

"... my heart rose to its feet, like the ashes of ash I saw rise in the heat. Settle soft and as pure as snow, I fell in love with the fire long ago..."

I tilted my head back to look down at her face—and God, those eyes of hers, with the setting sun hitting them just right through the window, transforming the color into the most vivid of greens, with rivers of gold flowing through them. I was swept up in them, in *her*. I could feel her body tense as she held her breath, anticipating.

Lowering my mouth towards hers, she met me in the middle—and we kissed, exploring one another as our bodies swayed, continuing long after the song had ended.

And this time, that electricity that had been flowing between us since the very start wasn't one that I was trying my best to ignore, telling myself it could only ever be a mistake.

Tonight, it felt healing, life-giving, as my heart continued its thaw. And I allowed the current to carry me away, off towards the places I finally felt ready to go.

Only now, I wasn't alone. She belonged there with me.

Chapter 24

Lizzie

It was nearly one a.m., and I'd been home for an hour—laying on my bed, surrounded by the smells of fresh paint and the night air flowing in through my open window—along with far too many thoughts and feelings to name them all.

For a minute, I'd debated texting my Dearie Girls. Just so I could have someone else look at all of this objectively and confirm if men like James existed outside of the pages of one of my books. To reassure me that what happened tonight wasn't just another one of my dreams.

And that feeling this way was ok and could actually be *real.*

God, I wanted to believe in it.

In the end, though, I'd kept my questions to myself—at least for tonight. I wanted to ruminate in this space for as long as possible, keeping it precious, with no room for doubt.

Because the evening with James had been, in a word, *perfect.*

I mean, first he cooked me an amazing dinner, not allowing me to do a single thing but sit there and enjoy it. It brought to light yet again how completely opposite James was from my ex, Randall—never in a million years would that man have performed even the smallest act of service for me, or anyone else for that matter. He expected it all for himself.

Now, for the first time within a relationship, I felt like someone's priority. And weirdly, I felt almost guilty about it.

Later on, as we alternated between moments of kissing and talking on his leather sofa, it felt like the walls had been lifted—finding ourselves in the sort of late night confessional you only experience at the tipping point, when you know deep in your soul that this, *this* was becoming something special. When you're in a moment where you feel like you can never possibly know enough about the person you're with—so you keep pressing forward, ever deeper, hungry for more.

It almost seemed like maybe he'd felt that way, too, as we wove our stories together, filling in many of the gaps from our previous conversations. We talked about our school years, favorite movies, and guilty pleasures. Memories of growing up on the lake, embarrassing moments, and the paths we'd taken up until now. Regrets of the past and hopes for the future.

We talked at length about the family we'd found in our friendships, where we both seemed to have lucked out—and of course, our grandmothers, both powerful influences in our lives. I was surprised to learn how close the friendship between these two women had been—and I made a mental note to ask GiGi more about it. Learning more about that time in my grandmother's life might make her feel closer, something that had seemed to be fading lately.

But the thing that struck me most was hearing about what James had gone through early on. I still couldn't believe what he'd managed to become, considering where he'd started. I mean, there *was* some solidarity in that pain, as we were both without parents. But losing both parents as a child—one by accident, the other by choice—was something I couldn't even begin to fathom. Sitting in that heartbreak alongside him had been gut-wrenching—but more than anything, it felt like I was right where I was supposed to be.

Now that I understood more of his past, it explained some of the guardedness I'd sensed at the very beginning—back when we thought we disliked each other, for one ridiculous reason or another.

It all seemed so silly now, looking back. First impressions can be so misleading and one-dimensional. And I'd made plenty of assumptions about this man at the start, based on practically nothing.

Because now I could see him so clearly—a thoughtful, hard-working, caring and sensitive man who'd grown into something greater than the sum of his somewhat broken parts. Thank God I hadn't turned down his offer that first day at the dock—otherwise, I might never have known *this*.

It made me wonder again what he even saw when he looked at me—an awkward, thirty-year-old woman, living on her own in an old cabin after losing her job, failing at the one thing she was supposed to be good at?

Damn, what a catch.

Of course, I knew I was oversimplifying myself in the cruelest way possible. And taking a break from writing wasn't 'failure'... *exactly.*

But looking at James—a man who'd known true trauma, yet still found a way forward to follow his dreams and start his own business, plucking up the courage to just go for it—had made me realize a few things about myself.

I hadn't been pursuing my dream with courage at all. All I'd been doing was floundering and running scared.

I'd thought I was supposed to fit within a very specific mold to be taken seriously as a writer, for anyone to believe in me or my abilities. So I'd worked my ass off trying to prove myself, all the while beating my head against the proverbial wall. And fear had been my fuel the entire time.

Now here I was, with countless years wasted on writing something that didn't feel authentic—that didn't make me feel *anything*, really, except inadequate.

It was why the words had refused to come. I'd been holding myself back, denying what I was supposed to be doing because I was goddamn scared. And it took this man to open my eyes.

But even while I worked to figure myself out, James somehow made me feel... I don't know... *better*, about all of it. Like I wasn't the mess I thought I was.

It was pretty ironic, considering the last man I'd dated had pretty much drilled into my head that writing what I loved would ruin me. But that was before he'd gone and done that himself.

Not that James and I were *officially* dating—were we? Despite all the objections I'd repeated like an oath these past two months, the reality was—I was acting like a chicken shit, yet again.

Because I wanted to be with him.

This was no longer about deadlines on a remodeling project or trying to be something I wasn't. I'd swam way out past the point of calling this thing between us a distraction or a complication.

Because if this evening had made anything clear, it's that I'd probably been feeling *more* for him longer than I'd realized. And it would be way too easy to just let go, to let myself get swept up in all of it. But *could* I do it, when I still felt a little afraid?

Lifting my hand to my chest, I fingered Grandma Cora's key necklace where it lay, the metal warm from direct contact with my skin. I'd been wearing the necklace nearly every day since discovering it hidden in her book. At first, I'd hoped it would serve as inspiration, a creative talisman of sorts.

Now I wondered if it had instead unlocked the barriers to whatever I'd been hiding from in my head, opening the door wide to whatever was blooming between me and James. I mean, when you think about it, hadn't the paper she'd enclosed read, '*Key to my heart*'?

I bolted upright in bed, my eyes fixed on the small painting of Lake Elska that the guys had discovered that morning. Even though they'd brought all the other furniture back into the room once they'd finished painting, I'd asked them to hold off on re-hanging the mirror. I was still so curious about why the painting was there, and if it was, in fact, a door—or just an odd sort of decoration. Knowing my grandmother, I wouldn't put either possibility past her.

But it was still weird that the painting *just happened* to depict the abstract heart-shaped lake from right outside my door—the heart of Dearing Creek. The unique shape was the reason for Lake Elska's name in the first place—taken from the Norwegian word for *'my beloved'*.

I mouthed the words from that slip of paper once again to myself. *'Key to my heart'.*

Had Grandma Cora been sending me some sort of message—a clue of sorts—when she made the plan to pass down both her books *and* this cabin to me?

Standing up, I crossed over to the painting as I slid the chain from around my neck. Leaning in close, I studied the image of the lake and then the frame itself, trying to spot the answer I was seeking.

And that's when I noticed a small heart built into the frame below the handle. It didn't seem to be made of the same sort of material as the rest of it—instead, the heart had a shinier finish and almost looked to be made of metal. Looking closer, I realized there was a tiny bolt attached to the top between the two crests. Pressing my finger against its lower pointed edge, I tried rotating the piece to the right—and it moved along with me, swiveling upwards to reveal a small keyhole.

Holy shit.

With a trembling hand, I inserted my grandmother's gold key into the lock, turning it towards the left until I heard a small click—and watched as the door slowly swung open.

James had been right—it *was* a safe. But the precious contents inside this one appeared in the form of two bundles of letters, each tied with a similar green velvet ribbon. Feeling like a kid at Christmas, I reached inside to pull out both bundles before scurrying back to bed, now completely wide awake.

Untying the top bundle, I opened the first envelope, labeled with one word, '*Dearest*'. Then carefully, I pulled out a short, handwritten letter:

October 15th, 1966

"Dearest Cora,

You've often said I was no romantic, but let this letter serve as a reminder – never again will there ever be a reason for you to believe I don't love you.

Because I will not allow another day to go by without proving how much I need you, how deeply you are cherished, and that my life with you is always my first priority.

For the truth is... you've always, always had my heart.

No matter what has transpired before, or what comes next... you can count on this.

With love,

Yours, Walter"

Dropping the letter into my lap, I felt a wave of emotion wash over me as I realized what I'd uncovered—an artifact from the love story I'd spent my entire life measuring everything else against.

I have no idea how she did it, but somehow—even from the great beyond—Grandma Cora knew exactly what I needed most.

Hope.

Despite having had almost no sleep the night before, I was up early the next morning, sitting at the kitchen table with my coffee—and Bucky snoring at my feet—when I vaguely heard the truck pull up out back.

I'd been sitting there for an hour already, skimming through Grandpa Walter's third letter for the fiftieth time and trying to avoid plowing through the entire pile of letters too quickly. This discovery had breathed new life into me, almost like having my grandparents back again—and I didn't want it to end.

So far, the first few letters in this first bundle seemed to be written by Grandpa Walter to my grandmother, but none from her to him. Had he kept her letters in a separate spot? Or maybe they were in the second bundle? I'd kept those bound together for the time being, like a simple ribbon could keep me away from temptation for long.

Needless to say, I was deep in a re-read when James and Jesse walked through the front door a few minutes later, clearly at the tail end of something funny. Glancing up, I saw James' face light up as soon as he saw me—that is, until Bucky ran over and tackled him with his aggressive brand of doggy love.

"Whoa, Buck, let me get a little more coffee in me first." He chuckled between kisses, ruffling my dog's head before pulling himself upright to smile shyly at me.

"Hey, there."

"Hey."

Jesse cleared his throat behind him. "So, uh, Lizzie... tell me, what are your intentions with our James here?"

I about choked on the huge gulp I'd just taken of my coffee. "Excuse me?"

James punched his friend on the shoulder, shaking his head. "Yeah, sorry about this idiot. Just to forewarn you, he's probably going to be insufferable for the foreseeable future."

"You think I'm bad? Just wait until Jack gets a hold of you." Jesse rubbed his hands together, grinning.

It was impossible not to laugh. "Don't worry... I think I can handle it." Catching James' eye, I smiled as I watched his posture relax again. I'd clicked with Jesse right away at the start of this project—but in the couple of months since, I could see he loved James like a brother. I had to imagine Jack was much the same.

For now, Jesse looked at the two of us, shaking his head with a grin. "So, I'm just going to start working in the bathroom... You two take your time." With a wink and a kissy sound, he wandered off, whistling as he rounded the corner. My eyes darted back to James, who shrugged sheepishly.

"I promise I didn't tell him much. But the smile on my face must've told him everything else when I picked him up this morning."

I mean, who could be mad at that? "It's ok, really. I don't mind." With a weird wave of nervous energy, I stood up, fumbling through what I should say next. "Anyway, uhhh… thanks for last night. I had a great time."

"Only '*great*'? You saying I need to up my game?" A smirk played upon his lips, hazel eyes dancing—and I couldn't help but smile again too as I felt my brief blip of anxiety melt away.

"Yes, I have impossibly high standards. But too late, Tate… you can't back out now." Raising up on tiptoe, I leaned in to give him a quick peck on the cheek—but before my lips could reach him, he pulled me against his chest, kissing me deeply. After what felt both like forever and far too short, he released me as I took a sloppy step backwards, breathless.

"Better?"

How stupid was the goofy grin on my face right now? "Definitely better."

"Good." He paused. "Is it ok that I did that here, on the job? Or would you rather we keep the weekdays professional? I don't want to make this stressful for you."

"No. As your client, I demand that you behave like a good boyfriend." Realizing what I said, I froze. "Sorry, I shouldn't assume... we never talked about being exclusive..."

He cocked his head. "Well, I'm not seeing anyone else. And I have no interest in playing games. How about you?"

I felt my cheeks grow warm. "Well, no..."

"Then it's settled... you're my girlfriend. If you have a problem with that, take it up with management." He grinned. "I better get back there. I'm helping Jesse lay the tile today." But before he could turn to walk away, I grabbed his arm. "What, you don't want me to work? Though you have a point, time spent kissing you is better than a finished remodel..."

I laughed. "Actually, I just wanted to show you something. Take a look at this."

Looking at me curiously, he pulled out the chair next to mine at the kitchen table, lowering himself into it as I handed him the letter I'd been reading. His eyes scanned it for a moment before glancing back at me. "Am I supposed to know who *Walter* is?"

"Probably not. But he's my grandfather. And... you remember that little painted door we found behind the mirror in my room?"

"Yeah?"

I held up my grandmother's key from where it once again hung around my neck. "Well... I unlocked it."

James' eyes widened. "So, it *was* hiding something, just like we thought." He glanced down at the letter in his hand again before his eyes returned to mine. "And this letter… was inside?"

Nodding, I smiled. "Yes… and about a dozen others. Plus a second bundle I haven't even unwrapped yet. And all of them so far were written by my Grandpa Walter, to my grandmother. I think they're like… love letters."

"Crazy." He shook his head. "I wonder what made him lock them up like that. How'd you figure it out, anyway?"

"Grandma Cora left a note in the box where I found her necklace that said, 'key to my heart', so I started wondering if she was referring to…"

"… Lake Elska, right. The painting." Grinning, he leaned over to give my hand a squeeze. "Well, I have to say, it's a pretty damn amazing thing to find. I'm happy for you, Red."

"Thanks." I smiled, then glanced down at my tingling hands, wondering how best to say the next part. "I want you to know, I'm really happy we're doing this. Dating, I mean."

"Good. Me too."

"Is it ok that I'm a little scared, too? I just… don't want to mess anything up."

I'd been avoiding his gaze, but when I looked up, his hazel eyes were filled with wordless emotion, crinkled up in the corners in that way that I loved. "Believe me, I don't want to mess anything up either." He took a breath, looking past me towards the window. "This is a first for me, you know. Wanting to be with someone like this.

Sometimes I've wondered if I ever would. But being with you, it makes me feel, I don't know, brave." His eyes darted back to mine. "I hope it's not weird that I told you that. I'm not always the best at talking about this stuff."

I felt a warmth spreading through me as the tingling in my fingers finally dissipated. I reached across to squeeze his hand. "Not weird at all. You make me feel braver, too."

"Good. Then we must be doing something right."

"I hope so." I smiled. "I like the idea of being brave together."

"Me too. Very much." He held my gaze for a moment, eyes intense, before squeezing mine back. "For now, though, I should let you get back to those letters. And who knows," he said, standing up from his chair, "maybe this will relight that creative spark you've been after." He leaned down to plant a kiss on my forehead before wandering off.

Watching as he disappeared around the corner, I lifted a hand to my forehead, the lingering warmth of his kiss making it impossible for me not to smile.

More than anything, I hoped he was right. About all of it.

Chapter 25

James

"I was wondering when you'd finally show your face around here."

GiGi stood in the doorway, one eyebrow raised as she attempted to look angry. But I'd had many years of experience learning to detect my grandmother's moods—or rather, knowing when she was actually messing with me.

Scooting past her, I kicked off my shoes before dropping down onto the same beige floral sofa that had sat there my whole life. "Yeah, yeah, yeah, go ahead, get it out of your system. I know you've been waiting to give me crap about that kiss you saw last weekend."

"Oh... a *kiss*, you say?"

It was Friday—also the Fourth of July—and I'd been avoiding GiGi's cabin all week, giving myself a chance to slowly settle into the idea of me and Lizzie before I let my grandmother latch onto it herself.

Ok, that was a lie—-once my brain had caught up with the rest of me, I'd been full steam ahead since that day in the lake, no settling in required. Which was, in a way, a little terrifying, too.

I'd wondered if I made her feel pressured by calling her my girlfriend the morning after our first date—but something about the way she'd looked at me suggested it hadn't been a mistake. That she wanted it, too.

Because no matter what, I didn't want to do anything that added to the anxiety I knew she struggled with.

Honestly, the fact that she'd admitted to feeling scared at all made me realize that I was finally ready to stop living that way. And the idea of the two of us learning to be brave together felt... I don't know, *pretty fucking incredible*. And so much less lonely than where I'd been all this time.

I don't even think I'd realized how much I'd been needing someone like her.

For once, I was starting to look ahead, rather than behind—and tonight, I'd be taking Lizzie out for a proper date. Well, not so much a *date* as a holiday cookout at Jesse and Tara's. Unfortunately, there'd be no official fireworks anywhere near Dearing Creek tonight, with the state in drought status after weeks with no rain—making anything fire-related a no-go.

But I had plans for us afterwards as well, which I hoped would keep us plenty occupied.

First, though, I better get this conversation with my grandmother over with. Catching the glint in her eye as she settled into the chair across from me, I realized all I'd done was delay the inevitable.

"The jig is up, GiGi. I've already talked to Jesse and Jack. I know all about this little side bet you three had going." Waggling a finger, I leaned in, eyes narrowed. "Which I don't appreciate, by the way."

She waved a hand, as though trying to shoo away any accountability for her nosey interference. "Calm down now. You're usually so predictable. Can't blame me for trying. 'Course I lost, so... thanks a lot for nothing."

I couldn't help it—seeing her face all screwed up in a frown like that, the laughter just spilled right out of me. A moment later, she was laughing too.

"Serves you right, GiGi. Though I have to admit... watching you lose kind of makes having to go through your little emotional manipulations worth it."

"No idea what you're talking about," she said, shrugging. "I certainly didn't force you to kiss Elizabeth that day. You did that all on your own, boy."

"Uh-huh, sure." Of course, she wasn't wrong. And even though I'd fought my attraction to Lizzie since our coffee shop collision, I didn't regret a single moment of the past week. Except for the fact that I wished I'd gotten over myself and asked her out sooner.

"Anyway, just don't go messing things up with this one, Tater. Take care... she's special."

I nodded, smiling to myself. Luckily, I'd already figured that one out on my own.

"Ok, I know I keep saying this, but that was probably the best burger I've had in ages." Lizzie sat back on the picnic bench across from me, a small bit of steak sauce caught in the corner of her mouth. Doing my best to hold back a smile, I offered her a napkin—which she snatched from my hand with a look of embarrassment. "Sorry, I just... get a little too excited about food sometimes."

"Oh, I've noticed," I said, grinning as I popped a few grapes into my mouth.

"Hey, I'll take it as a compliment," Jesse said as he sat back down in the seat next to me, reaching over to hand Tara a fresh glass of lemonade. "I've worked hard to maintain my *Master of the Grill* title around these parts."

Tara smirked at her husband, one hand resting on her baby bump as the other mussed his sandy blonde hair. "Oh, is that what you're calling yourself now?" She leaned in towards Lizzie. "Ask him how he is with *indoor cooking...*"

"Now listen, wife, that fire was not my fault..."

"Uh-huh, *sure.*" But by now, everyone at the table was laughing.

Jack took another swig of his beer before clapping a hand on Jesse's back. "Look, man... no judgment here. And you do make a damn good burger. But I hate to break it to you... Loon's Landing still has the best in the area."

I nodded. "He's not wrong. They might be even better than Mac's."

"You mean Mac's Bar, in the cities?"

"Yep."

"*Ohhh, boy*... then be glad my brother wasn't able to make it up here this weekend to hear that." Lizzie raised an eyebrow, smirking as she set down her fork. "Because those are fightin' words, where I come from."

"I think I can hold my own just fine, *city girl*."

"Reformed '*city girl*', thank you very much," she said, grinning. "As for the rest, we'll see about that."

Chuckling, I took a sip from my beer as I caught Jack's eye from where he sat on her left, grinning. I already knew that Jesse had grown to love Lizzie over the past couple of months, but it felt good to see Jack giving his official stamp of approval as well.

These guys were my brothers, after all. And she'd managed to slide into the entire group so easily, like she'd been a part of our circle since the beginning. It had been almost impossible to separate her and Tara since arriving a couple of hours ago. Watching her with these people I loved, it'd be damn near impossible not to fall for a woman like this.

But as much as I loved all this, I couldn't wait to have her all to myself again.

Shifting my eyes back to Lizzie, I watched as she took a sip from her hard lemonade, licking away a droplet on her upper lip while I did my best to hold myself in check. It was almost as though she knew exactly what she was doing to me—all of her warmth, her beauty, and the quirky little facets of her personality making me want to show her off and protect her and kiss her senseless, all at the same time.

It was unreasonable, really, how quickly I was falling. But not something I had any interest in fighting anymore.

Leaning my arms against the table, I looked across to my date. "So, you up for a drive?" I'd wanted to keep our first official public date casual, to take the pressure off both of us after the heavier, more intimate tone of our first date. It was good to have this time with friends on such a beautiful night, to see her relaxed and having fun as well.

But I still had more planned for her.

Lizzie looked at me, curious. "A drive? Where are you thinking?"

I bit back a smile. "Oh, it's a special spot. You'll appreciate it, I think. So... whaddya say, Red?"

"I say... I'm in."

I caught both Jesse and Jack shooting a knowing grin in my direction—but for once, I didn't care.

Damn it, I was happy.

Twenty minutes later—after a very *long* Minnesota goodbye and being loaded down with packaged-up leftovers in a cooler—we were making our way east along County Road Three. Looping around the lake, I drove until we reached a narrow gravel road that zagged off to the north, weaving our way through the pines until pulling into a small clearing at the top of a slope. From there, we had a view of most of the town—Lake Elska glittering at the heart of it all, the setting sun coloring it in shades of orange and peach with hints of gold. And by an odd stroke of luck, we were the only car up here tonight.

"*Oh... my God.*"

I glanced over at her in the passenger's seat, feigning innocence. "What?"

By now, though, Lizzie was smirking. "Did you seriously just bring me up to *Neckineezer Hill?*"

It was impossible to hold back the laughter. Neckineezer Hill—technically *Ebenezer* Hill, after one of Dearing Creek's earliest residents, though nobody ever called it that—was well known for being the premiere make-out spot of every coming-of-age teenager in the area.

And though I wouldn't admit it out loud to my date, I'd had my fair share of visits up here as well in my youth. Not that I gave a damn about any of them that came before her.

"Come on, Lizzie... let's go see what all the fuss is about," I said, giving her a wink.

Grinning, she grabbed her door handle and hopped out.

Pulling out the blanket and pillows I'd packed from the backseat, I made quick work of setting everything up in the back bed of the truck. "I'm actually surprised you've heard of this place, not being a local and all."

"Are you kidding me? Most of my best friends grew up here. Of course I know about this place." She glanced at me from across the truck bed, giggling. "I probably shouldn't tell you this, but Brooke actually lost her virginity up here. Not that she really keeps it a secret, anyway."

I laughed along with her as I lowered the back gate. "I'm sure whoever the lucky guy was considered it a badge of honor. Especially if he managed not to get killed by her brothers in the process." Reaching out a hand, I helped her step up onto the truck bed, and soon the two of us were settled into the cozy nook I'd set up for us.

Laying on my back and looking up at the sky, I watched as a lone eagle glided across the kaleidoscope of colors above our heads. It was beautiful how peaceful he looked, up there all on his own. Some creatures really were meant to go through life solo.

I used to think I was one of them.

Now, I turned my head to glance at the woman laying beside me. "So, how about you? Did you ever come up here with a boy during your hot cabin summers?" I'd meant it to be teasing—but even saying the words made something clench in my gut, irrationally jealous that she may have had a history of her own on this hill, too.

"Psssh… no boy wanted to make out with the awkward, nerdy girl with frizzy hair and way too many books." She sighed, eyes skyward. "I just lived vicariously through Brooke and Jules. They were the ones all the boys wanted, anyway."

"Their loss. Which one is Jules again?"

She turned to look over at me. "Jules Silver."

"Why does that name sound familiar?"

"Ever see *Anyone But You? Rome and Julia?*"

I grimaced. "Maybe now's the time I tell you I'm not… *super* into chick flicks."

"Well, you better get on board quick, because I love 'em," she said, nudging my foot with hers. "But anyway, Jules stars in both films."

"Your friend Jules is *that* Jules? Why didn't you tell me?"

She tilted her head with a smug smile. "Technically, I just did."

"Fair point, Blake." I elbowed her in the side, chuckling.

She was quiet for a moment. "I wish Ethan had been able to get up here this weekend. He's been so bogged down with some major tech project that he hasn't been able to get away. I really miss him."

"I get it. I mean, it's how I feel about Jesse and Jack. The world doesn't seem quite right when we're apart."

"Yeah, I can see that. With brothers, I think we both got pretty lucky." She smiled, squeezing my hand before redirecting her gaze upward again.

We lay like that for a while, watching as the sky shifted from gold to purples and deep blues, the moon becoming clearer as the sun dissolved below the horizon. It was easy being myself with Lizzie and not having to worry about hiding parts of me. Being up here together now, surrounded by nature and fresh air and stillness, I felt more happy and relaxed than I had... ever.

But not everything was still. Inside, the slow heat building was becoming harder to ignore.

Now that I had access to this woman I'd wanted for months, it had taken everything in me this week to hold myself back from finding excuses to touch or kiss her. And, of course, countless other things beyond that.

But I'd meant it when I told myself I wouldn't rush. With her, I wanted to be intentional, for her to know I wasn't in this to mess around. That what I wanted with her was *more.*

GiGi was right. Lizzie was *special.* She wasn't like any of the other women I'd been with—where it had never amounted to anything beyond a few casual dates and hookups. I mean, how could it have, when everything in me felt broken, discontent? Of course, I'd probably never given them a fair chance.

But it was about more than brokenness and boundaries. I hadn't felt anything like this with the others, not even an inkling of it.

Lizzie, though. It felt different with her, because… *she* was different. She was hauntingly authentic, in a way I'd never known anyone else to be. And with her, I felt different, too—more settled into myself, not feeling like I had to prove anything. Whatever this was between us, it mattered—for us both.

And I'd meant what I said the other day—being brave with her was something I was ready to do. So I would take things as slow as I could manage, until she was ready to believe it. She was more than worth the wait.

But in the meantime, I'd make sure that the girl who'd never had a chance to make out on Neckineezer Hill would know what it felt like to be the only one this man would ever remember kissing up here.

Reaching over, I brushed away a strand of hair that had fallen into her face when she'd turned her head. She was watching me too, I realized—her eyes darker now in this light but no less striking. I kept my hand near her face, running a thumb down along her cheek, grazing across those full lips of hers.

"Lizzie…"

"Yeah?"

"It's too bad I didn't really know you much back then."

"Why's that?"

My eyes locked on hers. "Because if I had, there's no way that frizzy-haired girl wouldn't have gotten her kiss." Then I leaned over, nibbling along her upper lip, coaxing her mouth open as the tip of my tongue found hers.

As a soft moan escaped her lips, I began kissing her more deeply, though every bit as slowly. Weaving my fingers through her hair, I pulled her in closer—our bodies side by side, not quite touching. I knew if I moved even a centimeter closer to this woman, any resolve I had within me would crumble.

Especially if she kept making noises like that...

Suddenly, a high-pitched whine pierced through the silence not far from my truck. Lizzie broke away, eyes wide. "Um... what the heck was that?"

Pulling away with a disappointed sigh, I raised my head to look around. The light had mostly faded around us now, making spotting anything out here tricky. "I don't know... probably just some raccoon or something." I'd barely finished my sentence, though, when the noise sounded again—whatever was out there, it must be closer than I'd thought. Grabbing the key fob from my pocket, I pushed the button to activate the headlamps, standing now to look over the truck cab as I peered off into the trees just ahead of us.

Then I heard Lizzie's voice behind me. "Oh, my God... is that... *Boner Jr. Jr.?*"

Sure enough, there he was, just past the edge of my headlight beams on the far left. Dearing Creek's most infamous mutt whore was going to town, humping a white fluffy dog I was fairly certain belonged to Bess and Tom Granger from a half mile down the road.

I turned back, doubled over with laughter as Lizzie released a loud snort of her own, clapping a hand to her mouth, as the doggy porn show continued to play out in front of us.

But before I could even begin to pull myself together, the ridiculousness of the situation only multiplied as we found ourselves startled by the flashing lights—and woop-woop siren—from the police car that had pulled up behind my truck in the chaos of the moment.

Holding up a hand to shield my eyes from the light, I squinted as a car door slammed and a tall figure approached.

Then I sighed, running a hand over my face. *Jesus Christ.*

"Good evening, what're you two up to tonight?" Lars Egge—sorry, *Deputy Lars*—strolled over to the truck, resting his arms against the side as he stared up at both of us. I'd known Lars my whole life, graduating from Lake View High the same year—but the guy had always been kind of a dipshit. And for reasons unknown, he'd always seemed to have it out for me and my friends. Giving him the almighty power of town deputy was a decision I still couldn't understand for the life of me.

Sighing, I hopped down onto the ground next to him. "Relax... we're not doing anything, Lars."

He cocked his head to the side, shifting his lanky frame away from the truck as he gave me a smirk. "Not what it looks like to me. You got fireworks up in there?"

"You know we don't, man."

He looked at me skeptically before glancing back towards Lizzie, still halfway up on her knees in the truck bed. "How 'bout you, ma'am... you ok?"

The look she gave him was clearly amused. "Other than being eye-assaulted by Boner Jr. Jr., yes... I'm perfectly fine." As if on cue, the two dogs scurried through the beams of the headlights, Deputy Lars shaking his head in annoyance before turning back to continue his interrogation.

"You're that Blake girl that inherited the cabin on the south side, aren't you? I'm Deputy Lars Egge... but you can go ahead and just call me Lars." He extended a hand across the open hatch towards her, which she leaned forward to accept hesitantly.

"Yes, I'm Lizzie. Nice to meet you... Deputy."

"*Lars*."

"Alright, then... *Lars*. Anyway, we just came out here to watch the sunset. It's such a beautiful night, we couldn't resist."

Deputy Lars nodded, a slow smile creeping across his face. "You picked a beautiful spot for it, best in town. I'd be happy to take you around sometime and show you a few other views that are almost as good..."

"Egge, are you *seriously* trying to hit on my girlfriend right now?"

Shifting his eyes back to me, the satisfied smirk on his face told me all I needed to know. And it made me want to slap the buzz-cut right off his head. Even still, he continued to flap his damn mouth. "Just trying to make sure the lady's ok and that you're not getting her into trouble up here, Tate."

I rolled my eyes. "I'm thirty-four years old, Egge. What the hell kind of trouble would I possibly be up to?"

"That's '*Deputy*' to you, Tate... and watch your tone. Don't forget, I'm an officer of the law." He patted his holster as he thrust his hips forward a bit, which might have been menacing if the man hadn't made it look so ridiculous. I glanced up at Lizzie just as she let out another little snort of laughter. Biting at the inside of my cheek, I did my best to keep my expression neutral.

"As if anyone around here could forget that," I said, not bothering to conceal the eyeroll. "Listen, just because your great-great-granddaddy used to own this hill doesn't mean you need to prowl around here all the time like it's sacred ground."

"Yeah, well... maybe it *is* to some of us. Regardless, the city park curfew starts at ten p.m."

I glanced at my watch. "And it's nine-fifty right now. Don't worry, we'll be on our way by then."

He eyed me for a moment, arms crossed. Then his posture relaxed as he looked back at Lizzie. "You make sure he watches the time, Ms. Blake. And when you decide you're ready for the company of a real man, you know where to find me." With a tip of his head, he strode over to his squad car, making sure to flash his lights and siren a few times as he pulled away, just to be annoying.

By now, Lizzie had hopped out of the truck bed to join me where I stood. Our eyes locked—and after a beat, we both dissolved into fits of laughter, echoing out over the ridge and down across the lake.

And even though I was still annoyed at being interrupted when I finally had Lizzie to myself, I knew it was another night with this woman that I wouldn't forget for a very long time.

JAMES: I've still got your sweater in the back of my truck.

LIZZIE: I know… I've already alerted Deputy Lars to send a squad car to swing by and pick it up. You're looking at hard time for petty theft, bud.

JAMES: Pretty sure you left it on purpose so you'd have an excuse to make out with me again.

LIZZIE: Maybe. Guess we'll find out in five to ten... or maybe two years, if they let you out on good behavior.

JAMES: Might be tough... I'm not always that good.

LIZZIE: Neither am I... ;)

LIZZIE: But don't worry... I'm sure Deputy Lars will be more than happy to keep me company in the meantime.

JAMES: Jesus Christ, woman...

Chapter 26

Lizzie

KAIT: Karaoke starts at seven p.m how many seats should I save?

JULES: Running to rehearsal but PLEASE promise me you'll record everything!

INDI: You know I'm in. Callum is hanging with his friends tonight, so mama bird's flying solo.

LENA: Ugh, I can't… I have to set up centerpiece arrangements for a rehearsal dinner because Bridget bailed on me again tonight. Sorry!

TESSA: I'm out too, ladies… Carlos is dragging me to some Mayo fundraiser. Besides, you know I won't sing in public anymore.

LIZZIE: Booo to Bridget and Carlos… though I seem to recall a stunning rendition of the Grease medley last year at the Beav.

TESSA: We don't speak of that night.

LIZZIE: lol. Anyway, I'll be there. And I'm bringing James. Is that cool?

KAIT: No. No boys allowed.

INDI: Kait…

KAIT: I kid, I kid. I love James. Plus, I hear he does a mean Bon Jovi. Tell him to bring the guys. But you have to sing your song, or no free drinkies this time.

LIZZIE: I'll think about it.

BROOKE: #jealous #sadinthecity

The next several weeks passed by in a blur, like summer was moving in double-time.

All around me, the final stages of my cabin renovation were starting to take shape, and I was amazed at how perfectly James and Jesse were making it all come together. It still felt like my grandparents' place: warm and homey, but modernized. The freshly painted walls and refinished hardwood floors gleamed in a way they never had before—and the guest bathroom had gone from its odd shade of yellow to a clean, crisp white and gray. The master bathroom was also nearing completion, and it was so bright and lovely, I could hardly stand it.

And my revamped kitchen now had an island—*an island!*

The furniture and appliances I'd ordered weeks ago had also started to arrive, and I'd slowly been adding my boho touches around the place. Just a few more weeks and all the work would be done. Looking around at what we'd accomplished so far, I knew Grandma Cora would approve.

Of course, like any home renovation, we'd hit a couple of bumps along the way. One of my brand-new windows ended up cracked by the refrigerator delivery man, so that had to be replaced. And even though Jesse had replaced portions of the plumbing at the start, a slow leak resulted in extra pipe replacements and, of course, more money spent.

Not that I was worried, of course. I knew how lucky I was to have that inheritance—and even though I'd hardly had to use any of it, the security of knowing it was there had changed everything for me. Including giving me time and space to recalibrate and figure things out with my writing—without the stress of a paycheck.

But I was starting to feel—I don't know—*guilty* that I hadn't told James about all of it. It's not that I was ashamed. But part of me wondered—would he see me differently if he knew about the money?

He'd never once questioned how I was supporting myself all these months while I wasn't working. Of course, I know I didn't owe him an explanation. But if we were going to be together, I didn't want there to be any secrets between us, especially this one. I wanted him to know I trusted him to know *everything*.

Because things with us had been going unbelievably well. By now, James and I were spending time together several evenings a week, neither of us wanting to be gone too long from the other. We'd gone out for dinners, made further attempts at tandem kayaking (which thankfully, I hadn't tanked... *yet*), took Bucky for long walks off in the woods past the cabin, and hung out with GiGi on her porch for drinks.

It was still that easy way between us, relaxed, comfortable, uninhibited, and fun—yet always with the crackling electricity that had only managed to amp up even more as the weeks passed. Plenty of kissing, holding, touching, snuggling together on the sofa—and wanting to do more, though we hadn't yet.

And as much as it was driving me crazy to wait—and how badly I really, *really* wanted to have sex with James—I kind of loved that we were taking it slow. No guy I'd ever dated before had been like that. But then, I probably hadn't felt comfortable enough with myself around *any* of them for it to have had a chance to be like this.

James made it easy, though. And instead of sending me into an anxious spiral, wondering if the reason we hadn't slept together yet was due to something inherently unsexy or *wrong* with me—like it normally would—I actually felt the opposite. Just from the way he looked at me, I knew James had to feel what I did.

But that physical pace between me and James wasn't the whole of it. Over the weeks, I'd been feeling a gradual shift between us as we inched closer to the end of our professional relationship. There was a depth and intentionality in our words and the way that we kissed—serious and caring, passionate and playful, all rolled into one. I almost couldn't believe it was real. *Almost.*

It was the first time with any man that I wasn't second-guessing myself in the relationship all the time, wondering if he cared about me, if I was too awkward, too *much*—or if everything I had to offer was enough. Because James was starting to make me believe that I *was*.

Somehow along the way, it was clear we'd begun growing into something greater than either of us had expected—especially for two people who were afraid of being hurt or screwing things up.

We were actually succeeding at being braver together.

Was it ridiculous to only know someone for three months and be feeling like this? I had no idea. No relationship I'd had before had come anywhere close—not even the three years I'd wasted with Randall, whose calls I *still* refused to answer, despite his persistence.

But for some reason, my mother's voice had been popping into my head again lately:

'Slow down, Lizzie, you're letting yourself get carried away again.'

How strange that it was her voice I was hearing—considering I'd never in a million years have considered asking my mother for relationship advice.

It had always felt complicated between the two of us, never easy. I mean, I knew she'd loved me in her own way. I just happened to also be the one who most resembled *her* mother, in both personality and appearance—a visible reminder of another relationship she'd struggled with, for reasons unknown.

Mom was much more like Grandpa Walter—sensible, grounded. My grandmother, on the other hand, sought the light, magic and romance in living a life full of wonder and possibility, trusting love above all else. Yet, even for being such opposites, the two of them balanced each other perfectly—a pair destined to be together. That's why it was the benchmark for love I'd always held for myself.

And I couldn't help but see them within James and myself. But was it too soon?

"Hey, Red... you're so quiet. Are you falling asleep on me?"

I craned my head back to catch James' sexy smile from where he lay behind me on the sofa, holding me in his arms.

"Nope, I never fall asleep while watching one of Jules' movies. It's part of our girl code."

"*That's* part of your girl code?"

"Well, it's really more of a bylaw. But I know it's in there somewhere."

"Noted." Smirking, he shook his head. "Just for the record... and I *might* regret telling you this... I'm not hating this movie."

I raised an eyebrow. "James Tate, are you telling me I've *actually* managed to convert you?"

"Maybe there's hope for this grump yet." He tossed a few kernels of popcorn at my face—one of which I caught in my mouth with a victorious grin as he chuckled, pulling me in closer to his chest. "Can't seem to help myself. What can I say, you do something to me, woman."

Giggling as he nuzzled my neck with a playful growl, it was hard not to believe I'd ever be happier than I was right now, with him. Like *this*.

I mean, yeah, maybe my mother would've been right and I was letting myself get carried away. But, somehow, I didn't think so. Not this time.

****

I was thumbing through the letters in my lap, gazing out across the lawn as I heard a door open. It was late Thursday afternoon, and the guys had already wrapped up work for the day. James would be back to pick me up in an hour for karaoke night at the Thirsty Beaver, but I was taking some time to myself now, out on the porch.

Bucky was curled up on the chair next to me, keeping me company. For some reason, he'd taken to sitting there rather than on the porch itself, like he thought himself human or something.

Such a weirdo... but then, so was I.

That day at the animal shelter, I'd known he was the one for me the second I saw him. And like any of us, he deserved someone who would love him for who he was—with all of his imperfections.

Reaching out to scratch his ears, I glanced back down at the letter I held in my hand. I'd finally allowed myself to read the last letter in the bundle that morning and had spent much of the day re-reading my grandfather's words—something about it was eating at me, though I couldn't put my finger on exactly what:

March 29th, 1967

"My Dear,

I'm sitting with you on the sofa at the cabin tonight, tired from tidying up the yard after the spring thaw. The fireplace is crackling near us, and you've fallen asleep beside me, legs spread across my lap.

And it struck me - you have never looked more beautiful. Pregnancy suits you.

Even though I grumbled about it, I'm glad you convinced me to drive up here for the weekend, just the two of us. I know it'll be a long while until it is ever 'just the two of us' again.

But I cannot wait until our child is born and we can show him this place that we love. To teach him that even when life takes an unexpected turn, love can still win in the end—if you have the will to fight for it.

For my part, your love has reawakened me and reminded me of all that I have... and all I could've lost.

I'll never make that mistake again.

I love you, my darling. Forever.

With love,

Yours, Walter"

I mean, it was a beautiful sentiment. And reading these letters had been helping me to envision my grandfather as more of a romantic than I'd ever thought him to be, despite his happy marriage.

But this letter was different from the others. Maybe it was because my mother was due to be born just a few weeks later—which I'm sure came as a surprise, as clearly Grandpa Walter had been expecting a son.

I felt like it was more than that, though. His words about *'unexpected turns'* or what he'd *'almost lost'*—they were pulling a bit at the foundation of what I thought their marriage, their *love*, was.

Perfect.

So when I heard the door open and saw GiGi come walking out, I decided to wander over. I'd been grilling her a bit off and on over the last several weeks about her friendship with my grandmother, and it had been amazing to get tiny glimpses of her as a much younger woman—ever social, up for shenanigans, and a steadfast friend. I'd learned she had been a coffee addict in her earlier days, just like me—and even back then had eagerly devoured stacks of romance novels. GiGi called her a *'hopeless romantic'*, and I realized how true it was.

And it was exactly what was inspiring me to start writing again. Because I'd decided to finally give in to what felt *true* to me and write a romance novel—this one based on my grandparents' love story.

But first, I needed to make sure I was telling the *right* story.

I tucked the letters back into my book bag, slinging it over my shoulder before heading out across the lawn, Bucky at my heels. For some reason, I hadn't told anyone but James about the letters yet. They were precious, and I just hadn't wanted to share those words with anyone else. Not even my friends, which was a first.

But maybe it was finally time to tell my grandmother's best friend, in the hopes that she could give me some clarity.

"Hey, GiGi... whatcha up to?"

She lifted her head from where she sat in her chair, smiling at me as she set down her crossword puzzle book. "Oh, not much, just gettin' my words done for the day. How are yours going?"

I made a face. "You mean my writing? Still on a break... but I think I might be ready to start up again soon."

"That's wonderful, dear." She glanced past my shoulder. "James already take off for home?"

"Yeah, a while ago... but he's picking me up later for karaoke at the Thirsty Beaver. We're meeting a few of my friends."

"Then I'll alert the townspeople that the Dearie Girls will be out in full force tonight," GiGi chuckled. "Can't believe you talked James into karaoke, though."

I grinned. "Actually, it was *his* idea. Well, sort of. I'm pretty sure Kait somehow got to him first. I was bragging the other day about being amazing at it, which I'm definitely regretting."

She shook her head, eyes twinkling. "Don't let him embarrass you. And make sure you pull him up there for a song or two. He actually has a pretty decent singing voice, which he certainly didn't get from me." She paused, her smile now thoughtful. "You two have seemed pretty happy lately. Things still going well, I take it?"

I felt my face flush. "Really well. Or at least, I think they are?"

"This would make Cora so happy, you know, seeing the two of you together. We always joked that we'd make it happen someday. Just never thought I could convince that boy to get out of his own way."

I smiled, thinking of my grandmother plotting out my romantic future. Somehow, the idea of it didn't surprise me. "Well, James is... pretty amazing."

"Ah, yes. He is. And I love him to death." She leaned in closer. "But he can also be a complete pain in the ass sometimes, so don't let him get away with too much."

"Don't worry, I won't." I laughed, taking the seat next to her. "Say, I wanted to show you something I found in the cabin."

"Oh, yes? What's that, dear?"

"Well, James found this weird little painting in the master bedroom, which turned out to be a door... to a hidden safe." Opening my tote bag, I pulled out the letter, handing it to her. "And inside, there were all these letters."

GiGi's smile—and the color from her face—faded. She took the letter from my hand, scanning the page before her eyes darted up to me, then back to the page again. "This says it's from Walter."

"Right... I think they were love letters to Grandma Cora, before my mom was born."

She looked up from the letter, her eyes almost... haunted. "How'd you get the key?"

"To the safe?" *Ok, now my Spidey-senses were tingling... along with my hands.* "My grandma had it hidden in one of the books she left to me. Why?"

"And were there any... other letters?"

I looked at her. "There was a second bundle, yes... but I haven't opened those yet. I've been trying to spread them out."

"Ok, good... maybe it's best to leave those, then."

"What... and not read them?" My eyes were wide now. "Why shouldn't I read them, GiGi?"

She shrugged, trying to sound casual—but I noticed her body was still tense. Something was definitely up. "No reason. I just thought Cora and Walter would have wanted at least a small part of their love story to remain private." Flashing me a smile that seemed more forced than genuine, she handed back the letter as she stood up from her chair. "Hope you don't mind, but it's time for my bath... and I'm sure you'll be needing to get ready for your date..."

"Yes, but..."

"G'night, dear." She disappeared into her cabin, the screen door slamming shut and punctuating her departure as I sat there, bewildered over the entire conversation—which hadn't at all gone the way I thought it would. And I hadn't even had a chance to ask her if she knew what Grandpa Walter might have been referring to in that last letter.

But the even bigger question now was—*Why the hell did GiGi not want me to read the rest of them?*

Chapter 27

Lizzie

"Alright, all you Thirsty Beavers! Next up at the mic is none other than… uh, Hank Ressler—singing 'Lucy in the Sky With Diamonds'! Let's give it up for Hank!"

"Jesus Christ, not again," Jack groaned as Kait rejoined us at our table near the stage. Hank had already made his way up, his gray-bearded face still flushed and sweaty from performing a rather painful rendition of 'Paradise By the Dashboard Light' twenty minutes earlier. "Kait, I'm begging you, put us out of our misery."

Kait shrugged, waves of highlighted brown hair dancing across her shoulders as the opening melody began playing. "You're welcome to finally get your butt up there, Jack. Unless you're too scared?"

"Picture yourself, in a boat on a river with tangerine trees and marmalade skiiiiiii-iiiesss…."

There was audible groaning throughout the bar, the loudest coming from Jack. "Ok, fine... *you win*. Put me up next. Literally *anything* would be better than this torture."

I glanced over at James sitting next to me and couldn't help but giggle at the expression on his face as Hank continued on painfully through the first verse. "How about you? I thought you and Jack were going to do a little Bon Jovi duet for us?"

James grimaced, tipping his head back to take another swig of his beer. "Is that a challenge?"

I batted my eyelashes. "*Maybe.*"

"Oooh, make her sing *her song* first, James, it's so good..." Indi said, grinning as she drummed her hands on the tabletop.

Kait perked up. "That's right, Lizzie. I seem to recall our deal. No song, no more hooch."

I raised an eyebrow at my friend. "'*Hooch*'? *Seriously?*"

She threw her hands up, laughing. "I don't know. I think I've had one too many Manhattans." She stood up. "I'm gonna grab some water from the bar. Anyone else need anything?" I was about to raise my hand when she pointed a finger to stop me. "Not you, missy, until I see you up on that stage. And you *know* what song is required of you."

Rolling my eyes as Kait walked away, I turned back to see James staring at me. "Alright, Red... time to fess up.

Why are you resisting? Are you a really terrible singer or something?"

"Nuh-uh, our Lizzie's the best," Indi interrupted as she leaned *wayyyy* across the table, clearly in need of water herself. "She's just..."

"... chicken." Kait had returned, passing a few glasses of water around the table.

"Well, I was *going* to say shy..."

I narrowed my eyes at her. "I am *not* chicken." Pushing back my stool without breaking eye contact, I stood up and turned to march towards the stage. Behind me, I could hear Indi squeak out a '*Whoop!!*' as Kait scampered ahead, yanking Hank's microphone cord from the speaker just before he launched into the chorus. He looked crestfallen as the bar erupted into cheers, though a moment later, Doris Minty had wrapped him in one of her signature boob hugs as consolation.

I took an anxious step onto the stage as Kait worked to pull up my music track on her laptop, wondering what the hell I'd gotten myself into. Seeing my face, Kait leaned over and whispered, "I'm sorry, sweetie, you know I love you. And you're a far cry from '*chicken*'." She shrugged, her eyes alight with mischief. "But I just really needed to hear your song tonight."

"I actually *hate* you right now."

"No, really... you *love* me. Break a leg, JT." Grinning, she backed away from the stage, giving me two thumbs up as she whisper-shouted, "*You are ah-ma-zingggg!*"

Clutching the microphone while simultaneously feeling like I was about to barf, I took a step towards the center of the stage while the opening beats began to play.

"Just somethin' about you... way I'm lookin' at you, whatever...keep lookin' at me... you're scared, right?"

Twenty feet ahead, James had a look of perplexed amusement on his face as I made my way through the first half of the song.

"Ain't nobody love you, like I love you...

You're a good girl and that's what makes me trust ya (hey!)...

Late at night, I talk to you...

You will know the difference when I touch you..."

And then, I felt something inside me shift. I don't know what it was exactly that made me just go for it—maybe it was the three glasses of wine. Could've just been the nostalgia of it all. Or perhaps my friends cheering me on, screaming out the backup vocals from their seats. Maybe I just *really* needed to let loose and forget any of the doubts I'd been having since that last letter.

But suddenly, I was seventeen again—memorizing the music video with my friends until we all knew the choreography verbatim.

It was almost like an out-of-body experience—half in memories, half out. But as I sang through my moves on that stage, front and center, all I could see was James. Now, there was *no* mistaking that grin—his entire face lit up as he witnessed the ridiculous, early-aughts spectacle before him.

"Maybe, we'll fly the night away...

I just wanna love you, baby, yeah, yeah, yeah...

Maybe we'll fly the night away...

I just wanna love you, baby…"

I probably should've felt more embarrassed. Any other time, my face would be on fire, my hands all numb and tingly, my guts in a knot at the idea of a room full of people watching me make a *complete fool* of myself.

But the man I'd come to care so much about was also right there—and for once, I just didn't care about all the rest.

As the song mercifully came to an end, Kait and Indi ran up to the stage, laughing and screaming, *"That was incredible!"* as I stepped down with a grin.

But as I looked across to James, I noticed his expression had changed—something had caught his eye across the room and his smile was fading fast. Walking over to the table as Kait cued up Indi's next song, I planted a kiss on his cheek and threw my arms around his neck. I could feel his body tense beneath mine—clearly, something was wrong. Pulling back, I turned my head to spot a middle-aged woman with dark hair looking in our direction from across the bar. But the pinched smile on her face was far from friendly.

I turned back to James. "Hey, is something wrong? And what's with that woman over there?"

He finally looked down at me, his smile making a brief appearance before his eyes darted back towards her again. "She's nobody, just a former client. Everything's fine."

Jack had walked around the table by now, throwing an arm around me. "Lizzie, I have to say... that was probably the best fucking rendition of a Timberlake song that I've *ever* heard. The fact that you haven't been signed by a label yet is criminal."

Tearing my gaze away from James, I grinned at his friend. "What can I say? This talent was literally *years* in the making," I said, giggling. "You guys are up after Indi, though. Don't forget."

"Oh, I haven't... James, which song are we doing?"

James glanced over at Jack, still distracted. "Whatever you want, man."

Jack gave him a weird look, then shrugged, walking over to talk to Kait as Indi began warbling through her second song of the night, her long mane of curly hair managing to look both wild and beautiful at the same time.

Still so unfair.

But as we drove home a half hour later—after the guys took the house down with their rendition of 'Wanted Dead or Alive'—I knew something was off. Whether it was about that woman who'd been watching us or something else, he was clearly bothered.

And it was *also* clear that he didn't intend to tell me why.

I sat on my bed early the next morning, Bucky snoring against me. I'd barely slept, my mind perseverating all night over the woman at the bar. I wished I would've thought to ask Kait who she was. Because she didn't seem like *just a client*. Not that I expected James not to have any romantic history—I wasn't one to talk. It just felt like there had to be something more going on.

But it wasn't only that situation that had kept me up last night. Sitting before me on the bed was the second bundle of letters, still wrapped tightly, ensuring their secrets remained hidden.

I hadn't been able to stop thinking about my strange conversation with GiGi since it happened. Nor could I do as she suggested—lock away the rest of the story about my grandparents, pretending I'd never found these letters in the first place.

But I still had to wonder—was she right? Was I invading their privacy? If that were true, why did Grandma Cora leave me her books as well as the cabin, knowing that their discovery was inevitable?

There was something she wanted me to know here, I was certain of it.

Slowly, I untied the bundle, opening the first letter in the stack. I noticed a difference in handwriting... but it wasn't my grandmother's.

May 2nd, 1966

"C –

I know I shouldn't be writing this letter.

But I can't help myself, nor can I pretend I have no desire to know you better.

One week ago, I met the most beautiful woman I'd ever laid eyes on. But what's made you unforgettable are these glimpses of who you are on the inside, through every conversation since.

Now that I know the depth of your beauty, the idea of you—of us—is even more impossible to shake.

Please, allow us to at least be good friends. I know it's unfair to hope for more. And I will respect your wishes.

But I am here, in any capacity you choose... if you're willing.

Yours,

M.H."

I was only vaguely aware of the letter falling into my lap, of Bucky tilting his head back to lick my palm—because inside, my mind was reeling.

Who the hell was M.H.?

Chapter 28

James

"Hey, man, where's your head at today?"

I looked over at Jesse, who had paused in caulking the shower door to stare at me. "Sorry, just feeling distracted. Did you need something?"

He shook his head, amused. "I was asking if the rumors were true that you and Jack blew the roof off the Thirsty Beaver last night."

Smirking, I continued to work on screwing in the brass light fixture Lizzie had chosen over the sink. "Exactly who'd you hear that rumor from?"

"Jack."

We both laughed, but my mind returned to last night, still alternating between moments of absolute joy in thinking about my girlfriend—and dread over watching Denise Kinney take in every moment of it.

It had been a great night, up until then. Everyone had been in good spirits, and Lizzie—*God, Lizzie*. Her actual performance during karaoke had been the icing on the cake, and even now I couldn't help smiling at her rendition of the boy bander classic.

Watching her up on that stage—relaxed, goofy and carefree, despite anything that may have been weighing her down—well, it made me never want to look away. She looked so radiant, *so happy*.

More than anything, I knew without a doubt that I would do damn near anything to make sure she always felt that way.

But then I'd spotted *fucking Denise Kinney*, looking on like a predatory hawk from her barstool perch. She'd been surrounded by her clan of Cabin Cougars—how most of us referred to the handful of middle-aged, upper-class women from the area all rumored to treat Lake Elska's summer season like their own personal buffet of man meat. Most were also married, but half of their husbands were just as bad—Joe Kinney, one of the worst.

And every single one of them thought their status made them untouchable. It was disgusting.

But it wasn't that I was worried about Denise wanting another go at me like she had before. Instead, the look on her face when she saw me with Lizzie made me realize she might still be harboring some bitterness, considering I'd used the excuse of 'professional boundaries' with her. And knowing what the Kinneys were capable of, it could make life a whole lot messier if she decided to act on it.

And I couldn't let anything happen to what I had with Lizzie. I'd do anything to protect it and her.

For the time being, though, it would be smart to keep a lower profile. Lizzie and I had been planning to run over to Heartwood for dinner later on, but maybe I'd see if she minded doing dinner here at her place instead. Prevent the possibility of running into Denise again so soon or exposing Lizzie to unnecessary stress.

Because she didn't deserve any of it.

Glancing over, I noticed Jesse had paused in his work, focused now on his phone screen, brow furrowed.

"Anything wrong?"

Jesse looked up, the worry evident on his face. "Look, I didn't want to tell you, seeing as we are so close to the end of Lizzie's reno… but I might need to take a day or two off. It's Tara."

I felt my heart quicken. "What's going on with Tara?"

Tucking his phone back into his pocket, he sighed. "Her doctor is concerned about both her and the baby. We already knew it was going to be more of a high-risk pregnancy anyway, because of her thyroid issues. But it seems like things are flaring up worse. Being on her feet all day at the clinic isn't helping things."

"Ok, so what can they do to help her? She's still got like three months or so left of her pregnancy, right?"

"They want her to go on bedrest, take an early leave. If she doesn't, they said she could lose the baby or have other complications." Jesse's usually happy face was solemn. "And I'm not willing to risk either one."

Tara had been a registered nurse for the past six years and loved her job—but it had taken her and Jesse a few years to finally get pregnant. Hearing this news must've been a tough pill to swallow.

"Jesus," I said, running a hand through my hair. "I'm sorry, man. Will the clinic work with you guys on it?"

"Oh, they'll hold her job and just bring in a locum to cover things while she's out; that part isn't a problem. But her current benefits will only cover sixty percent of her pay for eight weeks total. Whether it's bedrest or her maternity leave, that's the max."

"Shit, that's not even going to get her through the rest of her pregnancy, much less any time after the baby comes."

"Yep." Jesse shrugged, and I could see the stress written all over him. Between his career shift and a post-pandemic freeze on pay increases at the clinic, I knew things had been tight for them for a while. And I planned on giving Jesse a raise as soon as we completed Lizzie's renovation, along with every upcoming project. I could easily afford it, and he was family. He was worth it. They both were.

But I also knew I could do a lot more than that.

"Listen, I want to help."

"No."

"Jesse..."

"I mean it." His tone was sharp, in a way I rarely heard it. "This is why I didn't even really want to fill you in on what was going on. I knew you'd try and give us money. But I've got it."

"I know you do. But the money would make it easi—"

"James, I don't fucking need your pity."

"This isn't pity, man, I swear. I've got resources to share… and, you're family."

"Yeah, well, this is *my* family. And I know how to take care of them. Just worry about yourself, alright?" Jesse's eyes blazed, his fist balled at his side. "All I need from you is a day off to help get Tara settled at home."

The anger in him rattled me—I couldn't remember the last time I'd seen him like this. I was quiet for a moment as we stared at one another. "Of course, whatever you need."

"Thanks." Jesse turned away to continue his work on the shower, and I knew it was his way of putting a cap on the issue. I tried to refocus on what I'd been working on, but my head wasn't in it. A few minutes later, he spoke again. "I'm done here…. I'll clean up and head home." But he clearly wasn't asking. And before I could even think to respond, he was gone.

I stood in the silence of that room for a long time after he left, thinking about Jesse, and Denise—and for what seemed like the millionth time, how money seemed to do *nothing* but cause problems.

Chapter 29

James

A couple hours later, Lizzie and I were in my truck, headed seven miles west to a small Mexican restaurant in the neighboring town of Heartwood. After cleaning up back at my place, I came back to find Lizzie looking moody as well. She'd been out for a good portion of the day, so I hadn't seen her much—but one look on her face told me staying in tonight wouldn't do either of us any good. We needed a distraction—the *good* kind.

We'd been driving in silence for most of the way, the two of us stuck in our heads about one thing or another. Half a mile down from the restaurant, I couldn't take it anymore. Pulling over to the side of the road along a wooded stretch, I shut off the engine and looked over at her.

"I had a fight with Jesse today."

Lizzie's head turned towards me from her side of the vehicle, eyes wide. She knew how tight I was with both Jesse and Jack, how rare it was for us to argue. Or even for me to open up about the things that were bothering me. I'd like to think it was progress.

"Ugh, I'm sorry. What happened?"

"Tara's having some pregnancy complications, so she has to go on bed rest for her last trimester. They're holding her job, but her benefits plan isn't giving them much leeway. And she'll have nothing left for her maternity leave once the baby arrives."

"That's total crap. God, poor Tara." Her eyes were sympathetic. "But I don't understand... Why did you two fight?"

I sat there for a moment, trying to figure out the best way to tell her the rest of it. "I offered them money to help out with their finances."

"Wow, that's incredibly generous of you."

"Not really..."

Lizzie raised an eyebrow. "Yes, it *is*. When are you going to accept that you're a good man, James?"

"If anyone can make me believe it, it's you, Red."

She smiled at me for a moment, chewing on her lower lip in that way that drove me half-crazy. "I'd like to help too, if I can."

"No, that's not necessary. Besides, Jesse wouldn't take it, anyway. He turned me down flat."

"Maybe he's worried you can't spare the extra?"

"Trust me, that's not the reason." I took a breath. *Ok, here goes.* "Lizzie, there's something I haven't mentioned, something I should've told you a while ago now."

She looked at me. "Yeah... me too."

Now I was the one that was curious. "Really? What?"

Her cheeks flushed. "It's about my situation, why I moved up here. I didn't just inherit the cabin from my grandmother. Mariah, Ethan and I each inherited quite a bit of money as well after she and our mom passed away. We were the only living heirs, so everything went to us. But we had no idea they had so much stockpiled." Her eyes were avoiding mine now, and I watched her rub at her hands—in that way she did whenever she seemed anxious. "It's how I've been able to afford renovations on the cabin and why I could take time off to write."

For a moment, I didn't know what to say. This didn't seem real. How was it possible that we'd both landed in this place—taking different paths, but with the same outcome? It's almost as if it had been... written or something.

As she glanced back at me now, her eyes guarded, I realized it wasn't only feelings of grief, or imposter syndrome with her career, that she'd been battling with. There was shame in there, too. It was a feeling I knew all too well—and struggling in silence never did anyone a damn bit of good.

"Thank you for telling me."

"You're not mad?"

I chuckled briefly. "Of course not. Not in the least. Because... well, I've got money, too."

"I wasn't trying to imply that you're brok—"

I held up a hand to stop her. "Sorry, what I meant was... the coincidence is going to sound crazy, but I *also* inherited money. From my father, after he died a few years ago." As always, I felt the defensiveness rise up in me as I said it, like I'd somehow *asked* for any of this. But that argument was only ever with myself, not her. "He never remarried or had other kids, just ran his company, so... I was the only one left." Now it was my turn to look away, feeling the buzzing grow inside my head. "I'm... sorry I never said anything before. I don't really talk about it, not with anyone."

Eyes wide, she was quiet for a minute. "Jesse knows, though. Jack too?"

I nodded. "And GiGi, of course."

"And Jesse was upset because...?"

"I think he's struggling with feeling like he's not contributing enough to his family." Saying the words, I felt the sting of them—and knew I'd feel the exact same way as my friend. It was a feeling of pride, like he wasn't pulling his weight, at least in the way he thought he should be.

I'd tried offering him a larger salary when we'd kicked things off with Horizon Remodeling, and he'd refused. But I hadn't done it out of obligation. He was also a damn good plumber, and his skill set stretched far beyond that. This project at Lizzie's had more than proven his talents as a foreman, managing the contractors we'd brought on for various elements. Plus, it made me see that his work on finishings had become just as good as my own over the years.

Which is why I realized what I should've done from the very start. I should've asked Jesse to join me in this business as a partner, not an employee. It was something I'd be remedying soon—after we worked through the rest of this mess.

Because I couldn't afford to allow this money to create any more division in my life. It had been like a fucking noose around my neck for way too long, and I was tired of feeling like I couldn't breathe.

I was surprised, though—letting Lizzie in on my secret wasn't as hard as I'd thought it would be. If anything, the rope felt like it might've even loosened a bit. I wondered if it felt that way for her, too.

I looked over to Lizzie, who was still watching me—but all I could see was compassion, not judgment. I owned that one myself. That look in her eyes, I almost was afraid to hope for what it might be.

"You're a really good man, James, wanting to help your friends."

"I don't know about that," I said, shrugging. "Jesse and Tara, they're family. And I don't need all that money... might as well give it to someone who could make better use of it."

She gave me a small smile. "I get it. But... you should still talk it through with Jesse. They'll need your support in other ways now, too."

"Yeah, I know." I let out a breath I hadn't even realized I'd been holding. "Glad I told you, though. About the money, I mean."

"Yeah, me too." She paused. "I don't want there to be any more secrets between us, ok?"

"I don't either. I'll always be honest with you, Lizzie. I mean that." Then I realized—she was crying. "Oh, babe... I'm sorry, did I say something wrong?"

"No, no... it's nothing you did..."

"Well, did something happen? Does this have anything to do with why you were gone today?"

She nodded. "I went over to Indi's for a while, after I decided to open the second bundle of letters." Wringing her hands in her lap, she continued. "GiGi told me I should just leave it alone when I told her about them. But my grandpa's last letter was weird... I thought maybe going through the others would help me understand."

"And... did they?"

"No... I mean, I don't know." Her eyes squinched shut. "I think Grandma Cora might've had an affair."

"*What*? Why do you think that?"

"The other letters... they were still love letters but written in a different handwriting. And the few I've read so far were signed with the initials, 'M.H.'. So they weren't from my grandfather."

I reached out, wiping away a stray tear that had trickled down her cheek as she opened her eyes again to look at me. In the light of early evening, the flecks of gold in them burned. "I bet there's a perfectly good explanation for all of this. Why don't we both talk to GiGi about it? Maybe she'll remember something."

"But what if... it's true? I don't know if I'll be able to handle it."

"Well, then... we'll deal with that together, too. I'm not going anywhere, Red. I'm in this, with you." We gazed at each other for a moment. It felt like there was so much more to say—the words buzzing around inside of me, anxious to burst out.

But just then, the loud revving of a motorcycle interrupted us as it zoomed past and the moment was lost.

Giving her hand a quick squeeze, I turned the key in the ignition. "How about we grab dinner? I think we both need it."

"Yeah, sure... that's fine."

She turned back towards her window as I pulled out onto the road, thinking that if it hadn't been for that damned motorcycle, those words in my head might've spilled out, without knowing if it was the right thing for either of us.

An hour or so later, we were relaxing at La Cantina, munching on the last few tortilla chips from the basket after paying our bill. The mood felt lighter now after dinner and a drink as we chatted about any other topic except the ones weighing on our minds.

So basically the last thing I needed was Luke Hardon to spot us from across the restaurant, walking over in our direction with some leggy blonde in a short skirt—the latter of whom looked less than thrilled to be seen in a place known for their all-you-can-eat house-made chips and salsa.

I mean, fuck... this guy?!

"Hey, man, funny running into you over on my turf this time."

I raised an eyebrow. "Last time I checked, the Hardons don't own all of Heartwood. You just happen to live here."

"Sorry, wasn't trying to imply that we did. I don't often see you crossing the Dearing Creek city line, is all." But Luke was all smiles, his eyes darting over towards Lizzie as he extended a hand. "Hi, I'm Luke. I went to high school with James. You're Elizabeth, right? The one who bought the cabin over by Georgia LaMott's place?"

Lizzie smiled. "It's Lizzie, and yes. My family has owned that cabin for a long time, but none of us had been up here for years."

"Ah, I see. I'd looked into acquiring the land a few years ago as a business investment but was told the owner wasn't interested in selling." He shrugged with a laugh. "Guess it worked out ok in the end."

"Yes, everything worked out just *dandy*," I said, annoyed that he wouldn't take the hint and end the conversation.

I noticed Lizzie giving me a weird look before continuing. "So, Luke, what kind of work is it that you do?"

"I help run my family's third generation custom wood furniture business, mostly for high-end clients and commercial properties. My brothers and I do everything, start to finish—direct from the trees themselves."

"Wow, that sounds incredible. And is it all custom work, or do you have a shop as well? I might want to look at buying something for the cabin."

Luke grinned. "Only custom, but I'd be happy to help you out. Why don't you give me your num—"

I held up a hand, unable to listen to this conversation anymore. "No, that won't be necessary. Lizzie and I should get going."

His smile faded a bit; glancing at his date, Luke gave me a quick nod. "Of course. Just one last thing..." he said, leaning closer. For a second, my mind shot backwards twenty years again, hearing his voice heckling me in the hallways of Lake View High, along with the rest of his shitty, entitled posse. *"Quit walking around here acting like you're better than the rest of us, Tate. Everyone knows you're far from it..."*

But present-day Luke had lowered his voice. "It's good that I ran into you, because I wanted to give you a heads-up on something."

"Yeah? And what's that?"

"Have you done anything to piss off the Kinneys? Because my friend Sam is considering making an investment in some property they own... Apparently, Denise Kinney called him today and told him very specifically to avoid your company for any renovations, since I'd already recommended you to him. She said it would be a bad business move and could possibly affect the deal."

I felt the anger bubbling in the pit of my stomach, thinking about the incident at the bar the night before. Forcing a smile, I shrugged. "Can't think of why. Maybe he was mistaken."

"No, I don't think he wa—"

I glowered at him. "G'night, Hardon."

Luke's body language was now tense as well—but rather than argue, he nodded, grabbing for his date's hand. "Nice to meet you, Lizzie. Good luck with the cabin. Hope you both have a good night."

As they walked away, I could hear his date say, *"Please tell me this place has champagne. I need a buzz if we're gonna eat in a shithole like this, Luke..."* I smirked to myself before turning back to Lizzie, to see if she'd caught the woman's comment as well. But instead, I noticed she was staring at me with an odd expression on her face.

"What was that all about?"

"What?"

"Do you have a problem with Luke Hardon or something?"

I shrugged. "No, just don't like him or his family, is all."

"Why's that?"

"They're a bunch of rich assholes. They've got a ton of money, so they act like they own everyone and everything around here. Just like the Kinneys... and the Taylors too, for that matter."

Her eyes widened. "If you're talking about the Taylors in Dearing Creek... their daughter Tess is one of my best friends, remember?"

"Yeah, well, maybe that's true... All I know is, her parents and all the rest of them have treated a lot of people around here like shit over the years. Including my family."

She was quiet for a moment. "Well, what about everything we just talked about before coming here? You and I both inherited a lot of money... Does that automatically make us like all the rest of them?"

"What? No."

"How do you know for certain?"

"Trust me, I know." I raised an eyebrow. "Because we're different."

"Are we, though? Because from my perspective, you were pretty rude to Luke a moment ago. It seemed like he was genuinely trying to be nice."

I snorted. "Trust me, Luke Hardon hasn't been 'nice' a day in his life, unless it somehow benefited him. He treated me like shit all the time when we were kids."

"That may be true... and I'm really sorry you had to go through all that. But aren't you basically doing the same thing to him now?" She rested her hand on mine. "All I'm saying is, maybe he's changed. And maybe it's time to forgive and move on."

"No, these people will *never* change, Lizzie. You have no idea what we've had to deal with." The words were out before I could stop them, and I could see the hurt flash across her eyes. Standing up, I shoved my wallet back into the pocket of my cargo shorts. "Look, I don't want to talk about this right now. Let's head home... it's getting late."

"Yeah... fine."

But this time, the silence on the drive home felt *anything* but fine. Words both spoken and unspoken hung heavy in the air between us, both directions of tonight's drive overwhelming me with the weight of their revelations.

And I couldn't stop running through what Lizzie had said, what all of this meant—even with Luke's warning, coming out of nowhere. Even I had to admit that the guy had seemed like he was trying to help. But could a man like Luke Hardon ever actually change? And why now?

All of it left me questioning myself, and I had no idea what to do about any of it.

And most of all, I couldn't help but wonder... *What if she was right?*

Chapter 30

Lizzie

KAIT: Ground Control to Lizzie… where are you hiding?

LENA: We just want to help…

INDI: Sorry, hon… you stopped answering my texts. I had to call for backup.

INDI: (Please don't be mad.)

LIZZIE: Ladies, I'm fine. You can go back to your regularly scheduled programming.

KAIT: Sorry to say… but you're not very convincing, my dear. I call bullshit.

Another week passed, and I floated through it like a zombie—my mind and heart in a constant tug-of-war between the past and the present.

I hadn't been able to stop thinking about my conversation with James, or that incident between him and Luke at the restaurant. Since that night, each of us seemed to be giving the other a wide berth, both during workdays at the cabin and evenings apart. It wasn't silence, exactly—rather the sort of tip-toeing one does when they are afraid of saying the wrong thing, so they avoid talking altogether.

So much for being brave.

But as much as my mind needed space to process everything, the pause between us had only made me feel worse. I'd become used to our lives being mostly intertwined over the past month—and now that James and I seemed to be unraveling a bit, amongst everything else that was happening, it felt like I had nothing secure to hold on to.

And, well... *I missed him.*

I'd be lying, though, if I said his attitude towards people with money didn't bother me, even though I knew I was only looking at one piece of the story. I mean, he was right—I had no idea what had gone down in the past between him and Luke or anyone else, because this was the first I was hearing about it. And of course, some of his feelings about money had to be based on where his own had come from. He and I both carried baggage about what we'd been given. Maybe judging him in any of this was hypocritical.

But the real reason I couldn't get that night out of my head wasn't about the money. The fact that he'd just shut down, unable—*or unwilling?*—to talk through it at all the moment he'd gotten upset made me feel like he'd slammed a metaphorical door in my face. Considering how vulnerable we'd been with one other already, why was *this* any different?

Then there was the bigger question I couldn't think about, much less say out loud—How long would it take before James found something about *me* that he couldn't deal with, and just shut me out for good? Was it inevitable?

Because I had an entire vault full of flaws and crazy bits that had barely even come out to play yet. There was only one person on this planet, really, who'd ever seen them all. She just also happened to be the person who'd hidden away more of herself than I had ever realized.

So yeah, it wasn't only this situation with James that was messing with my head. It was also the fact that my grandmother—the woman I'd looked up to my whole life—wasn't the person I'd believed her to be.

Ever since opening that first incriminating letter, I hadn't been able to stop obsessing over it. I'd even gone ahead and opened several others as well—both praying for answers and terrified of what else I might uncover. The only thing I wanted to find was proof that I'd been wrong, so I could return to my happy little land of blissful ignorance.

But poring over the words on those yellowed pages again and again had only brought me to the same conclusion—that only a few months before my grandfather had composed his series of love letters to Grandma Cora, she'd somehow become involved with another man.

Which meant the vision I'd had of both my grandmother *and* their marriage was nothing but a steaming pile of lies.

It almost felt like she'd betrayed *me*, too—and *God*, did it hurt. She'd been the one I'd always felt sure about, especially when my world felt murky and hard. Now I was questioning everything—my beliefs about love, everything she'd taught me—and it felt like I was drowning in all of it.

And all I wanted was to be alone.

It's why I was lying by myself on Friday afternoon, holed up with my dog and my anxiety in the quiet sanctuary of my bedroom, now that James had wrapped up his work for the day and left for home. Minus Jesse, of course, who'd taken the day off to help get Tara settled.

As with the rest of the week, there'd been no goodbye kiss from my boyfriend—only another quick, cordial smile before he headed out the door, without a single word about anything that didn't involve the renovation.

It was the dance we'd been doing all week, and I'd hated every single second of it—even though yeah, I'd been avoiding the confrontation, too. Which was ridiculous, considering we were both grown-ass adults.

But as much as I wanted to get right back to where we'd been and fix it all, the emotional one-two-punch of everything still had me lying on the mat. And I was so damn tired of feeling defeated.

For now, I just sat here, reading through the words over and over and over, until they blurred together in a stormy cloud of betrayal...

"C-

How cruel is it that our paths crossed one year too late? But even if I can't have all of you, I am grateful for this... for our stolen moments, the feel of your hand in mine, the memory of you upon my lips..."

I looked towards the ceiling, repeating the same ques-tions I couldn't stop asking—"*Why, Grandma? Why did you do it? And why was it necessary that I ever find out?*"

Bucky whimpered from where his head lay on my lap, and glancing down, I scratched behind his ears as I reached for a tissue. "You hungry, boy?"

The buzzing of my phone laying next to the stack of letters on my bed yanked me back into reality. Picking it up to read the message, I rolled my eyes.

> *BROOKE: You're hiding out with a book under a quilt again, aren't you?*

> *LIZZIE: For your information, I do not have a book with me.*

> *BROOKE: Maybe not… but you're reading *something*, right? Still counts.*

> *LIZZIE: Wait, how d—*

My rapid-fire rebuttal was interrupted by a tapping on my bedroom window—bolting upright, I saw my friend's face peering through the other side, grinning and wav-ing like a beautiful blonde lunatic. Flipping her the bird while rolling my eyes, I shook my head at her—but even

I couldn't help laughing as I stomped my way over to unlock the back door.

I'd barely opened it before she pulled me into a tight hug. "Before you start bitching at me," she whispered into my ear, "just know—I brought reinforcements." Behind her, I could see Kait's car parked next to Brooke's Audi, with Indi, Kait and Lena unloading a handful of grocery bags.

As if on cue, everything before me turned all blurred and watery. Because it wasn't my usual solitary confinement that I needed after all.

It was the comfort of being surrounded by people I knew I could count on.

I could be wrong, but in my introverted, *bury-myself-in-anxiety* mind, it almost felt like... *progress.*

"Oh, sweetie... did you *really* think we couldn't tell something was up with you?"

We were all camped out in my living room, relaxing on my new furniture that had arrived earlier in the week with a spread of snacks and beverages surrounding us. I sat somewhere in the middle of my friends, having dragged my grandmother's traitorous quilt out from the bedroom.

Kait was looking over at Brooke now, with her usual expression that was half sarcastic eye raise, half smile. "Yup, we're all very fluent in Lizzie-speak. With you, 'I'm fine' basically means 'I've introverted and I can't get up'. If we'd waited much longer, you may have actually smothered yourself under that quilt."

"Alright, alright... I get it," I said, making a face as I pulled it tighter across my shoulders. "I'm sorry to make you all worry. Like I told Indi last week, I just needed time to work things out in my head."

Indi topped off my glass of Sauvignon Blanc. "And? Have you?"

"Well... no."

"Pretty much what we figured. Being stuck in your head never does you any good, darling. And that's why y—"

"... that's why we're here. To listen," Lena said, looking pointedly at Kait before passing me the bowl of tortilla chips. Bucky lay nearby, keeping one eye open for any extra crumbs that might fall his way.

Brooke leaned down and ruffled the top of his furry head. "What they said. Go on, spill your big ol' Lizzie heart."

And so I told them everything—James, the incident from the previous week, the discovery of my grandmother's letters, and how it all went from an incredible gift to something I wish had stayed hidden.

The one thing I'd left out was the book I'd been so excited to write about my grandparents' love story. All of the inspiration from a couple of weeks ago had, by now, completely evaporated. I mean, how could I even consider writing it—even if it *was* fiction?

As always, they listened, peppering my confessional with advice—Lena and Indi's thoughtful and patient, with Kait and Brooke's more lighthearted yet pointed. It was a balance in perspective these women had given me for so many years—as an anxious, often emotional person, it was one that I desperately needed.

And after a week where I thought I'd never be able to see clearly again, I felt the clouds start to lift.

Starting with James. I needed to stop avoiding the uncomfortable and talk things through, even if I wasn't ready for what I might hear.

As for the letters? Well, I had a feeling my neighbor might have some insight to share on that topic. And as much as I dreaded the potential of it dragging me down even further, moping around in this weird gray *ick* was doing nothing but keeping me all wounded and afraid.

Because if there was ever going to be any hope of me moving forward with my relationship, or returning to my writing, I needed to be brave—in all of it.

A couple hours later, the five of us were finishing off our fourth bottle of wine—and halfway through a sheet pan covered in our traditional favorite, *Nachos à la Kait*—when there was a loud knock at the front door.

"*Uh-oh... someone's hee-eeere...*" Indi croaked—a little too loudly—from her end of the loveseat, before popping another chip into her mouth.

Lena threw a pillow at her head from where she lay on the adjacent sofa, already circling the drain after two small-ish glasses of wine. "Quiet, Indi...You're gonna wake the neighbors!"

Kait had already tiptoed her way to the large picture window, shifting the curtains aside as she peered out into the darkness. "Oooh, it's for Lizzie."

"*Doi*, of course it's for me. I *live* here." I made a grab for Brooke's outstretched hand as she attempted to yank me upwards, the two of us dissolving into giggles as we nearly fell to the floor in the process.

It caused a domino effect as Indi also erupted into snorting laughter behind us, rolling down off the sofa and onto the floor. "'*Doi*'? Nobody has said '*doi*' since, like, nineteen ninety-three."

By now, Kait was tapping on the window, waving with a huge grin at whomever was standing on the porch. "I dunno... I hear '*doi*' is making a comeback." Laughing, she craned her head to look back at us, holding tight to the window frame. "But you better hurry, Lizzie... 'cause your boyfriend's here to make up... um, make out? No, wait, maybe both. Yeah, he definitely *better* do both..."

A moderately drunk Brooke now looped her arm through mine, dragging me towards the door in her excitement. "Oh, he wants to do allll the things with our Lizzo... but the question is," she said, gripping the handle as she swung the door open dramatically, "are you *worthy* of her, dear sir?"

There stood my super-hot boyfriend—looking equal parts confused and amused. "I, uh, think that's up to the lady of the house. But I'm trying to be." Biting back a smile, James' eyes scanned our group, now huddled together in the open doorway. "Looks like I'm missing quite the party."

For my part, I was biting my lip, for some reason still dealing with a case of the nervous giggles as I stared at him—irritated that he was making things hard for me, but, mostly, wanting to kiss him until neither of us could breathe. Because I was so *fucking happy* that he was here.

But no, talking to my boyfriend was a job for *serious Lizzie.*

And I had *serious* things to say. So I needed to stop laughing.

Like, now.

"No, this isn't a '*party*'... I'm *very, very serious*, James," I said, shaking a finger in his face for emphasis, laughter trickling out in spite of me.

I said I was serious, damn it.

He smirked as he took me in, arms crossed. "Yeah, I can tell." His eyes darted back to my friends. "How much wine have you ladies had tonight?"

"Not enough!" Kait hollered from the rear, and we all dissolved into giggles. Well, except for Lena, whose distinctive groan could be heard as she shuffled back towards the bathroom. "Want some?"

"No, thanks, I'm good," he said, chuckling. "But I'd like to borrow Lizzie… you think you all could give us a minute?" He glanced back to me. "Only if you're willing, of course."

"Alright, Tate," Brooke said, narrowing her eyes at him. "But just know, we're keeping our eyes on you. So you better not mess with our girl."

He held up a hand, now looking serious. "I won't, promise. I only want to talk."

I glanced back at my friends, feeling myself sober up the teensiest bit. "It's ok, guys, I've got this."

Kait reached out to squeeze my hand before ushering the others back inside. "Alright, then. Who *wants brown-ies?*"

As the door swung shut, I could hear the brownie chant begin as I turned to face James again—my face and hands all numb and tingly as I took him in. He gave me that same hesitant smile I'd seen on his face all week, and I realized he must be nervous, too.

"Can we sit down together, do you think? Down by the fire pit?"

I shrugged, trying to seem casual. "Sure, fine." Starting towards the stairs, I gave a slight wobble, feeling the familiar flutter in my chest as his arm wrapped around my back to hold me steady. We walked that way down the gradual slope towards the lake, neither of us saying a word until we were settled, side-by-side, on the Adirondack chairs.

Thankfully, it was James who broke the silence first. "So, listen... I'm really sorry for interrupting your girl's night, but I wanted to talk to you about the other day. Because it's been eating at me all week."

"Yeah?"

"Yeah. I know I came across as kind of..."

"Rude? Angry? *Judgey*?"

He chuckled again, but this time, the smile didn't quite meet his eyes. I hated how the darkness took away their warmth, leaving me guessing. "Yes. All of those things. And... I'm sorry. But you deserve to know why."

"Alright, I'm listening."

He took a breath. "So, after my mom died, and it was just me and my grandparents, I struggled... for a long time. All three of us did. I was so angry at my dad for walking away, for caring more about his company and his money than anything else."

I reached out to place a hand on his, saying nothing as he continued.

"Pops was working as master electrician for Hardon & Son's Design over in Heartwood, overseeing both the main facility and some of the machinery out in the mill. I was having a lot of behavioral problems after transferring to the elementary school here, struggling to make friends... Both GiGi and Pops were cutting their work hours a bit so someone could always be home right after school. After a few months of that, Robert Hardon got fed up with the schedule... and fired him. And not only that, he refused to pay out his pension. He left him with nothing."

I felt my breath catch in my throat. "What, really? That's... really shitty."

"That's one word for it. Pops had been with that company for almost twenty years by then, so it wasn't only about the money—it was his life, his identity." James clenched his other hand in his lap, his mouth forming a hard line. "The Hardons and the Ramseys are to Heartwood like the Taylors and Kinneys are to Dearing Creek—all wealthy and with businesses that employ so many people from this part of the state. It starts to feel like a handful of elitist people wind up controlling everyone else. Robert Hardon had plenty, and he could've shown some compassion for our situation, tried to work with Pops on it. But instead, he turned his back on a loyal employee, because it didn't suit his bottom line. He took everything from him. And Pops was never quite the same after that, even after finding work with my old boss, Mel."

"That must've been so hard... for your grandfather, for all of you. Especially on top of everything else."

He nodded. "After a while, it became easier to blame the money, I guess. Of course, it didn't help that I had assholes like his son Luke giving me shit all the time at school."

I watched his face as a few more of the missing pieces fell into place, anxiety blooming in the center of my chest as I called up my own memories of being teased as a dorky redhead back in middle school. "I'm sorry… kids can be jerks. Trust me, I've been there. But…"

James held up a hand. "I know… kids grow up. And people can change." He sighed. "I'm still not convinced that's the case with Luke Hardon, but… I guess I'm grateful for his warning about the Kinneys."

I cocked my head. "What's the deal with them, anyway?"

"Their house renovation was my last project with Mel. It had already been difficult, with all of their demands… but I was handling it ok. Until Denise decided to make me her latest conquest."

"Jesus."

"Yep. It's why I quit Aaronson Construction, and the project. When I turned her down, I knew it would end up being bad for me and Mel, so I quit. Just didn't think it would still be following me months later." He slanted a glance towards me. "But I guess seeing us together at the bar last week must've pissed her off."

I nodded, realization slowly dawning. "And people in town know you're my contractor. So now it's hurting your new business."

He shrugged. "Let 'em try. I wouldn't change a thing either way. Except to say, I'm sorry for how I acted... and I know I need to work through my issues with money. I'm working towards being better. I *want* to be better, for you. And for me too, I guess." Leaning towards me, he brushed the hair back from my face. "For now, I hope you can find a way to forgive me. Because I don't want to lose you, Lizzie. Not for pride, or any other reason."

His words hit right in the center of me—his gaze so humble, so imploring, it's no wonder the tears once again came easily. "There's nothing to forgive... I... don't want to lose you, either." I was so overcome with everything in my head and heart, I almost couldn't hold it all in—but the need to kiss this man *right now* won out.

Thrusting my body forward across the arm of my chair towards him, I unfortunately realized too late that four glasses of wine had killed whatever shred of depth perception and balance I had in me. As the chair flipped out from under me, James made a desperate grab to keep us both from toppling backwards to the ground. The effort came too late, though, as his chair tipped too—and with a roll, we fell onto the grass, me coming to rest on top of him with a thud.

We lay there for a moment in stunned silence: me, with my face plastered against the muscular curves of his chest—God, *how did he always manage to smell so amazing?*—and James, with one knee propped between my legs.

After a beat, I could feel his deep chuckle begin to reverberate through me as his hands came to rest along my back. "You ok?"

And before I could stop myself, I let out a loud, snorting laugh, dissolving into hysterical giggles that came pouring out of me, as the ridiculousness of it all carried away the tension that had been clenched tight in my gut all week.

At any other point in my life, I would've felt so damn grateful for the darkness right then—shielding my blazing red face and the humiliation of yet another clumsy, dorky Lizzie move.

But right then, I couldn't have cared less about any of it.

I mean, I'd like to think it was from unlocking a new level in my personal growth. But really, it had everything to do with who I was with.

And ok, maybe also a teensie bit from all that Sauvignon Blanc sloshing around in my belly.

Rolling off his chest and onto the ground beside him, I lay there as our laughter drifted off towards the shoreline. I could see the warmth in his eyes again—actually feeling it wrap around me, better than any old quilt ever could. With a slow smile, he reached a hand over to caress my face.

"God, you're beautiful, Red."

"Seriously? I'm a mes—"

He held a finger against my lips to silence my objection, pretending to look stern. "You're *beautiful*... and it's time you started believing it." He moved his hand away, lowering it to my back. "You make me feel so lucky, being with you. I can't imagine anything better than this."

Our bodies shifted along the grass, until no space remained between us. I didn't care that my friends were inside, wondering what the heck was going on—or that the cooler air hinted that it was much later than I'd realized.

I didn't want to be anywhere else than right here, lost in the feeling of him—in his breath, soft against my cheek. And all I could hear were the words that continued to echo through my mind—because they'd been my own, even before he'd said them out loud first. Along with many others I couldn't yet.

"You make me feel so lucky..."

The kiss that followed? Pretty sure that was inevitable. But maybe... *so were we.*

Chapter 31

James

I sat shaking on the sofa in my jammies, still feeling the chill all the way down into my bones as I waited for them to come back. For him to get here.

It felt like I'd been sitting here forever. Why was it taking so long?

It didn't matter. I wasn't ready for what came next, anyway. Would I even be able to look at him? I was afraid to see the same truth in his brownish-black eyes that I knew was already in my own.

Because it was my fault. I lost her. I let her die and couldn't bring her back.

Please, God, I'll do anything… just give me my mom back. I need my mom back.

The tears started up again, pouring up and out from the deep pit of grief I had stored up inside of me. Mama always told me it was ok to have big feelings—big love, big happiness, big sadness. It was a gift that let me know I was alive, she'd said.

This kind of sad, though, didn't feel like a gift. And without her, I didn't know that I even wanted to be alive.

If I could do any of it without her.

Dad wouldn't know how to help with that, either. The only big feelings he seemed to have for me were angry and annoyed, and all of that felt too much right now.

Still, he was my dad. That meant he loved me no matter what, right? Even when I messed up? Mama said he did. Maybe he still would, after this.

Unless... maybe I didn't deserve it anymore.

The door opened behind me, and there were GiGi and Pops, looking as cold and lifeless as I'd ever seen them. No more smiles or laughs. No more light. No more anything.

Maybe they'd lost their big love for me, too. Maybe the creek swallowed all of us up, along with Mama.

"GiGi... where's Dad? Is he coming?" My voice sounded so small I didn't think she even heard me. But then she shook her head.

It was the first time I ever remember seeing her cry.

I awoke as a stream of sunlight hit my eyes, disorienting me for a brief moment before I realized Lizzie and I must've fallen asleep next to her firepit.

The weight of the dream that I'd had on replay for most of my life still clung to me, like strands of a cobweb you didn't realize you were walking into—but now that you had, you couldn't quite shake off the mess of it all.

This summer, though, I'd been feeling its hold on me start to lessen. It happened slowly at first, in such tiny measures that I almost didn't even notice it. Weeks ago already, I'd stopped waking up in a panic in the middle of the night.

Now, I could already feel this most recent episode fizzling out in the background. Like it didn't have enough oomph left anymore to keep me caught up in it all day, like it once had.

The only explanation I could think of? All of it was changing because of her.

Laying here under the stars with her last night—talking and laughing together like we'd never stopped—had felt pretty fucking amazing. Working to make things right had been the hard part—but necessary.

She lay beside me now, mouth half open and snoring softly against my arm, as goddamn precious as she was beautiful. Seeing her like this, how could I not smile? Her body was curved against mine, her softness, as always, aligning with my harder edges—making it almost impossible to think of anything else. I didn't *want* to think of anything else.

The only thing in my head now was one simple truth—*God, I wanted this woman.*

Hard as it had been, I'd kept the promise I'd made to myself in the beginning not to rush things with her. Whatever was growing between the two of us, I'd wanted it to have a chance to be viable on its own before sex became a part of the equation.

At first, I'd wondered if maybe that was part of why none of the other women I'd dated had ever amounted to anything more—every time, we'd jumped ahead to the physical and things would fizzle out not long after.

Now I knew the truth—it was that they weren't *her.* And before Lizzie, I'd never bothered to want for more.

There'd been plenty of kissing these many weeks, of course—grazing my fingers along the soft surface of her skin, holding her to me in the way that we fit so well. Lying together with her in my arms, breathing in the scent of her—willing my hands and thoughts and lips not to ruin anything by rushing.

And it had been so damn hard.

But this was the first time we'd ever slept together, in the literal sense. I knew spending the night at her place or mine would be a slippery slope, a temptation I may not be able to hold myself back from.

I wondered if she felt the struggle, too—if she needed me the way I needed her. If she knew how I felt. Because I didn't think I'd ever be able to stop once I finally had her completely.

I almost didn't come here last night. I'd been stewing over what had happened that night at La Cantina every second of the past week, trying to find my way through it. At first, I was pissed off that Luke Hardon had showed up and ruined our date in the first place—and that I'd let him get under my skin, the way he always seemed to.

But the more space and breath I took away from the situation, it started to become clear that I'd, well, kind of fucked up. My default response to Hardon and others like him had always been resentment and anger—some of it warranted. But some of it, I now realized, wasn't.

And maybe the rest belonged in the past.

I'd been hung up on a rock this entire time—bitter about anyone and anything to do with money because of the damage I'd seen it cause. But as much as it hurt to admit it, it was possible for those who'd done wrong to change and make things right.

Even someone like Luke Hardon.

Even someone like me.

Sure, I hadn't wanted or expected a penny from my father after what he'd done. In my eyes, he was worse than all of them.

But now that I had everything he'd worked so hard for, everything he'd prioritized over his own family, it was pointless to hold on to the resentment, caught up in all the wrong things. Because money wasn't the problem.

The thing that needed to change was *me*.

I was tired of feeling the weight of it all, of drowning in my own bitterness. Maybe it was time to finally start doing something good with what I'd been given, instead of letting it drag me down further.

Or before it made me lose this woman I'd grown to care about more than I'd ever expected. So much so, that it scared me.

But I'd meant it when I said I wanted to be better for her. Now I needed to do the work to be worthy of it all. To be worthy of her.

And the first thing on my list was to follow through on my promise and help her figure out who the elusive M.H. was from those letters. Maybe solving the mystery would bring about answers and help her get through all of this without further heartbreak or disappointment.

For now, though—*holy shit, my arm hurt.* Plucking a dandelion from the ground beside her, I tickled it beneath her nose, smiling as her face wrinkled up in annoyance. And when her eyes opened, she looked downright annoyed—bringing my mind back to the first moment we met and how she'd ensnared me even then.

"What are you doing?"

"Waking you up, Sleeping Beauty. Unless you'd rather stay out here, sleeping on the grass all day?" Watching as the realization dawned in her widening eyes, I couldn't help but laugh.

"What... wait a minute... we were out here *all night*?"

"Yup," I said, tickling her again with the dandelion before tossing it aside. "Allll night, baby." Sliding my arm out from behind her, I rubbed my shoulder, flexing it before sitting upright. A moment later, she pulled herself up as well, groaning.

"Oh my God... my head..."

Grinning, I reached over to pull a stray leaf from her hair, which in the early morning dew looked like beautiful chaos. "Yeah, wine will do that to a person. I have a feeling you ladies enjoyed more than your fair share last night."

"Uh-huh." Lizzie had her head in her hands now, her words coming out in a muffled grumble. "Where are the others?"

"My guess is inside. If you'd like, we can head up and check on them."

I caught her grimace as she peeked through her fingers. "I'm already dreading it... but yeah, we probably should."

Chuckling, I helped pull her to standing and we made our way, hand in hand, up the gentle slope of her lawn towards the porch. I couldn't help smiling to myself as we walked, wondering how drunk she'd actually been last night and how much of our conversation she even remembered. But seeing her shy smile before opening the door, I had to believe I wasn't the only one replaying every bit of it.

Inside looked pretty much the same as the quick peek I'd caught the night before—empty wine bottles, half-eaten snacks spread across the coffee table, early-aughts club music still playing softly in the background. Except now, all the participants had scattered—Lena lay sprawled out on a sofa, with Indi, Brooke, Kait apparently claiming the beds. Bucky was lying curled up on his side by Lena's feet, one paw flung across his exposed ear like he was trying to block out the rumbling sound of her snoring.

Looking back to Lizzie with a smirk, she shook her head with a sigh and started cleaning up. Silently, I grabbed a trash bag from beneath the kitchen sink and began to help.

"Rise and shine, sleepyheads," Brooke trilled, padding barefoot from one of the bedrooms, looking remarkably refreshed. She gave us a sly look but said nothing, heading straight to the kitchen to begin washing dishes.

It wasn't until we'd almost finished up that the rest of her friends began to make their appearance—starting with Kait, grumbling and rubbing at her face as she shuffled over to where I stood holding the broom. "What're you still doing here, Tate?" She shot a look over to Lizzie. "Wait... did you two..."

"No, relax. We just, uh, fell asleep outside." Her cheeks had begun pinking up, and I had to fight to hold back the grin.

Before the interrogation went further, we heard the bathroom door open as Indi emerged, looking in far better condition than Kait as she shook her water bottle. "There you are. Why were you guys sleeping outside?" Without waiting for an answer, she tossed a few packets onto the table. "Girls, don't forget to take your electrolytes... gotta help those livers recover!"

As a loud grumble sounded from the sofa, I chuckled, turning towards Lizzie. "Listen, I'm going to let you ladies do your thing. But... can I see you later?"

"Definitely." She smiled, leaning upwards to give me a kiss before she froze, making a face. "Ugh, no... my morning breath might kill you right now."

"Woman, I don't fucking care." Pulling her in, I kissed her without an ounce of hesitation as her friends whistled and cat-called in the background, one of them shouting, "Get a room, you two!"

Of course, my mind was already there, making plans.

Because for her, it needed to be perfect.

Chapter 32

James

The next day, I was making my way through town towards Jesse's place, unable to wipe the smile from my face. Lizzie had come over the night before after her friends dispersed, and I'd had a whole night under the stars waiting for her—dinner by a roaring bonfire and a game of glow-in-the-dark frisbee target shooting out on the lawn. Watching her do her dorky little victory dance as she creamed me on the second round, face lit up in a huge smile, was *everything*—I could stand back and watch her like that all day, every day.

I had no idea how the hell we ever got so lucky to cross paths like we did—with everything afterwards leading us here. I'd stopped trying to pinpoint why things felt easier with her, because the answer was complicated—it was a million little reasons and steps that had brought us here, and not one of them made sense on its own. But now that I'd made it, falling with her seemed inevitable. I never wanted to let her go.

I'd never wanted to *not let go* before. I'd never wanted to *belong* to anyone before. To give up that kind of control.

But I was starting to realize, I already had with Lizzie—practically from the start.

I'd also decided to set up my two-man tent, with the best air mattress I'd ever slept on. I figured if things got late, she deserved a more comfortable and romantic re-do of sleeping outdoors than we'd had the night before.

But I couldn't deny I'd had other ideas in my head beyond sleeping. Something about the way she'd looked at me after we'd woken up on her lawn made me think she might be as ready as I was—it was all I'd been able to think about all day.

It became clear not long after Lizzie arrived, though, that our night wouldn't be playing out exactly as I'd hoped. She'd read another letter from M.H. before coming over, further proof that there'd been an intimate relationship between Cora and this mystery man in the early days of her marriage. Seeing the pain of it in Lizzie's eyes had been enough—and I knew I'd do whatever I could to be there as she needed me to be.

Because, God, she deserved it and far more. I'd shared more dark pieces of myself with this woman over the past months than I ever had with anyone. And not only had she truly listened and given me grace, she'd stuck around—challenging me to work through the areas where I'd become stuck. I was far from perfect, yet she'd convinced me, *somehow*, that this mess of a man was still worth caring about. And she'd done this even while starting her life over and dealing with the weight of her own losses.

I didn't know how I could ever be worthy of someone like her. But I wanted to be. And I was damn well going to do everything in my power to try.

So instead of making love to her under the stars, I simply listened as she worked through everything with the letters, keeping her plate and glass filled—and offering playful distractions—as we relaxed together. Seeing her start to relax, I knew I'd made the right call.

And holding her in my arms inside the tent as we fell asleep together for the second night in a row—our legs intertwined beneath the blanket as she snuggled in—it felt like home.

After a little kissing and cuddling after coffee this morning, we'd parted ways. She had plans with Brooke before she headed back to the cities, and I had something to take care of that I should have a week ago already.

Pulling into Jesse's driveway, I grabbed the couple of bags I had sitting in the front seat, making my way to their front door and ringing the bell. I had texted to let him know I was coming, and he'd responded with a simple "Ok", which was Jesse's way of saying he was still kind of upset about everything, but not mad enough to deny me access. I was sure Tara had probably nudged him a bit, too, knowing how stubborn we both could be.

I was grateful, at least, that he wasn't the type to get outright pissed, like me. Even angry, Jesse had always had the coolest head of the three of us. But his complacency had almost felt harder to take. I just hoped he'd be willing to hear what I had to say.

Jesse appeared at the door, acknowledging me with a slight nod of his head. "Hey, man."

"Hey."

"Well, come in, then." He held open the screen door as I passed through into their living room, immediately hit by the smell of pancakes and bacon coming from the kitchen.

I turned back to look at him. "Sorry, am I interrupting brunch?"

"Naw, it's fine. I told Tara you were coming over, and she insisted on cooking something. That nesting urge is running deep right now."

I chuckled. "Somehow, I'm not even a little surprised."

We found Tara parked on a bar stool at the counter, flipping a batch of pancakes on their electric griddle. "Hey, bro, hope you're hungry."

My eyes widened as I saw the tower of twenty or so pancakes already heaped on a platter next to her. "Who are you planning to feed, all of Dearing Creek?"

"She would if I let her," Jesse said, coming up behind her to plant a tender kiss on her cheek, his hands resting on her swollen belly. Seeing them together made me happy Jesse had found someone so perfect for him. It made me wish Lizzie was here, too.

But this was something I needed to take care of on my own.

Thirty minutes later, we sat around their table, plates still half full with pancakes, bacon and fruit. We'd been making small talk as we ate about random shit, both Jesse and I looking to avoid the elephant in the room. But it was time to face it.

Taking a deep breath, I began, "So, listen. I'm really sorry if I made you feel uncomfortable when I offered you that money last week."

"Yeah, I was." I saw him wince as I heard a kick under the table, and I had to bite back a smile as I saw Tara give him a threatening look. "But then my darling wife here reminded me you were coming from a good place." He sighed. "And I'm sorry for getting so mad at you. I guess... our whole money situation must've been bothering me more than I realized. It's my job to take care of my family, you know? All I seem to be doing is failing at it."

Tara reached across the table, squeezing his hand. "And I told my *exceptionally stubborn* husband that we aren't living in the year nineteen fifty-two. We're both responsible for providing and caring for our family." She turned back to me with a small smile. "Just because things are a little tight right now doesn't mean we won't figure it out. We always do."

I nodded. "Of course, I know that. If anyone can, it's the two of you. And you know I'd never intentionally upset either of you, right?"

"Yeah, we know. I just... can't have you throwing a bunch of money at us that I haven't earned," Jesse said, setting down his fork. "It doesn't feel right."

"I get it. You know that's exactly how it was for me when I found out about the inheritance in the first place. It felt like this... *burden*, something I didn't want or deserve." I took a breath. "But I've realized something lately. Money has been a negative thing in my life for as long as I can remember. It's made me resentful, angry... I don't want to feel that way anymore. And I'm definitely not going to let it hurt the people I love, either."

"I know. And for what it's worth, I'm really proud of you. I mean that."

"Good. Remember that feeling, because I have a proposition for you."

Jesse raised an eyebrow. "I told you, man... I'm not *into* you like that...*geez, stop asking...*" Tara slapped him on the arm, rolling her eyes as he started laughing.

I couldn't help laughing as well, feeling the tension finally lift a bit. "Thanks for the heads-up. I'll try to lower my expectations." Taking a quick sip of coffee, I continued. "My proposition is actually *business*-related. Because... I want you to be my partner."

Smirking as I watched the look of shock spread across Jesse's face, I took another sip of coffee.

I'd been thinking about this idea for a while, well before our argument. As much as I loved being my own boss and choosing the direction of the business, I also knew there were areas that weren't my strong suit—coordinating crews, scheduling. Even bringing in potential clients. But these were areas where Jesse, with his naturally outgoing personality and people skills, excelled.

Not only was this about getting to work alongside someone I loved and respected—it also made good business sense, if I wanted the business to grow.

And watching this potentially change the financial livelihood of my best friend and his family was worth way more than my bottom line.

"*Um, what's that now?*"

Grinning at my friend, I continued. "My *part-ner*. But only in business, so you can relax."

"Are you serious, man?"

"Yup."

"But... *why*? I have nothing to contribute."

"Is this about money again? Trust me... you have *plenty* to contribute. And you already have. You're a damn hard worker, and you're a natural leader with the contractors we've brought on. Plus, you know your skills have expanded way beyond plumbing over the last several years. You just didn't get enough of a chance to show it off with Aaronson's."

Jesse shrugged. "I'm just doing the job that's needed. And you're my brother. I want your business to succeed, so of course I'll work hard for you."

"Honey, stop it." We both glanced over at Tara, who had tears streaming down her face.

"Stop what?"

"Being so fucking *modest* all the time. You know James is right. You're fully capable of so much more."

"I don't know…"

"Well, *I do*. This is an incredible opportunity he's offering. We both know you can do this." Tara nudged him again under the table until he looked up. "And you better say yes, or you'll cause me undue stress. The doctor said I need life to be calm while I'm on bedrest, remember?"

I smirked. "Well played, Mrs. Sundgaard."

She shrugged, her smug smile spreading ear-to-ear. "I have my moments."

"*Jesus Christ*, I never stand a chance against you two."

"Is that a yes, then?" I held my breath, waiting for his answer.

His face broke out into his signature Jesse smile. "Fuck, yes. And I'm grateful, James. I won't let you down."

"Never have, never could." I grinned at him, starting to feel choked up. Clearing my throat, I continued. "I'll have the paperwork drawn up next week, and we can go over specifics. But just so you know, I have one small caveat."

He cocked his head to the side. "What's that?"

I reached for the envelope I'd set beside me on the open chair, sliding it across the table to my friend. "You've been working way above your pay grade all summer. And right now, since I'm still technically your boss, I need to make this right. So I'm giving you back pay."

Jesse gave me a look as he slowly opened the envelope, pulling out the check for twenty-five thousand dollars I'd had issued a few days ago, in the hopes this conversation would go well. Eyes wide, he slid it over to Tara, who promptly started sobbing.

"Damn it, James... don't you know it's rude to make a pregnant woman cry?"

"Yeah, sorry about that..."

But Jesse was looking at me, shaking his head in amazement. "I can't believe you."

"So, I'll see you bright and early tomorrow morning... ok, partner?" I stuck out a hand.

Jesse started chuckling as he grabbed it. "Watch your bossy attitude, or I'll have to write you up."

I joined him in laughter, even Tara—in between staccato'd hiccups as her tears subsided.

I was so glad I'd made this decision and only wished now that I'd done it sooner. Finally, it felt like all the parts of my life were exactly where I wanted them to be—and I'd never felt so unbelievably happy, at peace.

Now I just needed to help Lizzie find her peace as well.

That evening, I was back in my shop, hard at work on the final stages of the project I'd been working on for her off and on all summer. I'd kept it hidden, intending for it to be a surprise—but I couldn't wait to show her.

I heard the crunching of tires on gravel before I could see the car. Wiping the sawdust from my hands, I brushed off my clothes and stepped outside to see GiGi getting out of her car.

"Did I forget about dinner or something?"

Smirking, she pulled me into a quick hug. "Not this time, Tater. Luckily, I think you've learned by now not to stand up your dear ol' granny."

"Oh, believe me... I know the consequences that would be awaiting me if I screwed up like that again." Grinning, I pulled back. "So, this is just a social call, then? Or have you come to harass me about something?"

"No... I needed to talk to you about Lizzie."

Noting her serious face, I felt myself tense. "What about Lizzie? Is she ok?"

She waved away my words in annoyance. "Relax, Lizzie's fine. And I want to keep it that way."

"Um... that kinda sounds like a threat, *Don GiGi*."

She sighed impatiently. "Are you gonna take this seriously?"

"I am. But it would be easier if you'd just skip ahead to the point."

"Which I *will*... if you'd stop interrupting me, boy." GiGi paused, looking anxious. "It's about those letters, James. I need you to ask her not to read any more of them."

I crossed my arms. "Too late, she's already made her way through most of them... and she's pretty upset about it. So anything you can do to help clear things up would be great, like... who's M.H.?"

Her face was stoney as she looked off to the side, wringing her hands and muttering under her breath. *"God, why didn't that girl just listen and leave well enough alone?"*

"GiGi... what is this about?"

She met my eyes, now looking as if the fight had gone out of her. "No point in avoiding it now, I guess. We'd better go and talk to her before this whole thing blows up any further."

I stared at her, my head swirling with thoughts of what the mystery might be. All I knew was it took something pretty big for GiGi to get worked up like this. Giving her a quick nod, I felt the happiness I'd been sitting in for most of the weekend start to evaporate.

"Alright, then... let me grab my keys."

I wasn't usually the praying type—but as I followed my grandmother's silver sedan in my truck a few minutes later, I couldn't help repeating the words anyway:

Please God... don't let this hurt her.

Chapter 33

Lizzie

The sun was sinking lower on the horizon as I sat at my new writer's desk, Bucky snoozing at my feet as I looked out upon Lake Elska. I'd taken some time that morning after returning home from James' place to rearrange my furniture—for once, *wanting* the distraction. Now, the desk sat in front of the large picture window in my living room—a view I hoped would work some sort of magic within me.

When I'd first found out about my grandmother's affair, I'd thought that was the end of it. How could I write about love, when everything I'd believed had been thrown into a tailspin by those letters?

The rational part of my brain knew it was ridiculous and totally unfair to place the entire responsibility of my romantic belief system upon the shoulders of one woman, one relationship.

Which is why I was sitting here, trying to summon it back on my own. But not *really* on my own—-in the foreground of my thoughts, James was helping me.

I had to admit—everything about him made me want to believe in love the way I'd thought it could be. Because James was the first man ever to do it.

It was an embarrassing admission at thirty, even to myself. Especially for a woman who'd surrounded herself with the world and words of romance for most of her life.

In *real* life, however, I hadn't had more than a few relationships—and not a single one had seemed worthy of the words. The sad thing was, I thought I *had* loved them. And I'd been so damn wrong, about all of it.

But I guess when you want to believe in something badly enough, it's easy to write yourself a false reality where it becomes the truth. It's what I'd done with Randall, right? Ignoring all the evidence proving he was completely wrong for me, that he didn't love me. Convincing myself that I loved the man, more than the idea of him—-pretending that it wasn't also about my own confidence boost, being with a man like him. Hiding in the fiction, because it felt all warm and cozy and easier to believe.

Until it wasn't.

It would be easy, of course, to blame the poor examples I'd had in my life—most were a far cry from this vision of love I'd built up in my mind. I even wondered sometimes if my own parents had really loved each other in the end—because they never seemed particularly happy. And a marriage focused on status and elite social circles like my sister's—or even my friend Tess's—wasn't exactly the benchmark I was aiming for.

Which left me with my grandparents—and, well, we all know how *that* story turned out.

It's why I hoped I could trust in myself and what I felt growing between me and James. It was all the hope I had left.

And speaking of the devil, my eyes darted away from the lake as I saw the man himself walk past, hearing his knock at the door a moment later. Happy for the surprise, I opened the door to greet him—but something about his face told me this wasn't a social call.

"Hey." He leaned in, giving me a quick kiss on the forehead.

"Hey back. What's up? I didn't think I'd see you until tomorrow morning."

"Yeah, sorry." He took a deep breath. "So, GiGi stopped by my place earlier. She wanted me to discourage you from reading the rest of those letters... but then I told her you'd already gone through most of them." He craned his neck to look past me out the window towards her cabin. "Anyway, it seems now she's ready to talk."

I felt my heart thumping in my chest, so loudly I was certain he could hear it—but I nodded. Checking to make sure Bucky was still asleep, I followed him out the door and across the sloping lawn towards GiGi's cabin.

A few minutes later, James and I were sitting on the floral print sofa in her living room, awkwardly waiting as GiGi bustled back with a few hard ciders for each of us. Between how she was behaving and the apparent need for alcohol, I couldn't help feeling worried for whatever she was about to lay on us.

But I also needed to know what she'd been holding onto all these years. I needed the *truth*—even if it was hard to hear. Even if it hurt.

Taking a seat in her recliner after handing us each a can, GiGi took a sip from her own, then began. "I never wanted to keep any of this a secret from you, Lizzie. But Cora was very specific about her wishes, and she wanted them carried out in a certain way, especially when it came to you."

"What do you mean, *'her wishes'*?"

"About those letters, and her past. I've always known about it all, known she kept them hidden. I'm sure by now you've guessed why."

I nodded. "At first, I thought I'd just stumbled upon love letters from my grandfather. But the last letter that he wrote for her right before my mom was born made me think something happened between the two of them." I paused. "And then I started reading the other letters in the second bundle. I just... I *had* to know."

GiGi's eyes were sad. "I understand, dear. And I'm sorry you had to find out this way. But I won't lie to you. Cora did meet another man not long after she was first married to Walter."

I winced. Hearing confirmation of what I already knew still hurt, more than I'd thought it would. "But, why? I just don't get it. She and my grandpa always seemed so in love."

"And they *were*. What you grew up seeing was real, Lizzie. They truly loved each other, and there's nothing either would've done to hurt the other. But at the start, all of the change was hard on Cora. Walter was in the early days of growing his family medical practice, which had him gone for long hours, day after day. As a new wife, Cora found herself lonely, without purpose. At one point, she told me she even worried he was maybe having an affair himself with one of his nurses because he was gone so much."

"Well, did he?"

"No, he never did. But he was a workaholic... and he justified it, I think, because a thriving business was good for them both. I think he was really concerned about giving Cora a good life, since they both grew up without much. But also, Walter was really determined to prove himself in his field. Back then, he was willing to sacrifice time with his young wife to make it happen. That's why he secured the rental of the cabin. He'd spent a lot of time on Lake Elska as a boy and hoped to own a place there one day. When he saw how unhappy Cora was by herself all the time, he sped up his plans and found that cabin, which had just become available. He figured it would make her happy, as now she'd have a beautiful spot to spend her summer days while he was at the office in the cities."

I nodded as I felt James squeeze my hand—most of this I already knew. "Ok... so, then what?"

GiGi set down her can on the coffee table between us. "Well, you already know that's the year she and I met. She was such a lovely little thing, just like you—and far classier than I'd ever be. But she also had a spirit that I admired. My Sandra was close to turning one by then, and I'd been feeling a little isolated myself as a new mother. So as neighbors, Cora and I became fast friends. Every once in a while, Walter would drive up on the weekends... but his work kept him away most of the time."

"Ok. But then she met this 'M.H.' person?"

She nodded. "They met at the Spring Fling season opener dance that used to be held each year, over in the old event hall. At first it seemed fairly innocent, the two of them chatting, even sharing a dance. I didn't think much of it. But then came..."

"... the letters." My thoughts were swirling, hearing confirmation of what I'd suspected over the past week.

"How did he know where to send them?" James asked, his brow furrowed.

GiGi shrugged. "Small town. Everyone knows everyone else's business, so it wasn't hard to figure out. Cora was flattered, of course, by the attention... It felt like a dream. And you know how she loved her romance. But after a while, she started feeling anxious about it all. I think she told me about the letters because she needed someone to convince her to put the kibosh on the whole thing right away."

I took a sip of my cider, trying to calm my nerves. "And did you?"

"I tried. But when a couple more letters trickled in, she couldn't help but draw comparisons between him and Walter, who was very sensible... and even though he loved Cora, he wasn't much of a romantic. These letters helped to fill that need for her, to have the sort of romance she'd only read about. Especially because of her own rough upbringing."

Nodding again, I recalled the few vague details Grandma Cora had shared about her childhood, with parents who were miserable and overwhelmed in their poverty, always bitter and angry. "So I get that she liked the attention. But... why would she actually let things go as far as they did?"

"Because he was kind, affectionate, and showed her attention. All things a young wife craves." She gave me a sad smile. "Listen, she wasn't proud of what she'd done, for sneaking around, afraid of them being seen together. She truly loved your grandfather. But then..."

"What?"

GiGi hesitated. "She became pregnant."

"Right... with my mom. So that ended things, then?"

But then I noticed James giving his grandmother a strange look. "What aren't you telling us, GiGi?"

She drew in a deep breath, as if willing herself to go on. "Your grandfather was sterile, sweetheart. He couldn't have children. But they didn't find this out until after they'd already married."

I felt the blood leaving my face, my body. "So... I mean, what...?"

GiGi's eyes were bright now with tears. "Once she found out, Cora immediately broke things off. She was a wreck. And now she had to confess to your grandfather that not only had she been unfaithful, she was also carrying another man's child."

"Oh my God."

"Believe me, I know this comes as a shock. It was the wake-up call Walter had never expected. At first, he was so hurt, so angry... Cora apologized and begged for his forgiveness. Begged him not to leave her, swore her love to him. But even still, she didn't know if they'd make it. They holed up in that cabin together for an entire weekend, fighting and talking, crying and screaming. And by the end of it, they'd come to a resolution."

I tried to form the words to ask for more, but my voice felt caught in my throat. James, noticing this, squeezed my hand again once more and turned back to GiGi. "He decided to stay, then?"

She nodded. "Yes. Both were desperate to be parents, and he was willing to raise another man's child to make that dream come true. But he also realized his part in things, how his obsession with work and separation from his wife—while not an excuse—may have contributed to their divide. Despite everything that happened, he loved her. So they agreed to a fresh start."

"And the other man...?"

"He respected her wishes and agreed to sign off on any parental rights. Hard as it was, he agreed to walk away. But he also owned the land and the cabin as part of his business holdings, so he deeded them both to Cora, for the child he'd never know." GiGi let out a deep exhale. "He was actually a widower with two young sons already and didn't want to cause Cora any more harm than he already had. He's a good man, Lizzie. He knew he'd made a mistake, despite loving her."

My head was spinning now, trying to grasp everything GiGi was telling me. About my grandmother and the affair. That Grandpa Walter wasn't... really my grandfather at all. It was a lie that had spread its roots far and wide through all of our lives.

And then I realized—GiGi had been referring to M.H. in the present tense. Taking a breath, I found my voice. "Wait a minute... is M.H. still alive?"

She was silent for a moment as she looked down, wringing her hands in her lap in a way I knew well. My own were practically numb by this point, my face as well. But I had to know.

James beat me to it. "GiGi... who is M.H.?"

Finally, she looked up at us, tears now streaming down her face. "Mitchum Hardon."

Now it was James who was falling apart as I watched him collapse against the back of the sofa. "No. No."

GiGi's voice was soft. "I'm sorry... but it's true, Tater."

"A Hardon is *not* her grandfather. Those assholes cannot be her family. I won't accept it."

I looked at him, eyes wide. "My entire life has literally imploded... and *you're* the one who's unwilling to accept it?"

His hazel eyes flashed, though not with the comforting warmth I loved so much. This time, they were a wildfire, intent on burning everything around us. "Trust me... you are worth a billion of anyone in that family. You're better off not knowing them."

"And what if... I *want* to know them?"

The fire grew. "Why the hell would you want to do that?"

"I don't even know yet if I do, ok? I have no idea what to think or feel about anything. But I deserve the right to decide that for myself." The tears were flowing now. "Because Ethan, Mariah and I, we don't have any family left. Everyone who loved us is dead." I heard my voice crack, disintegrating into nothing, along with everything else.

"Well, those people will never be your family. The best thing you can do is walk away."

"Is this really about their goddamn *money* again?"

"Does it matter? I can't fucking do this."

It was as though I'd been slapped, the rush of burning pain spreading through me like a buzzing current as the air was simultaneously sucked from my lungs.

Is this what it felt like to lose everything?

Shakily, I stood up—insides twisting, face on fire, working to find enough breath for what came next. "Well, I guess that settles it then, doesn't it?" My voice was so low, I didn't know if he even heard me—but maybe, the words were meant more for me than anything.

I turned and walked towards the door, spinning around again as I heard James' footsteps sound behind me. "No. Do *not* follow me. I need... I need space." He flinched as he paused mid-stride, our eyes registering our mutual pain. But as I walked through the door, he didn't follow me out.

Choking on my sobs, I almost couldn't see well enough to make my way back home, between my tears and the sunlight having nearly vanished from the sky. But then a bright yellow sports car caught my eye behind my cabin, like the flash of a memory.

No... it can't be...

"Hello, Elizabeth."

Chapter 34

Lizzie

"Randall? What the hell are you doing here?" I wiped my face with the back of my hand—I could only imagine how I must look.

Randall Price—silver fox professor, former philandering boyfriend—was sitting on my porch, very much out of place in the rustic, Northwoods Minnesota setting he'd found himself in. He looked just as he had the night I'd left him and altogether too good for someone who'd cut me down completely. It's like he couldn't even have the decency to age horribly—or grow a giant mole on his face, *anything*—over the course of the past several months.

Why the hell did I care, anyway? I hadn't the energy to waste another second of my life on this man, much less care how either of us appeared to the other.

Probably didn't matter much anyway, once you've hit bottom.

Because right now, that's how it felt. I was on the verge of falling apart, of screaming and crying at the unfairness of every fucking thing that had just happened in the past thirty minutes—but no, instead I had to hold it together, waiting for this man from my past to explain why he'd shown up here in the first place.

Instead of answering my question, however, Randall stood up to embrace me. Taking a step backwards to dodge his outstretched arms, I saw him stiffen—but at least he didn't try again. Crossing his arms over his chest, he smiled. "It's good to see you again. I've missed you."

"Really? I haven't thought of you at all." Ok, that was only partly true. Though most of my thoughts had volleyed between humiliation and karma-filled daydreams, I'd gotten to a point where I'd been able to mostly forget about my time with Randall. Which, of course, was thanks to everything I'd experienced with James.

But that was, you know, *before*. Now he was sitting in the cabin a hundred feet behind me, having told me flat out that he was unwilling to accept my new reality.

He was unwilling to accept *me*.

"Listen," Randall continued on, ignoring the fact that I clearly didn't want him there, "I was hoping we could talk, that's all. Just fifteen minutes, and then I'll be on my way. I promise."

I should've said no. At that moment, I was barely hanging on to my emotions. But I was tired of fighting. Without saying a word, I walked past him to open the door, allowing him to follow me inside. In an instant, Bucky ran over, barking and sniffing all around him, with a nosedive straight to the crotch. Clearly, it made Randall uncomfortable, as I remembered his weird aversion to most animals in general.

In a moment where it seemed like I didn't have anything to feel happy about, I couldn't help but smile a tiny bit.

"Uh, *nice dog*. What's his name?"

I just stood there, arms crossed. "Bucky."

"Ah." He glanced around the room, gesturing. "And your place is... quaint. Is this really where you're living now?" Bucky released a low growl until I finally gave a small shake of my head.

Jesus Christ, did I look like I was in the mood for small talk? "How'd you even find me here, anyway?"

"You always talked about Dearing Creek... so I called a few places, asked around. Small towns, you know." As Bucky wandered off towards his spot near the fireplace, Randall gave me a hard look, finally noticing my tear-streaked face. "You seem upset. Is something wrong?"

Yes, everything. Thanks for noticing.

Thinking about James and everything that had gone down within the last thirty minutes, I dug my fingernails into my palms, willing myself not to start crying again. The last thing I wanted my ex to believe was that I was crying over him. "Randall, just cut to the chase... why are you here?"

"Can we sit?"

"Fine," I said, sighing. I wasn't in any hurry to make anything more comfortable for him—but suddenly, I felt the energy drain from my body, as though I could scarcely keep myself upright. Motioning towards the kitchen table, we settled ourselves into chairs across from each other. I just wanted to get this over with so I could be alone. "What is so important that you had to drive all the way up here to Dearing Creek, Randall?"

"Well, I've been trying to reach you all summer. You're a difficult woman to get a hold of."

I raised an eyebrow. "I thought I made it clear that I had nothing more to say to you."

"Yes, but I do. You deserve an apology… a rather large one. And I am deeply sorry, Elizabeth. You deserve far better than how I've treated you."

I stared at him for a moment, not quite certain if I'd heard him correctly. The Randall Price I knew never apologized… *ever.*

"Anyway… I want to make things right. Over the past few months, I've been putting some feelers out there, and I'm now connected with an acquisitions manager at one of the top publishing houses in the Twin Cities. I still happened to have some of your writing samples on my hard drive, so I took the liberty of submitting them on your behalf. And after reading through them, along with the synopsis of that Great Depression novel you've been working on, Mark indicated he would be quite interested."

"What do you mean, 'interested'?"

"My understanding is that they want to bring you into the fold, to publish your book. With some editorial guidance, of course. So, we need to start looking for an agent!" He looked both smug and triumphant, like a king who'd just presented me with a spare set of keys to his kingdom.

It was a place I'd convinced myself I didn't belong—both in Randall's world and among the ranks of published authors. Inside, I was still that awkward, anxious girl with her nose in a book, prone to disaster, a head and heart full of doubt.

Could that girl ever belong there?

I'd thought I belonged *here*—at my grandparents' cabin, in Dearing Creek, with James. It felt like my home, more than any other. Up here, I could *breathe*.

At least until the past several weeks, when the threads holding together the patchwork of my life had begun to loosen. Now, everything I'd been so certain of felt unfamiliar, distorted, barely held together.

Which left me here—struggling to make sense of my career as a writer, my belief in Grandma Cora unraveling, and now, tiny threads of doubt even weakening the certainty I thought I'd had with James.

"I... don't quite know what to say."

"What is there to say? This is a once-in-a-lifetime opportunity, Elizabeth. Say the word, and it's yours." He smiled, reaching across the table to rest a hand on mine.

As I recoiled from his touch, his smile flickered only briefly before returning. "It's what you've always wanted, isn't it?"

This is it, Lizzie... the dream.

I looked at him. "Why now, Randall?"

"What do you mean?"

"Why didn't you ever offer to help me before this? You've never once told me you thought my writing was good enough to be published, never even encouraged me to try. Not once."

He sighed. "Well, to be fair, I was initially concerned about your interest in those *romance novels*. But your other ideas, they're good. And I do regret not telling you, or leveraging my connections, sooner." He leaned in, eyes intense. "But I'm here now."

I considered his words for a moment. "And exactly what are you hoping to get out of all of this? If I agree to consider it?"

Randall hesitated. "Well, I'll be honest, Elizabeth. I'm hoping for a second chance, for us. But—" he held up a hand as I started to object, "—the offer stands, regardless of our relationship status. It's yours... you've earned it." He stood up, pushing in his chair. I could hear Bucky emit another low growl from over in the corner. "I need to head back, as I have an early lecture tomorrow. But our meeting with Mark is scheduled for nine a.m. on Tuesday. Here's the address." He set a business card on the table. "I'm being included in this meeting mostly as a professional courtesy... but rest assured, it's *your* meeting. Though I have a separate matter to discuss there as well."

I picked up the business card, not saying a word as I watched him make his way to the door. *Could this truly be happening?* He paused to look back at me one last time, flashing a quick smile. "I hope you'll consider my offer, Elizabeth. This could be an incredible next chapter. For both of us."

Moments later, with the roar of an engine, he was gone—though not really, because he'd left plenty behind for me to unpack. I sat at that table for a long time, one foot in the past and the other in the future—with no idea of which steps to avoid in the present so I wouldn't be hurt even more than I already had.

My mind drifted unwillingly to the past, to a time when I'd been so smitten with the suave professor who'd just walked out the door.

"You have a spark of talent in you, Elizabeth," he'd always say to me, giving me a slow, sexy smile from over his glass of Pinot Noir. And I'd believed him then. Or at least, I'd desperately wanted to. He was, after all, the expert.

But maybe he'd only told me what I wanted to hear. Maybe, those words were really meant to serve his own purpose.

So I had no idea if meeting with this publisher was the right move. Would it really be a no-strings-attached offer, like Randall claimed? Could I believe in anything he said anymore?

I mean, there was no way I'd allow myself to end up back with him—it wasn't even up for discussion. But what would it say about me, accepting a favor of this magnitude from someone who'd treated me as though I didn't matter?

And then, there was the whole issue with the Great Depression story concept I'd abandoned. Could I stomach the idea of returning to it, even if doing so could make me a published author?

After finally surrendering myself to the idea of writing what I loved, going backwards felt almost like... defeat.

Though considering everything that had happened to challenge my beliefs about love in the past few weeks, I was beginning to wonder if writing romance novels was something I even had in me anymore.

But the most important questions nagging at me, however, weren't focused on my career at all—they were all about the man I'd just walked away from. What would he think of me if he knew what I was considering? If I actually went for this, would the relationship I'd built with James still be here waiting for me? Could the rips between us still be repaired?

And if I didn't take advantage of this opportunity to achieve my dream, would I later resent myself—and my relationship with James—for not even trying?

Standing up slowly, I crossed over to the sofa where I'd tossed my phone before following James to GiGi's cabin. It felt like a century ago now, and all I wanted to do was sleep and cry, then sleep some more.

But first, I sent off three messages, the first to my brother—

> *LIZZIE: Yo, bro. I'm coming down to Minneapolis tomorrow afternoon. Do you have time (and free sofa space) for your favorite sister?*

> *ETHAN: Mariah, good to hear from you. How's the fam?*

> *LIZZIE: I hate you.*

> *ETHAN: Pretty sure you actually love me.*

> *ETHAN: And… yes to both. Can't wait to see you. Shoot me a text when you get here.*

Chapter 35

James

"No. *Do not follow me. I need... I need space.*"

Watching Lizzie storm out that door—and being told not to follow—felt like my heart being ripped from my chest.

Seeing her let some goddamn mystery man into her home not even five minutes later? I thought I was going to fucking lose it.

Because who the hell was he? Why was he allowed to follow and not me?

And most of all—*how the hell did we end up here?*

"James, I—"

I spun around to fix my eyes on GiGi, every part of me buzzing "No. You do *not* get to say anything right now. You held onto this shit all this time, and act like it's nothing? You know what that family did to Pops. I can't let them hurt her."

"Of course I know. And you have every right to feel confused, and worried about Lizzie..."

"*Damn right I do.*"

"But I don't regret keeping Cora's secret, Tater."

My eyes were wide. "Why the hell not?"

"Because of all this," she said, gesturing around us. "What good has bringing up the past done, other than to hurt you both?"

Glancing out the window one last time, I started towards the door. "You should know well enough by now, GiGi... secrets always have a way of coming out. But having it happen the way it did tonight may have just destroyed everything." I paused, looking back at her. "And *you're* the one who has to live with that."

Then I stormed out of the place I used to call home, away from the woman who had been both mother and grandmother to me for most of my life.

But before heading to my truck, I couldn't stop myself from crossing over to Lizzie's cabin. Her curtains were still open, and the light inside illuminated the scene of her and a dark-haired older man sitting together at her kitchen table. And I swear I could see his hand touching hers, almost intimately.

Never in my life had I been a violent or possessive man—but at that moment, I could've broken every goddamn finger on that asshole's hand and shoved them down his throat for holding what was mine.

Then again, maybe I was wrong. Maybe she *wasn't*.

I woke up the next morning to a loud knocking on my front door—glancing at the clock on my nightstand, I realized it was already after eight. I'd overslept, thanks to the handful of IPAs I'd had after getting back home the night before. I'd been so wound up that I'd needed to take the edge off—which apparently, I'd done a little too well.

Throwing on a t-shirt, I shuffled my way to the door, opening it to find Jesse's smiling face on the other side. Noting the scowl on mine, he raised an eyebrow as he walked inside. "Did I catch you at a bad time? Need a little more beauty sleep, Beastie?"

"Not in the mood," I said as I dropped down onto my leather sofa, Jesse taking the chair next to me. "Some really bad shit went down with Lizzie and GiGi last night."

"What happened?"

"Nothing I can get into right now." I rubbed at my face, trying to wake up, my head already pounding. "Listen, can you text Lizzie and let her know we'll be over in thirty minutes or so to start work? I just need a quick shower first."

"Yeah, sure, man. Whatever you need."

Twenty minutes later, I was sitting in the passenger seat of Jesse's truck, trying to think of what I would say to Lizzie once we arrived. I knew she had to be in shock after everything GiGi told us, because I sure as hell was. So I was doing my best to respect her wishes, giving her space to sort things out—while trying not to lose my shit over whomever it was that had paid her a visit last night.

But more than anything, I couldn't stop thinking about how our last conversation had ended, wondering if she was more angry at my reaction than the actual news itself. She had to know I was just angry, right? That I was still in this with her? Because I hadn't heard a word from her since.

And again, even if I had, what would I say? Was I sorry for how I felt about the Hardons? Or how having her in my life might mean welcoming them into it, too?

All I knew for sure was, this was the second time I'd let my personal resentment against that family drive a wedge between us. And this time, I'd hurt her in the process, something I swore I'd never do. I needed to get a handle on this, once and for all.

We pulled into her driveway a few minutes later, and the first thing I noticed was her car was gone. I glanced over at Jesse. "Hey, did you hear back from Lizzie?"

"Yeah, sorry... she said she wasn't around and to go ahead and use the spare key." Hoisting himself out of the vehicle, he slammed the door shut. I pulled my phone from my pocket, realizing I hadn't touched it at all since last night.

And what the hell—I *did* have a text from Lizzie. My phone must've been left on silent from when I'd been out breaking down wood in my shop the night before. I'd spent hours out there trying to keep myself from crumbling, or going to her before I could do so with a clearer head.

LIZZIE: Figuring some things out. I'll be back.

What did that even mean? Figuring what out—her family? Her future? Us?

And what do I say to that? Other than, '*I'm sorry. Please come back.*'?

But it was pointless debating, obsessing. Because with as fucked up as everything felt, her vague message and tone made one thing pretty plain—she needed space.

And not just from the situation—from *me* as well.

All I could do now was give it to her. Even if doing so felt like I could be risking the best thing I'd ever had.

JAMES: I'm so sorry. I'll be here, waiting for you… for as long as it takes.

Jesse and I worked hard all day long, finishing the last few touches on the master bathroom addition. I had to admit—of all the bathroom renos I had designed in my time, this is the one I was most proud of. Lizzie had opted for a large stall shower in addition to a corner jetted tub, everything in white and light gray tiles and warm wood. It was similar to the color scheme we'd gone with for her guest bathroom—but here, the upgrades were obvious. And the large, floor-to-ceiling window with built in shades gave the entire space a feeling of lightness and calm, grounded by the warmth of the wood finishings.

It would be pretty fucking stupid to ever compare the woman you loved to a bathroom, so I'd never making the mistake of saying this out loud. But the warmth I felt in this room—*the entire cabin*, really—was all Lizzie. Her compassion, her depth—even the color of her hair seemed threaded within the grain of the wood that ran throughout her home as a whole, polished with care and brought back to life.

But the woman herself was missing. And this '*giving her space*' crap was at least somewhat easier when I knew she was here, safe in her cabin.

Not knowing where the hell she was—or when I'd even see her again—well, that was *killing* me.

But now, we'd come to the end of the workday—and very soon, the end of this project. All that remained were the final walk-through and then the inspection, capped by installing the last piece I'd been working on all summer.

And then it would all be done.

I knew I should feel more excited now that we were on the cusp of completing Horizon Remodeling's first official renovation. I already had a few bids out on additional jobs, all of which seemed like a sure thing and would carry us well into the winter.

So my problem wasn't about the work. It was about not knowing what things would look like for me and Lizzie in the coming weeks. Because once things ended here, I'd no longer have an excuse to be hanging around, even when she was angry with me. Or to sense how she was feeling day to day and be there to help her through it.

It would be easier to disappear from her mind and heart completely.

I was stuck in my head on the entire drive back to my place, even as Jesse helped me to load up the piece I'd been working on in my shop these many weeks, then hauling it back to the cabin. I wanted to have everything in place for when she got back, whenever that might be.

Because she *had* to come back.

Standing back after we got it all situated in Lizzie's living room, Jesse wiped his brow with the back of his hand before turning to look at me. "She's a beaut, Tate."

I smirked. "Thanks."

"No, I mean it… For once, I'm actually not trying to make a joke. Lizzie's gonna love it."

"I hope so."

"And she'll be back soon enough."

"Yeah."

He was quiet for a minute. "You really love her, don't you?"

Giving him a quick glance, I shrugged before shoving my hands in my pockets, feeling the words I wished I could say catch in my throat. I didn't know why—but right then, with how unsettled everything felt between me and Lizzie, I felt naked and exposed. And all I wanted to do was surround myself again with the walls that had kept me safe all these years. It used to be my default, my comfort.

Now I wondered if all it had done was guarantee I'd always be alone.

Ignoring my silence, he pressed on. "It's obvious, dude… you're just… different with her. I mean, you're yourself, but… nicer."

Now I looked at him. "Gee, thanks."

Jesse grinned. "Again, not a joke. She's good for you. And I think you know it. Besides," he motioned now towards our focal point against the wall, "one look at all this pretty much says everything."

I grunted, feeling a bit of the Lizzie effect as my goddamn cheeks started to burn. I turned my face away from Jesse, but not because I was embarrassed.

It's because I didn't want him to see the truth.

Jesse took off for home a few minutes later, anxious for Tara's tater tot hotdish. We'd driven back to Lizzie's place separately, so I hung back for a bit. Now that it was early evening, the intense heat of the late August day had started to lift—and the traffic out on the lake was quiet for the first time in days.

I hadn't had a chance to get out there for the past couple of weeks, with everything going on. And right now, nothing sounded better than time by myself, on the lake that I'd loved my whole life.

Walking down to GiGi's dock while kicking off my socks and shoes, I pulled my kayak out from beneath the end of the dock. After a few taps to make sure no critters had crawled inside, I hopped into the cockpit and pushed off from shore.

A light breeze was helping with the temperature this evening—just enough to break the heat but not too much to cause wakes on the water. We were moving closer to the end of summer cabin season, and both Lake Elska and the town of Dearing Creek would soon settle into the quieter pace of fall and winter. The rental cabins would sit empty; the cafes and shops in town would no longer be packed with folks from the Twin Cities. This place would belong to us again—nature and the locals. And everything would reset, settling into hibernation until spring.

Not everything, though. Looking at my own life, things had changed pretty dramatically since the end of the previous summer. Back then, I was still working for Mel, overloaded with projects and ruminating over an inheritance I didn't want. I spent my free time right out here in my kayak, hanging with Jesse or with my grandmother. I had a handful of dates with some woman—whose name I couldn't remember—over in Heartwood, which never amounted to anything. Mostly because I wouldn't let it.

And I'd believed the only woman I'd ever care about was GiGi.

Now, it was almost like I'd finally gone ahead and updated my old reading glasses—and my world had gone from blurry to sharply defined. First, having Jack back home again; then, starting my business; and now, my life with Lizzie.

Before her was the part that seemed the most fuzzy—before we quite *literally* crashed into each other's lives and she went ahead and added all the details to a life that had never felt like much. I'd never expected to find peace, much less joy or beauty.

And now, here I was—pining after a woman I'd grown to care so much about, who I might've just allowed my stupid goddamn fears and ego to push away.

I glided along the water, hearing faint laughter coming from along the shoreline just off to my left along the western banks. The sun was setting in that direction, still above the treeline, so I couldn't quite make out who it was. But with that light shining in my eyes, almost blinding—it felt as though I were under some sort of interrogation.

I swear, I thought I was moving past all this shit. Until GiGi went and threw an emotional grenade on top of everything we'd built, and I allowed Lizzie to get caught up in it. Seeing her upset was the most painful part of it all. Though, I was beginning to think that my reaction to her newfound connection with the Hardons had been the thing that drove her away more than anything else.

I mean, I knew I'd overreacted. The Hardon name in particular was so triggering for me and my family, it felt out of my control. I didn't know much about Mitchum, the grandfather—other than that he'd started the company decades ago.

I wished that GiGi hadn't known about any of it. Even now, I still felt so angry... most of all, with myself. I hadn't been working through my past issues at all—instead, I think I'd just tried to pretend it no longer existed.

I rounded the bend and was almost back to the dock now, and I noticed GiGi had come out onto her front porch. I'd been hoping to avoid her tonight—I didn't think I could handle more confrontation so soon.

But as I dragged my kayak up onto the shore, I looked back again and noticed GiGi was no longer sitting on her rocker—instead she was laying, face down, on the porch.

I froze, my mind transported backwards fifteen years to the day I found Pops laying just like this out on the dock. It was my final glimpse of the only man who'd deserved the title of 'father'. The only man who'd bothered to stick around for me.

But now, here she lay. I couldn't lose her, too.

Running barefoot up the grassy slope, I screamed out her name as I pulled my phone from my pocket, dialing. Once I reached where she lay, I tried to rouse her, feeling for a pulse. It was there, but faint.

"9-1-1, *what is your emergency?*"

"I need an ambulance, right away. My grandmother... she collapsed. 103 Grove Avenue, south end of Lake Elska."

"*Can you tell me if she's breathing, sir?*"

"Yes, but I need someone—NOW!"

Dropping my phone to the step, I leaned my body over GiGi's and felt the tears begin to fall as, over and over, the words repeated in my head:

Please, God...I can't lose her, too.

Chapter 36

Lizzie

LIZZIE: *Perfect.*

BROOKE: *Good.*

BROOKE: *But, holy shit, though…*

LIZZIE: *Yup. #fml*

"*What… the actual… fuck.*"

I nodded at my brother, watching the same tidal wave of emotions cross his face as mine had done twenty-four hours earlier. "I know. It's… unbelievable."

"I feel like our entire lives were built on a lie."

"Pretty much."

Ethan stared at me across our corner booth at Amore Victoria, the same forkful of pasta still frozen in midair in front of him. "How are you this… *calm* right now?"

I raised an eyebrow. "Honestly? By this point, I'm starting to feel numb to it all." And it was true. I only vaguely recalled dropping Bucky off with Indi and Callum or the drive down to Minneapolis that morning—much less anything that had happened on either side of it.

At one point, I'd stopped at one of my favorite indie bookstores in Minneapolis, Tropes & Trifles—managing to leave with two sackfuls of romance novels I didn't even remember choosing (though even "numb Lizzie" had impeccable taste). Afterwards, I'd ended up at the Minneapolis Institute of Art for a couple of hours, wandering through the exhibits without really seeing—in a place that existed *solely* to be seen.

The one thing I knew for certain was when I woke up that morning, I couldn't deal with facing James—at least, not yet. Not when everything in my head and heart felt like one big, jumbled mess. So I'd packed a bag, heading out long before the guys were due to arrive.

And there'd been no response from James to the text I'd sent last night until finally mid-morning, though it didn't surprise me. What does one even say to, '*Figuring some things out. I'll be back.*'? If that had been me, I'd probably be dissolving into a whirlpool of anxiety right about now.

But at least when I'd finally heard from him, I'd felt a glimmer of hope. Like he still wanted me, in spite of everything. He hadn't given up, or walked away entirely. Even though technically, I'd been the one doing the leaving.

> *JAMES: I'll be here, waiting for you… for as long as it takes.*

How long *did* it take, exactly, to bring life back, when all you feel is numb? Because right before my eyes, the pages I'd already lived were being ripped out and burned, one by one—my biography rewritten in broad strokes, in a hand I didn't recognize. So you could say I was being reborn, but in the messiest, most painful way possible.

But at least I knew I wasn't crazy. Seeing Ethan's reaction confirmed that *none* of this was normal—nor had the way forward been written yet.

Which meant, I guess, that part was up to *us*.

"So, have you told Mariah?"

I gave him a look, already knowing how that conversation would go. "What do *you* think?"

"Come on, Liz... she deserves to know what's going on. We can't spend our lives tiptoeing around our sister just because she isn't the easiest person to deal with."

"That's putting it nicely," I said, muttering under my breath. But of course he was right. Taking a rather large sip from my wine glass, I pulled out my phone and dialed my sister. After two rings, her outgoing voicemail message began playing. I glanced over at him, mouthing *'voicemail'* with a know-it-all look on my face. As he rolled his eyes, I heard the beep.

"Yeah, hi... Mariah? It's Lizzie. And Ethan. Listen, there's some information I found out about Grandma Cora, and our family, that we think you need to know. But I don't want to just leave it in a message... so, can you call me back? Please. It's important." Hanging up, I set my phone back on the table, stabbing my fork into my bolognese. "You know she probably saw it was me and sent it straight to voicemail, right?"

"Maybe. But it was still the right thing to do."

"Yeah, I know," I said, sighing. "I just wish she didn't always make things so difficult."

Ethan shrugged. "Maybe that trait came from the Hardon side of the family?"

I reached across the table, smacking his arm. "Be serious." But it was the first moment since GiGi's living room that I'd felt somewhat lighter.

"So, how do we approach this with the Hardons?" Ethan asked, pushing back his empty plate.

"I don't know... I guess I haven't had time to form a plan yet. But I think I need to go and meet Mitchum, at the very least. GiGi said he's still living up in Dearing Creek."

"Alright. But I'm not letting you fly solo on this, Liz. You've had to deal with everything alone for months. We're in this together now. Ok?"

"Ok." But even though I appreciated having my brother alongside me, the person I most wanted was two hours north, hating everything about the family I'd just inherited.

Was it pointless to hope that he'd ever be able to accept any of this?

"Anyway, I'm sorry I haven't been able to make it up to the cabin all summer. The new website for that hotel brand was on a rush, and nobody on the team has been allowed time off. But now that it's wrapped, I can take a handful of days, spend some time up north. I've been dying to see the progress with the cabin, too. Is that ok?"

I smiled. "It's more than ok. I'd love it. But just be warned, Dearie Girls Weekend is a week from now… so I'm booting you out before then."

"Don't worry, I've learned my lesson on that one," he said, grimacing. "And hey, it's about time that I meet James too, don't you think? I need to do my due diligence, make sure he's worthy and all that brotherly stuff."

"Yeah, sure," I said, giving him a vague smile—inside, my mind was back on James, wondering where he was, or what he was doing. It had only been twelve hours since I left, and already I wished I was back home with him in Dearing Creek. And yet, I could still hear the words we'd both said in anger last night in GiGi's living room:

"Those people will never be your family. The best thing you can do is walk away."

"Is this really about their goddamn money again?"

"Does it matter? I can't fucking do this."

Was he sitting alone right now, wishing he could take it all back? Did he wonder how long it would take me to come back home again—or was he worried I might not at all?

He'd said he'd be there waiting for me, for as long as it took. He'd said those words, in spite of everything. I should trust in that, right?

But there was no point in driving myself crazy. Right now, my focus should be on the reason I'd made the trip here in the first place. Figuring out everything with James would have to wait until I returned home again.

"Anyway, I need to wrap up a few things tomorrow, but then I could head up on Thursday morning maybe? Does that work?"

I meandered back to reality, realizing my brother had asked me a question. "*Um, what?*"

"I asked if it's ok if I head up Thursday morning." Ethan gave me a strange look. "You sure you're ok?"

"Yeah, sorry. And Thursday is actually perfect...I have that meeting with the publisher in the morning, and then I'll be staying with Brooke for a couple of days. We can caravan up together."

"Sounds good. And again, I'm really proud of you for getting that meeting, Lizzie." His eyes, mirrors of my own, were encouraging. "It's about damn time someone noticed how talented you are."

I felt my cheeks flush. "Thanks. To be honest, it doesn't actually feel... real."

"Well, believe it... because it *is*." Ethan handed his credit card to the server as he returned to the table with our bill. "This'll be the start of something big for you, Lizzie... just watch."

I gave him a small smile, saying nothing. But I had to admit to feeling ashamed that I'd omitted a very important detail—that this entire opportunity had been orchestrated by my ex-boyfriend.

Everyone I loved now *hated* Randall—and even though I was hardly a fan of his either, I needed to have my head in the game for tomorrow. The rest would just have to sort itself out later.

Which, actually, was the *real* story of my life.

I walked out of the elevator at Everett Publishing, smoothing my hands over my hair one last time before walking into reception. Randall was already standing there with his back to me, looking exceptionally tall and put together as always. I bristled as I realized he was chatting up the pretty blonde receptionist, until I remembered—that was Old Lizzie's problem.

And I had no room in my life to waste another ounce of worry on Randall Price. I was here to get myself published—focused only on looking forward, not backward.

"Hi, Randall."

He turned with a slow smile at my voice, his eyes traveling up and down the length of me in that way I used to love. Now it made me feel, well, *nothing* really. Amazing what four months and a good man could do. "Elizabeth. You look beautiful."

Ignoring his compliment, I gave him a terse smile. "So, I just want to take a second to discuss how to approach this meeting with Mar—"

"*Randall, so good to see you!*" a voice called from the other side of reception as I saw a willowy, raven-haired woman cross towards us—wearing black stilettos and a gorgeous red sheath dress, perfectly matched to the shade of her lipstick. I suddenly felt very self-conscious, Ms. *Frumpy McFrumperson*, standing there in the wide legged beige trousers and dark blue blazer I'd grabbed without thinking as I'd thrown my bag together Monday morning.

"Loretta, what a pleasant surprise." As she closed the gap between them, Randall leaned in for the customary air kiss I'd always found so insufferable. But I noticed her lingering there a touch longer, making me wonder if the two of them had some sort of history.

Again, *absolutely* did not care. The only question I did care about? *Where was Mark, the guy we were supposed to be meeting?*

As the two separated, Loretta noticed me standing there, her eyes giving me the once-over before extending a hand with a slight smile. "You must be Ms. Blake. I'm Loretta Everett, CEO of Everett Publishing. Randall's told me a great deal about you and your... work."

Slanting a confused glance over to Randall, I forced a smile before shaking her hand with a firm grip. "Nice to meet you, Ms. Everett. Thank you for making time in your schedule to meet with me... I'm sure you're very busy. But I must admit, I'm a little confused. I thought we'd be meeting with Mark Hammer?"

"Our acquisitions manager?" Loretta waved a hand dismissively. "When I heard Randall Price had a fledgling author he was recommending, I knew I had to take the appointment myself. Especially as we have some other matters to discuss ourselves," she said, looking at him pointedly with the hint of a smile.

Randall nodded, returning her look. "We're very lucky she was able to fit us in, of course... Loretta's reputation in this industry is unmatched."

"You flatter me, Randall," she preened. "Follow me, please... and Molly?" She glanced over to the receptionist. "Please hold all of my calls. You do remember how, yes?" Molly nodded, now looking anxious as we followed Loretta down the hallway.

You and me both, sister.

Entering her lavish corner office, I wondered what the hell dimension I had just stepped into. The entire space—with vast windows, dark wood and gold accents—was decked out floor to ceiling in minimalist luxury, punctuated by the glass-topped desk at the center, and high-backed leather chair positioned behind it.

Lowering herself into her throne as Randall and I took seats across from her, Loretta zeroed in on me. "So, Ms. Blake... Randall tells me you have a degree in creative writing and have been working on your craft for years—but this would be your first official book. Is that correct?"

"Well, yes... technically speaking. I'd previously written a few novellas as well, though none were ever published."

"I see. What was the premise of these... novellas, if you don't mind me asking?"

Trying to ignore the familiar tingling feeling as it spread through the length of my fingers, I continued. "They were mostly... contemporary romance stories."

"Ah. *Interesting.*"

"But Elizabeth has moved far beyond romance tales, Loretta," Randall interjected, shooting me a look. "As I mentioned, she's been hard at work on her novel focused on The Great Depression. It's really quite good."

"Yes, I've read a handful of pages... I would agree, there's some potential there," she acquiesced, giving Randall a smile as though he were attending a slightly inappropriate parent/teacher conference. Then she redirected her gaze back to me. "What is it about this topic that most intrigues you?"

For a moment, my mind went blank. *C'mon, Blake... you can do this.* "Well, I grew up hearing stories from my grandmother. Her own mother and aunt had a tough life growing up in the thirties, pretty much having to raise themselves. It's what inspired me to make a relationship between two sisters the focal point, really. They're the heart of the story."

She studied me for a moment. "Relationships are what interest you most, then?"

God, this felt familiar. "Well, yes. But the historical aspect is important as well..."

The numbness was spreading to my face now. *She can see right through you, Lizzie.*

"Hmmm." Loretta allowed her gaze to linger a few seconds longer, before glancing down at the stack of papers before her—containing printouts spanning my writing career over the years. One student award, a couple of published short stories featured in my university's literary magazine, and this, the first few rough chapters of my abandoned novel.

But where was the heart in *any* of it? Especially in the story of the two sisters—whose relationship I'd barely begun to write, much less figure out. The only reason I could even call them *'the heart of the story'* was because everything else in it felt dark and lifeless. I still had no idea who those characters were, or why they even mattered.

Looking at that pile of papers, though, one thing was clear—everything that I'd written so far on a professional level, from those submissions to my time in marketing, had come from a place of technical precision, expectation, reader manipulation, and fear of judgment from so-called literary experts. Along with so much damn *doubt*.

And because of it, I'd spent so much time convincing myself that a true writer didn't write about things like romance—at least not one who wanted to be taken seriously. I'd talked a big game about being inspired by my grandparents' love story, but at the first sign of trouble, I let both my own romantic failings and the past cast a shadow over all of it.

I thought I'd been living my life as a self-proclaimed hopeless romantic. In truth, I'd let myself stop believing because I was afraid. Because I'd lost *hope*.

Even still—I *wanted* to believe all of it was real. And I wanted to believe that I'd found it for myself. With everything that had happened, could I even find my way back?

"Love stories are magical, Lizzie girl. They give us hope. Because all of us, regardless of who we are or where our stories began, need something to believe in. And all of us are worthy of being loved," Grandma Cora's voice echoed through my mind, saying the words I'd heard countless times before. The statement in itself was romantic, an ideal about love I'd grown up believing in. Those stories had made me believe perfect, infallible love was possible—not just possible—*probable*. I'd thought my grandparents were living proof.

Until they *weren't*.

But her words sounded different to me now. There was a rawness to them that only came from having gone through it all yourself—the highs and the lows, the unimaginable joy and the searing pain. From screwing it all up, to finding your way back again to what truly mattered. It takes courage and strength to live out our stories—but the grace comes when we can learn to love each other and *ourselves* through all of it. Especially the messy parts.

Like my grandmother... James... and even *me*.

That was true love, real and relatable. Those are the stories that mattered, that people needed to hear. And now I realized—it's what I should've been brave enough to share with the world all along.

My mind was brought back to the present by Loretta's pen tapping against the glass surface of her desk as she finished reviewing the paper in her hand. I wondered how much pressure it would take before the flaws became visible there, too.

"So, is this the sort of work we can expect if we were to sign you, Ms. Blake? Literary fiction, with a focus on social commentary?"

I hesitated for a moment, glancing between her and Randall. I knew the answer both were expecting. What kind of an idiot would shoot themselves in the foot in a moment like this?

Taking a breath, I shook my head. "Actually, no. The style of writing I'm looking to focus on is in creating stories about realistic relationships. Something that the reader can see themselves in that will give them hope. Stories... about love."

Loretta raised an eyebrow, considering my words. "It sounds as though you intend to write... *romance* novels, Ms. Blake."

I let the smile spread across my lips. "Yes, Ms. Everett. That's exactly what I plan to do."

Randall leaned closer, muttering, "*Elizabeth...*" like a warning from under his breath. I ignored him, my eyes locked with the CEO sitting across from me, feeling the numb and tingly sensations within me suddenly begin to dissipate. And for maybe the first time *ever*, I hadn't a shred of doubt.

It was Loretta who broke eye contact first, glancing over to Randall. "I thought you said she was a sure thing, Randall."

"She was... I mean, she still *is*, Loretta."

"What we had discussed was creating a strong lineup of new and promising authors, spanning the most important genres." Her red lips pursed. "And already you've faltered with the very first candidate, Randall?"

I looked at him. "What is she referring to?"

He held up a hand to silence me, turning back to Loretta. "Give me until tomorrow, and I'll present a suitable replacement to you. Already, I have at least half a dozen promising authors lined up who'd be thrilled to write anything you ask."

But she was shaking her head. "No, I need time to think—we may need to pause this relationship before it goes any further."

And then it all made sense. This had never been about helping me. As always, it was only ever about Randall. And based on how he was scrambling now, it was pretty clear he'd been promised some sort of monetary kickback in whatever arrangement they'd put together.

Had this happened a few months ago, I probably would've been destroyed. But now? All I felt was relief, like I'd finally been freed from my cage.

For too long I'd let imposter syndrome take the wheel, trying my damndest to seem interesting and impressive, just so I could feel *worthy* of an accomplished and cultured man like him or part of an industry like publishing.

But as I stared at him now, my ex was starting to look less like the handsome, polished professor—and exactly like a man I never should have wasted my time with in the first place.

Because Randall Price had never loved anyone but himself. And I'd *always* deserved better. It just took me too damn long to realize it.

Standing up, I gave the two of them a brief smile. "Well, I wish you both the best of luck with all of that." As I grabbed my purse and started towards the door, I heard both rise from their seats.

"Elizabeth, hold on just for a moment, ok?"

I turned, cocking my head slightly as I looked at him. "You know what, Randall? I don't think I will. And please make sure to lose my number, won't you? I assume you remember how."

And damn, it felt amazing, walking away from everything in that room.

Because finally, I knew *exactly* where I was headed.

Chapter 37

James

I'd been pacing near the nurse's station for nearly thirty minutes already, driving the staff crazy.

But I couldn't help it—with the way the adrenaline was still pumping through me, there was no way I could sit still right now. I'd followed the ambulance all the way to DCH Hospital—blasting my horn at all the jackasses who refused to make space on the road to pass—terrified that we'd never make it.

And now that we had, time had slowed to a crawl, forcing me into a goddamned eternity of waiting for any fragment of news that might give me cause to breathe again.

Because she hadn't looked good when they'd wheeled her through here. GiGi had still been unconscious, quieter than I'd ever known her to be. Paler, too. I still had no idea what had happened—all I knew was they were making me wait out here, wearing down a path on the laminate floor, as the doctors worked to figure it out.

Of course, that wasn't the only thing I knew. But facing the reality that all of this was my fault wasn't something I could deal with at the moment, when everything was falling apart. Finding a way to make things right with my grandmother would have to come after.

And the only *'after'* I'd accept would be the one where GiGi pulled through this ok.

Because if I lost her too, I'd never be able to forgive myself. Ever.

One agonizing hour later, Nurse Lynette led me back to her room in the ICU. She was the mother of one of the younger guys I'd worked with at Aaronson Construction—a very nice lady whom I still ran into around town from time to time. It helped to have a familiar face, even when I was at my worst.

When we walked in and I saw GiGi lying there, tubes and wires criss-crossing their way in and out of her from various machines, the steady whirring and beeping noises emitting from them screaming, *'You almost lost her'*, it was all I could do not to break down. Even as a boy,

I'd rarely cried. Apparently, it was only reserved for the women that I loved.

Approaching the bed after Lynette excused herself to answer a page, I at least found comfort in the fact that GiGi had more color to her now—thanks in part to the bruise on her forehead. But overall, she looked smaller, more fragile than I was used to seeing her. I lowered myself into the chair next to her, half expecting my grandmother to pop up with one of her sassy one-liners, telling me to wipe the frown off my face—truth was, I would've given anything for it.

Her eyes, however, remained closed, her voice silent. She was breathing, though, and her heart was pumping. So she was safe—for now.

But I couldn't breathe. Not just yet.

I heard footsteps coming up behind me, and a kind-looking man—maybe a decade older than me at most—approached the foot of the bed, extending a hand. "You must be James. I'm Dr. Addison, and I've been taking care of your grandmother."

Rising halfway from my seat to shake his hand, I nodded. "Thanks, Doc. How's she doing? And do you know what happened?"

"Well, Georgia appears to have had a TIA, or a Transient Ischemic Attack. Basically, a mini-stroke. But it appears that she passed out from hitting her head on the way down, rather than the stroke. Her MRI, however, looks good. Mostly just surface bruising."

"Thank God. Why isn't she awake?"

"We're just keeping her under mild sedation for the time being, nothing to worry about there."

Looking at her lying there on the bed, I was finding it difficult to do anything but worry. "So why did this happen in the first place?"

"Well, because of her heart disease, of course." The way he said it was so matter-of-fact, I knew I was the last one to be let in on this news.

"GiGi has... heart disease?"

"I've actually been seeing Georgia for this issue for over a year now, working on her risk factors and the lifestyle changes she needed to make." Dr. Addison frowned. "I'm sorry. I assumed she had told you."

I felt the fist in my gut clench tighter. "No. She hasn't told me anything."

With a sigh, Dr. Addison pulled out her chart from the pocket at the end of her bed, doing a quick review of her information. "Well, my guess is she hasn't been implementing any of the changes I'd recommended, either. Hopefully this will be her wake-up call to get serious about it." He glanced over at me with a slight grimace. "She was lucky this time, especially since you were close by. She shouldn't have any long-term damage from her TIA. But it could happen again, or something much worse... if Georgia doesn't start making her health a priority."

I could feel my own head starting to hurt, thinking again of how I could have lost her. *Why had she been so fucking stubborn and not told me about any of this?* "Got it. I'll make sure she does."

"Good. We'll keep her resting until morning. And assuming she's doing ok, I imagine we'll be able to discharge her by the end of tomorrow."

I nodded. "Thanks, Doc."

Dr. Addison replaced her chart, resting a hand on my shoulder as he made his way out. "Georgia is one of my favorite patients—definitely feisty, but she's a smart woman. As long as she starts making some adjustments, she should do ok." After a quick smile, he left the room as a familiar voice rang out behind me.

"You just can't find anything better to do with your time than hang out at hospitals, huh?"

Jack appeared next to me with two to-go cups of coffee, handing me one of them before dragging over a second wooden chair.

"How'd you know I was here?"

"You know how things work in this town. One of the nurses is good friends with Tara and let her know you guys were here, and then Jesse texted me right after." He shrugged. "Besides, GiGi's an institution around here—everyone probably knew within five minutes of your arrival, anyway."

Shaking my head, I took a sip from my cup—knowing my friend was absolutely right. "Thanks for this, man."

"Of course. I couldn't let you sit here all alone, drinking shitty hospital coffee. Serious moments call for Steamy Beanies' dark roast," he said with a wink, referring to the coffee spot on the other side of the lake.

"You know what I mean. Being here and everything."

Jack's face grew serious now as he gave a brief nod. "Not even a question. You and GiGi are family, probably more than my own." There was no joking between us now—both likely thinking back on countless times in the past where we'd each gone through shit. But like true brothers, we'd had each other's back every time. There was nothing I wouldn't do for Jack and Jesse or their families. And I was grateful to have it reciprocated.

Because with the way things seemed to be going over the last forty-eight hours, I knew I'd need their support now more than ever.

"By the way, Jesse said he'll try to stop by in the morning to check in. Tara wasn't feeling the best tonight, so he wanted to stick close."

"Is it the baby?"

Jack shook his head. "No... sounds like she was just dealing with some bad heartburn or something."

"I'll bet Jesse was trying out a new recipe on her again."

"Probably."

We smiled at each other for a moment before Jack continued. "I caught the tail end of your conversation with the doctor. How are you feeling about all of that?"

"Honestly? I don't know. I mean, I'm relieved that it looks like she'll pull through this ok. But I'm also pissed that she kept the fact that she has heart disease from me for an entire fucking *year* and didn't seem to be doing anything to take better care of herself in the meantime." I looked down at the paper cup I held in my hands, tracing the Steamy Beanies logo with my thumb. "What if she..." But I choked on the words, not able to find it in me to finish the statement. Almost like saying them out loud might give them more power, willing them into existence.

"I know. GiGi's a tough woman... she'll have to start listening to her doctor, so you know she'll grumble about that. But the world's not done with her yet." Jack's eyes were kind. "Have you talked to Lizzie yet?"

Lizzie. I'd thought about texting her a million times over the past hour—shit, even before the ambulance arrived. But her last message was still twisting around in my mind—*'Figuring some things out. I'll be back.'* So I didn't know if I should.

"James. I know something happened between the two of you the other night, but... she'd want to know."

Finally, I raised my eyes from my coffee cup, no longer surprised at my friend's ability to read my mind. "Yeah, maybe."

"There's no 'maybe' about it. You love her. And Jesse and I agree, it's pretty obvious she loves you. Despite you being a stubborn ass half the time."

"The love in this room is overwhelming." But still, there was that word again. *Love.*

Is this what love felt like?

Jack chuckled, but his eyes remained serious. "You know, I still ask myself all the time if I should've fought harder for Dana when she ended things. Maybe it wouldn't have changed a damn thing. But at least I'd have known that I tried everything." Glancing briefly at GiGi, he leaned closer. "We only get one chance to live this life, man. And even though you've been dealt a lot of shit throughout yours, don't let the past hold you back from being happy now. Trust me, you'll regret it." Giving me a pat on the arm, he did a scan around the room. "Now, let's see where we can wrangle some pillows."

My eyes widened. "What, you planning to stay or something?"

He grinned. "Of course. Can't leave you here to your own devices. And besides," he said, with a quick glance towards the door, "there's a cute nurse on duty tonight."

Shaking my head, I chuckled. "'Course there is." But we both left the real reason unsaid. After all these years, it didn't need to be. That's how it was with the family you choose.

After securing a pillow and a blanket each from Nurse Lynette, we sat there together in companionable silence, the soft whooshing of oxygen matching our own breathing. And I couldn't help but think how grateful I was that

GiGi would be ok. But even more so, how tired I was of being held captive to my bitterness.

With Lizzie, I could let go and feel happy. Maybe that's what mattered, more than anything else.

Chapter 38

James

Jesse showed up by mid-morning, with fresh coffee for both of us. And after Jack left for home, Jesse and I spent our time arguing good-naturedly about our individual job titles within Horizon Remodeling, now that we were officially going into a partnership together. My friend was in the middle of insisting upon calling himself 'Chief Turd Wrangler' when I heard a voice grumbling from the bed.

"If you two are gonna keep arguing over something so stupid, can you ask the nurse to give me the good drugs that'll knock me out again?"

Both of our heads whipped over to see GiGi laying there with her eyes open, giving us the same look she always had whenever she was secretly amused but pulled out her grumpy demeanor for appearance's sake.

I don't think I'd ever been so glad to hear her fake-complain at me in my whole damn life.

Eyes tearing up, I crossed my arms against my chest, taking a page from her book. "It's about time you decided to wake up. You think we've got all day to just sit around here?"

"Yeah, well... can't blame a girl for wanting a little peace and quiet."

"Yep... hard to come by, living in a small-town, on private lakefront property."

"And on *that* note," Jesse stood up, chuckling, "I'm going to run back home and check on my wife. Let me know if either of you need anything. And GiGi?"

"Yes, dear?"

"I'm really glad you're ok... don't ever scare us like that again, got it? But please, try to take it easy on our boy here."

"No promises. Give Tara my love."

Grinning as he looked over at me with an '*oh well, I tried*' shrug, Jesse retrieved his coffee cup from the floor and left the room. Soon, I could hear him chatting nearby with Nurse Abby, yet another friend of Tara's. I figured they were probably loading him down with workplace gossip to entertain his wife once he arrived back home—she'd been bored out of her mind already with her forced bedrest.

Turning back to GiGi, I realized she was eyeing me from the bed, her white hair spread wildly across her pillow. I wondered how getting her to make *her own* health changes in the coming weeks was going to go—probably not well.

But at that moment, emotionally strung-out and sleep-deprived, I didn't have the energy to figure that part out yet. All I could think about was how grateful I was to hear her voice, and how I needed to fix what I'd broken.

Sighing, I sat back in my chair. "How do you feel?"

"Not too poorly. Though, my head hurts." Reaching a hand up to her face, she touched her bandaged forehead gingerly before glancing back at me again. This time, her voice sounded less confident. "Was it my heart?"

"Doctor Addison said a mini stroke... a TIA, I think is what he said." I saw her eyes widen a bit, though she said nothing. "But you're going to be ok."

"I know."

"It could've been so much worse..."

"I know that, too."

I felt a lump form in my throat. "You really scared me, you know. I don't know what I'd do if I lo—"

She held up a hand to stop me, but her voice was gentle. "You didn't lose me, Tater... I'm still here. And I'm not planning on going anywhere, at least not anytime soon. But I *am* sorry for scaring you. And for... not telling you about the rest."

"You mean the fact that you have *heart disease*?" I said, eyebrows raised.

"Yes. I guess... I don't know, I was in some kind of denial. It hit close to home too, thinking about your Pops." She let out a long, shuddering sigh. "I know I need to make some changes in how I'm doing things. And I really will try. Starting with… an apology. For the other night."

I shook my head. "No, listen… *I'm* the one who needs to apologize. I mean, I was upset… but I never should have spoken to you the way I did. And God, maybe none of this would've happened to you in the first place if I'd handled it better…"

"Sweetie… this wasn't your fault." GiGi frowned, the concern visible in her eyes. "I only have myself to blame for not taking Dr. Addison's words to heart. Hearing yours wasn't what made me fall apart."

"But still… if I'd lost you, if that had been our last conversation…"

"Then, what? Do you think the entirety of our relation-ship is going to be summed up by one damn argument? I've loved you for your whole life, boy, and I don't plan on stopping. Not ever. And no matter what words get said, I know you love me, too. So, you need to let that nonsense go and forgive yourself."

Reaching her hand out towards me, I enclosed it be-tween mine without saying a word—her skin cold and delicate, with raised purple veins running through it. These were not the hands of a young woman, nor had I ever known her to be. Neither of us could stop the passage of time—and looking at her now, one might *al-most* believe the feistiness of the incomparable Georgia LaMott had finally faded.

But not if I had anything to say about it.

Then she continued. "I want you to know… it was hard on me too, carrying that secret all these years. And I spent too long being angry with Robert Hardon for firing your grandfather, when things were already so hard for all of us." I felt her hand shift slightly as she squeezed mine. "But holding onto anger and blame won't bring Pops back. What's done is done. All it can do now is keep stealin' from both of us."

"I know."

"I *hope* you do. Because I'm worried you've been wearing your resentment like a shield for so long, you might've forgotten what it feels like."

"I'm not following…"

"I'm talking about being brave with your *heart*, James. You have plenty of courage to spare for the rest of your life… you'll fight for anyone and anything you believe in. But when it comes to sharing your heart beyond me and those boys…" She took a breath. "Honey, not everyone you love is going to leave you."

The words were like a punch to the gut, so much so that I almost doubled over with the force of it. But seeing as GiGi hadn't moved a muscle, I knew it had to all be in my mind.

I wanted to fight what she'd said, deny it all, walk away. I almost did, feeling the sudden urge for air in a room that didn't have nearly enough. The oxygen machine was still making its *whoosh whoosh whoosh* sounds from over in the corner, and I wondered if instead it was on reverse, siphoning life from the space around us.

It made me think of my mother, for some reason. Is this what it had felt like, sinking *down, down, down* beneath the surface, the air being pulled from your lungs? I still remembered the feeling of gripping the edge of the ice with cold, wet mittens that day, saying my prayers to God to *please just bring her back.*

But she didn't come back.

My father left, too.

Then Pops.

And last night, very nearly, GiGi as well.

I somehow never doubted Jesse or Jack sticking around. We'd been through it all, together for most of our lives. And I'd do literally anything for either one of them. It felt, I don't know, *different* somehow. Safer.

But then there was Lizzie. I remembered again our first night together, at my house. When I'd shared with her about my mom, it was the first time I'd been able to open up about that to anyone, outside of my grandmother and the guys. And even with them, there were certain things I kept close to the vest.

With Lizzie, I'd at least been able to lower my shield most of the way. Inch by inch it had dropped, as we'd grown closer over the past few months. And she'd stood by me, through all of it. By this point, whatever protection still remained could easily collapse with the slightest breath—if I let it.

But now, she was gone—-and I \had no idea if or when she'd return. And after arming myself with the strongest fear and resentment imaginable for most of my life, letting go completely felt... *terrifying.*

What happens if I can't?

"Tater, it's gonna be ok."

I realized I'd been staring out the window this whole time, like maybe the answer lay there, out along the horizon. Shaking my head, I met my grandmother's eyes, all warm and watery, like home. Something about them made me wonder if those words had actually been intended for both of us.

"What if... I'm too late?"

"For what, sweetie?"

"To let go. To make it right. What if I've already lost her?"

I mean, maybe I had. And it would entirely be my own doing, my own fucking words and resentment that had sent her packing.

"You haven't lost Lizzie. You spoke from a place of shock and pain that night, not lack of love. It's clear as day that the two of you love each other. And I don't see that changing so easily, no matter *who* her family happens to be. But that doesn't mean it'll always be easy. The best things rarely are." GiGi smiled, squeezing my hand tighter. "Just promise me that when she makes her way back to you, your heart will be ready. Don't let anything hold you back."

I nodded, taking in her words, as I thought ahead to what mine would be.

I knew she was right about one thing. It was time for me to stop being afraid and tell Lizzie what she deserved to hear most—-the words that had been buzzing around in my head for weeks, but I'd been too afraid to acknowledge them.

Including, how much I loved her.

Because *of course* I did. I'd felt the words and thought them so much over the past month, especially over the past week. I'd kept pushing it away, admitting only that I cared about her but not letting myself go deeper. It had all felt too much, too soon. How could it be real?

But I knew now—my love for Lizzie was the most real part of me. It gave me purpose and made me feel alive. And it was the thing that mattered the most.

I needed to stop running from it. To be brave, like we'd promised each other we'd be.

I just had to pray I wasn't too late.

I've said I wasn't the praying type. The first time, it had done nothing to save my mother. Last night with GiGi, though, I had to believe my words had been heard.

Maybe it was worth another shot.

Chapter 39

Lizzie

"You know, this one has always been my favorite of hers."

Reaching into the giant bowl of popcorn parked between us, I snorted out a laugh. "No way. I mean, it's good, don't get me wrong... but *Anyone But You* is perfection."

Brooke tossed a piece of popcorn at me. "Agree to disagree. *Rome & Julia's* spicy scenes are far superior..."

"... yeah, exactly. I can barely handle seeing our Jules in sex scenes as it is, much less when they don't leave a single detail to the imagination. I mean, do we really need to see her nipples eighty-seven times in ninety minutes?"

She shook her head as she turned back to the screen, giggling. "You're such a prude sometimes."

"If being uncomfortable with watching a woman who is basically *our sister* having hot Italian sex is wrong, I don't wanna be right." But I could barely get the words out before laughing myself.

God, I'd needed this. Room to breathe, to laugh. To just *be* for a couple of days.

Brooke and I had spent the last two afternoons and evenings together after she'd wrapped up her crazy workdays. I was so proud of my friend and everything she was accomplishing in her career—she was the most driven woman I knew, pretty much succeeding at, well, *everything.*

If I didn't love her so much, I'd be mad jealous.

But that wasn't me. It never had been. Sure, I was passionate, bright, determined—but I was also quiet, sensitive, emotional. A dreamer. And I had never belonged in that world.

I was a writer.

It's kind of ironic, but I don't think I'd felt truly confident enough to own that title until finding myself at Everett Publishing the day before, walking away from both the CEO and a possible publishing deal. I'd spent too many years being told that path was impractical and difficult—of feeling ashamed about what I loved to write about, from people whose opinions I believed were the 'right ones'. After a certain point, I'd had trouble discussing it at all. Even with those closest to me.

Talking about the things you loved out loud made them real. And when they're real, it hurts far more when you inevitably lose them.

"Dreams are like wishes, Lizzie—both are impractical. And both have a way of fading away the moment you wake up to reality."

Those words of my mother's were always there, in the back of my mind. But I was done letting them mess with my head, or map out my entire life.

I would never be a serious literary fiction author. If that meeting had proven anything, it was to solidify what I'd already known for a long time. The words that had been itching for years to pour from my fingertips were the ones that had the power to make a reader laugh and cry—-and most of all, believe in love.

And if that meant people like Loretta Everett thought I didn't have what it takes to be published under a large publishing house, then it wasn't where I wanted to be. I only had to find the *right* publisher, who was looking for exactly what I had to offer. Or I'd just go ahead and publish the damned books myself.

Either way, I knew I could do it. Not only that, it felt *right*.

And I was done chasing things that weren't meant for me—including insufferable douche canoes like Randall Price. *(Though I had to admit—it felt so goddamn satisfying, seeing him scramble as his plan unraveled before his eyes yesterday. Now that was a scene I could rewatch—with a giant tub of popcorn—eighty-seven times in a row.)*

No, there was only one man I was willing to risk my heart with—which was a good thing, since he already had it.

I'd already forgiven James for the words he'd said the last time I saw him. Time and space had taught me I wasn't the only one who'd been hurt by the past that night. I just prayed he could forgive *me*, for leaving the way I had. Because I knew enough about James by now to realize what hurt him the most.

I wouldn't be one more person who left and never came back.

Talking through everything with Brooke had helped the final pieces click into place, and I finally felt like I could see the situation for what it was. Learning about my grandmother's biggest secret had been painful and shocking, the implications of it spreading far beyond what I ever could have imagined. I mean, I had an entire *family* I hadn't even known about until this week.

But as much as it hurt having pieces of my story turn out to be actual fiction, I couldn't blame James for the feelings the news had brought up in him, too. Considering what he and his family had already gone through, the idea of me having ties to a family that had caused him pain must've been hard to accept. Especially with the feelings it would inadvertently stir up about the wealthy father who had chosen money over his son.

Loss was complicated. We'd both lost many people we'd loved, and every bit of it had been hard. Some hurt more than others. As deeply as I missed my grandmother especially, I knew being left by choice had to hurt more than all the rest.

And if it was a decision between figuring out life solo or navigating the messiness of it all together, there was no question. I never wanted to be without him, because... I *loved* him. I could finally say the words, without feeling like they didn't measure up to some vague romantic ideal—-or rather, like I didn't measure up. All I wanted to do now was tell him how I felt, even if it also terrified me.

I just needed to get back home to Dearing Creek and find out if everything I wanted was still possible.

Brooke glanced over at me now. "So, have you texted James yet?"

Taking a sip from my wine glass, my eyes darted briefly to my phone, laying silent on the coffee table. "No."

"Lizzie," she said, sighing. "You can't keep avoiding this forever. I'm sure he's been worried. Your last message was so cryptic."

"Yeah, well... I did need time to figure a few things out," I said, shrugging. "But a text isn't going to cut it. I need to see his face, talk to him in person." *Assuming he even wants to see me.*

But I'd learned enough by now—sitting here, worrying over everything in my typical Lizzie fashion wasn't going to solve a damn thing. I had to hope that once I made it home, I'd find a way.

Because if I couldn't at least be brave enough to try, I didn't deserve any of it.

Chapter 40

Lizzie

Ethan's SUV pulled up next to my hatchback as I shifted it into park behind my cabin, breathing a deep sigh of relief. We'd made it.

My brother and I had taken off from Minneapolis late that morning, eager to get out of the city and back into fresher air. Well, somewhat fresher air, as it was already shaping up to be a hot and steamy day.

I was surprised by how different the cities felt to me now—so much louder and busier than it had ever felt when I'd lived there. In fact, from the moment I'd arrived on Monday, I had felt my anxiety spike. No particular reason, except for... it was no longer a place where I belonged.

But instead of excitement, I'd been dealing with even *more* anxiety for the entire drive back to Dearing Creek. Because when we'd stopped for coffee and pastries along the outskirts of the metro area, I'd received a text that had left my heart in a vice ever since:

JAMES: Sorry to bother you, but just thought you should know. GiGi was in the hospital here the past couple of days… had a mini-stroke. She's ok now, recovering at home.

JAMES: Hope you're figuring out everything you need to.

Standing there with my iced coffee and scone, the tears came instantly. All I could think was, *oh my God, GiGi,* followed by overwhelming guilt—*and I hadn't been there for them.*

His message, though, had been so formal, so detached-sounding, I didn't know quite how to take it. Maybe it was a sign he was still angry and didn't want to talk.

But that was the problem with texting, wasn't it? Words—more importantly, the tone behind them—could be easily misconstrued in so many ways. In reality, I knew he had to be doing everything he could to hold it together.

One very important thing, however, was clear—he'd at least wanted me to know what was going on. It mattered to him that I knew. So, maybe he *hadn't* given up on us?

The remainder of the drive, all I could think about was getting home to both of them. To make sure they were ok. To make sure *we* were ok.

And now that we'd finally made it here, I had no idea where to start. A quick glance over to GiGi's cabin told me she looked to be home, because her silver sedan was parked outside. Not that she'd be able to drive right now, anyway.

But there was a second car I didn't recognize—so she wasn't alone, but she also wasn't with James. I was a little relieved—I didn't think I could handle both of them at once without falling apart.

Who the hell am I kidding—I'm going to be a mess no matter what.

I heard Ethan's car door slam as I was getting out of mine. The air was even stickier up here, and I couldn't wait to get inside to the air conditioning—which I had to admit had been my best purchase ever. Deciding to leave my bags where they were for a moment, I called over to my brother, "Hey, do you mind hanging there for a bit? I want to give you the grand tour, but I should do a quick check on GiGi first."

Ethan shrugged. "Sure, that's fine. I'm going to head down to the dock, just grab me when you're done."

Watching his lanky frame stroll down the slight grassy slope towards the water, I smiled, then turned to make my way towards GiGi's place. It felt good having him here.

Once I reached her door, I raised my hand to knock—until I noticed a woman I didn't recognize near the kitchen window, giving me a quick wave. A moment later, she was pushing open the screen door to join me on the porch.

"Hi, dear, you must be Lizzie?" Looking to be somewhere around GiGi's age, the woman's eyes were kind. "I'm Marta, an old friend of Georgia's." Although, with her bright floral muumuu, chunky jewelry and her short and spiky gray hair, her eclectic style pretty much confirmed she was part of GiGi's circle.

"Yes, I am… nice to meet you. So… is she home?" I craned my neck a bit to look past Marta's shoulder but saw no sign of her.

"She is, just resting for a bit. I've been keeping her company to give James a break. But I can tell her you stopped by…?"

"No… I mean, that's ok. I'll just try again later." I paused, taking a breath to keep the tears from welling up again. "How's she doing?"

Marta smiled. "Much better, thanks to James' quick thinking. She'll have to make quite a few changes around here, and I'm sure she'll fight us on it…" she said, rolling her eyes, "… but, she'll be alright."

The tension in my chest lessened, just slightly. "Oh, thank God."

"Yes, she gave us quite a scare. But that tough old bird'll be around for many more years, I reckon." Marta winked at me, and I managed a small smile. Thanking her, I turned to head back, just as Ethan started making his way up.

Though as I grabbed my bag from my car, I couldn't help but still feel unsettled.

"Everything looks awesome with the exterior updates, Lizzie. Seriously, the place almost looks brand new. Even the porch doesn't sag and squeak anymore."

I laughed. "I know… is it weird that I was a little sad about losing that one? Even though the squeaks busted us every time we tried to sneak out at night."

"Yeah, and I think I got caught more than you and Mariah combined," he said, grinning. "Anyway, that was quick… How'd it go over there?"

"GiGi was resting. I'll have to go check on her later," I said, shrugging. I needed to put all of this out of my mind for the time being. Plastering a bright smile on my face, I pulled my keys from my pocket. "So, are you ready for the tour?"

"Bring it on."

Unlocking the door, we were greeted with the *woosh* of cool air as we set down our bags. He followed me into the kitchen as I opened the door of my beautiful stainless-steel fridge, pulling out two hard lemonades. "Want one?"

"Yes, thanks." I handed it to him as we both twisted off the caps, taking a long sip. He glanced around. "So, this would be the kitchen, I assume…"

I smacked his arm. "Smart ass. But," I said, spreading my arms out dramatically, "isn't it glorious? I mean, I have an island, Ethan. *An island.*"

He chuckled. "Now, don't go making me jealous, or I might just have to *move* to this island of yours."

"Always welcome, matey." I grinned, starting to relax more as we grabbed our bags, crossing through the living room and back into the bedrooms.

I can breathe now. GiGi is ok.

"Now, I'll go over all the amazing updates to the main living space in a moment, after we drop off our stuff. Go ahead and grab whichever guest bedroom you want... Oh, and make sure you take a peek at what we did with the old bathroom too. But first, come in and check out the progress on mine..."

I led him through the master bedroom and stopped short, surprised to find that my beautiful, en suite bathroom addition was complete. There hadn't been too much work remaining on it before I'd left, of course. And now, seeing the space all bright and shiny and beautiful, I could only think of James—and the hard work he and Jesse had put in to wrap things up while I was gone. Especially knowing everything he'd had to deal with since.

"Are you... crying over a *bathroom*, sis?"

I whipped my head over to look at him standing next to me, dabbing at the corners of my eyes with the back of my knuckle. "I'm not crying. I'm just... happy."

"Mm-hmm," he said with a knowing smile, turning to wander back out into the living room.

"Give me a sec and I'll be out... just need to freshen up a bit," I called out to him.

"Sure, no prob."

Closing the door, I splashed a little cold water on my face, drying off with a hand towel as I leaned against the counter to check out my reflection in the mirror. I looked tired—my long, auburn waves frizzy from the humidity, the rest of me a little wilted as well. But I knew the Lizzie staring back at me now was somehow changed from the one who'd left three days ago. That woman had been sad and confused, and desperate to feel like something in her life made sense.

I had no idea it was possible to go through so much in such a short period and to come out of it feeling somewhat ok… but I had. And not just *ok*. I felt pretty damn good about where I was, all things considered.

But until I saw James, I knew I wouldn't truly be able to breathe.

"Hey Lizzie, this is really cool…" I heard my brother's voice calling from the other room. Smoothing my hands over my hair (*pointless, because #humidity*), I walked out into the living room to see which upgrade he'd spotted first—and nearly lost it right there.

I had no idea how I'd managed to walk right past it in my beeline to the bathroom. Because the wooden book-case spanning the length of the room—shelves lined with what had to be every single book that I owned, including my grandmother's—was the most beautiful thing I had ever seen.

I mean, I remembered now that I'd requested a book-
case of some sort, way back in the beginning as we'd sat
at the kitchen table, planning out my renovation project.
But with everything since—refurbishing the cabin, starting and stopping my writing career; starting and *pausing*
the process of falling in love—I'd honestly forgotten all
about it.

But of course, James hadn't.

As if in a dream, I stepped closer to inspect it. Consist-
ing of three separate sections, the wood was stained in
a lighter neutral color, bringing out the natural grain of
the wood. But it wasn't just a basic bookcase—the front
of each unit featured an arched panel, with minimalist
carvings along the narrow sides that looked like—oh my
God. They were *river birch trees, my absolute favorite.* And
a nod to the Robert Frost poem I'd shared with James all
those weeks ago.

Well, damn it all to hell.

There was no point pretending to hold back now—the
tears were already flowing.

Reaching out, my fingers followed along the branches
as they curved upwards along each of the arches, discovering another surprise at their center—a small, simplistic
carving of heart-shaped Lake Elska, the place where it
all started. For me, for my grandmother, for the Dearie
Girls—and most importantly, for me and James.

It was the most incredible, stunningly beautiful piece
I'd ever seen before in my life, with James' touch evident

in every single intentional detail. It was... almost like a love story.

Our love story.

"Liz, seriously... are you ok?"

I was full-on snot-crying by now as everything from the past several months—hell, from the past seventy-two hours—overwhelmed me like a tidal wave. I didn't care about anything else. All I knew was I couldn't stay here, not after seeing what he'd done for me.

I needed to see him.

I looked over at my brother, who continued to eye me with concern. "I'm so sorry... I have to..."

"... go find James. Yeah, I figured," Ethan said with a knowing glance, our twin powers synching up in a way that always amazed me. "I wanted to go meet Tanner for a drink, anyway. You go do what you need to do, and I'll just... see you when I see you. Ok?"

Grabbing a tissue to blow my nose, I nodded. "Spare key is in the center drawer of the island. And if you need a towel..."

"... I'm a grown man, Liz. I'll figure it out," he said, laughing. "Go on, get out of here."

Five minutes later, I was on the road, making my way north towards James' property. It felt like the miles couldn't pass quickly enough, my need to see him was so great.

Please let him be happy to see me.

Chapter 41

James

I was sitting on my back patio in the late afternoon sun, sipping a cold beer, when I heard the sound of tires crunching on gravel—followed by the doorbell a minute later.

After bringing GiGi back home and getting her settled with her friend Marta, I'd gone straight home to take a shower and a much-needed nap. With two nights of shitty sleep under my belt, GiGi had kindly suggested that I was starting to resemble a character out of *The Walking Dead*. Which, considering how sleep-deprived I was, I didn't find nearly as funny as she did—especially when a glance in the mirror confirmed she wasn't wrong.

Both had done me good, though—at least now I felt somewhat human again. And now that my brain seemed to be functioning better, I was starting to form a game plan for not only finding Lizzie, but also telling her how I felt. About everything, but mostly... her.

Though in the meantime, I probably wasn't just hearing things with that doorbell. Taking my beer with me, I walked back inside, setting the bottle down on the table just before opening the front door.

That's when I really began to question if I was, in fact, dreaming. Because it was the only thing that seemed to make sense, seeing her standing out there on my front stoop—hair wild and wavy, her eyes shining, like she'd been crying—-and looking exactly like everything I'd prayed for.

But then Lizzie stepped forward, closing the distance between us to bury her face against my chest, arms wrapping around me so tightly I could feel her warmth, and I couldn't deny, this *had* to be real.

She was here. She came back.

"Red..."

"I'm so sorry I wasn't here for you, James. And GiGi. I read your text, and I... I couldn't get here fast enough..." Her voice cracked a bit as she trailed off, the words muffled against my shirt.

Breathing in the scent of her—*God, how did she always smell so good?*—I held her tight, still quietly disbelieving. "You... came back."

"I shouldn't have left in the first place. I'm so sorry."

"You have nothing to feel sorry for... How could you have known?"

"But maybe if I'd been here... if I hadn't fallen apart the way I did..."

"It wouldn't have changed anything that happened with GiGi." I pulled back slightly, still holding on, but needing to see her face. "It's my fault you left. I... I pushed you away."

She shook her head, tears leaving a trail down her face. "No, it wasn't. I mean, yes... I was upset that night. About everything and about what you said. But... we *both* had a bomb dropped on us. That secret hurt you, too. And instead of dealing with it, I ran."

"It's ok, Lizzie..."

"No, please listen. I need you to hear this. I wasn't running away from *you*. It was all the rest of it. And I needed space to work out the mess inside of me." I could hear the breath hitch in her throat as she leaned back into me. "Sometimes, my anxiety takes over, and all I can do is hide away from everything until I can breathe again. But this time, all I could think about was coming back home, to you."

I said nothing, just continuing to hold her. I wanted to tell her that I understood all of it. But I waited, knowing she had more to say.

Her voice was breaking apart now, piece by piece. "I can't promise we'll never argue again, or that I won't need to retreat from the world to sort things out, to recharge. I need that sometimes, and I think you do, too." She paused. "But I'm here for you, and I won't ever leave you. Because..."

I was afraid to hope for what was coming next, to believe it might be true for her, too. But before I could even think about what I was doing, I shook my head, and her words trailed off. Because right then, I realized—I couldn't wait anymore. I needed her to hear it first.

Or maybe it was more that for the first time in my life, I needed to be the one to *say* it out loud, without fear.

"I know." Moving my hand up to her face, I cupped my palm against her cheek, her own words seeming to fizzle out before they could reach her lips as we stood there, staring at each other. "I know *you*. At least all the things that matter. I'm so tired of being afraid, of feeling like something is broken in me. So here goes, me being brave... with you. Truth is, I love you, Red. I *love* you. And I'm pretty sure I have from the moment you smacked some sense into me with that door." I took a breath, but the words continued to tumble out, like they'd been waiting to for so long. "I've wasted so much of my life on the wrong things, but I've never been so sure of anything than I am about this. You're the one for me. The *only* one I want, ever. Even though you're so much more than I deserve, I won't stop working towards being worthy of you." As I looked at her, her eyes filled with tears, her body stiffening against mine. "I don't even care that it's only been a few months, or that it may not make sense to anyone else. Because you and I, we fit together. We make sense. And somehow, you've actually made me *believe* again, in everything. Even myself. If that isn't love, I don't know what is."

For a moment, there was only silence. Tipping her head downwards, I could feel her body begin to relax against mine as, slowly, she exhaled, her breath unfurling like a submission against my chest. Then I heard her whisper, "I... I love you, too. So much."

And there it was.

I could feel the cracks spreading as the force of her words coursed through me, the final walls crumbling down into dust. My protection was gone, every part of me exposed and raw and vulnerable. But as the tears came, I realized—the only thing I felt now was a deep sense of relief.

I was finally *free*.

And now, after spending a lifetime locking my heart away, afraid of trusting, afraid of losing—I wanted all of it. The love, the fights, the good and the bad, the passion and the pain. I wanted to feel all of it, knowing I'd not only survive but come out stronger.

But more than all that, I knew—I was worthy of it. Of being proud of what I was doing with my life, of being someone's priority—and the reason for them to want to stay. And even though I was far from perfect, Lizzie could see that in me. It was she who finally made me believe it. To *see* it.

And now, I had to make sure she believed it of herself, too. All I wanted to do was wrap myself around her, protecting and loving this woman in all the ways she deserved. To make up for everything we'd both lost along the way.

I would never allow myself to fuck it all up and lose something so precious ever again.

Lizzie tilted her face back up to look at mine, and I could see she was crying, too. But it was her smile that I noticed first—and the emotion that radiated from it was palpable. It was the last thing I saw before I brought my lips down to hers. Because I knew, finally, there was nothing holding me back now there, either.

I'd said the words, but now she deserved to feel them.

Chapter 42

Lizzie

Is this what it felt like to be loved?

I no longer had any frame of reference, I realized, beyond fiction. Because everyone and everything that came before James, before this moment, fell so far short that a fair comparison couldn't even be drawn.

It should hurt a bit—or maybe even feel embarrassing—to realize that I'd never been truly loved by a man before the age of thirty. But those feelings had no place in me anymore, or in this room.

The only thing I cared about now was how James was looking at me, with vulnerability and truth in his eyes as he said the words I'd waited my whole life to hear. How it felt as his mouth explored mine, deliberately, lovingly. Like we had all the time in the world, and yet, there would never be enough.

It was different, somehow, from the countless other kisses we'd shared before. Not exactly like the tenderness of our first kiss, or our make-out sessions, both teasing and passionate, or the long, lingering kisses that were clearly hungry for more, but afraid of what *more* might mean.

But this time, our kisses felt like a vow. A promise I could trust, knowing we were both invested in ways that had nothing to do with families or inheritances or circumstances.

Because the question I'd asked myself had been merely rhetorical. I finally knew the answer.

This *was* what it felt like to be in love.

How could it not, as I followed him into his bedroom, with the way his hands now roamed along my body, touching me as though it were the first time, knowing it could never be anyone but him? The way we slowly, deliberately undressed one another, pulling away only to slip the fabric over and away from our bodies. The way we gazed at one another with complete trust and joy, hunger and love.

We hadn't waited all these weeks because neither of us wanted this, or because something was wrong with me. In one way or another, we'd both been stuck, needing time for our heads to catch up to our hearts. To pull at the threads holding together our resistance and finally get out of our own way.

But there was nothing standing in our way now.

James lowered me onto his bed, his body leaning over mine as the slowly setting sun cast a glow across his pale green comforter and all over me. For a brief moment, I brought my hands to my chest, self-conscious, as though I were under a spotlight. But he gave a small shake of his head, smiling as he shifted my arms away. "Don't hide away, Red... you're beautiful. And I've waited so long to look at you."

And then he lowered his head to my breast, the scruff of his whiskers tormenting my already sensitive skin. I felt his tongue explore as my breath hitched, teasing my nipple while his hand gently cupped the other. Unable to stop myself, I threaded my fingers through his hair, the light in the room making it appear more golden than brown. Then my hands traveled down to his shoulders, his back, over the muscles that tensed and strained beneath his skin—wanting only to feel him, explore him, too.

Tipping his gaze up towards mine again, he gave me the sexiest grin I'd seen in my entire life as he began traveling downward, trailing teasing kisses along every inch of my chest, my stomach, my hips, and then...

"*Ahh!*"

I could hear his deep chuckle at my gasp as he kissed and explored the most intimate parts of me—nibbling, licking, then slowly sucking as I wriggled around, losing my mind. Feeling his breath against my thighs as he pulled back slightly, his fingers moved to gently part my lips before slipping inside. I arched my back, sucking in air as he slowly slid them out, then in again—teasing me with the rhythm, then pressing against my most sensitive spot as I felt myself quickly unravel, a low moan sounding in the back of my throat.

I had never had a man do this before, to pleasure me before taking his own. Not ever. I'd always been the giver.

But not with James.

Catching my breath as he pulled back, I watched as he slowly sucked the taste of me from his fingers. "God, I could taste you forever..." I felt the blush spread across my cheeks as his eyes met mine, the desire clear as the color deepened within them.

Reaching for him, he lowered himself until he hovered slightly above me, my hand tracing along his thigh down towards the hardness pressing against my leg, our breathing continuing to grow heavier. The need to feel him in me was almost uncontrollable now. I glanced back at his face with a slight smile and, as if on cue, he slowly slid inside of me, inch by excruciating inch, as we joined completely.

Hearing his moan, I wrapped my legs around him, already feeling on the verge of coming completely undone as we moved together in unison towards the edge, our eyes only on each other. And when we reached it together, the sounds and breaths and shuddering in that room confessed more than words ever could.

Afterwards, we held each other for a long time, our limbs intertwined, feeling like we could never be close enough. I lay with my head against his chest, listening to the beating of his heart as he stroked my hair. I never wanted to leave this place, this moment, where everything felt perfect, and made sense.

This was where I was meant to be, forever. With him, I could both lose myself and find myself again.

If this wasn't love, what was?

And now that I'd found it, I never wanted to run from it again.

Chapter 43

Lizzie

Friday, 3:12 p.m.

> *ETHAN: I know getting a text from your brother when you're probably in the middle of… you know… with your boyfriend is a buzzkill, but… you've been gone for almost 24 hours. Just wanted to make sure you're still alive.*

I set my phone down next to me on the sofa with a sigh as James continued rubbing my feet with one hand, holding a magazine with the other. An episode of Friends was playing in the background on the TV, though neither of us was really paying it any attention.

The two of us had been lounging around out here for the past hour, after a *very* late morning in bed—where we lost track of both the time and reality.

I don't think I'd ever smiled so much—or been so exhausted—*ever.*

Eventually, though, we'd made our way out of the bedroom to take what was undoubtedly the best shower of my entire life, and then, eventually, something to eat. And now, I was debating whether to text my brother back or stay here forever.

I mean, yes, my brother came all the way from Minneapolis to spend time with me. And I wanted to see him. But right then, the last thing I wanted to do was leave this blissful little cocoon James and I had been co-existing in for the past—*yep*—twenty-three hours.

"You should probably respond to him, don't you think?"

I nudged his chest with my toe, making a face. "Probably. Though I sorta wish he would just tune into our twin-tuition and realize I'll make it back home *eventually*."

James chuckled. "As great as that whole *twin thing* sounds, it doesn't sound like it works too well up here in the boonies. Maybe a text would be better."

"*Fine*," I said, grabbing my phone again.

LIZZIE: Yes, I'm alive. Very happily alive. Many times alive.

ETHAN: Yeah, yeah… I get it. Please, spare me the details. A simple thumbs-up would've done the trick.

> *LIZZIE: Let's consider it payback for calling me Mariah.*

> *LIZZIE: But… I am sorry for abandoning you for so long.*

ETHAN: It's ok, really. But do I finally get to meet the guy?

I looked up again at James, who was eyeing me curiously. "Would you be willing to have dinner with Ethan?

"Of course. I want to know anyone who's important to you, Red." He smiled at me, then paused. "Assuming he's not going to try and fight me to defend your honor or anything."

I smirked. "Not likely. I'm pretty sure I lost that sometime around one a.m., anyway."

He waggled his eyebrows at me. "Should we go back to the bedroom and look for it?"

"As tempting as that sounds, it might just kill me."

"What a way to go, though."

"Definitely. And '*death by sexual shenanigans*' would look great carved on our tombstones," I said, giggling, as I turned back to my phone.

> LIZZIE: Yes, I want you to meet him. Dinner at Loon's Landing at five? Oh, and remind me… I have some other news to share.

> ETHAN: You pregnant?

> LIZZIE: ETHAN MICHAEL.

> ETHAN: ELIZABETH GRACE.

> ETHAN: Sorry. Anyway, dinner sounds good. Tell him to be ready for an interrogation.

> LIZZIE: I'm rolling my eyes so hard at you right now.

> ETHAN:

Indeed rolling my eyes—but giggling in spite of myself—I tossed my phone down again. "Done. I told him we'd meet him at Loon's Landing in an hour."

"Great. I'm starving." He cocked his head, now growing more serious. "Still feeling nervous about tomorrow?"

After I was finally somewhat lucid this morning, I had called LakeView Assisted Living Facility and asked the front desk receptionist if Mitchum Hardon was accepting visitors.

My name—along with Ethan and Mariah's—was already on the list.

Did Grandma Cora assume we would end up right here? It seemed impossible, but yet... I had no other explanation. Yet another piece of my grandmother's past that was a complete mystery.

At any rate, I had been put through to Mitchum's voicemail, where I left him what I'm sure was a very rambling, anxious sort of message that made no clear sense—but it must have done enough, because I'd received a voicemail not even an hour later, inviting us to his place.

It was surreal, really, that this was actually happening. Looking at James, I shrugged. "Of course I'm nervous. What if this is all a huge mistake?"

Leaning over to squeeze my hand, James gave me a comforting smile. "It won't be. And if things go south, I'll be there, ok? And Ethan. You're not alone."

"I know." But my voice was small as reality started to weave its fingers back into our safe little haven. I wasn't ready to leave.

Sitting up the rest of the way, James pulled me towards him. "I mean it, you won't have to go through anything alone. You told me last night you would never leave, and neither will I."

I pulled back to look at him. "Even though the Hardons are now a part of my life?"

"Yes, in spite of that unfortunate detail," he said, making a face. Catching my annoyed expression, he laughed. "Ok, sorry... not the time for jokes." He took a deep breath. "I love you, Lizzie. That means loving *all* of you."

"I know... I love you, too. Even in spite of your lame attempts at humor."

"Just means I haven't peaked yet." He grinned as I settled back against his chest, his breathing deep and even. "Say, there's something else I wanted to tell you about. What do you think about... a library in Dearing Creek?"

"Um, do you even know who you're talking to? Libraries are my safe space... I've always thought this town needed something better than the tiny one at the community center."

"Good. Because I want to build one."

I sat up again, looking at him. "You want to build a library?"

He nodded. "My mom was a lot like you, always with a book in her hand. She was the librarian at my elementary school. Seems being with you has been bringing back a lot of memories of her I'd forgotten about."

I squeezed his hand, leaning forward to give him a brief kiss on his cheek. *How could anyone not adore this man?* "I love that you've been thinking more about your mom."

"It's been... cathartic, actually. Remembering her without it hurting so much." He took a breath. "That's why I want to build this library. To honor my mom, but also start doing some good with the money left to me. I think this would be something that would make her happy."

"I have no doubt it would. It's unbelievable, James. And so generous. Think of how it will impact the community, too."

"I know. She'd love that part especially." He returned my smile briefly, but his eyes were serious. "When I was at the hospital with GiGi, all I could think of was how I was losing the two most important women in my life, just like I'd lost Mom... all because I couldn't get over my pain and my fucking resentment. I'm done wasting another second on any of it. It's time that I start living for today, rather than being stuck in the past. And I don't want to fear it anymore, either. It's a part of who I am, just like my mom is. I know she'd want me to embrace everything I have, and not waste it. Most of all, my life with you." He squeezed my hand again. "Everything else we'll just figure out along the way."

I nodded, feeling the tears prick behind my eyelids. "Brave together, right?"

"Brave together." Then he leaned in and kissed me—slowly, lovingly.

And for a moment, it was just the two of us again, safe in our little bubble. But regardless of what happened tomorrow or in the days that followed, I knew he was right—together, we could face anything.

Together, we belonged.

The next morning, James, Ethan and I walked through the front doors of the main offices of LakeView Assisted Living, a few minutes shy of eleven. We were in the midst of another late-August heat wave, which was doing nothing to help me cope with what lay ahead. Because despite my bravery at initiating this meeting the day before, my anxiety now was set to bubble over—panic coursing its way through my veins, my hands and face half tingly and numb. I rubbed my fingers now as the receptionist gave us verbal directions to our destination, barely hearing the words myself, but thankful that the two men at my side seemed to be listening.

I was also glad that the two of them had hit it off so well the night before at dinner. At first, Ethan had a little fun with him, demanding that James make an honest woman of his sweet, innocent sister. But a french fry flung square into his face (*with strategic aim by said sister*) was enough to have both of them cracking up at my expense before diving into talk of kayaking, favorite bands, etc.

Ethan had also been surprised by my decision to reach out right away to Mitchum. And he was also the one who pushed me to finally leave another voicemail for Mariah, detailing everything that I'd uncovered and our plans for today. I knew it was the right thing to do, but it stung that she'd shut us out so completely all summer. We may not always see eye-to-eye on things, but still—she was our sister. We were all we had left.

Though I had to admit—as we now walked out of the building and back into the sticky air, following the side-walks past rows of single-level bungalows—along with many residents eyeing us curiously—I was beginning to doubt the sanity of my actions. I mean, I hadn't even taken the time to plan out what I was going to say to the man, how I would act. Should I be aloof? Angry? Accepting? What was the right thing to do here? What would be respectful, without betraying Grandpa Walter's memory?

But now that we'd reached the blue door of a beige home and Ethan had knocked, there was no more time to think or hyper-analyze. This was it.

The door swung open a moment later, revealing the smiling face and tall, regal posture of the man I'd been terrified to face—instantly taking my breath away, as all I could see in *this* face was our mother.

"Elizabeth, Ethan... hard to believe you're actually here, standing in front of me." Mitchum's deep timber of a voice was warm and his eyes were watery—not at all what I'd expected. But beyond the few assumptions I'd made based on who his family was, I hadn't known what to expect, not really. I stood there awkwardly for a moment, not quite sure of what to do next. Then I extended my hand awkwardly to shake his hand. "Nice to meet you, sir."

God, you're such a dork, Lizzie.

Face burning, I noticed Ethan giving me an amused look before following suit. To my left, I felt James squeeze my hand. But I barely felt it as my fingers were mostly numb by now.

But Mitchum took it all in stride. "No formalities needed around here, my dear. And who is your friend?"

"This is James. Though he's actually my boyfriend."

James stepped forward somewhat stiffly, reaching a hand out as well. "James Tate. My grandmother is Georgia LaMott. You might remember her?"

For a moment, the old man looked startled. "Yes, of course I know Georgia. Good woman." Then he brightened, motioning us in. "Anyway, please, come in. No sense catching up out here with all of my nosey neighbors lurking about." Glancing over my shoulder briefly to catch an older woman passing behind us with a walker, we followed him through the door.

Moments later we were all seated with glasses of lemonade and iced tea in a comfortable, well-decorated living room—the shelves and walls around us lined with framed photographs, old and new. The only sound, other than the ice clinking in our glasses as we took awkward sips, was the air conditioner whirring softly in the background. I thought back to the day James and Jesse had installed the unit in my own cabin and how grateful I was for the cooler air during that early summer heat wave. How I had hoped it might help cool down the simmering attraction I was already starting to feel towards my contractor back then.

For once, I was grateful my wish had *not* been granted.

But I had to say, I wouldn't have minded a little cosmic intervention to help settle my nerves right now.

Might as well get this over with.

"So, Mr. Hardon... you're probably wondering why we're here."

"Mitchum, please. And from your message, it sounds as though you have found your grandmother's letters." He chuckled. "Cora was wondering how long it might take you."

I froze. "Wait... you knew she had kept the letters? How much did she tell you?"

"Well, I suspect just about everything."

Ethan leaned forward in his chair. "Were you always in contact with her?"

"Not again until several years after Walter passed away. I assume you know enough about the early days, by the letters?"

I nodded. "Yes, and GiGi... I mean, Georgia... filled in the missing gaps. About how the two of you met, your secret relationship, and..." I trailed off, not quite knowing how much to say. Even though I ached to know *everything*.

But his eyes, though sad, were also kind. "Your mother, Cynthia."

I gave another small nod, though the words, '*How were you able to just walk away?*' were caught in my throat. I felt James' arm loop behind my back, pulling me in closer.

"I promised Cora I would never lie to you kids about our story, and you know much of it already. But I want you to know also that I truly loved her. I'd been a grieving widower for a few years, with two young boys... but I wasn't looking for love. Meeting Cora that day felt like fate and, well, it became quite impossible *not* to love her. She was the most beautiful, passionate woman I'd ever met, and our time together brought life back to me again." He paused, glancing out the window across the room, his voice sounding very far away. "We knew what we were doing was wrong. Cora had been so lonely as a young wife, all on her own, so unhappy... and to be honest, so was I. We let things go too far, and I should have been the one to stop it. But in the end, it was her."

Ethan cleared his throat, and I could tell he was affected by Mitchum's story as much as I was. "Did you ever get to see our mother?"

He shook his head. "No, I made that promise to your grandmother. She wanted things to work with Walter, and this was their second chance to have the family they both wanted. After the mess I'd created, I owed both of them that. And it was better for your mother. So as hard as it was, I honored her wishes." He turned his gaze back towards the three of us, his eyes locking with mine. "But I never stopped thinking of my little girl. Never stopped loving her, wanting her to be happy, secure. That's why I set up the fund for her."

"Wait, what?" This time it was James who spoke up, his hand tensing against my side.

"The fund. I contributed money annually for every year your mother lived to an account to help support her, along with giving Cora and Walter the deed to the cabin and the land surrounding it. It's how your parents were able to purchase their home outright, how her college tuition was covered... and I believe the rest was passed down to the two of you and Mariah?"

I felt like my head was about to explode—suddenly, the size of the inheritance that had been left to the three of us was starting to make a lot more sense. But now another question was burning inside me, and I needed to ask it—even though I was afraid to hear the answer. "Did... did she know about you?"

Mitchum hesitated for a moment, glancing down at his hands. "I didn't ever have reason to think so, based on our agreement. But, after your grandmother and I reconnected here last year, she shared that Cynthia had found her diary one summer when your family was here at the cabin. When she confronted Cora, she had no choice but to tell her the truth." He sighed. "Things were never the same between them after that. Cynthia, of course, blamed her for all of it and pushed her away. And it about broke Cora's heart. But there was nothing to be done."

"And the money?"

"She refused to touch it once she figured out where it had come from. She and your father had already paid for their house by that point—but the rest just sat there." He smiled sadly. "But I'm grateful it was passed down to you kids, at least. All I've ever wanted is for you all to be taken care of. Even if I couldn't be a part of your lives, I could at least do that much."

My mind was going in a million different directions as piece by missing piece of the patchwork of our lives was filled in—the money, our mother's resentment of Grandma Cora, everything. I couldn't believe the truth had come out, and yet, we never knew about it until now.

"Thank you for being honest with us. I can't deny it's a lot to take in, but... we know this must've been hard on you, too." Ethan flashed him a tight smile before taking another sip of his lemonade.

"Yes... you're a good man, Mr. Hardon."

I turned, almost not sure that I had heard my boyfriend correctly. But James was sitting there, looking straight at Mitchum with a serious expression. And from my perspective, I could see that his eyes were watery as well.

This day had been full of surprises for all of us.

Mitchum's expression was emotional as well as he looked between the three of us, nodding but looking unsure of what to say next.

It was then that I finally found my voice again. "We're grateful for everything you've done for our family, despite how things started. But I'm wondering... does *your* family know about all of this?"

"Yes, they do. I told my two sons once I brought them into the company many years ago, as I needed to provide an explanation for why I was transferring money all these years. Mitch Jr., my oldest, took it better than Robert did. Their children don't know yet. But I'd love for all of that to change, if it's ok with you."

I froze. "What do you mean?"

"I know you three have lost so much, but if you are willing, I'd love to welcome you into the family officially. You're all Hardons, and it's time the rest of the family knew it, too. But all of this is on your terms. Though, at the very least, I'd love to get to know you while I'm still able." He smiled tentatively, eyes tearing up once more. "Losing Cora for a second time has felt unbearable, but I'm still grateful I was given this time with her. I know you kids have lost so much, and that what I have to offer won't replace the people you loved. But we're here. And you're family."

Family. I felt the tears spring to my eyes, the truth of how much we'd lost still so fresh after all this time. But also, they were tears of hope for a new beginning.

"I think... I'd like to try."

"Me too," Ethan said, piping up.

Mitchum's smile grew. "I'm so glad to hear it. Oh, and before I forget, I have something for you, Elizabeth..." He rose from his armchair, walking over to a drawer in the credenza and pulling out an envelope and walking over to me. "Cora said it would be ok to give you this, if you ever came calling."

Taking it from his hand, I immediately recognized my grandmother's handwriting. My eyes darted back up to his face. "Is this..."

"... a letter from Cora? Yes. Though I regret saying it's only the last one she wrote when she ended things. I burned the others many years ago. It hurt too much to have them, knowing what I'd lost." He sat back down in his chair, sighing. "But I kept this one all these years, as a reminder that I was doing the right thing."

"Um, thanks. I don't know what to say." I was desperate to read the letter immediately, but instead, I tucked it away as he continued.

"You're welcome, my dear. I've been blessed with so much in my life.... My family, my business, and two great loves. I'm just grateful I can now share it with you."

And as we drove back to the cabin a short while later, Mitchum's words still rang in my head.

For too long, I'd been focused on what had gone wrong, on what I had lost. Of doubting what I believed in and what was right in front of me.

But now, I didn't want to waste another second of looking backward or trying to find perfection.

I already had everything I ever wanted.

Chapter 44

James

"I'd like to propose a toast, if I may." Mitchum Hardon raised his wine glass into the air as his eyes scanned the other guests at the table. We were seated in the rather impressive dining room of his former home—now owned by his eldest grandson, Luke, whom I never thought I'd share a meal with willingly.

Then again, there were many things I believed about myself before this summer that turned out not to be true—or at least, they no longer served me.

But none of that mattered anymore—I was done looking backwards. All I wanted was to continue doing the work on myself, so I could be the kind of man I wanted to be. Not just for myself but for the woman I loved. Beyond that, the only thing I cared about was making sure she had the support she deserved.

Like right now, at this dinner party Mitchum had arranged. It was a mere two days after he'd had a private conversation with his extended family about his past with

Cora, revealing he'd had a daughter they'd never known about.

I could only imagine how *that* conversation had gone down—discovering not only a secret family, but three new heirs to the Hardon fortune along with it.

Lizzie had been an anxious wreck the night before, and I had to admit, I was too. It was difficult to ignore the lifetime of beliefs about the Hardons I'd held onto so tightly—some true, others not.

But I had to hand it to them. Despite feeling some-what awkward, everyone tonight had, for the most part, been kind and respectful. Mitchum's sons, Robert and Mitchum Jr.—also twins, along with two of Robert's sons—were naturally less than thrilled about the family discovery. Robert had opted not to attend the meal at all—and given the history GiGi and I had with him specif-ically, I wasn't too heartbroken over that. His brother, Mitchum Jr., had decided to show up last-minute and had thankfully been mostly cordial. At least, so far.

But I was surprised that several of Robert's sons, including Luke, had made the effort to be here tonight—-Will, the second oldest after Luke, along with the twins, Ryder and Chase. Ethan was already chatting up Ryder, interested in his work in furniture design. The other two brothers were traveling, but there was already talk of another dinner in a few weeks. As all of the sons helped to run their third-generation high-end furniture business—Hardon Brothers' Designs—they all lived in the area. Seeing them around town had always been unavoidable. But I was mentally preparing myself to embrace it, for Lizzie's sake.

The biggest surprise—besides Mitchum himself—had been his granddaughter, Eve. The only girl born to a huge family of boys, Eve was laid back and friendly right off the bat, the only Hardon not involved in the family business or much interested in the trappings that came with it. She and Lizzie seemed to hit it off instantly—both likely grateful to have another female at this very male-dominated table.

Overall, most everyone had all been gracious and welcoming, despite the fact that this secret had dropped a bomb on their lives as well. There was still a lot to navigate, of course. But for now, this was enough.

Mitchum Sr. continued. "I know this news about our shared connection has been difficult for all of you, especially after so many years. While it will take time for each of us to work through the intricacies of what this means, I am grateful that, for now, we've all been able to come together to start finding our way." He paused, glancing over to where Lizzie and Ethan sat. "The two of you, along with your sister, are an equal part of this family. And I genuinely hope we can continue getting to know one another. No matter what, you will always be welcome."

I cast a sidelong glance at Lizzie, her green eyes alight with fresh tears. But she was also smiling. I squeezed her hand beneath the table, and I felt her squeeze it back. Seeing her happy and safe was everything to me. And I'd do anything to keep it that way.

Will, seated a few seats down, raised his glass as well. "I want to echo my grandfather's sentiment. You're family."

"To family," Mitchum Sr. said, smiling.

"To family," everyone around the table echoed, glasses clinking as the murmur of conversation picked up again. I noticed Luke had been uncharacteristically quiet since we'd arrived, probably still trying to figure out what this news meant for his place within their family dynasty. But he'd opened his home to us today, which was a step in the right direction. I had to give him credit for that.

His friend Sam, whom I'd met briefly months ago when we'd bumped into each other at Loon's Landing, was seated between Luke and myself. Turns out, he'd been in town fairly frequently lately, having officially purchased—as of last week—the old, abandoned resort property on the south end of the lake. As we all dug into our entrees, he leaned in.

"So, James... this dinner couldn't have come at a better time. I don't know if you heard, but I just bought the old Lake View Resort property from Joe and Denise Kinney."

"Yeah... pretty sure I heard something like that," I said, before taking another bite of my prime rib—which was perfectly cooked.

Of course.

"Luke said you might have," Sam said, smiling. "The Kinneys drove a hard bargain, but I think I still came out of it ok."

"Definitely don't envy you doing business with those two."

"Hopefully, I'll never have a need to again." He chuckled. "Anyway, I was talking with the guys at Aaronson Construction, but then Luke's brother Nash mentioned you started your own remodeling business and have been working on Lizzie's place. I guess he's friends with Lena Nelson, who knows Lizzie? Anyway, the word out there is you've done an incredible job on her renovation. And Mel over at Aaronson Construction said you're one of the best. I know a resort is a totally different beast, but... what can I say. As an entrepreneur myself, I prefer to work with small businesses. Would you have any interest in taking on some work over the next year?"

"Um, sure... what sort of work would you be looking to hire me for?"

"The entire renovation and rebuild."

My eyes were wide as I set down my fork. "Seriously?" *An entire resort?* This would set us up with work for an entire year at a minimum, probably more. My head was buzzing, already thinking about what Jesse would say, the subcontractors we'd want to bring on, the scope of the project. This could be career-making, and do so much to bring more revenue to the community of Dearing Creek, too. Combined with building a library, we'd be at capacity and would need to start hiring a handful of permanent employees instead of contracting everything out.

But that was the goal, wasn't it? To build and grow a business I could be proud of. I knew if Pops were still alive, he'd be telling me this was the moment, to just go for it and not look back.

And an opportunity like this almost seemed too good to be true. I wanted to say yes, immediately. But then, a memory floated to the forefront in my mind. "Thanks so much for the offer, Sam. It sounds really exciting, and I'm definitely interested... but I thought I heard a rumor about an issue with the Kinneys?"

"Yes, they seemed to think they could put a clause in the purchase agreement about who I could hire for the rebuild. But I spoke with my attorney, and he put the kibosh on that one." Sam rolled his eyes. "Last thing I need is some blowhard like Joe Kinney trying to make a mess of things. Lake Elska deserves a beautiful resort gracing its shores again, but more than anything, I want it to be a good thing for the community. That means hiring the best people who will not only work hard, but also have creativity and vision. Based on what I've heard, it sounds like you might be the guy."

For a moment, I couldn't speak—-thinking of my old boss Mel, overcome by the generosity he was once again showing me with this *massive* referral. "Well, thanks... I appreciate it. I'll need a few days to consult with my business partner, too, but maybe we can start with a meeting next week to discuss the scope of work?"

Sam grinned. "Sounds good to me. Here's my card." He handed me his business card, which I tucked into my back pocket with a smile as he turned towards Luke. I stared at my plate for a moment, still not quite believing this conversation had happened.

I'd had so much good come into my life ever since meeting Lizzie that it couldn't be just a coincidence. Opening my heart up to her had also opened my eyes, making everything appear in technicolor instead of the harsh black and white I'd lived by.

All I could think was how goddamn happy and grateful I felt.

How much I loved her already.

And glancing over at her now, I knew—with Lizzie by my side, life could never be anything but beautiful.

Two days later, Jesse and I had wrapped up three major milestones—first, officially putting our partnership into writing as we sent off the LLC amendment paperwork to the State of Minnesota, as well as adding him to my business account at the bank. The look on his face through all of it reinforced even more that I'd made the right call, having my chosen brother build this business alongside me.

Then the second milestone happened during our meeting with Sam outside of the old Lake View Resort property, which happened to be located only a couple of miles east of Lizzie's place. After taking a walk through the property and discussing Sam's vision, Jesse and I were in agreement—this was the project of a lifetime and we'd be idiots to pass it up. After Sam had his attorney email a preliminary contract for all of us to sign, the wheels were set in motion, with a plan to finalize the full contract and scope of work by the end of September and beginning plans for the indoor restoration and renovation by October. Jesse and I celebrated with Lizzie and Tara on Wednesday evening, all of it feeling a little too good to be true.

And then came the third milestone—because our resort project wasn't the only thing we had to celebrate that night. After Ethan had left to head back to Minneapolis, Jesse and I had spent a couple of days wrapping up the final touches at Lizzie's cabin. The renovation was now complete, and I couldn't have been more proud of how everything on Horizon Remodeling's first project had turned out. We'd done it.

It was probably annoying to everyone how much I smiled these days. Surly James had officially left the building.

Inside though, I couldn't help but feel it was all bittersweet. Bringing Lizzie's family cabin back to life had been the catalyst that brought us together, and I would always be deeply grateful for that.

But along the way, this experience had brought *me* back to life, as well. And now, the thought of not being with her every day automatically felt like a step backwards, even though it wasn't.

I knew Lizzie and I were built upon a more solid foundation than simply proximity. Even still, it was hard not to feel apprehensive of yet another change.

So once we hit nine o'clock—with our friends deciding it was time for bed—I suggested to Lizzie that we stop by the Thirsty Beaver bar for a drink on our way back to her place. As we wound our way along County Road 3 as the last bit of light faded from the sky, I couldn't stop myself from taking brief peeks over at her in the passenger seat. Even in the darkness, she glowed, as much about her beauty as the person inside. I doubted I'd ever stop feeling the way I did now—so goddamn lucky.

Ten minutes later we were making our way across the parking lot to the bar when I heard the sound of tires on gravel as a car pulled up behind us. Turning, I saw the tinted driver's side window roll down, revealing the face of one pissed-off Denise Kinney.

Shit.

"What a pleasant surprise running into you here, James."

From where I stood, seeing this woman was far from pleasant. But I plastered a smile on my face all the same, my arm looped protectively around Lizzie's back.

"Hello there, Mrs. Kinney. Nice night, isn't it?"

"It *was.*" Denise gave us a simpering look, eyeing up my date. "I see you're still running around with your clients."

"Actually, no... Lizzie isn't my client. She's my girlfriend. And we're just enjoying a night out to celebrate."

"Yes," Lizzie piped in, now wrapping an arm around me as well, "we have *loads* to celebrate tonight. Including how incredibly successful James' business has been as of late."

"Oh?"

Trying to hold back a smile, I turned my gaze back to Denise. "Yes, Horizon Remodeling just landed a massive corporate project. I assume you're familiar with the old resort on the south end of the lake?"

Denise's eyes were blazing. "That's... not possible."

But for the first time, I didn't feel defensive or angry. I felt... oddly calm—at peace—as I smiled at her. "Oh, I assure you, it's already in writing. Sam's a good man, making sure we moved quickly to get things in place before winter." I shrugged. "I hear you helped to convince him of my expertise, so thanks for the referral."

"I did no—"

"Anyway," I said, interrupting her, "if you'll excuse us, I want to enjoy the night with my beautiful date." Walking away, I could hear the tires of her car squeal against the pavement as the black sports car made its way down the road. Pausing before the door, I pulled Lizzie in tighter. "Is it wrong that I absolutely loved every moment of that?"

"Not at all. Though I'm pretty sure she's headed home for a temper tantrum."

Laughing, I pulled open the door, realizing for the first time that Denise Kinney and her kind no longer had any power over me. And damn, it felt *good*.

"Well, lookie here... two of my favorite peeps." Kait wandered up just as we grabbed the last two seats at the bar. "What're you crazy kids up to tonight?"

"Celebrating, actually," I said with a smile, feeling on top of the world. I'd always liked Kait but even more since getting to know her better over the past few months. "A couple of work milestones, and also the completion of Lizzie's remodel."

"Well, congrats! And not a moment too soon, considering that Dearie Girls Weekend kicks off in two days," she said, grinning. "Lizzie girl, you ready for this?"

"God, I hope so." Lizzie sighed dramatically, but her eyes had a twinkle to them. "What did I put you in charge of again?"

"*Nachos a la Kait*, fruit and four bottles of wine. But don't worry, I also picked up two boxed wines, too. Because you know Tess will bring the fancy shit again, and everyone will feel too guilty to drink it. Well, except maybe for Jules."

Lizzie snorted out a laugh, glancing back at me. "Remind me to tell you sometime about the truth or dare incident from three years ago."

"Still can't get that damn stain out of my carpet," Kait said, making a face. "Anyway, let me grab you two something to drink... the usual?"

"Yes, ma'am." As she wandered away, I smiled at Lizzie. "So I guess we better enjoy these last couple of days before I lose you to your posse... and what I'm guessing will be a massive hangover."

"Probably." She sighed. "Sorry, Tate, you got stuck with a lightweight."

"Oh, I think I've proven I can handle you just fine," I said, grinning wickedly as she blushed. I'd never tire of giving her a reason to. But as the giggles faded, she grew quiet while we waited for Kait to return with our drinks, chewing on her lower lip in that way that always drove me mad. Something was clearly on her mind.

"Wanna share what's going on in that head of yours?"

Her eyes darted back to mine. "Sorry. Just thinking about how I can't believe the work is done on my cabin. This summer went by so fast."

"Yeah, I've been thinking the same."

"I love everything... It really feels like my home now. You know how grateful I am to you and Jesse, right?"

"Of course I know. And you took a chance when you hired us. I'm the one who should be thanking you."

Lizzie gave me a small smile. "Neither one of us is very good at accepting gratitude."

I chuckled. "Yes, guess so." I hesitated for a moment. "Can I admit something, though?"

"What's that?"

"It's going to be damn hard not seeing your beautiful face every day. I've gotten used to being around you."

She blushed again, but this time, her eyes were glistening. "Me too."

It was then that Kait walked up with our drinks, setting them on the counter with a wink before darting off to deal with Hank and his friends in the corner. I took a sip from my beer, thinking of all the things I still wanted to say—but deciding now maybe wasn't the time. We were both exhausted from the past few weeks. This could wait. Even if I didn't want to.

"So I had an idea... maybe it's stupid, I don't know..."

I raised an eyebrow at her. "Knowing how much you think through everything, woman, I highly doubt that." But I could see her twisting her hands in her lap, which was always her tell. Placing my hand gently over hers, I gave her a quick smile. "What is it?"

She was quiet for a moment, then I heard her slowly exhale. "So I know we only live like four miles apart. We're going to see each other."

"Yeah..."

"And I know we're solid, both fully invested in us. So I'm not worried about that part. But... I want more."

"So do I."

She glanced up at me. "You do?"

"Yep."

"Ok, good. So... if I said I wanted you to move in with me... that wouldn't freak you out?"

I grinned. "Nope."

"You're a man of few words tonight, Tate."

"You want more words? How about this." Pulling her hands into mine, I turned to face her straight on. "I love you—your smile, your laugh, your nerdiness, your heart, the way your mind always seems to be racing ahead... even your anxiety. And definitely that body of yours," I said, grinning as her face grew redder. "All of it makes up the woman I was meant to fall in love with. So of course I want to be where you are. If I've realized anything over these past months, home is wherever I'm with you. And I'm done wasting my time pretending that's not the case."

Her eyes were teary now, but at least she was smiling. "God, I love you. And I'm pretty sure that's a song, by the way."

"Well, if it is, it's a damn good one," I said, chuckling. "But I mean it. And I was actually thinking along those lines myself... just didn't know if you'd feel ready."

"Nothing would make me happier." Then with a squeal, she threw her arms around me, nearly knocking me off my stool before I caught her, and we both started laughing. As she tilted her head back to look at me, her face was on fire. "Sorry! There I go, getting carried away again."

"I'm not sorry."

I mean, how could I ever be, holding this woman in my arms? Nor was I sorry for planting a kiss on her right there, in front of everyone—not giving a damn about the catcalls or the Dearing Creek rumor mill.

After years of never quite finding my way towards happiness, getting carried away with her—no matter where the current led us—was where I belonged.

Chapter 45

Lizzie

INDI: DEARIE GIRLS WEEKEND STARTS IN 24 HOURS!!!!

JULES: Eeeek!! My flight gets in at noon tomorrow. Brookie, you still picking me up to carpool?? And can we still swing by B & C to grab desserts??

BROOKE: Yes, my lovely little starlette… text me when you land. I've got two liters of Tito's and a ginormous pan of Crave sushi rolls, ready to go!

LENA: So, so excited! I've got all the soda and snacks. Mom is sending over a pan of K bars, too.

JULES: OMG… K bars?? #nailedit

LIZZIE: Gah!! I cannot wait to squeeze all of you! I'll be in hardcore riding mode all day until you get here, but then I'm all yours.

TESS: You have no idea how much I need this weekend with you ladies. Counting down the seconds. Brooke, can I catch a ride, too? I'll explain later. I'll make it up to the cities before noon.

BROOKE: The more the merrier!

*KAIT: Ummmm….is no one going to address the fact that our Lizzo just said she and her boyfriend are going to be *knockin' boots* all day until we arrive?*

KAIT: #majorovershare #pleasedisinfectall-surfaces

LIZZIE: OMG…I clearly meant WRITING, not RIDING. (Note to self: enunciate.) #voicetextingdidmedirty

INDI: HAHAHAHAHAHAHAHAHAHAHAHA #giddyup

BROOKE: #saveahorserideacontractor

LIZZIE: You are all uninvited.

KAIT: I only kid because I love… (But I'm not sleeping on sticky sheets. Just sayin')

I was sitting on the dock with my cup of coffee late morning, enjoying the break in heat we'd been having. Wide awake at dawn, I'd spent the past several hours writing at my desk, the words flowing through my fingers almost faster than I could type them. After being creatively stuck—and floundering in general—for so long, this felt nothing short of a miracle.

I had to credit it in part to my grandmother. I'd finally made my peace with her late last night when I decided to read the farewell letter Mitchum had passed along to me days ago.

"*Dearest* —

Do you remember that day at the cabin, when the rain was falling so hard that we both thought the roof might very well cave in on us? It was both exciting and terrifying, yet so life-giving after the long drought we'd been having.

I can't help but think now how closely that afternoon mirrors the path we've taken together.

When we met, I felt like I was losing myself. I didn't know my purpose or what came next. I was desperately lonely and disillusioned, and selfishly believed I was unloved as well.

Then you came along, and I felt wanted again. Loved. Alive. And a part of me never wanted it to end.

But the woman in me has realized, it must..."

I folded the letter, no longer feeling the need to re-read Grandma Cora's words for the millionth time. She'd said her piece and made the choices that were right for her and everyone involved. And she'd done everything she could to atone for her mistakes.

But she'd never needed my forgiveness. Instead, I'd been the one sending silent apologies up to the heavens, praying she could hear me.

I'd spent my entire life idolizing my grandmother—the one who knew me better than anyone. But it turns out, I was so busy looking for a role model that I hadn't bothered to really see who she was, deep down. Instead, I'd molded her into something unrealistic, like a false idol. Or maybe she'd let me, because she knew it was what I needed when life became too hard to face reality. To believe in a perfect love.

Like she also had with Mitchum, so long ago.

But Cora was just a woman, with plenty of life lived before I ever came along. Making mistakes along the way was part of being human. And I'd made plenty of my own.

But we'd both been blessed with far more in our lives than I'd ever recognized. Maybe it took ending the search for perfection for me to see it all clearly. That loss wasn't just about the losing; it was about what you do with what gets left behind.

And once I realized I was done living in regret, the words began to appear for me again. It was the moment I knew the story I needed to tell.

It wasn't just about my grandparents or the affair with Mitchum. There was some of my story in there as well—-how life and love can be both messy and beautiful. It was fiction, but at the heart of it was *truth*.

It was the story I was meant to write. And after everything, I finally felt like I was exactly where I was meant to be, doing exactly what I was meant to do, in the place where I belonged.

And by my side was the man I was always meant to love—imperfect, but perfect for *me*.

"Hey, Lizzie girl... you look like you're dreaming up something good down here."

My head popped up at the voice, realizing I'd been so stuck in my thoughts that I hadn't even noticed GiGi making her way down to my dock. I couldn't help but recall that morning so long ago when it had been her grandson sneaking up on me. I smiled at the memory and at her.

"Good morning. How'd you sleep last night?"

She waved me away. "Oh, just fine. You and James kept me up a little later than I'm used to these days, though. I still think he cheated in the last round of Skip-Bo."

I couldn't help but laugh, she looked so disgruntled. By now I knew her grumpiness was a form of love, and it made me love her all the more. Thank God she had come through her mini stroke without much for long-term effects, other than fatigue. But even still, both James and I had been keeping a close eye on her. I could only imagine how delighted she'd be when she heard he was moving in next door—but I was saving that one for him.

Then I noticed she was holding what looked to be a small book. "So, are you planning to do some reading down here, too? You're welcome to join me."

"No... just coming to give you something I should have a few weeks ago." She handed the book to me, with no words on the front cover—but when I opened it, I spotted my grandmother's name.

"The Diary of Cora Olsson - 1965-1967"

My eyes darted back to GiGi's, who was watching my reaction with a sad smile. "Cora asked me to keep this safe until the day you were ready for her version of the story. I'd say we've arrived there, don't you?"

I nodded, my vision blurring as I stood to give her a hug. Georgia LaMott was known for her feist and her strength—-but only a chosen few knew the vast capacity she had within her for love.

Releasing her slowly, I wiped my eyes with the back of my hand. "Thank you for this... and for everything."

"Of course, love," she said, touching my cheek tenderly. "You're mine now too, y'know. And family looks out for one another."

And before I could say anything more, I heard the sound of a car honking—spotting Indi as she hopped out of her car with Bucky. She and Callum had been watching him for me for the past two weeks, with everything else that had been going on—which Callum hoped was more of a trial run for their own dog someday. I knew my boy had been in great hands.

But that didn't stop him from barrelling down the lawn at full speed, nearly knocking me into the lake as he put his paws against my chest to kiss-attack my face. As I giggled under the assault, GiGi couldn't help but laugh as well.

"I'll leave you ladies to it… Oh, and have fun this weekend. Don't worry about keeping the noise down on my account. It's about time that cabin of yours was filled to the brim withlove and laughter again." Then, with a wink, she wandered back up the slope towards her own cabin just as Indi made her way towards me and Bucky scampered back up to his favorite spot on the covered patio.

"Sorry I'm early… but frankly, I just couldn't wait another second," she said, grinning. "And I figured you could use the help anyway before the rest show up."

Giving her a quick hug, I smiled as I looped my arm through hers. "There's no one I'd rather kick this weekend off with than you, darling."

And for a moment, as we strode up that hill in unison, I felt like we were thirteen again—full of excitement and hope for what came next.

By six o'clock, everyone had arrived—even the brigade from the cities, who came with far more luggage than necessary for a girl's cabin weekend. Not that anyone was surprised.

Now the wine had been poured, food spread out and the music playing, courtesy of Brooke's *Dearie Girls' mix*. I just sat there taking it all in—the newness of the cabin combined with elements of the past, surrounded with the familiarity of this group of women, whose bond only made sense to each other.

It felt like old times and yet, not at all. It was part of the beauty of the Dearie Girls. We continued fostering our friendships together through the years—through all the highs and lows, regardless of where our paths may have taken us. It was a rare thing, what we had. And I would never take it for granted.

As Brooke and Indi began their annual dance off while Kait and Lena worked in the kitchen, I sank onto the couch between Jules and Tess. "God, I've missed you two. I hate it when so much time passes."

"Me too, sweetie." Jules threw an arm around me to give me a squeeze, the scent of her perfume hinting at a sophistication that only existed on the surface. Beneath all of the glamor that came along with being an A-list Hollywood star, she was still the same Jules underneath it all—kind, goofy, sensitive and down-to-earth. "It's so good to be back. Especially here."

"That just means you need to get back more often," I said, playfully poking her in the side. "Are you planning to see your family while you're back in Minnesota?"

She hesitated before shrugging. To call Jules' relationship with her ultra-conservative parents and pastor brother complicated would be putting it mildly. "Who knows. Crazier things have happened, right?"

"Well, just know you can hide out here for as long as you want. At least until the paparazzi hunt you down."

She took a sip from her wine glass, half-smiling. "Don't tempt me."

Tess had been mostly quiet since she'd arrived, and as the chaos and laughter rang out around us now, I turned to study her face. She was staring at her wine glass, swirling the contents and looking as though her mind was far away. I nudged her with my elbow. "I missed you too, you know. What will it take to get you up here a little more often?"

Tearing her eyes away from her glass, she smirked. "What, and have to deal with *my* parents? Maybe we should take a trip somewhere instead." She sighed. "You know, just... get away from everything."

I eyed her curiously, but before I could say more, she stood up. "Ladies, we need our toast to kick off the weekend. Everyone grab a glass." She turned to me. "Would you like to do the honors?"

Amused, I picked up my glass as Brooke turned down the music, the others wandering over as well. "Um, ok." I looked around at these women, trying to think of the perfect words to say. Then I realized—they already knew the most important ones. "Seventeen years ago, I was an awkward thirteen-year-old, struggling to figure out who I was. That was the summer I found all of you, and it changed my life." I took a deep breath, then continued. "But I don't think I ever really felt settled in who I was, until now. I was struggling to keep up, to rebound from everything that had happened, and to trust in myself. When Grandma Cora gave me this cabin, it felt like my chance at a fresh start. But I had no idea how much it would change me for the better." By now, my vision was blurring—but this time, these were happy tears. "So I guess what I want to say is, I'm grateful. For this place, for all of you, for love... and for finally finding my purpose." I dragged a knuckle beneath my eye to stop a tear from falling, then started laughing. "Ok, enough of weepy Lizzie. Who's next?"

"I'll go," Tess said, wrapping an arm around my back. ""I'm grateful to have your love. I don't know what I would do without all of you. You're the family I never knew I needed."

Brooke smiled. "My turn. I'm grateful for this weekend with my sisters, wine and elastic waistband pants."

"Oh God, yes. To all of that," Jules said, laughing. "Oh, and K bars. Except I can't stop eating them... they're like crack. Please, somebody hide the rest."

Lena giggled as well. "I'll have my mom drop off another pan. But I'm thankful for a business that gives me freedom, and all of you, who accept me as I am."

"Same for me on the business front... the Beaver has never been thirstier," Kait said, with a snort of laughter as Lena groaned. "But I love you all. These friendships are what keep me sane. Well, mostly."

"And I'm grateful for the generous hearts of every single person here, and all the ways we show it to one another," Indi said, her eyes locking with mine.

Suddenly, a knock at the door made all of us jump. For a moment, nobody did anything. And then I remembered—*oh yeah, I live here.*

But nothing could've prepared me for what was waiting on the other side of that door.

"*Mariah?* And... Norah? What are you two doing here?"

My sister gave me a thinly-lipped smile. "I'll explain in a moment. Is it ok if Norah hangs out with your friends for a bit so we can talk?"

"Oh sure, come on in, sweetie," Indi said, coming up from behind me to take my niece's hand in hers. Norah glanced back at her mother briefly, who nodded. Indi smiled. "It's ok, Lizzie, go on."

With a quick, grateful look, I closed the door, leading my sister down to the Adirondack chairs around the firepit for privacy. She was quiet for a moment as we sat there together, looking out upon Lake Elska. And even though part of my mind was inside that cabin, I couldn't help but feel transported back to fifteen years ago, sitting here with my sister. Then finally, she spoke. "I'm sorry for ignoring your calls all summer."

"Well, thanks for admitting to it, at least."

She gave me a small smile. "I know it's time I stopped avoiding things. That's part of why I had to come here, to tell you in person." Leaning her head back against her chair, she sighed. "I was so angry that day in the lawyer's office, but it wasn't really about you or Ethan. This cabin was special to me too, but it hurt so much to come here after Dad died. It hurt to be around all of you, actually. Everything was a reminder. That's why I had to leave, to switch schools."

I looked at her. "And it's why you never come back home to Minnesota."

She nodded. "It's stupid, I know.... A thirty-three year old woman, avoiding her life."

"Well... I don't think I'd call it 'stupid'. Relatable, maybe." I shrugged. "But Mariah, we all wanted to be here for you, to be a part of your life. It felt like you just... wanted to forget about everything."

"Maybe I did. Not that it worked." She smiled ruefully. "I've missed so much, especially with you and Ethan. And losing Mom and Grandma... I just didn't think we could bounce back from that."

"You didn't lose me *or* Ethan, ok? We love you... even when you irritate the crap out of us."

That, at least, got a laugh out of her, the first I'd heard in years. "I deserved that. Anyway, about that day at the lawyer's office... I felt... betrayed, I guess. By Grandma Cora. I had kept her secret for so long, and then hearing about the cabin... it all felt like too much."

"Wait... hold on a second. What do you mean, you kept her secret?"

Her eyes darted over to mine briefly, then away again. "I know about the affair. And that Grandpa Walter was not Mom's biological father."

"What!? How did you know?"

"I overheard her and Mom arguing when we were all here one weekend. I was around fourteen, maybe? Apparently, Mom had found her diary under a loose floorboard. Grandma Cora admitted to everything."

It felt like my brain was going to explode. "So you held onto this all these years and never told me?"

She shrugged. "The two of you were so close. I didn't want to ruin anything for you. And besides, they never knew I'd overheard them. I figured it was just better for everyone if I said nothing. And when Grandpa Walter passed away, then Dad... there was no point in bringing up the past."

"Mariah... I'm so sorry."

"For what?"

"For you having to deal with this all on your own. It wasn't fair." I sighed. "I think I've been angry with you for leaving and changing. But I guess we all have, in our own ways."

"I'm sorry too, for not being here... and shutting you out. But I never stopped loving the two of you. You're... all that I have."

I smiled at her. "We love you, too. And I'm so glad you came here to tell me this, but..."

"... it's Dearie Girls weekend. I sort of figured that one out. It's ok... I can get a hotel."

"How long are you staying in town? Everyone leaves Sunday morning, and I want to spend time with you and Norah while you're still here."

"In town? Um... indefinitely."

"Say what now?"

"I left Brad. I just... couldn't do it anymore. That life. It was killing me. Ted was the final straw."

"Ted?"

"His personal assistant. Oh, and his lover for the past three years."

"Jesus Christ, Mariah."

"Yeah."

"And poor Norah…"

"That's why I knew I had to leave when I did. I want her to have not just a normal childhood but a happy one. And what better place than this? But don't worry, we're not moving in. I've already been scouting out houses." She turned again to gaze out at the lake. "It feels good to be home, though, doesn't it?"

I'd never pictured myself here again with my sister, finally feeling like I had her back again. Maybe that was always the way our story was meant to turn out.

And maybe, the rest was just waiting to be written.

"Thanks for doing this." James and I were standing together on the porch as Mariah loaded Norah back into her rental car behind the cabin. After a quick reintroduction, he was now taking the two of them back to his place for the weekend.

"Happy to do it. Besides, I need to get in good with your sister anyway, before we drop the bomb that we'll soon be shacking up together," he said, winking.

"Something tells me she won't be pulling out a shotgun anytime soon," I said, laughing. "Although she *does* own some very pointy stilettos."

He chuckled. "Noted. Now, come here…"

He pulled me in for a kiss as I heard the catcalls sound from inside the cabin. All that did was to spur him on as he drew out our kiss even longer—and *God, I could kiss this man forever.*

And as my friends grew louder and more obnoxious, I struggled to hold in my giggles—along with the overwhelming urge to just pull my hot boyfriend into my bedroom for a quickie.

Seriously, it's impossible for a girl to get any damn privacy around here.

But what did I expect, moving to a small town like Dearing Creek?

Certainly not privacy—much less finding love or a life that felt perfect. After all, I no longer cared about things like perfection.

But somehow I'd ended up there, all the same.

Epilogue

Lizzie

One year later

Was all of this a dream?

I had to wonder, considering how much had happened in a relatively short period of time.

James and I had been officially living together since the previous summer, practically the second after my last friend departed Dearie Girls weekend. It had been blissful—and a test in patience at times—but perfectly imperfect.

Mariah—now newly-divorced, with Norah in tow—had become a permanent resident of Dearing Creek as well after purchasing a home on the other side of the lake. Ethan was a frequent visitor as well, and I suspected it wouldn't take long before he joined us.

GiGi was her usual feisty self, now on an exercise and dietary regimen that only amplified that side of her. But having her grandson next door seemed to be the one change she embraced whole-heartedly.

Amongst our friends, relationships started and ended; babies were born, jobs changed. There were moments of loss and celebrations.

But those were stories for another time. Because at that moment, there was clearly one story in particular that required my attention.

"Lizzie, the line is now snaking all the way around the building. I'm going to tell them that the cutoff *has* to be nine o'clock." Elinor, my agent, had been practically bouncing off the walls of Lake Elska Community Library ever since the doors for my evening book signing had opened an hour ago.

Not that I could blame her. Despite doing my best to maintain my composure, inside, I was a ball of anxious energy.

I had, after all, been waiting for this day my entire life. My very first book signing, for the self-published book I'd poured my heart, soul and thirty-one years of living into.

There were many days I thought I'd never achieve my dream of becoming a published author, much less writing the types of books I cared about.

But as it turned out, sometimes believing with your whole heart can do magical things.

USA Today best-selling author.

Wall Street Journal best-selling author.

New York-freaking-Times best-selling author.

Words I *never* thought I'd see attached to the name 'Elizabeth Blake' were suddenly plastered on the cover of my book, blasting across my social media pages, on blogs and podcasts. What started as a boost during my book launch by a few well-chosen book bloggers ended up quickly gaining momentum with an obscene amount of sales for a debut romance author. And it didn't take long to catch the attention of a number of publishing houses as well.

Suddenly, I had both an agent—the amazing Elinor Wright—and a contract with my dream publishing house, Blossom Press. With their help, sales of my novel had continued to skyrocket, and a month later, Elinor was fielding non-stop requests for interviews and book signings from all over the country.

But there was never a question of where I wanted my very first book signing to take place. It always had to be the newly-opened public library, built by the man I loved to honor his mother and the community that took him in many years ago. Seeing him accomplish his dreams made me more proud of James than I could have possibly imagined.

Though, unfortunately, the setting I chose did nothing to settle my nerves—the anxious introvert, now forcing herself to be *very extrovert-y* for the sake of her book.

I'd been at it for an hour already, chatting with locals and signing books for readers who'd driven hundreds of miles to come here and meet me.

Me. Lizzie Blake. It still didn't feel real. And neither did my writing hand, which was currently going numb. But I had to make it another two hours. I couldn't disappoint anyone.

Taking a sip of water, I turned to Elinor. "Don't turn anyone away, ok? I can do this."

She smiled at me, shaking her head. "Alright, you're the boss." Then she hustled away, disappearing into the crowd. The next woman in line approached the table—middle-aged, looking anxious as she clutched my book in both hands.

I smiled at her. "Hi there. So glad you could make it."

The woman set her book on the table, her face brightening. "Thanks. I wouldn't have missed it. I'd love it if you could sign my copy, if you don't mind."

"Of course, happy to. Who should I sign it to?" As I opened the front cover, I heard her speak again.

"Delores Walton, please... and... do you mind if I ask you a question?"

"Sure."

"Great! First of all, I loved your book. But at the end, things felt sort of... unfinished for Grace and Marcus. I mean, did they ever get married?"

Looking up again to hand her the book, I bit back a grin. It was a question I'd been asked countless times, so I already had my answer prepared. "Well, that was sort of my intention with the ending. Grace was finally confident in who she is and happy with her life, *and* with Marcus.

She didn't need for him to rush off to put a ring on it in order to feel secure in their relationship. She already knew he loved her."

"Are you sure about that?"

But the question wasn't coming from Delores. James stepped out from behind her, a copy of my book tucked under his arm.

I grinned at him. "Yes, sir. I'm quite sure."

He cocked his head. "So what you're saying is Grace isn't looking to get married."

I crossed my arms. "No, I didn't say that..." I noticed that the steady hum of conversation amongst the throngs of people filling the library had started to diminish. I was now becoming more aware of the many ears now listening to our conversation.

"So if Marcus had proposed to her at the end of the story, she'd have been happy about it?"

"Well, yes... but that's not exactly the point..."

"Maybe it should be." James' eyes twinkled as he took in my narrowed eyes, knowing he was driving me crazy. Part of me wanted to kiss him, and the other part wanted to yank that book from his hand and swat him with it.

"Do you want me to sign your book or not?"

"I thought you'd never ask." With a flourish, James held the book out in front of him and I grabbed it, whipping open the cover to write some sassy comment inside.

Of course, that *was* my intention, before I saw the gorgeous, emerald-cut diamond staring at me from the ring box hidden inside.

Eyes wide, I looked up to see him smiling at me—though this time, I could tell he was running on a similar nervous energy.

"Ever since the day you ran into me with that door and flung tampons at my head—"

"—I did *not* do that..." My face now completely ablaze, I could hear giggles coming from the women towards the front of the line.

"—agree to disagree, my love," James said with a grin as he continued. "Anyway... after that day, something changed in me. At first, I thought it was simply about starting fresh and healing from the past. But I quickly realized what I ran into that day was *hope*. Hope for what my life could be, if I'd only just open up my heart to it."

"James..."

Ever so slightly, he shook his head. "I spent decades of my life running on fear and resentment. It took nearly losing everything for me to realize I didn't want to live that way anymore. To realize I *deserved* more. You're the one who helped me to see it, Lizzie. You're the one who taught me to trust another with my heart again, to believe that I was worthy of happiness. And that I didn't have to be afraid anymore. Because I wasn't alone. You were by my side."

I wasn't even bothering to stop the tears now. "Seriously, James..."

He held up a hand. "Not yet. Because you need to hear how you've made everything in my life better, made *me* want to be better, just by being *you*. Beautiful, kind, dorky *you*. I need you to know how your laughter fills my soul, how you overwhelm me with your capacity for empathy and love, how you amaze me with your incredible talent and terrible kayaking skills..."

There was more laughter now, but as I glanced around, I could see a few of the women were wiping their eyes. *Was this actually happening?*

"More than anything, I love that we are both building our life together, every messy and beautiful part of it. I don't care what came before, nor do I need to know what comes next. And all I need is you. Well, and an answer to my question." He reached forward to pull the ring from the box, which I realized I was *still* holding in front of me, completely caught up in the moment. Setting it down, he slid the ring onto my finger. A finger, I realized, was not tingly and numb with anxiety. Because, with James, all I felt was *him*. "Lizzie Blake, will you marry me?"

"Yes, you idiot. Of course I'll marry you." And as the room erupted into cheers, he came around the table, pulling me into his arms, one eyebrow raised as he held back a smile.

"Are those the best words you have in your arsenal after a proposal like that? Seriously, woman, I thought *you* were supposed to be the writer."

Grinning, I cocked my head to the side. "Oh, I am. I just thought you'd appreciate me skipping ahead to the best part."

"Touché." And with a wicked smile, James leaned in and kissed me, like he did all the other times—with his whole heart. But underneath it all, I could hear the unspoken promise of forever.

I said a silent prayer of thanks to my grandmother, who knew from the start what we'd need most to carry us through life—*love*. True, unconditional, intentional, and steadfast love. The kind that not only lifts you up and carries you away but holds you together when everything else is falling apart.

And thanks to the man in front of me, I now knew she'd been right all along.

THE END

Also by

OTHER BOOKS BY FARRAH JANE:

WEAVERVILLE, CA SERIES:

Baby By the Rebel
Bound to the Cowboy

EVELETH, MN SERIES:

Do-Over With My Best Friend's Brother
Do-Over With the Nanny

WISHING, OR SERIES:

Undoing the Playboy
Undoing the Rockstar

Undoing the Baller

DEARING CREEK, MN SERIES:

Lake I Love You

**LET'S STAY CONNECTED – JOIN MY EMAIL NEWSLET-
TER FOR NEWS & EXCLUSIVE BONUS CONTENT!**
https://bit.ly/FarrahJaneNewsletter

About Farrah Jane

Farrah Jane is a Midwest-born-and-bred author of smart, from-the-heart small town romance, filled with swoon-worthy, complex heroes and sassy, relatable heroines who'll feel like your new best friend.

A total nerdy introvert, you'll usually find Farrah reading/writing #alltheromance, wandering around in trees somewhere (*probably not lost*), listening to eighty-seven different podcasts, diving into her best-ever brownies (*I will die on this hill*), dreaming of her next travel adventure, or spending time with her favorite people on her gorgeous patio or cozy couch.

Farrah migrated from small town life to the outskirts of the Twin Cities, Minnesota, where she currently resides in her forever home with her husband, son, daughter, & two rescue pups.

LET'S STAY CONNECTED – JOIN MY EMAIL NEWSLET-TER FOR NEWS & EXCLUSIVE BONUS CONTENT!
(I promise, never spammy or lame!)
https://bit.ly/FarrahJaneNewsletter

FOLLOW FARRAH!
TikTok:
https://www.tiktok.com/@love_farrahjane
Happy Hour on the Patio (VIP Reader Group):
https://bit.ly/FarrahJaneHappyHour
Instagram:

https://www.instagram.com/authorfarrahjane
Facebook:
https://bit.ly/FBFarrahJaneAuthor